# Smitten

## Also by Colleen Coble

The Lonestar novels
*Lonestar Sanctuary*
*Lonestar Secrets*
*Lonestar Homecoming*
*Lonestar Angel*

The Mercy Falls series
*The Lightkeeper's Daughter*
*The Lightkeeper's Bride*
*The Lightkeeper's Ball*

The Rock Harbor series
*Without a Trace*
*Beyond a Doubt*
*Into the Deep*
*Cry in the Night*

The Aloha Reef series
*Distant Echoes*
*Black Sands*
*Dangerous Depths*

*Alaska Twilight*
*Fire Dancer*
*Midnight Sea*
*Abomination*
*Anathema*

## Also by Kristin Billerbeck

*Split Ends*

The Ashley Stockingdale Series
*What a Girl Wants*
*She's Out of Control*
*With This Ring, I'm Confused*

The Spa Girls Series
*She's All That*
*A Girl's Best Friend*
*Calm, Cool, and Adjusted*

## Also by Diann Hunt

*Bittersweet Surrender*
(available as ebook only)
*Be Sweet*
*For Better or For Worse*
*Hot Tropics & Cold Feet*
*RV There Yet?*
*Hot Flashes & Cold Cream*

## Also by Denise Hunter

The Big Sky Romance series
*A Cowboy's Touch*
*The Accidental Bride*

Nantucket Love Stories
*Driftwood Lane*
*Seaside Letters*
*The Convenient Groom*
*Surrender Bay*

*Sweetwater Gap*

Colleen Coble,
Kristin Billerbeck, Diann Hunt
& Denise Hunter

# Smitten

*Love is on the way*

**THOMAS NELSON**
*Since 1798*

NASHVILLE   DALLAS   MEXICO CITY   RIO DE JANEIRO

Published in Nashville, Tennessee, by Thomas Nelson. Thomas Nelson is a registered trademark of Thomas Nelson, Inc.

Scripture quotations are taken from THE NEW KING JAMES VERSION. Copyright 1982 by Thomas Nelson, Inc. Used by permission. All rights reserved; and HOLY BIBLE: NEW INTERNATIONAL VERSION®. © 1973, 1978, 1984 by International Bible Society. Used by permission of Zondervan Publishing House. All rights reserved.

Kristin Billerbeck is represented by the literary agency of Alive Communications, Inc., 7680 Goddard Street, Suite 200, Colorado Springs, CO 80920, www.alivecommunications.com.

Publisher's Note: This novel is a work of fiction. Names, characters, places, and incidents are either products of the author's imagination or used fictitiously. All characters are fictional, and any similarity to people living or dead is purely coincidental.

ISBN 978-1-61793-851-1

*Printed in the United States of America*

# DEAR FRIENDS,

· · · · · · · · · · · · · · · · · · · · · · · · · · · ·

*H*ave you ever noticed that life's biggest blessings are often unexpected? That's how it was with both our budding friendship and the origination of *Smitten*.

In the mid-1990s, God began linking us together, first Colleen and Kristin, and a year or so later, Denise. Bonded by our fledgling writing careers, we attended writing conferences, connected daily via e-mail, and eventually wrote a few romantic novella collections together. Our relationship deepened and became the kind of friendship we knew could only be a God thing.

Years later, our careers budding just as our friendship had, God brought us Diann. The lonely business of writing was lonely no more—it was a party for four! Diann frequently teased us about being "left out" of our previous novella collections, as if she were our group's third wheel, but nothing could have been further from the truth. The fact was, we fit together like pieces of a heavenly puzzle.

Although our genres took us down slightly different paths, we were constantly connected by love and support—the kind that got us through bouts with cancer, family crises, and all the other storms that came our way.

When the opportunity arose to collaborate on a collection, we were ecstatic. Do what we loved with the people we loved? How could we turn that down? Besides, it was Diann's dream, and we (including Thomas Nelson) couldn't have been more eager to grant it.

Hours of brainstorming and hundreds of e-mails later, *Smitten* was born—a story that follows a fledgling town and four friends as each finds her true love. To make things simpler (not to mention more fun), we endowed our heroines with a healthy dose of our own personalities, so as you meet them you'll also be meeting "us." (We hope you'll like us.☺)

In many ways, this collection is a celebration of our friendship, a celebration of enduring love, and a celebration of God's unexpected blessings, all wrapped in one simple book. It's our greatest hope that you, our readers, will feel a part of it all as you join us on our journey to Smitten.

Love,

Colleen, Kristin,

Diann, and Denise

# CONTENTS

# Natalie: Birthday Wishes

## Colleen Coble

# CHAPTER ONE

. . . . . . . . . . . . . . . . . . . . . . . . . . .

*N*atalie Mansfield's heart swelled as she stood on the perimeter of the town square and watched her niece and the other children decorate the town for Easter. A gigantic smile stretched across five-year-old Mia's face as her Sunday school teacher lifted her to place the lavender wreath at the top of the clock.

Mia saw her and waved. "Aunt Nat, look at me!"

Natalie waved back, her smile broadening. "She's growing so fast," she told her great-aunt, Rose Garner. "I love her so much."

Black threaded Rose's silver hair, and her smooth skin made her look twenty years younger than her seventy-eight years. "I still remember the first day I laid eyes on you."

"How could you forget? I was a morose ten-year-old who snapped your head off every time you spoke to me."

Her aunt pressed her hand. "You changed our lives, honey. Now here you are providing a home for your niece. A full circle, just like that wreath. I'm so proud of you."

Her aunt's words made Natalie's heart fill to bursting. Being part of their family, along with her four cousins, had healed her heart. "You gave me the only stability I'd ever known. I want to do the same for Mia."

Aunt Rose wasn't listening. A small frown creased her brow. "Something's wrong."

Natalie looked at the men standing a few feet away in

3

front of the hardware store. Their heads were down and their shoulders slumped. The dejection in their stances sent her pulse racing.

She recognized one of her coffee shop patrons, Murphy Clinton, and grabbed his arm as he walked past. "What's happened, Murphy?" she asked.

He stopped and stared down at her with a grave expression. "The mill's closing."

"That's not possible," she mumbled. Her thoughts raced. The mill was an institution and the main employer in Smitten. If it closed . . .

He finished her thought. "This town is finished."

The aroma of the freshly brewed coffee overpowered the less appetizing smell from the drum roaster in the back room. Natalie let her cousin Zoe handle the customers at the bar, as Natalie took the hot beverages to the seating area by the window where she and her friends could see white-topped Sugarcreek Mountain. Spring had come to their part of Vermont, and the sight of the wildflowers on the lower slopes would give her strength.

"So what are we going to do?" she asked, sinking onto the overstuffed leather sofa beside Reese Mackenzie.

"Do? What *can* we do?" Reese asked. Her blond ponytail gleamed in the shaft of sunlight through the window. She was the practical one in the group. Reese was never afraid of hard work, but while Natalie saw only the end goal, Reese saw the pitfalls right on the path. "We can't *make* them keep the mill open."

While rumors about the mill had been floating for months, no one had really believed it would fold. The ramifications would be enormous. Natalie's business had been struggling enough without this added blow.

She took a sip of her mocha java. A little bitter. She'd have to tweak the roast a bit next time. "If the mill closes, the town will dry up and blow away. We can't let that happen." If Mountain Perks closed, she didn't know how she would provide for Mia.

And she wasn't leaving Smitten. Not ever. After being yanked from pillar to post with an alcoholic mother until she was ten, Natalie craved the stability she had found here with her great-aunts and extended family which included her three best friends.

Julia Bourne tossed her long hair away from her face, revealing flawless skin that never needed makeup. "This is one of those things outside your control, Nat. I guess we'd all better be looking for jobs in Stowe."

Shelby Evans took a sip of her tea and shivered. Her Shih-poo, Penelope, dressed in a fashionable blue-and-white polka-dotted shirt, turned around in Shelby's lap and lay down on her navy slacks. "I don't know about you all," Shelby said, "but I wanted my kids to grow up here."

The women had no children of their own—and none of them was even close to thinking about settling down—but that was a moot point for Shelby. She had a storybook ending in mind that included a loving husband and two-point-five children for each of them. Natalie was sure her friend would find that life too.

Natalie moved restlessly. "There has to be something we

can do. Some new export. Maple syrup, maybe? We have lots of trees." She glanced at Julia. "What about your New York friends? Maybe you could ask some of your business friends for advice."

Julia shrugged her slim shoulders. "They know spas. I hardly think a spa is going to save us."

Reese had those thoughtful lines on her forehead. A tiny smile hovered on her full lips, and her hazel eyes showed a plan was forming. "We don't have time for exports, but what about imports? Tourists would love us if they'd come visit. We have heart." She took out her ever-present notebook and pen and began to jot down ideas.

"They come to ski in Stowe anyway," Shelby said. "All we have to do is get them here."

Natalie rubbed her forehead where it had begun to ache. "But what do we have to offer that's different from any other town?"

Julia crossed her shapely ankles. "Smitten is cute with its church and all, but cute doesn't bring tourists. I can't even get a decent manicure in this dinky town. People aren't going to pay for ambience. We need some kind of gimmick."

Reese tapped her pen against her chin. "I have an idea," she said. "Everyone jokes about the town name. Why not capitalize on it?"

"How do you capitalize on a name like Smitten?"

"What does Smitten make you think of?" Reese asked. "Love, right? What if we turn the town into a place for honeymooners?"

Shelby adjusted the bow on Penelope's head. "I went to Santa Claus, Indiana, once. Tons of people, even in July."

Natalie swallowed a groan. They'd all heard about Santa Claus too many times to count. She needed to derail Shelby before she broke into a rendition of "Jingle Bells." "We could have love songs playing as people strolled the streets."

Julia snickered and nodded toward the man striding past outside the window. "I have a feeling Carson would have something to say about that. He hated all the jokes about his name in high school."

Natalie followed the angle of Julia's nod. Her gut clenched the way it always did when she saw Carson Smitten. He was a man who attracted female attention wherever he went. He looked like his lumberjack great-grandfather, with his broad shoulders and closely cropped dark hair.

He had all the single women in town drooling over him. Except for Natalie, of course. If the other girls knew what she knew about him, they wouldn't think he was so great.

"I'm still thinking about my idea," Reese said. "This will mean new businesses, new jobs, lots of revenue pouring in. We'd have to get the entire town on board."

Natalie's excitement level went up a notch as she imagined the town transformed with its new mission. "The town meeting is coming up. I can present the idea there."

"It's a good thing you're a selectperson," Shelby said. "People listen to you."

Natalie dug paper and a pen from her purse, a Brighton that Julia had given her for her last birthday. "There needs to be a cohesive plan. What would this love town look like? Besides romantic songs playing over speakers around town." She peered at Reese's list and copied down the items.

Shelby retied Penelope's bow. "We need a lingerie shop

that sells perfume," she said. "Fudge. Some plush hotels and bed-and-breakfasts with tubs for two." Her smile grew larger. "Maybe old-fashioned lampposts along the path around the lake. You could put outside tables on the street and white lights in the trees. Flower boxes all around town."

"And we'll need more restaurants," Julia added.

Natalie eyed her. "You said a good manicure was impossible to find. What if you started a spa?"

Julia's perfectly plucked brows lifted. She grabbed the tablet and pen from Natalie. "I don't know. I'd like to move back to New York eventually."

"The honeymooners won't spend *all* their time in their rooms," Reese said, her eyes gleaming. "We offer great outdoor activities. The skiing here is as good as anywhere in the country. People just don't know about us." She gestured toward the mountain. "And look at that view."

Natalie groaned. "The last thing I'd want to do on my honeymoon is go skiing. I'd rather sit holding hands across a linen tablecloth with a lobster in front of me."

"But I'd go skiing in a heartbeat," Reese said. "Our big draw is our outdoor beauty. We don't have an outfitters shop. We'd need that." She jotted it down on her paper. "You know how I've been saving for a shop like that for years. Maybe now is the time."

"Now *is* the time," Natalie said. "Sometimes you have to take a leap of faith. We're going to push you until you do it."

"I love it!" Shelby stood and paced by the window. "Maybe my etiquette school can be part of it too. I can coach women on how to put on the best parties and cater to the society women who come to town. Maybe teach ballroom dancing."

"And your designs," Natalie said, unable to keep her voice from rising. "Those cute outfits you make for Penelope would sell like hotcakes." She glanced at the picture of herself with Mia hanging on the wall. "I have to do what I can to save the town. I want Mia to have the security I've never had. A-And I've been thinking. I want to be Mia's real mother. I'm going to see about adopting her."

Her announcement left her friends with mouths gaping. She glanced at Shelby, whose soft heart she knew would be the first to agree with her.

Shelby's dark eyes glistened. "Oh, Nat, that's just like you! You have so much love to give. Mia's a very lucky girl."

A lump formed in Natalie's throat. "Starting the adoption is going to be my birthday present to myself. Every day I wake up and wonder if Lisa is going to take her away from me someday. I can't live with that fear."

Julia grimaced. "Lisa is never going to own up to her responsibilities, but I'm glad you're going to make sure Mia is safe."

"I'll be praying for you," Reese said softly. "There will be lots of frustrating paperwork. Let me help you with that." She flipped the page on her notebook. "And it's all the more reason for us to get this idea sold to the residents. You don't want Mountain Perks to go under."

This was not going to be an easy sell to Carson Smitten. Natalie stared out the window again and watched the man yank on the door to his hardware store in his usual confident way. She had no doubt she could convince the rest of the town over his objections. After all, what did they have to lose?

Smitten Town Hall was packed. Carson Smitten scanned the rows of people. Folks were talking excitedly, mostly about the mill news that had been announced two days ago. There looked to be a lot of interest today in the things listed in the warning that had been published thirty days earlier. Once the moderator had been selected and brought down the gavel, the participants recited the Pledge of Allegiance and began to go through the list of items in the warning. Things went smoothly with no surprises until Natalie Mansfield took the mic.

Dressed in jeans and a red sweater that showed her curves to advantage, she stepped forward on the stage. "We've all been reeling with the news that the mill is closing," she began. "I have a proposal to bring to the town. A way to bring major tourism to Smitten."

A wave of murmurs rose, and people leaned forward. Burly George Metcalf called out, "If you can save my plumbing business, I'll eat dirt."

She smiled. "It won't take that, George. But make no mistake—it's a major change."

Carson narrowed his gaze on Natalie. He liked looking at her. He'd always been drawn to her dark-haired beauty, but she'd been distant with him ever since that fiasco with her sister, Lisa.

Natalie moved to the podium, and the screen behind her illuminated. The picture that came up showed Smitten, but a very different one from the rough lumber town that now existed. Was that a skating rink? Carson studied the screen, intrigued by the picture-perfect town.

"We've all heard the jokes about our town's name, but it could be the thing that saves us." She turned to look up at the screen. "We can cater to lovers, honeymooners, those celebrating their anniversaries. We'll have love songs playing in the streets, encourage more businesses that accommodate couples."

Carson shot to his feet to object, but before he could voice his opposition, others got in ahead of him. The town meeting buzzed with excitement as voters threw out ideas on how to make this idea credible. Terms he'd never associated with his town were bandied about. Terms like spa, candle shop, *lingerie shop* of all things. It was insane.

He finally got the mic. "We don't need a new marketing plan. We need a new industry." He glared at Natalie, who leveled a stare back from calm brown eyes. She'd done this on purpose just to rile him. He knew it.

"But don't you see—this *is* a new industry. It's tourism, one of the best kinds. Instead of the mill ruling our lives, we'll be in charge."

"It's a good idea," Harold Warren shouted from the back of the room. "We can sell our town. I've lived my whole life here, and I don't want to leave."

"Me neither," a woman's voice chimed in. "We'll need a publicist. I can help with that."

Someone else volunteered to be on a task force. In spite of Carson's resistance, the proposal went to a vote and passed. All around him he heard people laying plans for how they could contribute to the idea. He couldn't believe it. Grabbing his jacket, he stormed from the building. Out in the town square he sank onto a park bench and rubbed his forehead.

How could they jump on such a crazy idea so quickly? Love capital. Good grief. They'd be the laughingstock of Vermont.

A female voice spoke behind him. "Can I talk to you for a minute?"

He looked around to see Natalie standing behind the bench with her navy peacoat in her hand. She was the last person he wanted to talk to. "I think you've said it all," he said.

She ignored his comment and joined him on the bench. A light scent, something flowery, wafted from her hair. He nearly rose and walked away, but courtesy demanded he at least hear her out.

"It's clear you hate the idea," she said.

"You're getting people excited about an idea that won't work. We're not a touristy town. We're blue-collar workers. We need another plant, maybe a furniture manufacturer. Something we can *sell*."

"Think about it, Carson. This is totally unique. People will eat it up. What else do we have going for us?" Her voice held excitement.

He struggled to ignore her enthusiasm. She'd always been persuasive. "Recreational stuff like skiing, hunting, and fishing. We can work on that." He glanced at her. Big mistake.

She leaned toward him on the bench. "We've worked on that for years. It's no secret your fishing cabins are only half full most of the year. And you're practically running your hardware store by yourself."

He winced. "We can brainstorm ways to do a better job."

"We've tried that. There's too much competition, even here in Vermont. But no one else is doing this. No one else *can* do it. We have the name and the great setting. All we need is to work together."

"It's *my* town, Natalie. My ancestor built Smitten. I'm not going to stand back and watch you make a joke of it."

She nodded toward the hall. "The meeting is breaking up, and I have another appointment. Let's talk at the coffee shop when you come by in the morning. I have some ideas to discuss with you. Please."

"No, Natalie, you're wrong about it. All of it." Just as she was wrong about him and her sister.

Her hand touched his. "Come on, Carson, I'm not going to bite. What do you have to lose?" She bit her lip. "I know Mia is an issue between us."

"She's only an issue because it's clear you believe your sister's lies," he shot back. "And what makes you think you know what's best for this town?"

Her dark eyes studied him. "Just because you're a Smitten doesn't mean you're the only one who cares about this place. Can't you put our differences aside and work with me for the good of the town?"

Good of the town? When she put it like that, it made him sound like he was being petty. Which he wasn't. She just didn't know what was good for the town. This was his town, passed down from the original Carson Smitten in the 1700s. If he had a prayer of saving Smitten, he had to derail this crazy plan.

"No thanks," he said.

Her dark eyes widened, then thick lashes shuttered the disappointment in them. She'd thought he'd agree, hadn't she? She'd clearly thought she could convince him.

# CHAPTER TWO

. . . . . . . . . . . . . . . . . . . . . . . . . . .

atalie held Mia's hand as she led her to the children's area in the back of the coffee shop. "You play here for a little while, honey. I've got a meeting."

Mia sat down at the low table. "Can I make a wreath?"

Ever since Aunt Rose had taught them how to decorate a Christmas wreath from ready-made grapevine wreaths, Mia had made one every week. The Easter wreath adorning the town clock was the little girl's creation as well. And it was while helping her niece make that wreath that Natalie had first decided she wanted to change their relationship. The three of them had been sitting at a table in front of the fire, and Natalie had looked at her aunt Rose and Mia with their heads bent together. In that moment she'd known this was what she was supposed to do. It was time she quit looking over her shoulder for Lisa to show up.

Natalie smiled. "I'd like that, honey. I'll be right over there." She pointed to the seating area.

Her stomach was jittering with the beat of Ben King crooning "Stand by Me" that was playing from the speakers, and she shot up a quick prayer for help. What had she been thinking when she decided to ambush Carson this morning when he came in for his coffee? Last night it had seemed a good idea to let him meet Mia and talk to him about the town at the same time.

The bell on the shop door tinkled, and Carson's broad shoulders blocked the sunlight. No wonder Lisa had lost all sense. The man was downright gorgeous. No one could have muscles like that and not work out, but Reese said she'd never seen him at the gym. Maybe he had barbells at home.

Natalie told Zoe she could take a break, then stepped to the counter to wait on Carson herself. At least the shop wasn't full of customers. Carson tended to stop by after the first rush was over.

His extremely male presence made her want to back away, but she held her ground. "Black coffee?"

He nodded. "You're running the place yourself today?"

"Zoe's on break." She poured him coffee and slid it across the counter to him. "My treat." She pushed his two dollars back into his hand. "Any new thoughts about our plan after sleeping on it?"

He eyed her over the top of his steaming cup. "A little sleep isn't going to make it logical. You've got the whole town talking about it. I stopped by the bank this morning, and the manager mentioned two people had already been in to apply for business loans."

She nodded. "Bet Ellie Draper was there to get her fudge shop up and running." The woman had been making fudge as long as Natalie could remember. It was about time she turned it into a career.

"How'd you know?"

"She mentioned it when she got her coffee this morning. She'll be right next door. We're going to do a joint café area outside."

"You've got it all figured out," he said. "But I've got my own ideas. We need something that isn't a pipe dream. There are leading manufacturers who are scouting for towns where taxes are low and workers are abundant. I'm working on figuring out some incentives to offer. That will save us. Not making a mockery of our name."

"Aunt Nat?" Mia stood at her feet, holding a grapevine wreath covered with dried lavender and baby's breath. "I have my wreath done."

Natalie sneaked a peek at Carson's granite jaw. Surely he'd see how cute Mia was, with her dark curls and dimples. Carson was staring at her, or maybe at Mia. Natalie couldn't tell. "This is Mia," she said. "Say hello to Mr. Carson, Mia."

"Hello," the little girl said.

Natalie's brown eyes studied him. "Is the wreath for me?" she asked Mia.

Mia nodded, her dimples flashing. "It's for the door of the coffee shop. Aunt Rose said the wreath means forever and ever. I want Smitten to always be here. So I want to put up a wreath to show God we know he's going to take care of us."

Natalie stared at the slightly lopsided wreath. "That's very sweet, honey." Oh, the faith of a little child. Even Natalie wasn't sure this would work. She *hoped* it would, but that was as far as it went.

"Can I put it up now?"

"Sure. There's a hook on the door that I use for the Christmas wreath. If you can't reach it by yourself, I'll help you in a minute." She watched Mia carry the wreath to the door.

"You planned that, didn't you?" Carson said the second Mia was out of earshot. His dark eyes were intense. "She's cute, but she's not mine, Natalie."

"That's not what Lisa said."

"I might not be perfect, but I'd never in a million years abandon a child of mine. All I did was give Lisa a ride that night when her car broke down. I never so much as kissed her." He jumped to his feet and strode toward the door. "Oh, what's the use," he muttered.

Well, she'd blown that battle. On both counts.

The town square was filled with people as Carson walked to work the next morning. Two men were putting a park bench under the old green clock. Other men were hammering together wooden flower boxes while women painted ones that were already done.

Zak Grant, a longtime friend, motioned to Carson as he neared the door to Smitten Hardware Store. Zak was thirty-two, just like Carson. They'd been friends since Carson knocked Adam Denton off Zak in the playground when they were in kindergarten. The two could have been brothers—both tall and strong. Both had dark hair and eyes. And both had come to the conclusion that the perfect woman didn't exist for either of them.

Zak stopped in front of Carson. "Spill it, Carson."

"Spill what?"

"Don't act like an idiot. Well, more than usual anyway. Why did your uncle close the mill? It's been three days. You have to have talked to him by now."

Carson stepped past Zak and unlocked the door, then motioned him inside. "Let me get things opened up first."

He got the computer booted up, then turned it over to Candy, one of his employees. "I'll be in the back," he said.

Zak followed him into the storeroom at the back of the store, past rows of steel shelving units that held overflow merchandise. Carson flipped on the coffee machine and motioned to Zak to have a seat at the break table. "What's up?"

Zak pulled out the steel chair. "Did you see all the craziness out there? It's like the whole town has gone mad."

"When people are desperate, they'll do anything," Carson said. "Folks are hurting."

"But a resort town focused on romance? Come on. Have you talked to your uncle?"

"No, it's none of my business. If he closed the mill, it's because he had no alternative."

Zak nodded. "Maybe it has nothing to do with the economy, though. Maybe it's just that he's getting older and isn't up to it anymore."

Zak had a point. Uncle Howard had been battling diabetes and never seemed to feel like doing much of anything. "But he loves his employees. If there were any choice, he would have kept it open."

"We could do something with it," Zak said. "You and me. A wood chip mill maybe."

"Come on, Zak. I don't know a thing about running a mill."

Zak folded his arms across his chest. "I'm a fourth-generation logger. I know everything there is to know about wood and mills."

"There's a lot more to it than running the equipment. There's vendors, suppliers, payroll, selling the product, marketing, overseeing everything. It's a big job."

"You've been in business for ten years. And we can get help. Would you at least talk to him?"

"I don't have time to run my own businesses *and* the mill, buddy."

"Just call him," Zak urged. "See what he has to say."

The last thing Carson wanted was to get involved with his uncle's business, but he supposed he owed the town that much. People had already been asking him if he knew why Uncle Howard had made his decision. He pulled out his phone and called his uncle's cell.

"Hi, Carson," his uncle's voice boomed. "I wondered how long it would take before you broke down and called to get the inside scoop."

The two men had always been close. Uncle Howard had helped raise Carson after his dad was killed in an accident at the mill, and had given Carson his dad's share of the mill to start a hardware store in Boston. When this place in Smitten had come up for sale, Uncle Howard called him and invited him to come home. Carson owed him a lot.

"People are asking," Carson said. "You okay?"

"As okay as I can be," his uncle said. "I thought about filing for Chapter 11, but I don't have it in me to fight any longer. The economy has taken its toll, and I don't see any possible way of pulling the mill out. It's been running in the red for five years."

Five years. How had his uncle kept it open that long? "I had no idea," Carson said.

"Helen's asthma has gotten worse too, and the doctor says she needs to move to a warm, dry climate like Arizona."

"But will you have enough money to live on?"

"Don't worry about us, boy. I've made prudent invest-ments. We're losing the mill, but thanks to the smart thinking of those ladies, I've already got an offer for the property."

"What? Who would want it? And why?"

"Some big investor from New York wants to build a resort on it. It would take years to get up and running, though. They'd have to level the buildings, get architect drawings done."

"You've accepted the offer?"

"Not yet. I'm thinking it over. I wanted to give you a win-dow, Carson."

"What kind of window?"

"Time to renovate your cabins into some high-class lodg-ing. You've got the premier spot right on the lake. Folks love that rustic feel if you can combine it with inside luxury. At least that's what Helen tells me." His voice held laughter. "I can help you with funds for that."

"I don't want to take any money from you."

"Consider it an investment. When it's up and running you can pay me back."

Uncle Howard was an astute businessman. If he saw the potential, maybe it wasn't as crazy as Carson thought. He ended the call with a promise to stop by and talk about it.

"The place is bankrupt," he told Zak. "And he already has an offer for the property. He's moving to Arizona."

Zak leaned forward. "He's taking the offer?"

"Thinking about it."

"Get him to put it off. Let me find out what it will take to get a wood chip mill going."

"I'll talk to him." Carson knew if anyone could make a

go of a wood chip mill, it would be Zak. He'd taken a ram-shackle building and turned it into a thriving bar and grill for the workers at the mill. He cared about those men and their families.

"I wish that whole romance thing wasn't so crazy," Zak said. "At least we'd have some hope." He stomped off and slammed the back door behind him.

Carson poured a cup of coffee and thought about his uncle's offer. Maybe he'd do some research about destination tourist spots. He took a sip from his mug and grimaced. It didn't compare to Natalie's brew.

# CHAPTER THREE

· · · · · · · · · · · · · · · · · · · · · · · · · · ·

*T*he town square had been transformed in a week. Natalie surveyed all that had been accomplished. Reese was everywhere, organizing and directing where things went. She had an eye for color and form. Spring flower boxes had been built, park benches had been put into place, and the center commons area was spotless. It didn't look like their ideal yet, but it was a start.

Natalie crossed the grassy area toward her shop when she saw Carson locking the door to the hardware store. She changed course. "Can I talk to you for a minute?" she asked him.

He glanced at her and nodded. At least he wasn't frowning. He put his key in his pocket and folded his arms across his chest. "Your minions got quite a bit done today," he said.

"They're not *my* minions. They're just people who have caught the vision." She tucked her hair behind her ears. "Look, I didn't come here to argue with you."

"Then why did you?"

"I wanted to apologize." That set him back on his heels. When he raised a brow, she rushed on. "I was out of line the other day. Your private affairs, er, business, has nothing to do with me. I shouldn't have said anything about Lisa."

"No, you shouldn't have," he agreed. "It has nothing to do with you. And spreading gossip isn't very Christlike."

"I wasn't spreading gossip! I've said nothing to anyone but you. Lisa said . . ."

"Lisa lied," he said. "Look, you've made your apology, such as it is. I have things to do this evening."

He was right—her apology left much to be desired. She held out her hand. "I really am sorry. I shouldn't have had Mia there."

His warm hand closed around hers, and his touch made something in her stomach flutter. *What on earth?* She pulled her hand away.

"Tell me something," he said. "Does Mia ever ask who her father is?"

"If you aren't her father, why do you care?"

He wagged his finger under her nose. "You just can't stay out of my business, can you?"

"You brought it up."

"I asked a simple question."

The man was going to drive her crazy. "She has asked. And I've distracted her and never told her."

Relief glimmered in his eyes. "Just because I care about the kid's feelings doesn't mean she's my daughter."

"I know." She didn't want to talk about it with him anymore. It made her feel sick in the pit of her stomach to think that he was Mia's father—which made no sense. She wished his denial were true. But why would Lisa lie about such a thing?

"Can I buy you a coffee to make up for it?" she asked. "I made some new cranberry bars today that turned out pretty tasty."

He hesitated, and she thought he was going to refuse, but he finally nodded and fell into step beside her across the pavement. They'd worked down the street from each other for several years, but their relationship had been cool and guarded. Maybe that was all about to change.

He stopped and touched the wreath on the door. "Looks like Mia managed to get the wreath up."

"She's so proud of it."

The aroma of coffee greeted them when she pushed open the door to the shop. She ducked behind the counter and got their coffee and snack while Zoe waited on a customer. Hmm, not many of the cranberry bars had been sold. She joined Carson, who was waiting for her on the leather sofa by the window. She watched him eagerly when he took a bite of the cranberry bar.

His mouth puckered. "I think it could use a little more sugar."

She bit into hers, and the tart flavor puckered her lips too. "I don't remember them being so tart this morning. Maybe cranberry flavor develops. I'll use more figs next time." She took another bite and managed to swallow it. "You don't have to eat yours. I've got a fresh batch."

He popped the last bite into his mouth, but his eyes widened.

"We've gotten off to a bad start."

"You might say that."

She hardly knew what to say to that. "I think that is going to change now," she said. "We'll have to work together on the plans. The town voted for it."

His lips flattened. "It does appear I have no choice unless I resign as a selectperson."

"Are you going to do that?" She couldn't lay a finger on why the thought dismayed her.

He said nothing for a long moment. "No. I'll abide by the people's wishes even though I think it's going to fail. That'll be a lot of money down the drain."

"Good. I'd hate for you to quit," she said. She bit her lip when he stared at her. He'd probably dislike her next question, but for the good of the town, she had to ask it. "I've been meaning to ask you something. Is there any chance your uncle might help us?"

"In what way?"

"W-With money for renovations downtown? Do you know if he's heard of our plans?"

He looked down at the coffee cup in his hand. "He knows."

"What's he think of it?"

"He thinks it's brilliant."

She couldn't help the smile that sprang to her lips. "That's wonderful!"

"He's going to Arizona, though, so don't count on much help from him. Knowing Uncle Howard, I'd guess he'll give some kind of a donation. What needs to be done first?"

"Reese is keeping a list, so check with her, but I know we need more sprucing up of the buildings downtown. Painting, cleaning, sidewalk repair."

"We need to put up some volunteer sign-up sheets in the church and the town hall," he said.

"Reese already took care of that. She has lists of the types of workers we need, like electricians, plumbers, painters, or whatever."

She watched animation brighten his eyes. He could bring a lot of enthusiasm to the project if he fully believed in it.

Carson sat back in his chair and rubbed his eyes. The numbers didn't look good. The moonlight glimmered on the lake just outside the window, and he saw swans gliding by on the glasslike surface. He opened the French doors and stepped out onto the deck. The scent of the cattails in the shallow water just offshore came to his nose. Frogs croaked, and one splashed off to his left.

He settled into one of the Adirondack chairs and let the lake's magic soothe him. His cell phone rang, and he answered it. "Carson Smitten."

"Hello, Mr. Smitten, I need to cancel a booking," the woman said.

He placed the voice, and his heart sank. "Sorry to hear that, Mrs. Deshler. All of them?"

"I'm afraid so. We decided to go to Stowe instead. I called in time to avoid a charge, isn't that right?"

"Yes. If you cancel thirty days or more before the date, there's no cancellation fee." He made a note to release the ten rooms she'd booked and hung up.

He'd been counting on that booking to pay his staff. There was money in his savings to cover it, but it didn't make him happy. If the woman had waited one more day, he could have collected a cancellation fee. Rebooking that many cabins this quickly wasn't going to be easy. With the sounds of the lake in his ears, he sat and prayed for direction.

Another sound came to his ears, and he lifted his head. Was that the doorbell? Before he could heave himself out of his chair, he heard boot heels clacking along the wooden floors. Only one person's footsteps sounded like that.

He rocketed out of the chair and turned toward the door as his brother stepped through. "Sawyer!"

The two embraced, then Carson held his brother at arm's length and inspected him. His hair was a little longer under the cowboy hat, but his blue eyes were alert and mischievous. He wore a bright blue shirt with fringe, well-fitted jeans, and snakeskin boots.

"Same old Carson," Sawyer said. "Town looked good as I blew through. I stopped at the coffee shop for a latte, and Zoe told me what's going on. Pretty exciting stuff!"

Sawyer always looked on the bright side. His dreams had taken him to a television talent show, where he'd found success beyond his wildest expectations. Well, maybe not beyond Sawyer's expectations. The guy put his heart into everything. The country was beginning to pay attention to his cowboy love ballads.

When Carson said nothing, Sawyer glanced around. "I hear you need to renovate the cabins."

"I like them the way they are," Carson protested. "And I don't have the money for the kind of renovations you're talking about." He put all the disgust he could muster into his voice.

Sawyer's grin vanished. "Listen, buddy, I'm the reason you don't have the money. You've poured so much cash into my dreams that there hasn't been any left over for you. I want to pay for the renovations. It's the least I can do after all you've done for me."

"That's way too much," Carson protested. "You're still getting your career going. Besides, I didn't give you what it's going to cost to update this many cottages."

"Including college, you've given me over fifty grand through the years."

Carson hadn't had any idea that Sawyer was keeping track. "It wasn't a loan, little brother."

Sawyer lifted a brow. "I know. That's one reason I made sure I kept track. And one of the many reasons why I love you."

Uncomfortable, Carson looked away. Singing love songs every day had made his brother more open about his feelings. "Ditto. But I don't want to take your money."

"You don't want to renovate at all, I hear." There was amusement in Sawyer's voice.

"I'm sure my reaction is all over town."

Sawyer frowned. "But it's a great idea. We've had to endure all those jokes about our name. Might as well put it to work. What do you say? Let's do something with this place."

"I'll think about it. What are you doing here anyway?" Carson asked, indicating the other chair on the deck.

His brother dropped into it. "I have a gig in Maine, and I had the bus go through here so I could show Kate where I was from."

"Who's Kate?"

Sawyer's grin came. "My fiancée."

# CHAPTER FOUR

. . . . . . . . . . . . . . . . . . . . . . . . . . . . .

*N*o one missed the big bus lumbering along Main Street as the women sat on Natalie's porch with their drinks from the coffee shop. The shiny paint on the sides depicted the face of the town's one claim to fame—Sawyer Smitten, the Cowboy Lover. Since he'd won the big *Country's Best* talent contest the year before with his cowboy love songs, he'd put Smitten on the map.

Natalie couldn't bear to look at Reese, focusing instead on the hummingbirds buzzing around the feeder near the blooming azalea bushes. She dreaded telling her the news she'd heard this morning from Zoe.

"Sawyer is in town," Shelby said, stating the obvious. "I've been praying for him. And for you, Reese, that you would find someone ten times better." She knelt to pick up Penelope, who was whining at her feet.

Reese's cheeks reddened, and her expression was guarded. "I saw him last night at the coffee shop. I managed to slip out the back door when he came in."

Julia set down her mocha java on the table beside her. "And we're just now hearing this?"

"He was with a woman." She studied her fingernails.

Natalie opened her mouth and closed it again. She squeezed Reese's hand. Sometimes a touch was the only comfort she could offer. That and prayer. "Zoe told me it was his fiancée."

Reese's smile looked forced. "I'm okay, Natalie. Really. I'm not going to lie and say it doesn't sting a little."

"What's she like?" Julia asked. "What kind of purse was she carrying? Was she wearing Louboutin shoes? I've been trying to save up for a pair."

"I didn't look at her feet," Reese said dryly. "I only got a glimpse before I rushed out. She's very pretty. Blond hair, green eyes, I think."

"Hmm, sounds like someone else we know," Julia said, exchanging a long glance with Natalie.

"She did look a little like me, except my eyes are hazel," Reese said. "I guess Sawyer is attracted to a certain type."

"You're really okay?" Natalie asked. Reese tended to keep her feelings to herself until things got so bad they erupted out of her.

Reese squeezed her hand. "Really."

"Zoe said she told Sawyer about our idea for the town," Natalie said. She'd been dying to tell the girls what she'd heard.

"What did he say?" Reese asked.

"He was excited about it." Natalie glanced at the other two. "I think he might have his wedding here." She couldn't help the triumphant smile that lifted her lips.

"What?" Julia scooted to the edge of her chair. "Celebrities will be swarming Smitten if Sawyer gets married here! What can we do to convince him? If I decide to do the spa, I'll be able to name the celebrities who have visited. It could make my spa a national destination!"

"Zoe said Sawyer was going to talk to Carson about it," Natalie said.

"We don't have housing," Julia said, pausing to turn a gloomy face Reese's way. "Without housing, the wedding won't happen here."

"They could stay in Stowe," Shelby suggested.

"We want the business," Julia and Natalie said together.

The bus *had* stopped at the coffee shop. Natalie could make out its shiny paint two blocks down. "Sawyer will forget it once he starts looking into things. He'll need lodging for everyone. Close lodging."

"Maybe he'll talk Carson into renovating the cabins," Shelby said.

"You're such an optimist," Julia said. "No one can talk sense into that hard head of Carson's. Not even Sawyer."

"I don't know," Natalie said. "Shelby might be right. Carson would do anything for Sawyer. And Carson *has* agreed to stay on the council to help. That's a start."

The women fell silent. "How can we help that decision along?" Shelby asked. "What if we all talked to him?"

"He'll feel ganged up on," Natalie said, shaking her head. "I wouldn't want to do that to him. Let's just pray and let God take care of it."

Julia's eyes widened. "You're attracted to the guy. It's written all over your face."

Natalie opened her mouth to deny it, but closed it again. How did they know when she hadn't realized it herself until this minute? Something about Carson intrigued her. And she didn't *want* to like anything about him. Not after what he'd done to Lisa.

"Okay," she said finally. "Maybe I am. But nothing can come of it." She bit her lip. "There's something I haven't told you. It felt too much like gossip."

"About Carson?" Shelby asked.

Natalie nodded. "Lisa told me he's Mia's father."

Reese froze, then twisted her ponytail in her fingers. "You're kidding. She just told you this?"

Natalie shook her head. "No, I've known about it ever since she got pregnant. She said he brought her home one night, and it happened then."

The girls looked a little hurt that she'd kept something so important from them. "You know how I hate gossip," she said again.

"What does Carson say?" Shelby asked. "Knowing you, I assume you talked to him about it."

"I talked to him about it a week ago. He denied it."

Julia held up her hand. "I'm sorry—I know Lisa is your sister, but, Natalie, *think*. When has Lisa ever told the truth?"

Natalie looked down at her hands. "I can't believe she would lie about something that important." She told her friends about her discussion with him in the coffee shop.

"There you go," Julia said. "I bet Lisa is the one who lied."

"I'm not convinced," Natalie said. "And I wouldn't date a man I couldn't trust. No matter how soft I go in the knees whenever he looks at me."

"Oh, honey, you've got it bad," Shelby said. She sounded wistful. "Good for you. I have a feeling God is going to surprise you in this relationship."

Natalie squinted at the bus again, still parked in front of her coffee shop. "Look, let's skip Pilates today. I want to talk to Sawyer."

The girls turned to follow her gaze.

"But it's your day to choose our exercise," Reese protested. "It's not a good idea to skip a day."

"We'll work extra hard tomorrow."

Shelby turned pleading eyes toward Reese. "Let her go, Reese. She's right. We need to talk to Sawyer."

"You go, then. I don't want to. I'll see you later." Reese jumped to her feet and headed down the street in the opposite direction from the coffee shop.

Natalie's heart hammered against her ribs as she hurried back to the shop, accompanied by Julia and Shelby. She stepped inside Mountain Perks. Sawyer was hard to miss with his bright shirt and cowboy hat. His fiancée *did* remind her of Reese, but Natalie's attention went to Carson, who was coloring with Mia.

He put down his crayon and got up when he saw them. "There you are," he said, putting his hands in his pockets. "Got news for you. Sawyer is going to have his wedding here. We wanted you to know since it might figure into your plans somehow."

Natalie's heart skipped, and she told herself it was only the good news. "That's fabulous! Thanks, Sawyer." She stepped forward to hug him. "We're so grateful."

"It'll be great publicity for Smitten. Get things off with a big bang."

"You like our scheme?"

"I love it. And the media will descend here for the wedding. All my guests too. I need your help to convince my brother he has to get the cabins renovated for them."

"I think you'll have more luck with that than me." She stepped back and smiled up at him. "You look every inch the rising country singer. Are you really the one who used to bring me wilted daffodils?"

"Guilty as charged," he said. "I backed off when Carson gave me the evil eye."

*Evil eye?* Natalie glanced at Carson. Surely Sawyer hadn't meant Carson liked her in that way.

Carson's smile vanished. "We need to go, Sawyer." He nodded to Natalie. "See you later." The bell over the door tinkled as they stepped back into the sunshine.

"Well, well, well," Shelby said, smiling. "Did you all see what I saw? Carson has a crush on Natalie."

"That's so not true," Natalie said, leaning down to pick up the crayon that had rolled to the floor. It was still warm from Carson's fingers.

"Sawyer said Carson gave him the evil eye for giving you flowers. What do you think he meant?"

"Oh, stop it! He was kidding. And I was only sixteen, and Sawyer was thirteen."

"And Carson was seventeen," Julia said. "Did he ever ask you out?"

"No," Natalie said. She wasn't about to tell them he'd asked her to get a Coke and she'd turned him down because she was giddy about going to the prom with Chris, a senior at the time. Carson had never asked again. What would have happened if she'd said yes that day?

Shelby eyed her over the top of Penelope's head. "You're afraid of being like your mother, aren't you?"

Her friend's perception shouldn't have startled her. Shelby had an uncanny ability to read her mind.

"It's easy for guys to hide who they really are."

"You have much better judgment than your mom," Julia said. "And I'm a discerner. There's nothing fake about Carson."

"My mother swore that was the case about husband number three. And four. And five," Natalie said. "I don't want anyone to deceive me."

"So you're going to be single the rest of your life, just to be safe?" Shelby asked. "What kind of life is that?"

"As you just said, a safe one," Natalie said. "Besides, you girls are blowing this out of proportion. Carson isn't interested in me." She picked up a plate of gluten-free cranberry bars. "Here, try these. Cranberries are good for you. They're full of antioxidants and protect against heart disease and cancer. I put more figs in them, so they're sweeter than the last batch."

Julia shot to her feet. "Uh, I have to go."

Shelby hugged Natalie on the way out. "Trust God," she whispered. "He might be opening a door for you."

Natalie nibbled on a cranberry bar and watched her friends through the big window. There was nothing wrong with being sure you knew someone before getting involved. Not that she was "involved" with Carson. They were just going to work together.

Carson didn't like his attorney's expression as he shut the door to the office and indicated a chair. It was just a little too eager, and the message Brian had left on Carson's cell phone had been too bright as well.

"Been a good day?" Carson asked. He wasn't about to even look at the way his morning had gone. The store had been packed with people working on their property and talking about the pros and cons of the romance idea. Good for business, but it made him uneasy. What if they were all hitching their dreams to a falling star?

"Amazingly good," Brian said, rubbing his forehead. "We have to talk, Carson."

"Not sure I like the sound of that. Is there a problem?"

"There's an offer for your property at the lake."

Carson sat back. "I'm not interested in selling. Who is it, and why do they want it?"

"An investor from New York. He heard about the idea to renovate Smitten and wants to build a big hotel."

"Bad news sure gets around."

"You're still opposed?"

"It'll never work. If they wanted to make us more like Stowe, catering to the outdoor types, I'd be hopeful, but this is a really nutty idea."

"I disagree," Brian said. "I did some research on towns that have a theme, and their tourist business is booming. The town is really onto something big here."

First his uncle, now Brian. Carson had always admired his attorney's business head. If the guy was in favor, he had to at least listen. "Got an example?"

Brian nodded. "Take the Poconos. They were a resort destination once upon a time, but bookings had diminished. Then in the sixties some of the lodging places started putting in things like heart-shaped tubs and publicizing it as a honeymoon place. *Life* magazine ran a story about the tubs and the honeymooners. Tourism boomed. There are other towns that advertise something special like German culture or Christmas year-round. Hershey, Pennsylvania, is the chocolate capital. If we specialize on romance, it could be our salvation."

"Come on, Brian, it's peanuts! A few tourists wandering in to see what all the hoopla is about. They'll just wander right back out, and we'll have spent all this money for nothing. The mill employed five hundred people. We won't replace that many jobs with this idea."

"Put your personal feelings aside," Brian said. "Think about it. You sure you don't want to sell? The guy is offering an outrageous amount of money." Brian named a figure that made Carson gasp.

But he would never sell. The place had been a camp for fishermen since the 1800s.

"If you aren't going to sell it, the guy offered to invest in your business," Brian said. "I think you have to consider it. Your cabins are a crucial piece of the overall plan. We need the lodging for this to work."

"I have lodging."

Brian's nose wrinkled. "Old cots and rough sheets. No woman in her right mind would agree to stay there."

Maybe today's news would lift that glum expression from Brian's face. Carson stretched out his legs. "Sawyer stopped in on his way to a concert."

"I wondered if that was his bus I saw this morning. I only caught a glimpse."

"He just headed out. He asked me if things would be up and running in time to have his wedding here. He'd like to do his part with some publicity."

Brian's expression brightened. "Good idea!"

"Yeah."

Sawyer's face was often on the front cover of magazines. With that kind of promotion, the town would see some major tourism.

"It could be the big break we all need. A love capital suits his image too, since he focuses on love songs and not drinking ones," Brian said. "It all ties together."

"So you really think this idea has merit?"

"It's either this or we all pack up and move out." Brian stared into his computer screen. "I ran some numbers for your renovation. It will be expensive. The guy's offer might be something you want to accept."

Carson didn't want to get on board with this idea, but did he have the right to kill it? If there were no decent lodgings for tourists or for Sawyer's wedding guests, the plan would fail. Did he want to be responsible for the town's demise if this scheme actually would have worked?

Carson thought of the amount he had in savings. "It will be tight. I just did some improvements to my hardware store."

Brian pursed his lips. "I could loan you the money on a one-year note with a promise to repay after the wedding. A week of full cabins at the prices you could charge would go a long way to paying off the loan."

"Sawyer has offered to help out. My uncle too. I'm still not convinced. And the cabins are still going to look like, well, cabins," Carson said. "No matter what I do."

The camp had been on shaky ground for several years, but he kept hoping his ads in fishing magazines would pay off. But spring was here, and the bookings hadn't picked up. Yesterday's cancellation would really hurt.

Brian shrugged. "People love the look of cabins. They just want the amenities inside."

"I'm not sure how to begin," Carson said. "I guess I could hire a designer."

"Or talk to Natalie. She's got a notebook of pictures that shows what she has in mind."

Carson kept his expression passive. "I'll figure it out." He left the office with a promise to drop off estimates of how much he would need by tomorrow.

No way would he go crawling back to that maddening woman and ask for her list of suggested changes. Never mind the thought that being around her gave a blip to his pulse.

# CHAPTER FIVE

. . . . . . . . . . . . . . . . . . . . . . . .

*I*t was a gorgeous spring day with crocuses popping up and a light breeze playing through the treetops, but Natalie's heart wasn't in the experience when she thought of what she should be doing. "I can't believe you talked us into this, Reese Mackenzie," she grumbled. Her breath whooshed out of her mouth as she trudged up the mountain slope to keep up with her friends. "How could you inflict this torture on your best friends? And you know I hate heights."

Reese widened her eyes in mock innocence. "It's good for you, Nat. Just walking isn't strenuous enough for optimal health. And we all know how health conscious you are."

*Hoist by her own petard.* "Oh, sure, throw that in my face."

Reese gave a cheeky grin and blew her bangs out of her eyes. "Besides, any excuse to forget about my job is a good time."

"Still hate it, huh?"

"My boss is a dragon. I just get things organized, and she dumps a bunch of files on my desk that are totally mixed up. I never feel like I'm making any progress."

Natalie stopped and bent over as she tried to draw air into her burning lungs. "That's gotta be totally annoying. You, Miss Organization Extraordinaire."

Reese grinned. "Okay, maybe I take it a little far, but things run better when they are orderly."

"I'll agree with that." Natalie straightened and glanced

at the path down Sugarcreek Mountain. "Have we climbed high enough for our first excursion? I'm done in and ready for coffee."

Reese checked her watch. "Twenty minutes up and another fifteen down. Perfect." She waved at the other girls. "Back to the coffee shop!" she called to them.

Natalie stumbled down the path behind her friends. When they reached the lane back to town by the lake, she squinted in the sunshine. "Here comes Aunt Violet. So much for coffee."

The woman was dressed in bright pink shorts with a matching shirt that clashed horribly with her red hair. She waved at Natalie and her friends. "I've just had the best idea!" she said as she reached the group. "My sisters and I are going to play every Friday and Saturday night in the town square."

The Garner Sisters were a Smitten institution. Aunt Violet had played the cello once upon a time in the Boston Symphony, and Rose and Petunia were accomplished on violin and viola.

"What a great idea!"

"I ordered some Frank Sinatra love songs," Aunt Violet said, then crooned a few lines of "The Very Thought of You."

Natalie barely held back a wince. The woman's singing didn't match the skill of her cello playing.

Shelby unzipped her sleek jogging jacket. "Uh, maybe you ought to learn some more current ones. Our honeymooners will probably be in their twenties and thirties."

Violet stiffened. "Classics never go out of style." She glanced around the lake. "I'll see you later, girls. I have a lot to discuss with Rose and Petunia." She hurried off to meet up with the other women.

"I *need* coffee after that," Julia said.

Natalie led the way to the coffee shop. "I have a new treat for you to try too."

Julia groaned. "Give it up, Nat. Those gluten-free things you make are horrible."

"This one wouldn't have gluten in the normal ones. It's a special energy bar that's packed with antioxidants. You'll like it. It's a blueberry bar. Sweeter than the cranberry ones."

"Gag," Julia muttered. "I'm not trying it." She stopped and stared toward the green clock at the town square. "Here comes Carson. Maybe he's reconsidered what you said."

Heat sprang to Natalie's cheeks. Was she *blushing* at the thought of talking to him? Julia gave her a curious glance, but she ignored it.

Carson appeared to be a man on a mission. A frown crouched between his brows, and his eyes were cold. As the women approached, he gave them all a nod, then focused on Natalie. "I need to talk to you," he said.

"I'm all ears." She kept her tone light and turned to her friends. "I'll catch up with you at the coffee shop."

Carson waved a hand toward the park bench next to the flagpole, and Natalie walked with him toward it. She sank onto the bench and tugged her jogging jacket a little tighter.

He stared down at her. "I want to talk to you about your ideas."

His face did *not* just turn red. Natalie stared at him. He definitely seemed discomfited. "My ideas about what?"

He dropped beside her on the park bench. "My fishing camp. I-I've reconsidered. I'm going to do some renovations."

She wasn't sure she'd heard him right. "Renovations?"

He nodded. "You know, the romance stuff." A pained expression haunted his eyes.

She would not laugh. She *would not*. "I see."

He shifted uneasily. "I wondered if I might get that list from you? Of suggested changes. I'm going to get started right away, and I need to get some quotes for materials."

"No problem, Carson," she said. "I'm glad to help." She wanted to ask him what had changed his mind, but looking at his tight lips, she didn't think she'd get an answer.

"I realized we need to work together on this," he said. "We're both selectpersons, and we'll need to present a united front if we want this to be successful. I need to be all in if we have a hope of making it work."

The very thing she'd wanted to say to him yesterday but hadn't had the chance. "Our first committee meeting is tonight at Smitten Community Church. I'd hoped to enlist your help."

"I'll be there." He stood. "Can we get that list now?"

She was dying to find out what had brought about his decision. Maybe he would spill the beans over coffee.

Carson glanced at the list Natalie had given him. The things his cabins should have were all well and good, but he had no idea how they should look. What made a rustic cabin into something luxurious? Not just the items on this list.

His office was a jumble of papers and fishing gear. Even this place would have to be brought up to elegant standards. He had no idea where to begin. Maybe he needed to hire that designer Brian had mentioned.

He heard a door slam and saw Natalie get out of her small red Dodge. The thrill that shot through him at the sight of her dark hair was downright alarming. He met her at the door. "Natalie, I wasn't expecting to see you."

She tossed her hair away from her face and smiled up at him as she extended a cup of coffee. "I brought a peace offering."

"I thought we'd made up already." He took the coffee. "Come on in, and don't mind the mess." She followed him inside. He scooped old fishing magazines off the chair on the other side of his desk.

She settled onto the chair. "I probably should have called, but I wanted to ask you what your timetable was for the renovations. Sawyer called about an hour ago, and his agent thinks having the wedding here is a terrific idea."

"I know. I talked to him too." He ran his hand through his hair. "I just don't know that these cabins can be turned into what his friends will expect. It's pretty overwhelming."

"I thought it might be." She pushed the notebook in her hands across the desk to him. "I thought you might enjoy looking at these pictures of luxury cabins."

He flipped through the pages. The first few showed the interior of various cabins. The pine was lighter than his, which had been stained dark. What did he do about that?

She stared at him. "You're frowning. You don't like them?"

"They're okay," he said. "But they don't look anything like the interior of my cabins."

"Yours don't have to look exactly like those. The pictures are just some ideas the girls and I have collected. Would you mind if I took a look at your cabins?"

Why not? He could use all the ideas he could get. "Be my guest." Tucking the notebook under his arm, he led her to the door and out into the yard, patchy with bald spots.

The blue of Timber Lake glimmered through the pines. The expanse of water beckoned to their right, with thick trees crowding the banks. A beautiful sight.

Natalie stared. "I never get tired of this view," she said. "You should maximize it so visitors never forget their first glimpse."

He took in the blue of the lake with the trees crowding the shore. Ducks paddled in the shallows, and the air was filled with the crisp scent of pine and water. Pretty as a painting, but he'd seen it so often he took it for granted.

She pointed at the sign at his drive. "The sign should be discreet, an engraved wood one, maybe. Landscaped with flowers and shrubbery that tell customers this is a special place."

"The sign is looking ratty," he admitted. He hadn't even looked at it in years. The thing was peeling, and the *e* in "Smitten Fishing Cabins" was nearly worn off. There had once been a picture of a largemouth bass on it, but now only bits of the green paint remained.

Natalie glanced at him. "Have you given any thought to a new name? You can hardly call it anything to do with fishing. How about Smitten Cove? It has a romantic sound."

He liked it, but he wasn't about to capitulate yet. "I'll think about it," he said. At least his drive was paved. If it had been gravel, she would have wanted changes there too.

He watched her stare around the place and tried to see it with her eyes. The cabins were in good repair—he'd made sure of that. New windows two years ago, the chinks between the logs were tight and even, and the roofs had all been done just last summer.

"You need some landscaping, but the exteriors look nice," she said. "Some redwood stain and they would be perfect." She advanced to the first building. "How many cabins do you have?"

"Twelve."

"Is there a building you can use for a convenience store?"

He pointed to the larger building to his right that they'd just exited. The neon sign declaring it an office was only half lit. "I have a bait shop in there too."

"It should have a cutesy name that lets customers know they can get supplies there like cold meds, hand lotion, snacks, that kind of thing." She stepped to the nearest cabin. "You have a key?"

He brushed past her and pushed open the door. "I don't keep them locked unless they're occupied." The stale air rushed past his face as if to let her know there was seldom someone inside.

She followed him. "Nice big space," she said. "And there's a fireplace. Bedrooms?"

"Some have one bedroom and some have two," he said. "Separate bedrooms plus a living space and kitchenette."

"The walls all need lightening up," she said. "The easiest thing to do would be to whitewash them. Then you could put in light pine furnishings."

He hadn't thought about whitewashing. At least he wouldn't have to sand all the wood. "What about the kitchen?"

She wrinkled her nose. "The wooden counters were a nice

touch once upon a time, but they're stained and warped now. I'd take out the kitchens. Cheaper than replacing, and you'd have room for the tub where they once were. Besides, honeymooners aren't going to want to cook. The plumbing is already in place, and the tub would have a good view of the fireplace."

She was good. He was beginning to catch her vision for the space. "The bedroom is through that door," he said, pointing to their left. She stepped into the next room, and he heard her gasp. "It's a little rough," he said.

The room held four cots, all with older bedding. The legs on the cots were metal, and some were rusting. The pillows were misshapen and the bedspreads were faded. The space felt dark too.

"All of this has to go," she said. "Whitewashing in here too. The floors need to be sanded everywhere and refinished a natural color." She pointed. "Bathroom through here?"

"Yep." He followed her to the small space and glanced around. The china sink was a little stained. The shower was a plain twenty-four-inch enclosure.

"This all needs to be gutted," she said. "You need bigger showers, preferably tiled or with marble or granite."

"This is all going to be expensive."

"You need top-quality materials in here, but it will pay off."

"What if it doesn't? I'll have to pour a fortune into this many cabins. If your idea fails, we'll all lose our shirts."

She turned toward him, and she was close enough that he could see the gold flecks in her brown eyes. "Catch the vision, Carson. Close your eyes and see it."

Her voice was so persuasive that he nearly shut his lids. He forced himself to glance around. For just an instant, he could see firelight gleaming on polished wood floors, the luxurious fabrics on the furniture and windows. "Okay, I'm on board," he said.

# CHAPTER SIX

. . . . . . . . . . . . . . . . . . . . . . . . .

*N*atalie finished her notes at the counter of the larger two-bedroom cabin while Carson watched. She put her pen back into her bag and held out a paper to him. "Here's the list of things that I suggest."

"You're good at this, Natalie. I can see why you've made a success of your business."

Before she could respond, her cell phone rang. She dug it out and saw it was Lisa calling. *Not now.* She was tempted not to answer it, but it might be important. "Hi, Lisa," she said into the phone. She turned away from Carson's shuttered expression.

"Nat, you have to help me." Lisa's voice was strident.

*Uh-oh.* Natalie hated to deal with her sister when she was agitated. "What's wrong?"

"I'm in jail."

*"Jail?"*

"In Chicago," Lisa said. "The idiot cop said I was loitering. I was just sleeping on the park bench. That's not a crime. I need some money for bail."

The only time Lisa called was when she needed money. "Aren't you even interested in how Mia is doing?"

"I'm sure she's fine. She has you, after all. I'm going to need two thousand dollars."

"Two thousand! I don't have that kind of money." There

was something suspicious here. Loitering wouldn't demand that much of a fine. "Were you selling drugs, Lisa?"

"Of course not."

But there was a defensive note in her sister's voice that made Natalie's heart sink. *Tough love.* Her pastor had told her she had to quit bailing Lisa out. Every time Natalie had resolved to do just that, she'd weakened when her sister begged for help. This time Natalie couldn't do it, though.

"Natalie, are you there?"

"I'm here. I can't help you, Lisa."

"You have to send me the money. I'll take Mia away from you if you don't!"

Natalie's lungs contracted. Losing Mia was her biggest fear. She should have gotten legal help ages ago, but she'd been busy with life and her shop and hadn't done it. One year had slipped into the next. Even though she'd made the decision to pursue adoption, she hadn't called an attorney yet.

"I don't have the money," she said softly.

"Well, you'd better find it!"

The phone slammed down in Natalie's ear. Her thoughts racing, she put her phone away.

Carson's brow was furrowed as he stared at her. "Lisa is in jail?"

"For loitering, so she says, but I think it has to be more than that. She wants two thousand dollars, and I don't have it."

"You're white as a sheet," he said. "What else did she say?"

His observation surprised her. Why would he care? "She threatened to take Mia if I didn't help her."

He nodded. "Ah. I'd hate to see that happen. Mia is a darling."

She glanced at him intently. Was he admitting he cared about his daughter?

His frown darkened. "And no, she's not my daughter, Natalie. I'd just hate for any child to be dragged from pillar to post with Lisa. She's unstable."

"I know," she admitted.

"You know she's unstable, yet you believe her accusation of me."

Natalie couldn't hold his gaze. "Mia looks like you," she said.

"Oh, good grief," he said. "She has dark hair and eyes, but so do you."

"What about a paternity test?" she asked.

"What's the point? I know the truth." He put his hands on his hips. "This bothers me for more reasons than you know. I'm not that kind of man, Natalie. This goes against everything I believe about relationships and marriage. I wouldn't do what she's accusing me of doing."

Her cheeks burned at the hurt in his eyes. Was it put on?

"Anyone who really knows me wouldn't believe it. If Mia were mine, I would do my duty by her. But *she's not mine, Natalie.*"

She wished she could trust the conviction in his voice, but Lisa had given too many details for Natalie to get the words out of her head. "Forget it," she said. "Let's wrap up here so I can get back to my shop. This is my problem, not yours."

He pocketed his hands. "What are you going to do about Lisa?"

"I don't know yet. I'm not going to give her money, though."

"Talk to Brian," he urged. "You shouldn't have any trouble getting legal custody. Lisa has abandoned Mia and is in jail."

"I'll call him. I want to adopt her, make her my real daughter. I want to tell her on my birthday."

"When is that?"

"May tenth."

"She's a lucky little girl," he said softly.

She glanced around the cabin. "We'll need you to have these ready by Sawyer's wedding on Valentine's Day. You think you can make it?"

"Less than a year, but I'll do my best."

"Listen, I'd like to help," she said, wanting to make up for how abrupt she'd been. "I'm pretty handy with a paintbrush."

"I hate painting," he admitted. "That whole whitewashing thing sounds tricky."

"It's not," she said. "I did my sunroom last winter. If you want to come by this weekend and see how it looks, come ahead."

"How about Saturday? What time?" he asked.

Mia would be at her friend's house for lunch but home by dinner. "How about six?"

"I'll stop by," he said. "Can I bring a pizza?"

"I can't eat gluten," she said. "I'll fix us a pizza that I can eat if you're game."

He grinned. "Will it kill me?"

She smiled back at him. "You won't even be able to tell the difference."

Carson had seen whitewashed wood before, but Natalie's offer was irresistible. This week's meeting had opened his eyes about her. He liked her presence, her enthusiasm. And he was man enough to admit to himself that he was attracted to her.

Her home was a gray two-story with white trim and a wide front porch. He noticed a lavender wreath on the red front door when he rang the bell. *Mia's handiwork again?* The door opened, and Natalie's smiling face welcomed him. The scent of pizza hung in the air.

"Nice place you have here," he said, following her into the foyer.

The oak floors appeared to be newly refinished. Gray-green walls were decorated with pictures of Mia at various ages from babyhood to the present.

"I love decorating projects," she said, leading him into a large living room that opened into the dining room and kitchen.

He glanced around the room in the same color scheme. A comfortable-looking sofa in gray-green tweed faced a matching love seat. Yellow pillows brightened the neutral color. He started toward the sofa, then changed his mind and headed for a leather chair. "You did all this yourself?"

"Oh yes. That's half the fun. I even sanded the floors, though I could hardly move out of bed for days afterward."

"Surround sound?" he asked when he saw tiny speakers.

She nodded. "And streaming video to the TV. I love technology. The pizza is almost ready."

"Dare I ask what the crust is made of?"

Her eyes were amused. "I'm not going to tell you until you take a bite."

"That's what I was afraid of." He heard small feet on

hardwood, then Mia burst into the room from the hall. "Aunt Nat, I got orders for two more wreaths. Two!"

Natalie put her hand on Mia's curls. "That's wonderful, honey."

How many little kids cared about things like this? Natalie was doing a great job with the child. Carson settled on the sofa. "Are those your wreaths I've seen on the front doors around town?"

Mia nodded as she knelt in front of the coffee table and opened her coloring book. "The wreaths stand for eternity. We want Smitten to be here forever. Do you need one, Mr. Carson?"

"I'll see about getting a hanger for one on my door."

"Dinner's ready," Natalie called from the other side of the granite breakfast bar. "Mia, wash your hands and show Mr. Carson to his chair."

"You'd better wash your hands too," Mia told him.

Grinning, he followed her to the powder room off the hall. An apple-scented candle burned on the granite cabinet top in the bathroom, and the scent made him think of his grandmother's pie. The hand towel had a Cinderella design. He handed it to Mia to dry her hands, then washed his own before following her back to the dining room.

The pizza looked and smelled good. Natalie had prepared a salad as well, and two bowls held olive oil and Parmesan cheese for dipping bread into.

He eyed the bread basket. "I thought all bread had gluten."

"That's gluten-free French bread," she said. "We have mocha soufflé for dessert." She pointed to the head of the table. "You can sit there." She dished some pizza onto his plate.

"Thanks." The crust almost looked like—vegetable something. He sniffed it suspiciously, but it smelled fine. He took a bite. The spices and cheese hit his tongue. "It's really good. You going to tell me what's in the crust now? It sort of looks like potato."

She settled into the chair to his right. "Cauliflower, egg, and cheese. I know it sounds terrible. That's why I never tell someone what's in it until they taste it."

He demolished half the pizza and salad by himself. When was the last time a woman had cooked for him? He couldn't remember anyone inviting him for a meal except his mother and other relatives. The women he'd taken out over the years had expected a meal in a nice restaurant. Cooking seemed to be a dying art.

What would it be like to have a family to come home to every day? He'd always thought he liked his privacy and independence, but tonight, watching Natalie and Mia, he wasn't so sure.

"How are your friends' plans coming?" he asked Natalie after she brought out dessert.

"They're discussing how they might contribute to the idea. Julia wants to open a spa for sure. She has some friends in New York who might be able to advise her. She's going to fly there next month and talk to Dev about it. She's hoping to talk him into coming here and telling her what to do."

"A spa. Seems nuts that anyone would pay good money for someone to put goop on their face."

"We girls like to look beautiful."

"You already are," he said. The words were out before he could stop them. He was gratified to see her blush.

She rose and took his plate. "We ran into Aunt Violet a couple of days ago on our hike. She and her sisters are going to be playing love songs in the town square."

He picked up the nearly empty bowl of salad and followed her to the kitchen. "I actually like that idea. Your aunts are all good. Violet used to travel the world with the Boston orchestra."

"Just don't let her sing," Natalie said, smiling. "She'd drive away our visitors. Want to see the sunroom?"

He set down the bowl and followed her to the French doors. Without looking at it, he already knew he was going to like it. He liked everything about this woman and her talents.

# CHAPTER SEVEN

. . . . . . . . . . . . . . . . . . . . . . . . .

*H*aving a man in her home alone should have discomfited her, but her ease with Carson surprised Natalie. They'd talked and joked over pizza as if they'd done this a thousand times. She stepped into her sunroom and glanced at him to see his reaction.

He stared around the space. "Very nice. I see what you mean about whitewashing. The wood grain comes through it enough to give it texture." He glanced at the floors. "You refinished these too?"

She shook her head. "I had them put down new. This used to be an enclosed porch. I had more windows put in and a floor laid. The knotty pine was already here, but I wanted it to feel open, light, and airy."

"It does. I like the colors. The gray-greens are peaceful."

It felt feminine to her, so she wasn't sure how a man would like it. She indicated the cushions on the wicker furniture. "Shelby made those for me for my birthday."

"You have good friends."

"I do." She settled into the big chair, and he followed her lead and sat on the sofa. "I have coffee on. It should be ready in a few minutes."

"I took the liberty of talking to Brian about Mia for you," he said. "I hope you're not offended."

It took a moment for his words to sink in. "You mean the custody issue?"

He nodded. "I know it was none of my business, but you need to do something, Nat."

It inexplicably warmed her that he used her nickname. "What did Brian say?"

"That Lisa abandoned Mia and hasn't paid for any care for her, correct?"

She glanced toward the kitchen to make sure Mia wasn't close enough to hear. "She never even calls or sends birthday or Christmas gifts. Mia hasn't seen her since she was two weeks old."

"You're a remarkable woman."

"Anyone would have done the same." Though his praise made her flush, she couldn't look away from the warmth in his gaze. What was happening here?

"I don't think so. Most would have turned Mia over to Child Protective Services. So you've been her mom for five years. There shouldn't be any trouble getting custody. Then Lisa can't threaten you any longer."

"I'll make an appointment with Brian and get it started. Thank you for that push. I needed it."

"You've been shoving me lately. I thought I'd return the favor." His grin told her he didn't hold any grudges about it.

"I think it was Sawyer who changed your mind," she said. "Not me."

Before he answered, the French door opened and Mia stepped through with a tray in her hands. "I brought you coffee, Aunt Nat. I wasn't sure how you liked yours, Mr. Carson, so I brought sugar and cream." She carefully balanced the tray as she came toward them.

"I'm not used to being waited on by such a pretty girl," Carson said. "I drink my coffee with cream, so you're pretty *and* smart."

Mia smiled and moved a little faster. Just when Natalie feared she might take a tumble and spill it, Carson took the tray from her hands.

"Looks like you're going to join us for coffee?" He glanced at Natalie with a question in his eyes.

"She likes only a little coffee and a lot of cream," she said.

"You're corrupting her early."

She took the cup he offered. "What? Coffee is a good antioxidant."

They sipped from their cups in companionable silence. Neither of them seemed to feel the need to fill the quiet with meaningless words.

"Want to watch a movie?" she asked.

"*Finding Nemo!*" Mia said.

"You've seen that movie a million times," Natalie said.

"I've never seen it," Carson said.

"Oh, you have to watch it," Mia said. "I love the turtles."

He glanced at his watch. "I have nowhere I have to be. If it's okay with your mom."

Natalie caught her breath at his slip of the tongue. She hadn't said anything yet to Mia about her intentions.

But Mia just shook her head. "I wish Aunt Nat was my mom."

She'd never said such a thing before. In the past she'd always just asked why her mother never came to see her. At first Natalie had assumed Lisa would return for her daughter any day. As the little girl grew old enough to understand, Natalie had been careful to show Mia pictures and to talk about her mother. But as the months turned to years, Mia had shown less and less interest in a woman she had never known.

"She's a mom in every way that counts," Carson said, rising from his seat. He took Mia's hand. "Let's see what Nemo and the turtles are up to."

Natalie followed them into the living room and started the DVD player. The movie was already in it since Mia watched it so often. As the movie played, Natalie sneaked peeks at Carson's obvious enjoyment of the little clown fish's quest.

When the credits played, she told Mia to go get ready for bed and found Carson's gaze on her when she glanced back at him. "What?" she asked.

"You're a lot like Marlin," he said. "You never give up, do you? And you'd die to protect those you love. I like that about you."

He stepped forward and cupped her cheek in his hand. A surge of emotion welled in her at the touch of his lips on hers. Her fingers clutched his shirt, and she kissed him back.

He was smiling when he lifted his head. "Can I take you out to eat one night when the craziness dies down? We can go to Burlington."

"I'd like that," she said, breathless.

When the door closed behind him, she sank onto the sofa, her knees trembling too much to support her. She was playing with fire. And she liked it.

But feelings like this were what had led her mother into trouble so many times. How did Natalie know she wouldn't be as easily deceived?

Carson grinned at the smear of paint on Natalie's cheek. Their relationship over the past two weeks had fallen into an easy camaraderie that surprised him. She'd given up her Saturdays to help him, and had shown up at eight this morning to whitewash the walls.

"I can't believe how much bigger this place looks," he said. "When you called this morning and said you'd like to do one of the living rooms, I didn't see any way you'd get it done in a day."

The cabin already looked like a different place. An old friend, Griffen Parker, had come back to town, and Carson had hired him to tear out the kitchens and install the tubs and bathrooms. He'd been working on this cabin for a week, and the place looked bigger, airier.

She held her roller in the air in a victorious gesture. "I'm the best painter in town. I love it." She climbed down the ladder and put the roller in the pan. "I'm ready for some lunch." She sniffed. "What did you bring us? I can't put my finger on it."

"I hope you like Mexican. I got *arroz con pollo* and made sure there was no gluten in the spices. Rice is okay, right?"

"I *love* Mexican. I could eat it three times a day." She went toward the folding table and chairs by the window where the boxes of food sat.

He followed and shoved open the sliding glass door to the deck overlooking the lake. The fresh scent of the water rushed in to push back the smell of paint. She was already seated, and he pulled out the other chair.

He dug out plastic utensils and they ate in silence at first until he glanced at her. "Did you hear any more from Lisa?"

The smile froze on her face, and she put down her fork. "She called twice after that, but I didn't answer. What more was there to say? I don't have that kind of money, and even if I did, I'm not going to give it to her."

"Did she leave a message?"

Her eyes shadowed, Natalie nodded. "She said she'd contacted an attorney."

"Did you see Brian?"

"Yes, he drew up papers for me to sign. He's been swamped with all the stuff here." She held his gaze. "Lisa said she might go after money from you."

"She won't get it," he said. "Tell me you don't still believe her."

She poked at her Mexican rice with her fork and didn't look at him. "She's just like our mother. Easily deceived by men and always making the same mistakes."

"I *wasn't* a mistake she made. I never even knew her outside of high school glee club, Natalie." He put down his fork. "I thought you knew me better now. Recognized the kind of man I am."

She looked up then, and her eyes were haunted. "What kind of woman would accuse a man of something so bad if it were all a lie? And why would she contact a lawyer if she weren't sure of her proof?"

"You think all men are deceivers and hiding who they really are?"

She put down her fork. "I don't know. Maybe there are good men out there. And it's just not in my genes to weed them out."

He should have been offended, but he found himself intrigued by experiences that had affected her so dramatically. "Your mom died when?"

"I was ten. My aunts took in the three of us." Her brother, Paul, had left town for college and gone on to be a top architect.

"What do you remember about your mom that affected you so much?"

She looked down at her hands. "The front door was a revolving one of man after man. She was married five times before she died."

"And Lisa is just like her?"

She nodded. "I don't want to be like them. Every day I ask God to help me see things more clearly than Mom and Lisa. To open the eyes of my heart."

"Yet you fail to trust him to do just that," he said softly.

Her cheeks reddened as though she'd been slapped. She said nothing as she rose and turned back to her paint pan.

"Prove you trust him and go out to dinner with me this weekend," Carson said. "Give me the benefit of the doubt."

He'd moved from the thought of "someday" going on a date to actually asking her out this weekend. Roller in hand, she stared at him, biting her lip ferociously.

"I'll pick you up Friday at seven."

"You're on." She turned back to her work.

He picked up a paint roller and joined her. Maybe he'd given her food for thought.

# CHAPTER EIGHT

· · · · · · · · · · · · · · · · · · · · · · · · ·

*N*atalie watched Julia lean on the counter and stare at the pastries on display. "Try the peanut butter cookies. They're fabulous."

Julia straightened and shook her head. "I need to lose three pounds."

Natalie knew better than to object. Julia maintained her weight like a drill sergeant. "I have a date with Carson," she announced. She'd been dying to tell her friends.

Shelby nearly choked on her latte. "A real date?"

Natalie nodded. "Dinner and everything."

"What about Mia?" Julia asked. "Who's watching her?"

"I thought I'd ask Zoe."

Julia shook her head. "Let me. I'd like to do it."

"You're sure?"

"Mia and I are buds. I'm in the mood to watch *Finding Nemo* again."

"I need help with what to wear."

"That's Julia's forte too," Reese said. "You don't believe Carson's Mia's father anymore?" Her voice rose over the sound of the beans Natalie was grinding.

Natalie's elation faded. "I still don't know what to think about that. I'm giving him the benefit of the doubt as I get to know him." Zoe came in from the back room then, and Natalie froze. Surely she hadn't heard them talking. While her cousin wasn't a gossip, she was blunt and often said things without thinking of the consequences. "I'll let you take over, Zoe," she said, shooting a warning glance at her friends.

Julia shoved items of clothing aside in Natalie's closet. "What do you mean you didn't tell him Friday was your birthday?" She wore slim-fitting slacks and a bright green sweater that showed her figure to advantage.

"I didn't want him to make a big deal of it." Natalie pulled a box from the top shelf and opened the lid. She lifted out a black snakeskin heel. "How about these Pliners that you got me last year for Christmas?"

Julia glanced at them. "I love those on you. They make your legs look fabulous. You need a short skirt."

"Not short!"

"Trust me on this—men love short skirts." Julia held up a black skirt that had a flirty ruffle on the bottom. "This is perfect."

"I've never worn it. Don't you think it's a little, well, daring for me? Maybe even too young?"

"You're thirty, not fifty. You're young enough to wear anything. Let's figure out the top." Julia rummaged again until she found a red lace top with a V-neck. "I've never seen you wear this either. It still has the tags on it. Hey, wait a minute. I bought this for you last year for your birthday."

"I hate to remind you, but I'll be thirty-one on Friday. And yes, you got me the top."

Julia put her hands on her hips. "I bet I got the skirt too."

Natalie suppressed a smile. "You have a good memory."

"Well, you're wearing it on Friday. He'll be speechless." She perched on the rose coverlet on the bed. "I don't know how to tell you this, Nat."

Natalie's smile faded at the serious expression on Julia's face. "What's wrong?"

"I was in the bank today and overheard two women talking about Carson being Mia's father."

The strength went out of Natalie's legs, and she sank onto the bed beside Julia. "Zoe must have overheard us."

Julia nodded. "It's probably all over town by now."

"I hope Mia doesn't hear about it."

"You probably ought to warn Carson."

The thought of telling Carson made Natalie spring to her feet and pace the lavender carpet. "He's going to think I was gossiping."

"It's not like you're a couple. Not yet anyway."

"We might be heading that way." Natalie settled on the carpet with her legs crossed. "I don't know what's happening between us."

"Do you trust him?"

"I want to. I'm trying to. Working together has made me see he's got integrity. How could a man of integrity ignore his daughter?"

"You know what I think."

"That Lisa lied. I'm beginning to wonder myself." She decided to change the subject. "At least the town project is moving along. I think we're going to do this!"

Julia's expression turned thoughtful. "You know what would be great? If Sawyer would write a song to go with the town."

Natalie gaped when the suggestion took hold. "That's a *great* idea! Can't you just see what kind of attention that would bring us? I wonder if he would do it."

"Carson could ask him. He might make it a song about his fiancée and how smitten with her he was when he first laid eyes on her." Julia sighed. "I don't think I'll ever feel that kind of overwhelming attraction. Men are pigs."

Natalie laughed. "You haven't dated the right one yet."

"And I'm not likely to in this hick town," Julia said gloomily. She sprang to her feet. "I'd better run. We'll come to the coffee shop for our birthday cake and party before the big dinner."

"You *will* be gone before he comes, right?" Natalie gave an inward shudder at the thought of the girls being there when she left with Carson.

"We'll be perfect ladies. Shelby has been coaching us."

Natalie walked Julia to the door. "That wasn't a promise."

Julia's smile was impish as she opened the door—and ran smack into Carson. He caught her before she could fall. "Sorry," Julia said, laughing. "Hi, Carson. Bye, Carson!"

Natalie's stomach fluttered at the warmth in his gaze. "I wasn't expecting to see you today," she said, stepping aside for him to enter. How on earth could she tell him that she and the girls had inadvertently started a terrible rumor?

"I'm on my way to work, so I can't stay," he said. "I found this under my door." He showed her a note from the school that had been colored in crayon.

*Dear Mr. Smitten, You are invited to Smitten Elementary for a tea to honor our girls and their fathers on May 2 at 2:00 p.m. We hope you can come. Love, Mia*

The *Mr. Smitten* and Mia's signature had been written in block letters.

Something kicked in Natalie's chest. "Oh dear," she said softly. "I'm so sorry, Carson. I never meant . . ."

"You told her I was her father?" His eyes showed hurt.

Natalie shook her head violently. "No! The girls and I were discussing it at the coffee shop. We didn't know anyone could overhear, but I think—"

"Someone did," he finished for her.

She could barely force herself to look him in the eye. "I think so. I'm so sorry. Truly."

His lips flattened. "It's a little late for an apology." He stared down at her. "You still don't trust me, do you, Natalie?"

"I-I want to," she whispered. "I'm trying. Lisa is my sister, so it's hard for me."

"It wasn't easy for me to trust you either. Did you think about that at all? It would have been easy for me to think you're just like her, since you're sisters."

She shuddered at the bleakness in his face. "I'm sorry, Carson. I didn't want to hurt you."

"You're one of the few people who can," he said. He held up the note. "What do I do about this?"

"If you show up to the tea . . ."

"People will assume even more that the rumors are true,"

he said. "I know, but I can't let Mia feel she has no one who would come with her."

Her earlier doubts resurged. Would a man care like this if he weren't Mia's father? "I can't let you do that, though," she said. "You know how a small town is. It's going to be bad enough for you without this. I'll talk to Mia. Maybe I can get my brother to come from Boston and go with her." She doubted Paul would be able to come, though. He often traveled with his job, and chances were he was out of town.

He turned toward the door. "Maybe."

She didn't want him to go with the tension between them. "Before you go, Julia had a great idea. What if Sawyer wrote a song called 'Smitten'? And sang it for the first time at the wedding?"

He turned back toward her, but his expression was guarded. "It would be good for his career and good for us too. A win-win situation. I'll give him a call tonight and ask him."

"We thought so too, but I don't know how long it takes to write a song and get it produced and ready for distribution."

"I don't know either, but Sawyer will do what he can, I think. I'll let you know what I find out."

He hesitated, and she thought for a moment that he was going to say something about what she'd done. Then he twisted the doorknob and stepped back into the sunshine.

"See you Friday," he said.

"See you," she echoed. Should she even go?

The work on the cabins was coming along, and the hardware store was busy with customers. Carson had been asked to order material for the new fudge shop going in next to Mountain Perks as well as the remodel of the bookstore down the street.

He stuck the cloth he'd been using to wash the front window into his pocket when he saw Mia and Natalie crossing the street in his direction. When it was clear they were coming to the hardware store, he stepped out onto the sidewalk to greet them.

Mia carried two lavender wreaths in her hand. "We came to bring you a wreath," she said, holding them up for his inspection.

"Very nice," he said. "Let me get a wreath hanger and we'll put it up."

Natalie's expression warmed. "I wasn't sure if you were ready for one or not."

"After seeing my cabins being wrecked and rebuilt, you should know I'm ready."

He left them on the sidewalk while he fetched what he needed to hang the wreath. Conscious of Natalie's gaze on him, he attached the hanger to the door, then took the wreath and positioned it.

"Perfect," he said, stepping back. "Go inside and tell Candy to give you a sucker, honey."

"Cherry ones?" Mia asked.

"You bet. Take two." He opened the door for her and caught another whiff of the lavender.

Rose Garner came toward him. Her smile brightened when she saw them together. She glanced at Natalie. "I'm glad to see you don't believe that nonsense circulating through town, Natalie."

Natalie's face went pink. "Aunt Rose . . ."

"Now, honey, we both know Lisa. It's not being disloyal to speak the truth. I'm glad you finally have seen through your sister." She stared at Carson. "You be good to my niece, Carson Smitten. And I'll be glad to welcome you into the family."

Now it was his turn for his face to flame. He didn't know what to say. "Uh, thanks, Ms. Garner."

She patted his cheek. "Glad to see you have a wreath on that door of yours."

"Thanks to Mia, of course."

"I think I'll take Mia for ice cream, if you don't mind, Natalie," Rose said. "Is she around?"

"That's fine." Natalie barely mumbled the words. "She's inside."

"I'll bring her back later." Rose headed for the door.

No way did he want to discuss their relationship with Natalie. Not now. "Sawyer called yesterday," he said. "He was excited about the song idea. He'll see what he can do. They were working on the guest list. So far it's at five hundred people."

She clapped her hands. "Yay! This is going to be big, Carson. Which means maybe two hundred and fifty people will show up. You can usually assume half of your guest list won't be able to make it, especially for a destination wedding." She pursed her lips. "Though that statistic may not hold true for a celebrity wedding."

"He told me to count on about three hundred. The most my cabins would hold is a forty-eight, if we stuffed people in four to a cabin. And people won't be willing to do that unless entire families are coming."

"So we have a problem," she said.

He liked the way she said *we*. "Any ideas?"

She chewed on her lip and looked up and down the street. "We need some kind of hotel."

"But could it even be built in time?"

"Probably not."

"I have an idea," he said slowly, the seed taking root. "I have some acreage south of town. Uncle Howard wanted to do all he could to get this off the ground. I could ask him if he'd be willing to help me build a larger lodge there. Since I already own the land, things could proceed much faster."

"A large enough lodge is going to be expensive. Can he afford that?"

He shrugged. "I can only ask."

"It will mean losing control over your property and taking on your uncle as a partner. Are you prepared to do that?"

She seemed to really care how he felt. The realization warmed him. "I'm finding I'd do just about anything for you," he said.

A flush stained her cheeks, but she didn't look away. "I'll help all I can."

"I'll need it. This is a much bigger project than cabin remodels."

She chewed on her lip. "My brother is an architect. He's done big hotels for major chains. I could ask him if he'd do some freelance work."

"You're kidding. That's thousands of dollars."

"I think he'd be willing to help. We could give him some free advertising by telling the media he designed the lodge. I think he'd do it for a song."

He held her gaze. "You're a good woman, Natalie Mansfield. When you believe in something, you are all in, aren't you?"

"Isn't everyone?"

He shook his head. "Too many people quit when the going gets tough. You just get more determined."

Her blush heightened. "Some would call that hard-headed. Or stubborn."

"I'll tell you a secret. You're the reason I believe this will work. You could sell refrigerators to the Eskimos."

She smiled. "I think I've heard that before, only it's been said with less respect."

"That might be why we've butted heads now and then in the past—you're not one to sit back and take orders. You like to make things happen."

"Guilty as charged," she said. "There is nothing that irritates me more than whiny quitters."

"I hope I'm never one of those," he said, grinning down at her.

"People look up to you," she said. "I've always respected you and known you put careful thought into your decisions."

"Even though you didn't always agree."

"Even though I *often* didn't want to agree." She diffused the words with a smile. "I didn't like admitting you were right. It's a character flaw I have to work on. Among many."

"I don't see any flaws," he said softly.

The connection between them broke when he was summoned inside to help a customer. Natalie went to the park, where she took out her phone and called her brother, Paul. When she explained what she needed, he was quick to offer to help.

"Can it be built in time?" she asked.

"If we get right on it," he said. "It's not like it's a mega-hotel. Average time to build a hotel is about a year, but many have been built in a much shorter time. Heck, the Ark Hotel in China took only two days!"

"I doubt we have that kind of labor," she said, smiling at her brother's optimism.

"So it's going to be a romance capital," Paul said, a smile in his voice. "And the avowed spinster is spearheading the project. Rather ironic, don't you think?"

*Spinster.* She winced at the ugly word. "I've never been against marriage."

"No, you're just afraid of making a mistake like Mom and Lisa."

"You're hardly a poster child for commitment," she said.

"You never know," he said. "Even this old dog could change his spots. You could too if you learned to trust a little."

"Well, back to the hotel," she said. "Let me give you Carson's number. You can discuss with him what he wants."

Was that what she was doing with Carson? Learning to trust?

# CHAPTER NINE

$\mathscr{M}$ia already had dinner, Nat," Julia said. She was dressed in expensive jeans and zebra shoes that matched her top.

After a visit with Julia, Mia would spend hours trying on her clothes and wanting different things done to her hair. Today Natalie had been talking to Brian about legal custody, so she had needed after-school care for Mia, and Julia was quick to come to the rescue.

Natalie hung her light jacket on the hook by the door. "Where is she now?"

"In her bedroom. I want to say good-bye before I leave." She paused. "You still need me on Friday, right?"

"Yes, if you're free."

Mia came running down the hall and hugged Natalie.

"I'm always free for Mia." Julia held out her arms to hug Mia good-bye, then went out the door.

Natalie steered Mia toward the kitchen. "Did you leave me anything to eat?"

Mia nodded. "I didn't eat all the chicken. It's still warm."

"What a good kid." Natalie put the last of the grilled chicken on a plate, then joined Mia in the living room. The thought of talking to Mia about Carson made the idea of food unappealing. She wanted to protect the child all her life, but she knew hard truths had a way of coming out. And pain molded character.

Natalie settled on the sofa with one leg folded under her. Sunlight still streamed through the picture window. "Did you have a good day at school?" she asked.

Mia nodded. "Mandy's mommy brought in cupcakes for her birthday." She sat down on the sofa and leaned against Natalie. "Can I call you Mommy, Aunt Nat? I don't think my mommy is ever coming back."

Natalie had been about to take a bite of chicken. She lowered her fork and embraced Mia. Brian had been very confident, but what if he was wrong? She hated to get Mia's hopes up. She'd hoped to be ready to spill the news on her birthday, but it didn't look like it was going to happen that quickly. "I'm your mommy in every way that counts," she said. "To me you are my Mia and no one else's." She smoothed Mia's curls.

Mia buried her face against Natalie's side. "I don't have a mommy *or* a daddy," she murmured.

"I'm going to make you my own little girl," Natalie said, her throat tight. "I've asked a judge to let you be my daughter."

"Truly?" Mia's face lit. "Forever and ever?"

Natalie hugged the little girl to her, and Mia gripped her with a fervency that touched her. "Forever and ever."

"I love you, Aunt Nat." After a final squeeze, Mia let go. "Do you know who my daddy is?"

Natalie's hand froze on top of Mia's hair. What should she say? She looked into Mia's innocent eyes. "I don't know, honey." She wished she could say with firm assurance that Carson wasn't Mia's father.

The hope in Mia's eyes dimmed. "Mandy at school said it was Mr. Carson, but I didn't believe it," Mia said. "He would have come to see me if he were my daddy. I asked him to the tea. Do you think he'll come?"

"I think he'd like to, but it might make people think badly of him."

Mia frowned. "I don't want people to talk mean about him."

A shadow moved past the window. Natalie saw Carson walking toward the front door, then the doorbell rang. The surge of pleasure she felt at his appearance shocked her. Was she as easily influenced as her mother? As Lisa?

Mia slid from the sofa. "It's Mr. Carson! I'll get it." She ran to the foyer, and Natalie followed. "Come on in," she told Carson.

Her mouth went dry at the sight of him. He wore jeans and a red shirt that made him look incredibly handsome. She'd never noticed how thick his hair was, how long his lashes were.

"Hope I'm not intruding," he said.

"Not at all. We're glad to see you." She led him to the living room, then pointed to the sofa. "Have a seat."

He settled on the sofa and lifted Mia to his lap. "I came by to tell Mia I'd be honored to attend the fathers' tea."

Mia smiled, then her grin vanished. "Aunt Natalie told me that it might make people say mean things about you. I don't want you to come if that's what will happen."

His eyes widened, and he glanced at Natalie. "A friend told her the rumor," she mouthed.

His eyes held a shadow. "I don't care what people say,

honey. I'd rather make you happy than worry about wagging tongues."

Mia's smile returned full force. "Pinky swear, Mr. Carson?"

She held up her pinky finger, and he linked his with hers. "Pinky swear," he said, his face serious. He glanced at Natalie. "I did a lot of thinking today. Some things are too important to take the easy way out."

Could he possibly be all he seemed? Where were Natalie's faith and trust? Maybe his accusation at the cabin was right. "I'll do what I can to head off the rumors," she said.

He went still. "Now that I've met this munchkin, I kind of wish the rumors were true."

Mia threw her arms around his neck and planted a kiss on his cheek. "I love you, Mr. Carson."

His eyes misted as he hugged her. "I'd walk on hot coals to hear that."

As Natalie watched them, she allowed herself to wonder what it would be like for the three of them to be a family. She shook off the ridiculous notion.

Natalie had arranged to meet the girls at the coffee shop for a quick birthday party before her date, and they'd come bearing gifts. The table was decorated with a chocolate gluten-free cake and balloons, and she'd had the barista make her friends' favorite beverages.

She unwrapped a blue package first. It was a CD. "Christmas music?"

Shelby's dark head bobbed, and she smiled proudly. "It's the California Raisins! I had to order it online since it's not being made anymore, but it's the best Christmas CD *ever.*"

"It's May," Reese pointed out.

"But Christmas is coming! And it lifts my spirits no matter what time of year it is." Shelby began to sing "Santa Claus Is Coming to Town" in a rich alto.

Natalie contorted her mouth trying not to laugh, but a giggle escaped anyway. "Only you, Shelby." She hugged her friend. "Thank you. I'll think of you when I listen to it."

"Okay, that's not all," Shelby said. "But it was my favorite gift. Here's the other." She handed over a bag that contained three books. One on the behavior of five- to ten-year-olds, a children's story about adoption, and another book on building an adoptive family.

Natalie squealed. "Shelby, how did you find these?" She hugged Shelby again.

Shelby smiled. "Glad you like them."

Natalie opened the gift from Julia, a stylish pink backpack. "I can put Mia's things in it when we travel or go to the park."

"That's what I thought," Julia said.

Smiling, Natalie glanced at Reese. "I suppose you have a motherly item for me too?"

"We have to celebrate with you." Reese handed over a bag.

Natalie peeked inside and pulled out a Pilates DVD for children ages five to ten. "It's perfect! I might actually be able to do this one."

"Glad you like it," Reese said. "And by the way, you look totally hot tonight. Is that the outfit Julia got you last year?"

Natalie exchanged a long glance with Julia. "Yes. You don't think it's a little—well, sexy?"

"Legs like yours should be flaunted, not hidden," Julia said. "The only thing I would have added is fishnet stockings."

Natalie shuddered. "I think I'll stick with bare legs, thank you." She glanced at her watch. "He'll be here in half an hour." The skirt ended just above her knees, so it wasn't that short. But she felt so vulnerable in it.

"I want to see his face when he first spots you," Julia said.

"I don't think so. Having you all here will make me too self-conscious. I can't even remember the last time I had a date," Natalie said. "I'm out of practice."

Shelby hugged her. "I'll be praying for you, friend, but you're going to have a great time."

Shelby always reminded Natalie that God was in control. Natalie picked up a knife and cut into the birthday cake. "Who wants a piece of cake?"

Julia sprang to her feet. "Let's listen to that Christmas music. What's on that CD?"

"No cake for me, thanks," Reese said. "I'm trying to shed a couple of pounds. But you go ahead."

Natalie took a bite. "Come on, girls, it's really good. Honest. It tastes just like one made with wheat."

"I'll have some," Shelby said, her eyes sympathetic. "I found a great recipe. It's made with almond flour mixed with rice flour and pea protein. And it's chocolate, so it has to taste great."

Natalie took another bite. "It's delicious, Shelby. Thanks for going to all that trouble."

"Anything for you, my friend."

Natalie glanced toward the door to the kitchen. "Now to just figure out those cookies. I have a sample batch you can try."

Reese sprang to her feet. "I need to leave."

Julia headed for the door. "We know you don't want us here when Carson comes. I'll pick Mia up from Rose's tender clutches."

Natalie laughed. "Chickens." She saw them to the door, then rushed to the mirror where she fussed with her hair and touched up her lip gloss one last time. The bell over the door reverberated through her midsection moments later, and she gulped. It was so silly to be nervous. Her feet wobbled in the high heels as she went to see if it was Carson.

Carson wore jeans and a blazer over a white shirt. His short curls appeared to have been newly trimmed. He held out a bouquet of daisies. "You seem more like a daisy kind of girl than one who likes roses," he said. "Happy birthday."

"I *love* daisies," she said, taking the flowers. "How did you know it was my birthday?"

"You mentioned it once, the first time you came to my cabins."

And he'd remembered all this time? "Let me put them in water." She carried them behind the counter, trying to stay out of Zoe's way, and dug a vase out from the cabinet. She was conscious of his presence as she filled the vase with water and arranged the flowers. "Beautiful," she said, placing the vase on the counter.

"Yes, beautiful," he said, his gaze on her and not the flowers. "I have something else." He pulled a small box from his pocket and held it out.

Jewelry. It had to be jewelry. Did that say something special about their relationship? Her hands shook as she took it and untied the ribbon. She lifted the lid of the black box, and a locket glimmered inside. "It's beautiful," she breathed.

"Open it."

She lifted the locket and opened it. Mia's face smiled back at her. Her vision blurred. "Oh, Carson," she said softly. She looked up at him. "It's perfect."

"On the other side you can put one of the two of you together."

"How did you get the picture of Mia?"

"Your aunt Rose helped a little."

The bell on the door jingled again, but she didn't look to see who had come in until a man cleared his throat and spoke.

"Hey, Carson. Candy said she thought you were here," Brian said. He didn't smile, and his eyes were troubled.

"We were about to head out to dinner," Carson said. "What's wrong? You look upset."

"I had a call from Lisa," Brian said. "We dated in high school some, so I guess she thought I'd help her."

"What did she want?"

"She asked me to try to get some money from you. That you should want to bail your child's mother out of jail."

Carson's hands curled into fists. "You've got to be kidding."

"I wish I were."

Carson rubbed his head. "What does she hope to gain by this?"

"Your guess is as good as mine," Brian said.

Surely Lisa was certain of her facts or she wouldn't have taken this to a lawyer, would she? Natalie didn't want to believe Carson was Mia's father, and in fact, she was ready to trust his word totally. But hearing this news made her want to take a step back.

"So what do we do now?" Carson asked. "I'm not giving her a cent. And it goes without saying that I'm not Mia's father."

Brian's face filled with relief. "I'd take a blood test, then. You'll have proof if she presses the situation."

Carson sighed and dropped his hands to his sides. "I don't think I should have to prove myself. My word should be enough."

Carson glanced at Natalie, and the indecision she saw in his eyes made her wonder even more. Why would he even hesitate to agree to a blood test? Unless he didn't want the truth to come out.

# CHAPTER TEN

. . . . . . . . . . . . . . . . . . . . . . . . . . . .

*T*he Sentry was a nice restaurant, and their table looked out on Lake Champlain, but Natalie only wanted the agonizing evening to be over. Her seared ahi tuna looked and smelled delicious, but she couldn't have said what it actually tasted like. Conversation had been stilted.

Carson took a sip of his Pepsi, then set it down. "You've been weird all evening. You don't believe Lisa's accusation, do you?"

She gulped a mouthful of water to give her time to form an answer. "I guess I'm surprised at your reluctance to take the blood test. It's the only way to end the gossip."

His face hardened, and his eyes narrowed. "So you *do* believe it."

Was that hurt in his voice?

"I don't believe all of it," she said. "But I have to think there was more to your relationship than a casual ride after her car broke down. Th-That's just crazy to accuse you with no more than that."

She saw him swallow hard. His lips flattened.

"After what you know of me, you'd actually believe that?" He leaned forward and stared at her. "Even a kiss to me means *I love you*. I take that pretty seriously. I haven't had sex with any woman, Natalie. God says it's sin, and I want to go to my marriage bed as pure as my wife. I feel stupid even admitting that to you. Guess I've been so careful for no reason, when the woman I love is so quick to think I have no morals."

*Did he just say he loved me?* She opened her mouth, then closed it again, unsure how to respond.

His chair scraped on the floor as he pushed back from the table. "There's no more to say. Let me take you home." He left money on the table and headed toward the door.

Silently she rose and followed him to the car. Everything in her wanted to believe him, but it would be stupid to ignore the evidence. She'd seen her mother do it time and time again, each man worse than his predecessor.

"I'm sorry," she said when he dropped her in front of her house. Her door opened smoothly, and she thought he might ask her if he could stay so he could explain more, but he simply wished her a good night and drove off. She stood and watched until his taillights flashed at the stop sign, then disappeared into the fog.

Her vision blurred. No matter how attracted she was to Carson, she was determined not to be deceived by appearances. Ten years from now she didn't want to end up in divorce court because she married a man who wasn't what he seemed on the surface. Swiping the moisture from her cheeks, she took a deep breath and entered her house.

"Is Mia in bed?" she asked Julia.

Her friend nodded. "She was so sweet tonight. She prayed for Carson."

"Why?"

"She didn't tell me, but it was cute to hear her talk to God like he was her best friend." She went toward the door. "How was your date?"

"Don't ask. I'll tell you when we're all together tomorrow."

Julia hesitated, then nodded. "See you tomorrow. It's Shelby's day, so we only have to walk."

Natalie locked the door behind Julia, then went to check on Mia. The child was sleeping on her side with one arm flung over her head. The covers were twisted. Natalie straightened them, and Mia opened her eyes.

"You're home," she said, rubbing her face. "Is Mr. Carson here?"

"No, he left."

"I tried to stay awake so I could talk to him."

"You really like Mr. Carson, don't you?"

"I love him," Mia said solemnly. "Even if he isn't my dad."

*So do I.* The realization that her feelings were much more than mere attraction made Natalie sink to her knees by the bed. What would Mia think if she knew Carson should be part of her life but had rejected her? What if she heard about the paternity suit? Natalie prayed she would never find out. "Did you have a good time with Julia tonight?"

"Uh-huh." Mia rolled onto her back. The moonlight touched her sweet face. "We prayed for Mr. Carson too. God told me to."

"He told you to pray?"

Mia nodded and sat up. "Mr. Carson was sad tonight. It hurts him that people lied about him. I'm going to make sure all my friends know the truth."

*Truth.* It sounded like it would be so easy to discern, but it wasn't always possible to see beneath the smiling surface. How could Natalie ever tell when to trust and when to dig deeper?

*Carson prayed over dinner tonight.*

Okay, so her mother's men never claimed to be Christians. Still, Natalie had seen her share of hypocrites in her life. Some had been in her own church.

She sighed and kissed Mia. "Time for sleep, honey."

"I love you," Mia said, her eyes already closing.

"Love you most," Natalie said, knowing she'd get the last word in since Mia's breathing had already deepened.

She eased out of the room and shut the door behind her, leaving only a crack so there was a bit of light. In the sunroom, she dropped onto the sofa and stared into the dark night before sighing and picking up her Bible on the stand beside her. She hadn't had time to do her devotions this morning. Or rather, she'd let herself get distracted.

The bookmark was in Hebrews. She began to read chapter 11, and the first verse hit her heart.

*Now faith is the substance of things hoped for, the evidence of things not seen.*

She'd seen the evidence of Carson's life. Did she need more than that? *Substance.* There was substance in Carson's life too. He'd told Mia he didn't care what people said about him. Maybe he really didn't care because he knew the truth and where he stood with God.

She wanted to *know.* Stepping into the unknown scared her, but maybe it was supposed to. Wasn't that what faith was all about? Still, she didn't want to be stupid about it. There had been too much of that in her life. She grabbed her concordance and looked up references to faith. The first one she went to was Matthew 8:26.

*But He said to them, "Why are you so fearful, O you of little faith?" Then He arose and rebuked the winds and the sea, and there was a great calm.*

Fear. That's what had been ruling her life. She was afraid of being abandoned. Wasn't there a scripture about perfect love casting out fear? She found it in I John 4:18.

*There is no fear in love; but perfect love casts out fear, because fear involves torment. But he who fears has not been made perfect in love.*

"Help me trust, Lord," she said, closing her Bible. No matter how hard she tried, she couldn't uproot the love she felt for Carson. And fear was what held her back. How could she fix it?

The crowd had gathered on the lawn outside the town hall. Most were careful to avoid the newly planted flowers in the planting bed. The doors would open shortly for the Planning Commission meeting. Natalie glanced at the big green clock. Ten. The sunshine strengthened her resolve in spite of how many more people were here than she expected.

She hadn't seen Carson in a week, and her stomach was in knots as she spoke to several people on her way to the door. She didn't see Carson's dark head towering above the crowd, and for a fleeting moment she almost hoped he wouldn't show up. The janitor was unlocking the entrance when she reached it, and she was the first one to step into the hall. She barely had time to take in the empty room before people crowded in behind her and filled the seats.

This was not going to be as easy as she thought. The

other selectpersons took their places at the table on the plat-
form. Carson still wasn't here. What if he didn't come? Maybe
he didn't want to be anywhere near her. Her breath whooshed
out when she saw him step through the door just before time for
the gavel to fall.

He didn't look at her as he took his seat and banged the
gavel. "This meeting is called to order."

Natalie sat at the end of the table. She glanced at him
from time to time as the meeting progressed from approving
plans for an ice cream parlor to denying a request for a casino.
Whenever Carson spoke, she saw the townspeople whispering.
They'd heard the news about Lisa suing for support for sure.
It seemed not to bother Carson, but it hurt Natalie. She'd been
just as quick to believe it.

She listened with keen interest as various townspeople
spoke on ideas to help further the town goals. The hands on
her watch crept closer and closer to eleven thirty, when they
would have to vacate the room for the meeting of the Parks
and Recreation committee.

The gavel came down on the meeting. It was now or never, but
she was beginning to wish she'd chosen a different way to do this.

Her knees shaking, she rose. "I have something to say before
we dismiss," she said. Those standing in the audience glanced
at her, then sat back down. "I know you've heard about my sister,
Lisa's, accusations against Carson Smitten."

Carson's head swiveled. His eyes narrowed, but he didn't say
anything. The others on the board stared with wary eyes.

"I want to publicly say that I don't believe Lisa." She turned
and held Carson's gaze. "All of us know Carson Smitten to be
a man of integrity. I've learned he is also a godly man and one

who takes responsibilities seriously. If he were Mia's father, he would step up to the plate by himself."

Carson's jaw dropped. He half rose, then sank back in his chair, looking stunned. Natalie glanced into the audience. Several in the room began to nod and whisper. She saw smiles and a few disbelieving expressions.

"Anyway, that's all I wanted to say. We've always been a close-knit town, one that has believed the best in people. Let's do that now. Think of what you know about Carson and trust your instincts about him. I should have done the same right from the start."

One by one, the people began to rise and filter out of the room. Several approached the table and thanked her for being so up front. Others shook Carson's hand. Natalie wanted to run when she realized she was alone with him, but she hadn't come this far to turn into a coward at the last minute.

She gathered up her purse and notes and turned as he approached. Everything she wanted to say dried up on her tongue.

His hands were in the pockets of his jeans. "Thanks for that. You didn't have to do it."

"I meant it. I realized how wrong I've been." She wetted her lips and stared up at him. "I was afraid."

"Afraid?"

"Afraid of becoming my mother and sister."

"You're nothing like your mother. Or like Lisa."

"At some point my mom should have realized she couldn't trust her instincts."

"I don't want this hanging over your head. I had a blood test this morning."

"You didn't have to do that."

"I did it for you." His hands came down on her upper arms. "If you'll take Mia in to give a sample, you'll see that the results are negative."

"I don't need to do that." The warmth of his hands on her arms penetrated her blouse and reached her skin. His eyes were so warm, so approving. As if he could see into her soul and loved everything about her. Her pulse jittered in her throat.

His right hand came up to cup her cheek. "So your instincts tell you I'm trustworthy?"

Speechless, she nodded.

"You'll believe anything I tell you?"

Again she nodded. A smile began to tug at the corner of her lips. Where was he going with this?

"Then believe this, Natalie Mansfield." His head came down, and his lips captured hers.

The warmth of his lips coaxed a response from her in spite of her fear. She wound her arms around his neck and kissed him back, letting go of her fear and uncertainty. He lifted her off her feet and continued to kiss her until she was breathless.

When he let her feet touch the ground again, he cupped her face in his hands. "I love you, Natalie. You can take that to the bank."

"That's worth more than my house and bank account combined," she whispered. "I'm sorry . . ."

He put his fingers on her lips. "I'm sorry we never did this years ago."

"Me too," she whispered.

He took her in his arms again, and before all thought fled, she wondered what the girls would say.

# Julia: Small Town, Big Dreams

## Kristin Billerbeck

# CHAPTER ONE

. . . . . . . . . . . . . . . . . . . . . . . . . . .

*J*ulia Bourne paced in front of the metal hangar at Smitten's regional airport. *There's nothing to be nervous about*, she told herself, but her body wouldn't comply. No amount of positive thinking would allow her to relax. Her dress, a simple cotton sheath from Tahari's previous season, clung to her in the sticky June heat. She wished she could stay cool under pressure like one of her New York socialite clients, but Julia wore her nerves like a conspicuous piece of jewelry.

It was bad enough she'd had to endure the stares of the town as she walked about in stilettos, but to convince Devlin Stovich that Smitten was ready for an upscale spa seemed utterly ridiculous at the moment. One local coffee shop and a few dessert places didn't exactly scream Fifth Avenue. She felt like a child wobbling about in her mother's high heels, and her hometown felt like preschool next to the sophistication of New York City. At that moment she wanted to abandon the whole scheme and beg Devlin to let her have her job back.

Unfortunately, that wasn't an option. Julia's mom still needed her. Smitten's mill was closed now, and all that remained of the once bustling logging town were the Sugarcreek Mountain Ski Resort ten minutes outside of town and one square block of struggling but infinitely quaint shops and a few modest inns. Julia and her friends were convinced that the town's only hope of success was to redefine itself as a romantic destination, worthy of hometown hero and country singing sensation Sawyer Smitten's Hollywood-style wedding. Any romantic destination needed what Smitten had to offer: gorgeous scenery, outdoor activities for both summer and winter, and, naturally, a high-end spa. She tried to summon her friend Natalie's enthusiasm for the future as she waited.

Julia held her breath as the Learjet glided elegantly onto the runway, the same way a flock of geese landed on a summer lake. She tugged at the collar of her fitted dress and wished she'd worn something more appropriate for life in Smitten. Devlin would know it was last season's dress, and there was no sense putting on airs when asking for money and his support. Reality required a certain humility. She needed to stay in Smitten for her parents' sake, and Smitten needed to find a new industry for its future. Tourism seemed the logical choice.

The private jet unfolded from its side like a metal yawn and thrust down a set of stairs. Julia's heart pounded at the sight of Devlin's tall, intimidating frame. He'd come without an entourage, and for that she felt grateful.

Even her best friends didn't understand the honor of socialite Devlin visiting their town, but the full weight of it pressed on Julia. She paced some more and practiced the breathing techniques Devlin had taught her for dealing with a particularly difficult client. *Breathe in, hold for three seconds, exhale deeply, forcing out the air.* To Smitten, Devlin was just another prospective businessman. To anyone in the spa business, he was a rock star. She watched him leave the plane.

Devlin Stovich's awkward looks worked for him. His

dirty blond locks curled around his strong jawline. There was almost a comical air to him, as if he were playing a 1950s Julius Caesar role, but his charm gave him that "it" factor that invited awe and commanded respect. He always wore silky black slacks with a black turtleneck, like a theater arts major. In the summer he switched out his turtleneck with a short-sleeved knit—also in black. Whenever he left the spa, he threw a gray linen sport coat over his uniform, and what seemed a lack of creativity became fashion-forward. For as trendy as he appeared in Manhattan's Upper East Side, he looked equally ridiculous in Smitten.

She'd lost sight of him, when suddenly large hands surrounded her waist and lifted her up from the floor, twirled her around full circle, and placed her back down in her original spot.

Devlin laughed heartily. "I will never get tired of that, lifting that lithe, tiny figure. Julia, you are the picture of health." He kissed her on both cheeks, as was his custom. "I think country life agrees with you. Look at your skin." He brushed her cheek with his thumb. "It's like pure springwater. I wish I could take credit for it, but in Manhattan we can only work with what we have, and we'll never have this clear air."

"You *can* take credit for my skin. I'm using all your products, and it doesn't hurt that I learned from the best."

"Always my best cheerleader. It's so dreary in the spa without your perky personality." He gripped both of her hands. "Come back to me."

"Is that a marriage proposal?" she answered flirtatiously.

Devlin grinned. "I'm not the marrying kind, Julia, or I might say yes. I see far too many beautiful women in a day to stay true to one. But if I were going to stay true, you'd be my girl."

"Such an offer. Too bad I'm not a gambling woman."

"I wouldn't say that. I saw the size of this town from the air. An upscale spa here?" He shook his head and stared across the expansive but empty parking lot. "One of my estheticians will quit eventually. You can come back to New York then."

She frowned. "I've made a commitment, Dev. Smitten needs me. Manhattan needs you. We have to face that what we have is unrequited love," she joked in her best dramatic voice.

"I miss you, Julia. You always manage to see the beauty in everyone. That's what I saw when I discovered you behind the makeup counter at Nordstrom. The way you had with people. You had that old woman on the stool, do you remember?"

"No, actually, I don't."

"She was not an attractive woman, clearly a tourist from the heartland. She didn't have a stitch of makeup on, and I think she was wearing sweatpants. You used eye makeup on her, and the blue of her eyes was suddenly obvious to me. I'll never forget that. I saw her."

Julia couldn't help but feel sorry for Devlin and how much his prejudice kept him from seeing. "All your clients are beautiful. I don't see what you thought I could add."

"You saw potential in average people. It made me realize I might be missing clientele who would feel comfortable with you. You could take Quasimodo and find something about him that's attractive."

She couldn't find her voice. Quasimodo equated with a woman who didn't dress in St. John knits and fill her face with Botox? She would never understand how Devlin saw the world—or she prayed she wouldn't, anyway. She wanted to tell him that not noticing "normals" was pure narcissism on his part, and *noticing* them not any extraordinary ability at all. But that wouldn't serve her purpose, so she kept her mouth shut.

Devlin walked outside the hangar and into the parking lot, where he shielded his eyes. "Like this place. I see the natural beauty. But, Julia, what do you *do* here with your days in the middle of nowhere?"

"I take care of my mother. I hang out with friends. I make plans for the future of a history that's in my blood. Life moves more slowly here, I'll give you that. But it moves deeper as well."

"If you say so." Devlin placed his hands on his hips and surveyed the expanse of open space, his line of sight to the pine trees and mountaintops. "What makes you think there's enough clientele here to support a spa?"

"W-Well," she stammered, "there's not yet, but the town is changing, and our tourism is growing rapidly. Sawyer Smitten is getting married here, and that announcement alone has put us on the map. His fans will come, as if they're on some kind of pilgrimage. Our bed-and-breakfast hasn't had any vacancies since the announcement, our coffee shop has a steady business, and at night the town is lit up with sparkling lights. There are carriage rides, and in the spring there'll be tours of the maple sugarhouses. All that's missing for after a day on the lake or the slopes is a spa."

He didn't look convinced, so she kept talking.

"With Sawyer's wedding, we are prepared to wipe the Poconos off the map as the East Coast romantic destination."

"I've always appreciated your enthusiasm, Julia, but a spa

needs steady clientele. It needs customers who value—" He pulled his critical gaze away from the mountains and looked back at her as if he were ready to get back on the plane that moment.

"It's more than my friends and me, this town project. Sawyer's speaking out about his wedding and what his hometown means to him. This is a calling. There's a little girl in our town, Mia, who prayed that—"

He held up his flat palm, as he always did when she said anything remotely faith based. Dev's religion was beauty and eternal youth. He had no interest in anyone else's belief system. "I believe in you, Julia, but there's a long lead time and tons of start-up capital that come with the spa business. I'm sorry, I just didn't see the potential here from the air. Maybe you can convince me once we get downtown. Smitten doesn't happen to have a Ben & Jerry's, does it?"

At least Devlin's sweet tooth would keep him from getting directly back on the plane.

She shook her head. "Ben and Jerry's headquaters is just south of Stowe, though. We have a shop called Sweet Surrender that would give Serendipity a run for its money. I'll take you there as soon as I've shown you the location possibilities for my spa. We also have Piece of Cake and the Vermont Creamery. Smitten is a sweet lover's paradise."

He didn't look convinced, which only made Julia speak faster and her dress feel stickier.

"I know when you see the potential of our downtown, you're going to be impressed. You have vision, Devlin, and that's why I called you here . . . because I think this is an incredible opportunity."

"Somehow I doubt that, but for you I'm willing to take a look." He brought his lips near to the crook of her neck and whispered the rest. "For you, I'd do a lot of things. Just say the word."

She forced a smile, but shivered involuntarily at the reminder of how uncomfortable Devlin could make her. She'd invited him, so she put on her game face and focused on his strengths. Devlin knew how to run a successful spa, and he had the money to invest. In fact, the amount she needed was less than his annual summer rental in the Hamptons. She suddenly wondered if she wasn't selling the soul of Smitten for money.

"So who is this Sawyer person, and why should his wedding make any difference to this town's tourism?"

Julia's mouth dangled, but she snapped it shut when she realized he really didn't know. "He's a country-singing sensation. Well, maybe not a sensation, but he's on his way. 'You Turned My Heart to Sawdust'? 'Sugar, You're Sweeter Than Maple Syrup'?"

"Are you singing me a song? Or is this some strange mating call of Smitten folks?" He laughed. "I'm kidding. Tell me about this sensation I've never heard of."

"He crossed over into pop after winning *Country's Best* on television. He's had concerts in New York too." She felt protective over Sawyer's image. He'd been the most popular boy in her high school when she was a freshman and he a senior. He wasn't the cocky type at all, and though music was never "cool" in school, Sawyer possessed that star quality that would have made it cool if he'd played on the badminton team. "He won a talent show and became an overnight hit!"

She felt an urge to tell Devlin how ignorant he could be

about pop culture, but it wouldn't have done any good. Dev wouldn't serve Madonna at his spa because he found new money vulgar. He catered to the elite of Manhattan and made no secret of his disdain for the self-made man.

They'd been standing outside of her car for several minutes now, and at some point, she'd have to admit to owning the Subaru. She should have borrowed Shelby's car for the occasion. Shelby's classic styling may not have been practical when they were hiking outside of town, but her Lincoln would have proven infinitely more upscale and appropriate for Devlin's appearance in town.

"We need four-wheel drive here," she explained, rather than saying, *Yes, this is my beat-up Subaru, get in.* "For the winters."

"A four-wheel drive and everything. You're a regular Sarah Palin."

She knew he hadn't meant it as a compliment, but she ignored that fact. Unlike Dev, she could camouflage herself in either place, the city or Smitten. There was something to be said for not carrying your location on your person.

"We're not going to shoot our lunch, are we?" he quipped.

"Get in the car, Dev."

Once inside the car, she turned the key in the ignition, and Third Day blared from the stereo system. Considering the band also sang Sarah Palin's theme song from her reality show, Julia thought it best just to shut off the music.

As they approached the town, her heart swelled with pride. Smitten's Main Street belonged on a postcard. Its brick Main Street and sidewalks ended at the old-fashioned, whitewashed church, where the traditional steeple and cross rose high into the bright blue sky. In the afternoon, the cross displayed its shadow across the village, as if Smitten's church stood sentry over the town's history and future.

"You say there's skiing in the winter?"

"We have a lake. There's waterskiing in the summer as well, but yes, both downhill and cross-country in the winter. Mountain biking on the fire trails. It may not look like much yet, as far as the shopping and conveniences go, but the women of Smitten have our minds set. We come from a long line of tough stock, and I daresay nothing will stop us."

"I hope for all your sakes you have enough capital to keep going until the town finds its footing."

She pulled her car up alongside the coffee shop. "This is my girlfriend's coffee shop. There's open retail space alongside her there." Julia pointed. "Natalie is very proactive and always searching out the latest coffee-roasting techniques. Anyone in Manhattan would be quite comfortable having a hot cocoa or an organic green tea in there. Don't you think that would be a nice location for a spa?"

He shook his head. "Coffee fumes aren't right for your location, and I can tell from here there's not enough water available for a spa. It would cost you a fortune to get that place piped."

"H–How can you tell that?"

"Easy. It's what I do. And what if your friend burns the beans? Have you ever smelled that? It could ruin the day's profits for you."

She didn't want to admit that she had.

"Aromatherapy is going to be a part of your business, so you have to take that into account. Drive up the road here, away from the church. I think off the beaten track would be better. Like the latest nightclub, it's almost a well-known secret. I know you can take the ugly duckling and turn it into a swan, Julia, but you can't pretty up strong smells that don't belong in a spa experience. What's up this way?" He pointed to the end of the street.

"Natalie's an excellent chef too!" She didn't want to mention some of Natalie's infamous tries at the perfect gluten-free cookie. "Maybe you're right. Off the beaten track might be more relaxing."

"Drive up here a little bit. The downtown is perfect, might be found under 'quaint' if you looked it up in the dictionary. We want to make the most of that aspect. In Manhattan, you want to be right in the midst of things, but not here."

"No?"

"No," he answered firmly.

"I'm so excited you see the potential. It confirms what we've thought all along. Smitten's an old logging town, you know. The idea of bringing anything feminine into this town is offensive to the men, but we know this is our future. We can't cut down trees any longer, so we've got to create a green economy out of the beauty here."

"Stop!" Dev said as they reached the end of Main Street. "What's that building?"

He pointed to a rustic, log cabin–looking building that defied the rest of Smitten's idyllic downtown, like a permanent stain on its cuteness.

"That? That's the Smitten Grill." She said it as if she had a bad taste in her mouth. "It closed a little while after the mill, but the owner opens it during ski season generally." One side of her lip lifted. "If you think upscale clientele would despise the scent of brewed coffee, imagine what they'd think here with scorched meat." She let out a nervous laugh and hoped he'd join her, but he was still mesmerized by the restaurant.

He put his hands in the shape of a picture frame. "No, this is it, Julia! I can see it here. There's so much potential. You realize that you can't copy a Manhattan spa and plop it here in the country."

"Naturally," she said. "No plopping."

"You have to know what would work here in Smallville. All this enchanting nostalgia is money in the bank if you know how to take proper advantage. Pull over."

She steered the car to the curb. Devlin didn't wait until the car was at a full stop before he leapt out and walked along the boardwalk under the shingled overhang.

*Can we go now?*

"That's another thing," she yelled out the window. "Everywhere else in town has brick sidewalks. Those old planks probably have dry rot, and you'd be looking at a lot of extra costs on the building."

"Nonsense." He jumped on the wide wooden planks. "They're in perfect condition."

Dev's sleek black image looked wrong against the rustic wooden lodge. As though Matt Damon had strode into a Yosemite Sam cartoon. She shuddered as she stepped out of the car.

"The Smitten Grill isn't exactly a place the women in town frequent." The dark-stained wood exterior made it the town's eyesore and something the girls and she hoped to eliminate with enough time. It was nowhere to be seen on their future maps.

"All the better to bring some masculine energy into the mix. Couples' business is going to be tantamount in a tourist town. You do realize that?"

"We have an appointment up the street in ten minutes." She turned her wrist toward Devlin.

"We'll be there. Let me just see inside here. Humor me, if you will."

"If we hurry, maybe we'll have time."

Devlin pressed down on the door's spring button, and to her dismay it sprang open. "After you."

She stepped gingerly onto the cracked cement floor covered by sawdust, which crept inside her peep-toe heels. Like a cat on a hot sidewalk, she lifted her feet gingerly, anxious to get the tour over with as soon as possible. She searched the room with wide eyes. Stuffed animal heads stared at her from the walls, burned-out neon signs surrounded them, and primitive wooden stools set at burled-wood tables dotted the room. "Well, you've seen it. Not exactly a place Smitten is proud of, and you can see why."

"If it's closed, I can't imagine the owner wouldn't want to rent it out. Make some money." Devlin walked toward the bank of dirty windows. "Is that a pond in the back?" He fluffed a gray handkerchief from his pocket and wiped the window.

"Whitetail Pond. Named for the deer that came to drink there before the sludge from this place probably poisoned the water."

"Julia." Dev pushed off from the windowsill and stared at her with his intense blue-green eyes. Eyes that had broken lesser women's resolves. "I think you're totally missing the vision, and that's not like you. You take ugly things and make them beautiful. That pond alone is sheer, feng shui perfection. Imagine a rock waterfall just over there." He pointed to the corner, then turned on his heels. "Or a fireplace back there where clients wait or relax after their treatments in their white, fuzzy robes. The gentle, soothing sound of trickling, clear water, the warming scent of maple syrup. Soothing couples' massages out on the deck in the summer. Think like one of my students. Think outside the box and you'll see there's no place in town for this spa other than right here. I don't understand how you're missing this."

"Outside the box? I can't think at all in here. All I want to do is grab some bleach and grease-cutter. Do you mind if we get on to the next building? I have an appointment."

"Julia, forget the appointment. Work with me here. You've got all the elements built in." He took her by the hand and walked around the expansive room. "Wood . . . water . . . fire would be easy enough to put in . . . metal . . ."

Devlin went on in his Eastern meditation trance, and she questioned his involvement for the first time. She could handle his flirtatious passes, but not actually meddling with the location or "feel" of the spa. Maybe she had been in New York too long. She certainly knew Devlin's belief system to be different from hers, but for the first time, she questioned if she'd truly relied on faith for Smitten's future rather than Devlin's money. She slipped off a heel and emptied it of sawdust.

"Can we talk about this after we've seen the other building? I told Ms. Draper we were coming. She owns the fudge shop and keeps the key."

She didn't want to mention that the people of Smitten didn't bow out of appointments. It simply wasn't done.

Besides, she wanted to get out of there before—"Zak!"

She felt the blood drain from her face at the imposing sight of Zak Grant. He hadn't changed at all, and she willed herself to lose the swirl in her stomach that made her feel like a prepubescent girl at a Justin Bieber concert.

Zak Grant, with his sleepy-eyed gaze and stretched, taut T-shirt. She searched for an excuse as to why she'd entered his antlered, medieval lair. He raked his hand through his thick, boyish curls, and she noted that being out of business had apparently left Zak plenty of time to build up his muscles. He was built like a Vermont maple: tall, filled out, and sturdy. She felt sawdust invade her shoe again and twitched her leg trying to get it out.

"Julia," Dev's smooth voice chastised. "You look like a dog being tickled on its belly." He chuckled.

She glanced at Zak, who bit his bottom lip. "Do you own a broom, Zak?"

"I do. You looking for a job? I was just thinking I should hire someone."

"You two know each other, I assume," Devlin said, eyeing what he must have seen as competition. The truth was, any normal fifty-year-old man would know he was no match for the athletic perfection that was Zak Grant, but Devlin's delusional view of himself trumped his reality.

"This is Smitten. Everyone knows each other," she said. "I'm sure Zak has lots of work to do. We'd best get out of his way." She grasped at Devlin's elbow. "Zak, this is my former boss from New York, Devlin Stovich. Devlin, my brother's best friend, Zak Grant."

The two men shook hands.

"Julia's going to open a spa here in town." Devlin's eyes narrowed.

"So I heard," Zak said. He rubbed his three days' worth

of stubble. "What kind of treatment would you give me?" He bent toward her and rubbed his jaw. "Do I have sun damage?"

"Can we get out of here now?" she asked Devlin. "There's no texture here. Wood on wood. Oh, and while you're at it, add some wood."

"That's part of the beauty of it. You could so easily add the other elements. This pond, it's positively picturesque. Man-made?"

"God-made," Zak clarified.

"I can see the brochures now. From across the pond, we see the massage tables on the deck in the distance. Can't you see it, Julia?"

"No." She crossed her arms in front of her.

"A few orchids in the background, some rock water features . . ."

"Sounds like you have big plans. That right, Julia?" Zak, with his barrel chest and dark, earthy green-brown eyes, stared at her with his meaty hand wrapped around some blueprints. His muscles bulged out of his dark gray T-shirt, and she wondered if he had added to his wardrobe at all since high school.

She thought all those nasty things rather than remember his stinging rejection as one of the popular boys in school to her quiet, pensive geek. She used to spy on him when he'd play basketball in the backyard with her brother, but he'd never noticed her. Just like that woman in Nordstrom, she'd been invisible to Zak.

"Looks like you've plans of your own." She nodded at the blueprints in his hand. "Sorry to have bothered you." She hooked her arm into Devlin's.

"Are you renting the place out?" Dev asked Zak.

"Only half of it. I'm using the other half for my office. I live upstairs."

"Unemployed bodybuilders need an office?" Julia regretted her words immediately, but she couldn't take them back.

Both Zak and Devlin gazed at her as if she were the devil himself.

"Still as charming as ever, huh, Julia?"

"What do you plan to rent the place for?" Dev asked him.

"More than she can afford." His steely gaze rested on her in a silent challenge.

"I'm considering investing in her business," Dev said, handing Zak a business card from a jacket pocket. "But only if she's smart about it."

"It's more than either of you can afford."

"I doubt that. I take it you two don't care for one another," Devlin said. "But you seem to be a businessman, Mr. Grant, and I'd consider it a great favor if you'd reconsider Julia as a tenant. I wholeheartedly and enthusiastically believe in her abilities as an esthetician."

"An esta what?"

"Julia, look here. These cabinets are already built in. I'm seeing earthy browns under soothing candlelight, cedar and sandalwood as signature scents. Or perhaps maple, if you want to go for that local flair. Muscle repair massages after skiing, with mountain arnica extracts and oregano . . . Surely even you can see the need for that, Mr. Grant."

"Nope. Oregano goes on food, not me. If Julia wants to make me spaghetti sauce with it, we can talk."

Zak's refusal seemed to ignite Devlin's competitive nature. "Mr. Grant, wouldn't you like to see the women of

Smitten looking younger with antiaging facials after a day in the sun? It repairs the collagen with licorice extract."

"What? Food *on* people instead of *in* people isn't right for Smitten. We don't go for all that froufrou stuff you city people like."

"Detox? Surely a bodybuilder knows about detox. Julia could do the best detoxifying treatments there under the crackling fireplace." He pointed toward the corner.

"There is no fireplace," Julia said dryly.

"There will be. An exfoliation treatment with the local maple sugar scrub. Julia, Zak, this is a gold mine. What's it going to take to get you two to see it?"

"A miracle," they said in unison.

"I need to get back to work." Zak tapped his blueprints against the wall. "Let yourselves out when you're done."

Julia watched him stride to the back room, untouchable as ever.

# CHAPTER TWO

. . . . . . . . . . . . . . . . . . . . . . . . . . . . .

*Z*ak's fists tightened and the blueprints crumpled in
his right hand. He dropped them on a nearby table.
*Devlin.* What the heck kind of name was that? His name was
probably really Irwin or Gilbert.

Julia had returned to Smitten months ago. Zak promised
her brother, Greg, he'd check on her, but he'd avoided her.
Julia wanted a bigger, better life than he could ever provide,
so why tempt himself? She was sophisticated and elegant, and
seemed to want a different world than what Smitten could provide. She probably never would have come home if her mother
hadn't broken her ankle and needed her help. He didn't want
to watch her leave again.

He heard the door slam out front and made his way into
the main section of the restaurant. He could still smell her
perfume lingering in the air. He had to go after her. The
deck door latched behind him, and he turned to see her
standing on the deck overlooking the pond, deep in thought.

Tension tightened at the base of his neck as he pushed
the door open and followed her out onto the deck. The sun
sparkled in reflection off the pond, and she brushed off an
Adirondack chair and sat, never noticing him.

"Julia?"

She looked up at him, her eyes filled with tears.

"Where's Devlin?"

"He left."

"How?"

"He took my car. I'll get Natalie to drive me to the airport later and pick it up." She sniffled, and his fists tightened again at the idea of that city slicker making his Julia cry.

"I'll take you to the airport."

"I thought he was the answer. My dad offered me the money if I stayed in Smitten, but he doesn't have that kind of money. It's nothing to Devlin, so I thought—"

"It's more money to his kind than you realize. Besides, think of the pressure with that tool in your business. It's hard enough to make a go of it here in Smitten. You don't want that guy telling you what works in New York City. You know this town. You know how things work. When are you going to trust yourself?"

She laughed through her tears. "Thank you, Zak. My faith is wilting. I need to have a job if I'm going to stay here and take care of my mother. What else do I know how to do? Maybe I should go back to school and become an accountant."

He looked down. "You can do anything you want to do, except for maybe shoot a basket." He winked at her. "And if you want to set up here, I am going to be renting out half the building. You're welcome to it. Maybe that turkey is right about something. It is a beautiful setting here."

"I don't need charity, Zak. I pictured the spa closer to town. Nearer to the main businesses. Devlin said if I wasn't going to take his advice, there was no sense in his wasting his time on me. Then he just left. He took my car while I stood idly by. That's not me."

"The location isn't that far from town. Certainly within

walking distance, and the horse-drawn carriage could bring people from the bed-and-breakfast here. You wouldn't be alone out here if you worked nights, if that's what you're worried about. The restaurant will open again soon after the upgrades."

"You're upgrading?"

She looked up into his eyes, and he knew he would remember that innocent, hopeful look for the rest of his days. It melted his heart.

"The town's getting older, and people want chairs, not stumps to sit on."

She grinned. "And the sawdust?"

"So 1990."

"You mean 1890."

"I'm a fourth-generation logger, Julia. I didn't know anything about opening up a restaurant. I just saw a need and I filled it."

She stared off toward the pond. "I like it out here. It's so calming." She lay back in the Adirondack chair and let the sun soak into her perfect, clear skin. Her complexion was her own best advertisement.

"You look like you belong here. The queen of all you survey." A trout leapt from the water and created a ripple over the previously glassy-calm pond. "See, even the fish agree."

She stood abruptly and brushed off her backside. "I'd better go. I'm back at square one now."

"What's that you're carrying?"

"It's a wreath Mia made for me. Like the ones in town, it's supposed to be a wreath of faith for Smitten's future. I think I should just give it back to her."

"Why won't you take me seriously? You think I'd offer half my building to just anyone?" He missed the lighthearted Julia who smiled constantly and giggled girlishly like she always had a secret. She'd changed since coming home. "The Julia I used to know wasn't afraid of anything. I know she's in there somewhere."

"Don't worry, Zak." She rested her hand on his. "I'll tell Greg you did your part and offered me the help."

"It isn't that," he protested. "I don't understand why you're waiting for some guy to tell you what you already know. You can make the spa work here. You can do whatever you set your mind to. What do you need that guy's permission for?" His jaw clenched at the thought.

"Devlin threw an adult tantrum and said if I didn't see the spa here in this building, there was no hope for me. If Devlin doesn't think it will work here, how can I gamble my father's money?"

"Your father believes in you. Devlin's a toad. Why do you care what he thinks?"

She rose. "I'd better let you get back to work. I need to go ask Natalie for a ride to the airport."

"You said yourself that I had nothing to do. Sit down, Julia."

To his surprise, she sat back down, and he sat in the adjoining chair, turning it to face her and watch as the sun highlighted the coppery strands in her dark hair.

She leaned forward and rested her elbow on her crossed legs. "I need to find the right place. Smitten needs more romance if we're to attract tourists after Sawyer's wedding. This building is dripping masculinity, so I appreciate the offer, Zak, I really do, but—"

"That was the idea. A place for a man to get decent grub and get back to the mill before he was missed. Not much need for prettying it up back in the day." He leaned back in the chair and kicked out his legs. "But times are changing. I don't need so much space now, and you said yourself this place could use a woman's touch. So be an accountant and do the math. It all adds up."

Julia seemed like a lost child, nothing like the arrogant little schoolgirl who wanted a bigger life. It was as though New York had stripped her confidence away. He never thought he'd miss that obnoxious know-it-all, but he did. It was like a part of her had disappeared.

Julia stared into Zak's handsome face, the murky depths of his dark eyes. He'd always been a mystery to her, and she supposed he always would be. Why now? Why did he want to help her now? Was it guilt over Greg not being here to help?

She eyed him suspiciously.

"This isn't the right place for the spa. Now if only I can convince my one and only investor that I'm correct, I can get on with things."

"What if he's right?"

"He's not."

"Just tell Devlin you're not going to sissify the building and slather cream on a bunch of loggers. I want to put them back to work so that maybe their wives can afford such a luxury." His cocked eyebrow took her right back to high school when she'd watch him and his popular friends horseplay in the cafeteria, and she was invisible.

With as much time as Zak spent at their house, being Greg's best friend, he never once spoke to her outside of the safety of their home. She wondered if he realized that. How he became someone different, someone aloof and out of reach when anyone was looking. His deep hazel stare out from under his mop of dark brown hair still intimidated her. It always had. She felt smaller in his presence, and the words she wanted to say, the coolness she wanted to display, never managed to show itself when he was around. Today, in fact, marked the most she'd ever said to him in public, and that was only because Devlin had stripped away her choice. She sucked in a deep breath to find her voice.

"It always was like you to make fun of what you don't understand." She straightened her shoulders and stared over the pond rather than meet his eyes, but she felt them upon her. "I don't intend to 'slather cream,' as you put it, on loggers. I intend to, along with the rest of Smitten's women, make this town the romantic capital of the East Coast. Any town oozing this kind of quaintness and a ski lodge needs an upscale spa."

"No one 'needs' a spa. You've been living in New York for too long if you believe that. This town needs to work. That's a need, but I'm willing to support you rather than bring in outsider money. That will only corrupt Smitten."

"Devlin has a few million dollars that make that statement patently untrue. Plenty of his clients believe taking care of themselves is a necessary part of life."

"Patently . . . what?" He shook his head at her.

"Why have you always been so mean to me?"

"Mean to you? When was I ever mean to you?"

Her breathing quickened. "Never mind. I thought maybe Devlin's professional eye saw something I'd missed here, but my first thought was correct." She stood and brushed the back of her dress again. She bent her leg and leaned against the top of the Adirondack while she emptied her shoe out again. "You probably think Sawyer's wedding won't put us in the spotlight, but I can tell you, romance means something to women, and this wedding means a great deal to Smitten."

"On the contrary, we're already on the map. Sawyer did this for Smitten, you know. He loves this town."

"All the men do, right? I know how you feel about the women's plans for Smitten."

"I don't think you do," he said in a low, lumberjack growl. He tugged at her hand. "Sit down a minute."

She felt the hair on her arms stand on end. She refused to sit, so he stood closer. So close that she could feel the heat from his expansive chest. "I need to go. If Devlin leaves with all his money, so do my hopes."

"We all have plans for Smitten. You girls aren't alone in what you want. You realize that?"

"I do, but what you've done in the past hasn't worked, Zak. It's time we did something different." She pulled open the door and walked into the darkened restaurant.

Zak was right on her heels. "You girls, we appreciate what you're trying to do, but, Julia . . . that guy." He bounced his forefinger toward the door. "He's an interloper you don't need. We don't need. You bring in foreign money and you answer to it. That's the last thing Smitten needs. We're hanging on by a string as it is, and I don't like the way he talks to you. Who the heck does he think he is? When have you ever been a quiet little mouse of a person? He ruins you, Julia. Don't you see that?"

"You're wrong about Devlin. He's just used to having his way, that's all. You should understand that. He runs the most successful spa in Manhattan, and he wants to create the same sort of ambience here." She gazed across the room. "Clearly, no matter of plastic surgery is capable of making that happen in this building. But don't get me wrong—I wish you all the luck in the world with whatever you have planned. I'll just get out of your way." She walked toward the door, and again he grasped her wrist.

"I'll lend you the money to do what you need to do here."

She couldn't pry her eyes from his hand wrapped around her wrist. Had he ever touched her before today? "Where would you get that kind of money?"

"That's a personal question, and the answer is none of your business, but I have it, and in case you haven't noticed, the banks aren't too keen on lending when you don't have any collateral. Especially to a new business in a town as dead as a doornail."

"No offense, Zak, but I'd rather have an 'interloper's' money than answer to you. If you believe my idea is so ridiculous, why would you want to lend me money to make it happen?"

That wasn't actually the truth, and she went hot with guilt, but she didn't correct herself. Zak scared her with his bravado, and she saw herself sweating over a spreadsheet trying to explain the cost of organic cleansers.

"Don't be proud, Julia. Why would some guy from New York want to start a business in this Podunk town? Does it occur to you to question his motives?"

She blinked away her rising tide of emotion. "I was his best student. I learned the spa business faster than anyone he'd ever hired. He recognizes vision, what we women of Smitten are doing to change the village, and he sees the financial opportunity."

"You believe that," he chuckled, "then I have a very successful mill I'd like to sell you. Well, it was successful fifty-odd years ago."

"I don't have any reason to question his motives. I love this town. And with the passion I feel for Smitten and for taking care of oneself with clean living, how could I fail?"

Zak held open his hands. "Look around you. Are you saying I didn't love this town? And what do you see? A shell of a functional business. Ski season isn't enough to keep us going all year long. In the meantime, I work on ways to get that plant back open while you girls pin your hopes on a dream. Without a new hit song we can't even count on Sawyer, if the truth be told."

"That's why we have to do something different. We prayed, Zak, and I believe God wants us to do this. He wants to see Smitten flourish, and what better way than to blossom in love?"

"If only wishes were dollar bills . . ."

"Zak." She let her hand grasp his. "Are you worried?" Because she didn't think she could take seeing Zak falter.

She watched his Adam's apple twitch.

"I am worried, but that doesn't mean I've given over reason. Lose that guy, Julia. You got his advice, that's all you need. He says the spa should be here. If you want help, take mine. You know I'd never do anything to hurt you. Your brother would have my neck."

She wanted to agree, but she didn't dare. Zak Grant would break her heart again and again. He'd never look upon her as more than a little sister, and she didn't want that kind of help. *Charity.*

"I need to get over to the coffee shop. Sorry to have disturbed you." She ran across the darkened restaurant, and her heel caught in the plank floor. The ground rose up to meet her, but Zak's bulging arms came out of nowhere, caught her, and set her upright. He kept his hands around her waist, and she didn't dare move, didn't dare breathe. She hoped he couldn't feel how hot she was from nerves under her dress.

"Julia, I think he's right."

"Who's right?"

"Devil, or whatever his stupid city name is. This place has everything you need for a spa. I'll rent you half the building, help you make the improvements, and if you don't make it, you can turn it into a dog wash and bathe the hounds of Smitten. It won't hurt me, and if you owe me money at the end, you can work it off washing dishes. Or maybe we could use the hot tub to soak the ribs in beer overnight. You're going to have a hot tub, right?"

"It has everything, except for an ounce of femininity, a total renovation, a water fountain, a fireplace, a—" She felt his arms release from her waist.

"I told you I'd help with that, but you do what you need to do. You've known me since grade school, and if you don't trust me by now, you never will."

She tried to make sense of her thoughts. "Precisely. Who I've known is a guy who pulled my ponytail, tattled on me to Mrs. Swindoll, and forgot he ever knew me once he joined the football team and I the chemistry team."

"Okay, I'll give you that. But I pulled your ponytail because I thought you were cute, and you ignored me. I tattled on you to Mrs. Swindoll because you let her class turtle go during logging season and I didn't want it to get hit by a truck. The least you could have done was let it go near the pond! And when you joined the chemistry team, I knew you were too smart for my blood. Your brother always told me so. All right? Trust me now?"

"You pulled my ponytail because you liked me?" She tapped her peep-toe shoe on his work boot.

"Wipe that smile off your face. I was young, and I'd never seen a girl with dimples, or one whose bow matched her dress every day. I was, in a word, smitten."

"Smitten?" She grinned in the way that accentuated her dimples in all their glory.

"Stop." Zak shook his head. "Dimples are a birth defect, you know."

She sighed.

"Besides, then your brother told me you picked your nose and wet your bed."

"He what? You didn't believe him!"

"Maybe I did. I was ten. It sounded reasonable."

"I have to go."

He paused, his mouth slightly open, but he said nothing. She'd never seen Zak Grant display the slightest sign of vulnerability, and the sight caught her off guard and forced her to question what she knew to be true: that the men of Smitten were he-men, woman-haters of *Little Rascals* lore, who needed to rule over women to be in partnership with them.

"If Devlin won't give you the money and you won't take

it from me, will you run back to New York and leave your mom?"

"Well, I have to find a way to support myself. If I can't do it here, I suppose I will run back to New York. I can't babysit Mia forever, even though I love that little girl like she's my own. She'll be back in school in the fall and Nat will have no need of me."

He nodded, his jaw set.

"Tell me something—does that sound committed to this town to you?" He waved her off, grabbed up his blueprints, and disappeared through the kitchen's double doors.

That wasn't how she thought at all, but what good would it do to explain it to Zak Grant? He'd made up his mind about her a long time ago, and as his "little sister" all that was left for her was to watch him date the town's next beauty queen.

Julia walked out the door. She'd have to hike the quarter mile of Main Street to the coffee shop in her stilettos, feeling utterly ridiculous. She couldn't get her mind off of Zak and his warped opinion of her. Not that it should matter.

She squeezed the lavender wreath Mia had made. The little girl's faith reminded Julia that the women of Smitten weren't acting alone.

She walked back to the plank sidewalk and placed the wreath on the red double doors of the Smitten Grill. Did the wreath belong there? Had pride clouded her judgment? She left it there on the door. She could always get it later.

# CHAPTER THREE

. . . . . . . . . . . . . . . . . . . . . . . . . .

*J*ulia walked slowly up Main Street, her heels clacking along the brick walkway. She noted how beautifully the town was coming along, with the giant clock in the center of town garnished with a giant version of Mia's wreath. That little girl was really something special.

The window boxes outside the brick storefronts were brightened by spring flowers, and the renewed life of the town felt palpable. As she approached the coffee shop, she rehearsed what she'd tell Natalie. She had no answer for her. That's what Zak had done to her thinking process. He took it, shook around everything she knew to be true, and left her dizzy with confusion. She never should have stepped foot into his grill.

She noticed her Subaru parked outside the coffee shop. Apparently Devlin hadn't made it all the way to the airport after all. No doubt his sweet tooth got the best of him.

She had two possible investors, but both of them wanted something from her that she wasn't prepared to give: her independence.

She'd work on Natalie first. Natalie Mansfield was one of her best friends. Every week the two of them, along with Shelby and Reese, did some sort of exercise together to keep each other motivated. They shared prayer requests, joys, and failures. Sadly, there'd been too many failures of late, and her spa dream was rapidly joining that list.

Julia cupped her eyes and peered inside the coffee shop. Natalie's curvy figure could be seen inside, bustling about in her typical manic display of energy. Natalie liked to mother the world, and any patron entering her coffee shop automatically gave her that right—or so it seemed to Julia. No doubt Devlin had received an earful of opinions in his quest for caffeine. She could only hope the earful included how the Smitten Grill would never work for a spa. She stepped out onto the brick street and wished again she'd dressed more practically, but she gazed at the church and focused on the cross. "Here goes nothing."

She pushed open the door, and the bells rang as the scent of freshly roasted coffee beans invigorated her senses.

"Julia!" Natalie welcomed her. "I wondered when you'd get here. How did it go?"

"Hi, Nat, is Dev here? I'm assuming you know his entire background by now. He said he was going straight to the airport. I guess the scent of your coffee lured him inside."

"I'm not sure of his net worth, but everything else, yes." Natalie grinned and pushed her long dark hair behind her ears and closed her Mac laptop. "He's in the back room, using my desktop. His smartphone wouldn't work here, and he needed to check e-mail."

"You didn't tell him about Smitten's intermittent Internet service, did you?" she whispered.

"It's not intermittent in here," Natalie snapped. She was the town's resident tech expert and managed to find ways around the town's ailing infrastructure, but she kept her secrets quiet and sold more coffee as the only working Wi-Fi spot in town.

"You let a complete stranger into your office on your computer?"

"He's your mentor. Hardly a stranger. I explained to him that our Internet could be a little spotty, but I had my ways around that. Don't worry, I let him know your spa would have no trouble either. Not if I have anything to say about it."

And she did. Natalie loved her technology, and if there was a new gadget available, she found a need for it in the coffee shop. No doubt Natalie had probably already picked out the spa's computer software.

"I suppose Dev told you where he wants me to put the spa."

"He did. I told him there was no way. Zak Grant is enough to keep that from happening, but that building! I asked him if he went in or was going by the outside, which isn't nearly so bad. The mere idea of us helping you clean that place was reason enough for me to set the guy straight."

"He sees potential there." Julia shrugged. "I don't see it, but I can't just ignore his advice." She leaned in to whisper, "Not if I want his working capital."

Natalie shook her head. "It's terrible advice. I took him next door and showed him the building I want you to put the spa in. There's an art gallery interested, but I'm sure with you being the hometown girl, they'd give you first crack at it."

"And?" She felt grateful that Natalie had taken on the necessary battle and had time to wear Devlin down.

"He said there wasn't enough square footage, that the water lines weren't running where you needed them. He said walls are cheap, but water lines cost a fortune. He didn't like it at all. But you can't let that stop you."

"In other words, he won't invest in that space. Only Zak's."

"Well then, you'll have to find the money elsewhere. You can't go into that building. It's oozing testosterone. I told him about our romance theme, but he didn't seem to get it." She cupped her mouth. "For a city guy, he can be kind of slow."

"Zak offered me the money."

"Zak?" Natalie gasped. "Zak Grant?"

Devlin appeared in the doorway of the back room. "Natalie, thanks for the use of your computer and the great coffee. Have you tried her blueberry muffins, Julia? They rival anything in New York. I'm impressed."

"And they're gluten-free," she and Natalie said together.

"But don't try the cookies yet," Julia warned with a wink.

"They were lovely." Dev took Natalie's hand and kissed the back of it in his European way. Natalie turned bright red. "Julia, the pilot's waiting for me. Did you want to drive me so you'll have your car?"

"Uh, yeah. Sure."

"I expect I'll hear from you soon about your decision. I have another protégé I'm considering for investment, so I trust you won't keep me waiting."

The way he said it made it clear that her decision had better line up with his, and just by her sheer inner will she wanted to deny him. Someone needed to. Natalie gave her a look that told her to stand up for herself or she would take the reins.

"I'll tell you right now that I don't think Zak's place is right."

Dev's cheek flinched, but otherwise his face remained motionless—the way Botox intended. "I thought you might say that. While I find your little town very charming and full of potential, it's apparent that you're not in a place of humility where I can work with you . . . mold you, if you will. Therefore, I believe it's best that I withdraw my offer of financial backing for your spa."

Julia swallowed hard and tried to have faith. If Dev wouldn't back her, it only meant God had something different in mind. In the meantime, Natalie looked ready to leap over the counter and take Devlin Stovich by the throat.

After a cleansing breath, Julia replied, "I understand. Smitten is best left to Smitten, I guess. But I feel bad for bringing you out here. Are you hungry? Did you want to grab something to eat before I take you back to the airport?"

"I think I've had enough of small-town life for the year. I'll eat when I get back to the city."

"Good luck finding a gluten-free muffin that tastes like mine," Natalie mumbled.

"Dev—"

"Don't say a word, it's fine. I understand how difficult it is to make changes when you're used to life moving at a snail's pace. You're not ready for my help, and I understand that, but I can't condone it by leaving the option open."

"No, that would be downright human. We can't have that." Natalie opened her laptop again and rolled her eyes. "Would you like me to call you a cab? We have them here, you know."

Julia just wanted to get him out of town before she changed her mind. And before Natalie made it virtually impossible for her to ask Devlin for anything again.

"My car's right out front. I can have you at the runway in ten minutes." She bit her lips down together to maintain a professional front.

Devlin managed to make her feel like a child desperate to win a parent's approval, but suddenly his confirmation seemed unimportant. She couldn't have voiced why, but something in Zak's grit, in his immediate dislike of Devlin, gave her renewed determination. Zak believed in her. Somehow that knowledge provided the boost of faith she needed at the moment.

Dev went outside and waited by the car. He flipped his linen jacket over his shoulder as Zak's pickup pulled up. Zak got out and approached Devlin. Julia watched the entire scene paralyzed, as if they couldn't see her if they glanced in the coffee shop window. The two men had words and then shook hands. She wondered if her fate hadn't just been decided.

"I need to go." She grabbed a muffin from the counter and raced outside to the two men she'd disappointed.

Her meager savings, earned in New York, wouldn't be enough to open the spa to the level of elegance that she wanted, or at all, if she was honest. But she realized in that moment that answering to a caveman, be he a well-dressed and charming caveman like Devlin or a rugged, hard-bodied Neanderthal like Zak, was not the vision she had for her business. Or her future. Her friends' shared vision for Smitten was based on faith, and either she trusted in God's ability to rescue Smitten, or she didn't.

"Julia," Zak said as she approached the car, "stay and enjoy your coffee. I'll be taking Devlin to the airport."

"What? I—"

"I'll see you when you're back in New York, Julia." Devlin slunk into Zak's oversize pickup, and the two of them sped away before she had a chance to say another word.

She walked back into the coffee shop and slipped her heels off. "What do you think happened there?" she asked Natalie.

Natalie stood by the espresso machine. "The usual?"

Julia nodded. "Make it a triple. Two shots of espresso couldn't possibly save this day. I'll never get the money now. I wish I were more like Reese and planned everything out since I was a child. Maybe then I wouldn't be in this mess."

Natalie grinned. "If this mess includes being rescued by Zak Grant, I'd say there are a lot of girls who'd like to be in your shoes." She wiggled her eyebrows while she drew the espresso.

"Ever since you and Carson started dating, the rest of us will never hear the end of your romantic notions. Just because it worked out for you in this town doesn't mean the rest of us have any hope. Smitten is home of the spinster, may I remind you. If there's one thing unemployed loggers avoid, it seems to be taking a wife."

"Dark thoughts like that do nothing for our romantic destination idea."

"That's just it. It's a destination, meaning you bring the guy with you. He's certainly not here."

Natalie laughed as she poured Julia's espresso over ice. "It will all look better after you've had your coffee. Everything does."

"I thought today was the start of something new, but I feel further away from my goal than when I began. At least I had hope this morning."

"It's always darkest before the dawn. How's your mom's therapy going?"

"She's home now. Someone comes to the house once a day to work with her."

"How's your dad doing?"

"Without his slave, you mean? He's trying to train me up to be a 'proper wife,' which resembles an Egyptian slave according to him, but I'm managing. I mean, he's managing."

The two friends laughed, and Julia lifted her cup. "Cheers!"

"To new beginnings and hot barbecuers."

"Zak is only interested in boosting Greg's morale. The day he looks at me as more than Greg's little sister is the day of reckoning. None of us will need businesses by then."

"What would Shelby say if she heard you talk like that?"

"She'd probably plant buttercups in my front yard and tell me to spend more time in prayer."

"Then maybe you should do it."

"I wonder if Shelby's attitude would be so happy-go-lucky if she were approaching thirty and living with her parents."

"We'll pray," Natalie said. "The answer will come."

Julia wished it would come in the form of Zak Grant, but her life didn't work out that way. Julia Bourne, eternal member of the Chemistry Club, invisible to the Available Men Club.

# CHAPTER FOUR

· · · · · · · · · · · · · · · · · · · · · · · · · · ·

*S*ince Julia moved back to Smitten, she'd lived in her lavender childhood bedroom at her parents' house. Nothing made her feel the angst of her day's failures like coming home to Mom and Dad's. Life at home served as a constant reminder as to why Smitten needed a change from its current male, chest-beating administration to a fresher, more feminine way of life. She entered the traditional Colonial, built in 1900, and cringed at the familiar mint-green carpet (over original hardwood) against the peach walls with her father's periwinkle blue recliner set smack-dab in the middle of the room. Directly under the blaring television set.

"Hey, Dad."

He rustled under the newspaper and cast off another section. "You're home early."

Since her father's retirement from the mill, Julia didn't know if the recliner actually sat upright any longer. It was a wonder he didn't develop boils on his backside.

"Yeah."

Her mother's habits harked back to the time when the house was built. She always wore an apron and saw her life's work as bringing Dad sustenance and fresh reading material. If others needed a reason as to why Julia despised the thought of marriage, they only had to look inside her family home, where her mother worked as if she had seven dwarves by her side and her father slept as if his life depended upon it. When her mom broke her ankle, Julia had rushed home from New York. Clearly, her father might have starved had she left him to his own devices. He didn't even operate the microwave oven. That was, as he put it, women's work.

"I'm back!" she called to her mom, and her dad startled in his chair.

"I heard you the first time," he grunted.

"I was talking to Mom."

"Oh, hi, honey!" Mom came from the kitchen and wiped her hand on her apron, her other hand operating her crutch.

"Mom, sit down! Didn't the physical therapist tell you not to overdo it?"

"Nonsense. How did it go? Did Devlin give you the money for the spa? What did he think of Smitten? Did he like the place you picked out? How long will you have to wait to get started?"

"There was a complication or two." Julia helped her mother to the sofa. "Please sit down, you're making me nervous."

"Oh? Complications?" Her mom sat gingerly. Julia raised her mother's leg onto the sofa and fluffed the pillows.

"Well, one complication, really. Zak Grant."

"Oh, Zak. How is he? It's been so long since we've seen him, hasn't it, Hal? He never comes around since Greg deployed, and we miss him terribly. Did you tell him we missed him, Julia?"

"I didn't really get the opportunity."

"Did you know he sent me roses in the hospital? Such a thoughtful young man, and he should know Greg doesn't need to be here for him to come to dinner. He always loved my cooking."

Her dad groaned. "He probably thought how ridiculous the idea of a spa was in a man's town and told your boss that, right? You should know, I agree with Zak. The last thing this town needs is another girly shop. There's enough ways to spend our money as it is."

"It's not only a man's town, Dad. The mill is closed. Remember? Tourism, the ski lodge, and the lake are our future now. A romantic destination spot," she said for the eight hundredth time or so.

"Future," her father spat. "I worked in that mill for forty years—you don't have to tell me about the future. We built this town! Men built this town!"

"Yes, Dad."

"Why can't you just get married like the rest of the girls in your class?"

"Not all the girls are married. None of my friends are married."

"True. All the ones you hang out with are spinsters. That should tell you something about how you pick your friends."

"So you were saying," Mom interrupted to spare them both. "You saw Zak? Is he still so handsome? I thought for certain that pretty Hastings girl would snatch him up." Mom looked at her father. "I suppose that makes Zak a spinster too."

"Heh-heh," Dad said. "The Hastings girl probably got tired of waiting. Why would Zak want to marry? He lives the perfect life, knows how to cook for himself—"

"Well, he certainly doesn't know how to clean." Julia rolled her eyes. "Another benefit of women in your life, Dad."

"He could ask any girl to come over and clean for him, I'll bet."

"Dad, do you have to be such a chauvinist?"

"What? If that pretty Hastings girl didn't tempt him, who else is left?"

The pretty Hastings girl knew enough to get far away from Smitten. Julia turned back to her mother. "As I was saying, I ran into Zak because Devlin thought his grill might be a good spot for the spa."

"The grill is a good spot for the grill!" Dad smacked the newspaper on top of his belly and sat up.

"Hmm. That chair does sit up. Anyway, I'm not sure what happened, but Zak and Devlin had words. Next thing I knew Devlin left for the airport in Zak's pickup, and I was right where I started."

"If that sissy boy left mad, it's probably because Zak told him how things are here in Smitten. We don't need no gussy-up place."

"Thanks for the encouragement, Dad."

"Hal, what did you offer her the money for, if you're going to talk to her like this?"

"Because I want her to get married and have a good life, but if she refuses, she's my responsibility. I won't have anyone saying I don't take care of my family."

"I can take care of myself, Dad. It isn't 1850. I lived in Manhattan and supported myself. Surely I can find a way to do it here."

"If you weren't so independent, you'd be married by now. Who do you think will marry you when you're running your own business, making a mockery of the men in the town?"

"Well, Julia," her mom interrupted again, "I don't know what happened today, but I know Zak wouldn't do anything to hurt you. He must have had his reasons for sending this man away."

"The men of Smitten, Zak in particular, think there's hope for that mill, Mom. We women are trying to do something different, and that doesn't sit well with the guys, so they want to be certain they can shut down anything we run in the future. Who is he going to sell ribs to if we're bringing in a higher class of clientele who prefer fresh-roasted espresso and brie-and-apple platters for appetizers?"

She neglected to tell her mother of the offer Zak had made concerning her spa. She knew it was a lie of omission, and guilt swelled in her heart.

Her father laughed. "The men who got talked into this cockamamie trip in the first place, that's who. If they can't say no to that, they'll certainly put their foot down on sissy food and get themselves a steak at Zak's." Her father tugged at the lever on the side of his chair and fell into his familiar reclining position.

"Zak offered me half his restaurant for the spa, but with that he has the power to shut it down at any time."

"Zak wouldn't do that, Julia. Why are you so suspicious? Why can't you trust him?"

"I don't know, Mom." *Because he broke my heart. Because he never noticed that I'm a girl, and not just Greg's helpless little sister.* She tapped her mom's good leg. "Are you hungry yet? Should I start dinner?"

"Yes," her father called across the room. "Mom's hungry."

Her mom smiled. "I'm getting around better. I baked a peach pie today, mostly while sitting at the kitchen table, but nonetheless we'll eat dessert like kings tonight."

"I'll go start dinner."

"Wear an apron," her dad said. "What?" He looked at her mother. "It's good practice for her."

"Don't listen to him, Julia. He's just trying to get a rise out of you."

The roar of an old muffler stopped her mom's words midstream. Mom hobbled to the front window and pushed the floral curtain aside.

"Mom, you're supposed to stay off that foot."

"It's Zak," she said as she replaced the curtain. "Speak of the devil. Oh my, he's still a sight. I'll never understand why you never looked after him, Julia."

"Indeed," Julia said. "I'll be in the kitchen." She started for the door.

"You stay here and apologize, young lady. If he offered you part of his building, he obviously deserves a thank-you. He still drives that old orange pickup? I suppose it suits him."

"I wonder what Devlin thought of that jalopy."

"Any man who can't appreciate a classic pickup ain't worth his weight in salt," Dad said.

"Julia, don't be rude now," Mom said. "I'm sure he's here to see you. He hasn't been to visit your father and me since you and Greg left. Be polite and invite him to stay for pie. I'm sure he doesn't get much of that now that the grill is closed for the season. He'd probably appreciate a home-cooked meal. What were you planning for tonight?"

"It's not closed for the season, Mom. It's closed, period. Roasted chicken, and I'm sure he has a date or somewhere to be."

"Pshaw!" Her mother opened the door and her arms, and

Zak caught her unsteady stance. "Zak Grant, how dare you wait so long to come by and see us? You'd think we live in Russia the way you disappeared."

Zak helped her mother to the sofa and saw her safely to a seated position.

"Don't hurt the boy," Dad said. He thrust himself forward out of the chair and slapped Zak hard on the back a few times. "Good to see you, kid."

"You too, Mr. Bourne. Mrs. Bourne, you're as beautiful as ever and light as a feather. I'll never understand how you do it, cooking as well as you do. You and Julia look more like sisters than mother and daughter."

Julia rolled her eyes. Zak held out his arms. "Don't I get a hug, Julia?"

She crossed her arms and plopped onto the couch beside her mother. "What did you say to Devlin when I was in the coffee shop and you were on the sidewalk?"

"Julia, don't be rude," her mother said.

"I said nothing he didn't already know for himself."

"Julia wanted to know if you could stay for pie," Mom interjected. "I made one this afternoon."

Zak grinned. "You're in luck, Julia. I can stay for pie."

"Here." Her mother removed her apron from her seated position and handed it to Julia. "You don't want to get that pretty dress dirty."

Julia rose and grasped the proffered apron. "Let's go. This is the closest to Betty Crocker you'll get me, so enjoy it while it lasts."

"Oh, I will," Zak said.

As he followed her through the swinging kitchen door, she

added, "I'm making a roasted chicken too, but you'll be gone before it's ready."

◈

Zak sat down at the small maple table under the rustic copper lantern. Like most kitchens in old homes, the space was confined and claustrophobic, stuffed full of oversize appliances that early settlers never could have imagined in a house at the time.

"The kitchen looks nicer than I remember. Did your mother redo something in here? It seems bigger."

"I took all her cookie jars down. The original subway tile shows now. It's gorgeous, don't you think?"

"There's more light too. Is that a new window?"

"No, it's the original," she said. "I took down Mom's curtains and made that window treatment. It allows more light inside."

"Careful, Julia. You're sounding remarkably Martha Stewart. I might want you to bake me something yourself."

Julia pursed her lips.

Zak leaned back in his chair with his hands clasped behind his head. "Would you like me to tie that apron for you? You know how I love a woman in an apron."

Her stubborn glare returned. "I've got it, thank you."

"The kitchen looks great. Imagine what you could do with my place and your spa. You just have that way of finding the beauty in things."

"It's just a woman's touch. Something you're not familiar with down at the grill." Julia pulled a plate down from the knotty-pine cabinets and set it on the peach tile countertop. Her gaze seemed wary, mistrusting. "Why would you want a spa in your restaurant?"

"You've been in New York too long; you've become suspicious in nature. I told you, I'm remodeling, and I don't need all the space. It may as well be a spa. No doubt it will be something frilly, with all you girls have in mind."

She opened the drawer and pulled out a fork, pointing the utensil toward him menacingly as she spoke. "I always felt stir-crazy in this kitchen, but I never understood why until I grew older. Things should match. My mother's purple floral plates, the red-lined curtains with the peach tile . . . How did she miss it?"

He shook his head. "I never noticed it, but I do notice the improvements."

Her eyes lingered on him in a way he felt to his toes. For a moment she softened, and he remembered how she used to look up to him like he was royalty. Until he'd grown too big for his britches in high school and treated her like a serf in the high school caste system.

"I used to wonder how my mom could spend every waking moment in this mismatched kitchen without ending up in the loony bin. It drove me insane to be in here. Now I see she just loved what she loved and she didn't care if any of it matched. It's funny how two people can be from the same blood and so very different."

"Can you bake a pie like that?" Zak asked, staring at the freshly baked crust before him.

"No, I can't bake a pie like this, now that you mention it. Does that disappoint you?" Julia cinched the apron around her waist. "Not for a lack of my mother's efforts, mind you. I just never took to baking. I can mix up a facial concoction to perfection just by reading a client's skin type, but baking is such an exacting art form. Mom says I'm too sloppy to bake the love in that's needed."

"Doesn't bother me in the least. You look great cutting the pie in those heels. That's enough for me. Any man, actually."

She flicked a heel off and tossed it at his shin. Then she took off the other one and sliced the knife into the pie. Without washing her hands.

"That's a state violation," Zak said. "Not washing your hands. You did that on purpose, didn't you? To see if I was paying attention."

"Sue me." She put the plate in front of him and sat down at the table. "Are you going to tell me what all that was about this morning? Why didn't you trust Devlin? You didn't, right? From the start, I could tell."

"No ice cream? I like my pie à la mode." He slid the plate toward her and smiled. "With coffee. Nothing like a little pie à la mode with coffee. Just the right amount of sweetness, tartness, tasty bitterness. It excites the senses, all the taste buds."

"Except salt." She held a saltshaker over his slice of pie. He swept it from her hand and leaned in close to her beautiful complexion. She wasn't taking any of his hints, so he'd have to be more straightforward. He needed her to understand that he'd changed; he wasn't the kid who'd pulled her hair and treated her like a second-class citizen anymore. Though as he smelled the sweet sensation of her shampoo, he quickly remembered his promise to Greg and backed away.

"Why?" Her voice was no more than a whisper. She

cleared her throat and said it again with force. "Why did you do that this morning?"

"I Googled your friend."

"That's a lie. You couldn't have Googled him. The Internet was down. That's why he stopped at Natalie's place and I was able to catch him before he left town."

"That's not a lie. I don't lie." He took her wrist, kicked out the chair with his foot, and told her to sit. "I didn't say I Googled him today. Why are you so suspicious?" he asked again, but he knew what he'd done to make her suspicious. He felt red with shame for asking the question.

"Why would you search him at all? How does who I work for evoke one smidgen of concern on your part?"

"Because I promised your brother I'd look out for you while he was gone, and when you ran off to New York, how was I supposed to do that? Google was my only option."

She winced. "I didn't need anyone to keep an eye on me. I needed an investor, and you sent Devlin and his money packing."

"I offered you that. Devlin is not necessary."

She exhaled loudly. "Who are you to tell me Devlin isn't necessary? Why is everyone trying to tell me how to run my business? Maybe I want to do this alone. Did anyone think of that?"

"That's not the way we do things in Smitten."

"Maybe that's the problem. I understand Greg asked you to look after me when he deployed, but I'm a grown woman. I don't need looking after."

"Everyone needs help once in a while. No one is an island."

"Have you met my parents? Maybe I want to be an island."

"If that were true, you wouldn't be here to take care of your mother. You wouldn't be starting the spa to pull off your friends' girly idea. You're more of a team player than you care to admit. I'm only asking to be on your team."

She laughed for a moment, but it wasn't her springtime, happy laugh. New York had changed her in some ways. Her laugh employed a sarcastic bent.

"No offense, Zak, but commitment isn't your best attribute. How long until you'd want your money and your building back? You flirt a good game, but I need something solid as the foundation for my spa. You can see that my parents don't really have the money to lend me, even if they did offer. That money is for Greg when he gets home from serving our country."

Her words stung. Mostly because there was truth in them.

"I deserved that, but I'll be there. I promised Greg."

"Don't trouble yourself. My bed-wetting, nose-picking, turtle-stealing self will find a way to make it work."

She charmed him. She always had, if he were honest. He pushed his plate closer toward her. "The pie's getting cold. I like it when the ice cream melts over the top of it. Sweet and tangy, warm and cold. Like I said, a taste sensation."

She narrowed her wide, childlike eyes. "You think you're cute, don't you?"

"I think I want some ice cream on my pie and you're not being a very good hostess. I might have to tell your mother."

She pursed her lips together and walked to the freezer. She yanked down on the handle and pulled out the frozen vanilla, covered with freezer snow. She banged it down on the counter. "Mmm. Ancient ice cream. Nothing like a little freezer burn to go on your fresh pie."

"Looks like you have time to make the coffee." He grinned, hoping for more time to convince her he meant what he'd offered.

Julia opened the yellow Tupperware canister and scooped coffee into the percolator. She measured water and set the pot onto the stove, and though she'd never admit it, she did it with the skill of a professional.

"I know Greg meant well, but I lived in New York City by myself. Surely you don't think I need looking after in Smitten." She sat down again at the table and rubbed her feet. "Stilettos and Smitten do not mix."

"You're going to wash your hands this time, right?"

"You can't tell me you care about sanitizing. I saw the grill today."

"There's a reason it looks like that."

"How did you come by Devlin's name to Google him?"

Zak chuckled. "This is Smitten, Julia. Not New York. If I want to know anything about anyone, I need only to visit the coffee shop. Nat isn't exactly shy with details."

*Natalie!* She should have known. "Why don't you visit the coffee shop now? I'll pack your pie, and by the time you get there, the ice cream should have defrosted. You'll bring my mother's Tupperware back, won't you? I'm afraid she'd never forgive you if you didn't return her Tupperware. I don't care how young you say she looks. Tupperware is sacred."

He leaned back in his chair and took her foot into his lap. Just the touch of her felt electric. He rubbed her arches, and she closed her eyes. He hoped there were more nights like this in their future. "You have to stop wearing those shoes. They can't be good for your back on the brick sidewalks."

"Julia!" Her mother entered the kitchen, and Julia pulled her foot to the floor. "Haven't you gotten that boy a slice of pie yet? Honestly, if you were one of his waitresses, he would have fired you by now."

"On the contrary, Mrs. Bourne, I'd never have hired her. She has a bit of an attitude, I'm noticing." He winked, but Julia slapped his arm.

Julia padded to the counter in her bare feet and pouted. "The vanilla is frozen solid. How old is it?"

"That's why you wait to cut the pie. Put it in the microwave for thirty seconds. Go on."

Julia did as she was told while Zak rested his chin on his fist. She set the microwave as her mother instructed, then pulled out the tub and plunked it in front of Zak's pie. "Your ice cream, sir. No charge for the freezer burn."

"Well, serve it to him properly. Honestly, Julia, you'd think you were raised in the barn. Zak likes a dollop of Cool Whip on his pie, don't you, Zak?"

"I sure do, ma'am."

"You sound like Gomer Pyle," Julia told him. "Mom, how can you fall for this?"

"Well, go-ol-ly," he answered.

"Have you heard from Greg lately?" Mrs. Bourne asked. She stumbled about the small kitchen on her crutch.

"Just a text now and again. He might be home for Christmas, but I'm sure he told you that already."

"Yes," Mrs. Bourne said. "What's this I hear about Julia's spa being in your grill?"

"My spa is not going to be in his grill!" Julia protested.

Zak thrust out his lower lip. "Your daughter's a stubborn woman. I offered to do the build-out for her and use local workers. She wants to bring in foreign money, and who knows where she'll get the labor. Tell her it's all right to accept help when you need it. It's the Smitten way. I think she forgot that while in New York."

"New York is not foreign. Last time I checked it was part of the US of A."

"Your mom knows what I mean."

"Does my mom know you lie like a rug?"

"Julia, why wouldn't you take Zak's help?" Mrs. Bourne asked.

Julia rolled her eyes.

Why wouldn't she take Zak's help? Where did she start?

"Mom, Zak has plans for that grill, and if he gets it running again, I'll be out of a business after putting all that money into his spot."

"Zak wouldn't do that, would you?"

"I might. If we had enough business." Zak raised his brow. "But not without finding the spa a new residence."

"See," her mother said. In one fell swoop, with one arm, her mother scooped up the ice cream, plopped it on the pie, scooped up a dollop of Cool Whip, and shook the spoon so the pie looked like something on a television commercial. "The coffee will be ready in a minute."

"I'll get it, Mom. Can you leave us alone for a minute? I want to talk to Zak privately before he goes."

Her mother smiled coyly, as if romance were in the air. "Oh my, yes." She hobbled quickly out of the kitchen.

"For an older woman on a crutch, she scurries about pretty good where you're involved."

Zak grinned. "Not everyone is immune to my charms."

"What did you say to Devlin?"

"I just let him know I knew the truth about where his money came from and what ulterior motives he might have."

"All right. I admit you know more than I do, and no doubt I've been blindsided by something you're delighting to tell me. Do you want me to beg?"

"That would be kind of fun."

"I'm not going to."

"I figured as much."

She hated that Zak knew something about Devlin she didn't, but in fairness, she'd never seen Devlin turn on her as he had that morning. Three years and one incident seemed forgivable, but even if Zak thought the women's ideas for Smitten were inane, she knew enough to know he'd never let anyone hurt her. That was a privilege he reserved for himself.

"Ask him yourself, Julia. If you're so convinced of Devlin Stovich's character, ask him what I told him. See if he's man enough to tell you. If he's not, you have your answer about his character." Zak hadn't touched his pie. "Let me help you."

"No," she snapped without thinking.

"You say you want the spa. I can give it to you. If you really want it, why won't you take it?"

"I don't want your help. That's all. I don't need to explain my reasons."

"I promised your brother I'd do whatever it took to keep you here while he's deployed. He doesn't want your parents to worry."

"Ah." She nodded. "So this is all about Greg. Your word to him. It never had anything to do with helping me, is that right?"

"I didn't know you'd show up in my grill today. You came to me, and I took it as a sign from God that it was time to do my duty."

"Your *duty*?" She couldn't bear to look at him any longer. Besides, she couldn't have independence and Zak Grant, so she was only making herself crazy. "The coffee cups are hanging on the backsplash. Help yourself."

It took every ounce of self-control she possessed not to break at his words. *Hope* was her problem, believing there was something more to Zak than the shallow, callous tool he was. As part of his man code, he'd look after her. When Greg returned, Zak would be released from any responsibility and from her life. He'd never looked at her as a woman, and why she had for a moment believed otherwise was a mystery. Besides, she didn't want to end up like her mother, waiting on some man hand and foot.

Zak stood and blocked her way.

"Move, Zak."

"That didn't come out right."

"It didn't come out covered in your smooth, milk-chocolate words that have my mother completely snowed, you mean."

Julia slipped from his grasp and scrambled out of the room as if he carried a contagious disease. Her rejection stung.

"Julia, wait!" He followed her into the living room and watched her shadow disappear up the stairs. Back in the kitchen, he bent over and picked up her scandalously high stiletto. He studied the shoe and wondered how a girl like her had ever come from Smitten in the first place. "Julia," he whispered to the ceiling. "I'm doing this all wrong. Help me out here, God! Help me get through to her that I've changed."

# CHAPTER FIVE

. . . . . . . . . . . . . . . . . . . . . . . . . . . . . . .

*J*ulia stretched out her right leg and set her foot on the split-rail fence. She bent over at the waist in a long, deep stretch, and her muscles groaned in protest. She'd been the first to arrive that morning along the river walk, and with so much pent-up energy she'd already jogged a mile. She wouldn't mention that to the girls. They already saw her as an overachiever because her workout wear always matched. So she stretched rather than explain her ruffled appearance.

Shelby arrived next, decked out in pink leggings with new blinding-white tennis shoes. In her arms she carried Penelope, her white Shih-poo, who also wore pink "shorts" with a cutout for the tail. "I've never been on in-line skates before," Shelby announced.

"That poor dog. Can't you give her some dignity?" Julia asked.

Shelby kissed the dog's ear. "Don't listen to her. She's grumpy today, and she doesn't realize how a new outfit makes you feel!"

Shelby lived in a special place Julia liked to call Fairy Tale Land—where, if it were an actual place, it would always be Christmas. It would smell like cinnamon, and women would still wear velvet dresses with lace collars and stockings every day. To a stranger, Shelby might appear snooty, but to anyone who knew her—and that included all of Smitten—she simply spread sparkle dust and sunshine wherever she went. The consummate optimist, Shelby ran an etiquette school at the edge of town to teach younger girls how to view the world through rose-colored glasses.

"I heard it didn't go so well with your boss. I'm so sorry to hear it. But that's hardly a reason to put us all on skates. If God meant for us to roll around, he would have created us with wheels instead of toes."

"The loss of Devlin's money only means I'll have to try something different. And you'll be fine on skates. We have to give Reese the motivation to open up her outfitting shop. She's got to try out the best equipment. This way, we can help motivate her *and* get exercise."

"Or we can keep the medical clinic in business with our broken limbs."

"We'll have fun. If everything in that store isn't planned for the next ten years, she'll never get started. It's our duty to skate. And ski. And whatever else Reese needs to convince herself it's a foolproof plan."

"I don't understand why Reese has to be so athletic and organized. Can't she open up a nicely stocked soap store? She's clean too."

"That gets in the way of my business," Julia said.

"Maybe you don't have to start the spa as large as you planned. Just rent a little room somewhere and do facials and makeup to begin with?"

"That's a good idea, Shelby. Maybe I set my sights too high. The way Devlin looked at me at the end of the day was enough to make me question the whole plan."

Shelby put the dog down on the pathway. Penelope picked

up her paws anxiously in a strange circle of movement. "Penelope doesn't like the way the path feels on her paws."

"If you get that dog shoes, I'm not exercising with you."

"She has snow boots for the winters."

"Of course she does. I draw the line at flip-flops." Julia laughed. "There's Reese." She raised her hand. "Over here!"

Reese approached them with a giant plastic box on wheels trailing her. Her blond ponytail bounced with each step. Petite and athletic, Reese Mackenzie really required a more active power-exercising group, with more energy and fewer words, but socially the women all fit together like a well-cut puzzle.

Reese gnawed on her thumbnail as she approached. She set the box to rights and grinned. "They're all here. The best brands of in-line skates on the market. We only need to decide which two my potential store will carry." She opened the top of the box and pulled out four pairs of skates. "There are knee guards and wrist guards too."

"What if I fall on my dog?" Shelby asked. "What's going to protect her from me? Did anyone see that *MythBusters* where the frozen turkey fell and killed a dog? They proved it. Imagine what I could do to Penelope!"

"You're not going to fall. We'll go slow," Reese said.

Shelby pointed out Penelope's new outfit. The dog's rhinestone collar glittered in the morning sunlight. "I think we should just walk. We've got a lot to talk about, after all. Julia's boss was here yesterday. We have to hear about the spa."

Reese sighed. "It will take less effort to skate than run. We can talk fine while we skate briskly. What we're looking for is a smooth, quiet ride."

"Maybe you can ride smoothly. For the rest of us, that remains to be seen." Shelby looked down at the dog again. "How briskly?"

Natalie appeared on the path. "We ready?" She looked at the skates. "Hmm. Not much to those, is there?"

"You'll be fine," Reese said. "Let's buckle up." She pointed to the bench and pulled out a pair of skates and pads for each of her friends. "You want to make sure they're tight enough so that your balance isn't thrown off," Reese said. "We need to move fast enough to see which brand works best, since this is where most of my potential customers will skate—along the river walk."

"I feel old," Natalie said. "I'm a mother. There's something inherently wrong about a mother putting on roller skates."

"In-line skates," Reese corrected. "Come on, we're not going to Sawyer's wedding with any extra weight."

"Reese, you haven't an ounce of body fat on you. You're not going anywhere with any 'extra weight.' Don't rub it in." Natalie changed the subject. "You girls aren't going to believe what a jerk that guy from New York was. Did Julia tell you? Honestly, if I weren't a Christian woman, I might have lobbed one of yesterday's muffins at the back of his head."

The girls giggled. "Does that mean he's not investing in Smitten's spa, Julia?" Reese asked.

"We wouldn't want his money even if he was willing," Natalie continued. "I'm telling you, girls, I'm surprised he wasn't run out on a rail. He nearly was, and not by me!"

"Oooh, gossip. What did you do, Julia?"

"Not Julia. Zak Grant! He came to Julia's rescue just like in an old John Wayne movie."

"Oh, Natalie, he did not. Honestly, I wish I could see the world the way you do."

"Zak?" Reese smiled. "I always thought he had a thing for you, Julia. Was he jealous, Nat?"

"He looked like it. He came to the coffee shop, and he and the New York guy had words outside. Then Zak pushed him into his truck and took him to the airport. He didn't even let Julia say good-bye!"

"Oooh, *words*," Shelby said. "Did Zak look angry?"

"He was facing away from me, but I'll tell you what, that Devlin character looked intimidated. He may be hot stuff in New York City, but in Smitten he's just a wee little man. No competition for our loggers."

"Who wouldn't be intimidated by Zak? He could beat down half of Smitten!" Shelby said, and they all looked at her to see if she'd really said that.

"That's not the way it was at all," Julia said. "Natalie loves life in this small town because of the great drama she imagines going on."

"I forgot the best part," Natalie said, undeterred. "Zak offered to invest in Julia's business himself, but get this: both men wanted to put the spa in the Smitten Grill."

"Eww!" Reese said. "That makes me want to take a shower right now."

"See?" Shelby said. "A soap shop. Far more realistic than an outfitters store. And it would be a lot easier on my body."

"Relax, all of you. It's not going to happen," Julia said. "Neither guy gets what we want to do with Smitten. Shelby had a good idea that maybe I should start smaller. You know, not bring in all the equipment and ambience just yet. Maybe just one facial chair and product. That way I can save up and get an employee so that by the time Sawyer's wedding happens we can do the couples' massages."

"Doesn't sound like much of a spa," Reese said. "Sounds more like a bad slumber party."

"Which is the type of spa I can afford to back on my own at the moment. If we hope to get this romance destination spot off the ground, I need to get cracking."

"So take Zak's money," Natalie said in her drill sergeant tone. "Duh."

"I'm not taking Zak's money."

"He said he'd help her," Natalie said to enlist the support of Reese and Shelby. "He wouldn't offer it if he didn't have it and wasn't willing to lend it to you. Zak's not stupid. He must believe in it even a little to offer you the money."

"He might," Shelby said. "He's got a good heart. I personally think he's always had a thing for Julia, but he laid off because of Greg."

"Oh, Shelby, you think the Grinch has a good heart!" Natalie snapped.

"Well, he did at the end. Remember? *Fah who for-aze, Fah who for-aze* . . ."

Julia groaned. "Forget about Zak! I'm not taking his money! Help me think! We're on a deadline here, and Zak is not the answer."

They started slowly on their skates. Reese took Penelope's leash until Shelby found her footing.

"I feel ridiculous with this dog. Can we go faster? I need to get a workout," Reese said.

"You can go faster. Penelope and the rest of us are going as fast as we can," Shelby said.

"Then can I pick her up?" Reese asked.

"What kind of walk would that be for my baby?"

Reese sighed and skated ahead, forcing the dog to run. "I'm thinking for you, Julia! Just trying to get a workout and see if these in-line skates will work for the shop!"

"So does this mean I'm at square one?"

"It means you need to swallow your pride and call Zak. We're all doing our part to make this happen, so call him and do your part," Natalie said. "Is there anything besides pride that's keeping you from taking the money?"

"Well, there's that and the idea of cleaning that disgusting grill. What if I fail? What if I can't make the spa work, and I'm indebted to Zak Grant?"

Natalie raised her eyebrows as she skirted along the path. "I can think of worse people to be indebted to. Maybe he'd take payment in massages."

"That just sounds wrong, Natalie," Shelby said.

"Well, then you'll have to answer to Zak Grant, and I would think that would be reason enough to succeed. Provide the motivation, if you will," Reese said.

"That's encouraging," Julia answered.

"It's supposed to be," Natalie said. "Zak's not your enemy. And he's not your father. You can't be afraid of every man on the planet, Julia. If you trust yourself and your own abilities, you have no reason to. For one thing, I can't for a minute see Zak in an armchair like your dad. The man never sits down."

"Thank you, Dr. Phil."

"I think she's only saying that Zak would try to help you. I don't think he'd try to control you like that former boss of yours. If Natalie says she wanted to hit him with a muffin, I have to believe he's worse than all the men in Smitten." Shelby skated faster and chastised Reese. "Give me my baby back. You're practically dragging her!" Shelby picked up her dog and cuddled her close while they moved slowly along the river walk.

"I should just go back to New York and find another job in a spa," Julia said.

"And leave us? And all this?" Reese raised her arms to the blue summer sky and skated backward as she spoke.

Reese was right. Julia couldn't bear to be alone amid so many people again. She had missed her family. Her friends. She felt at peace in Smitten, and she had to find a way to make her life here work. Faith. She knew it rested on faith, but fear kept pushing it away.

As she watched Reese get smaller in the distance, she wondered if it was fair for her friend to assess a pair of skates worn by the rest of them. Clearly, they had no athletic prowess compared to Reese. Julia looked at Natalie, brimming with confidence and success. Her life was full now, with Carson's and Mia's love. And Shelby, so full of lollipop thoughts that nothing dared harm her . . . Shelby had been through so much and still stood tall. Julia felt weak by comparison. She wondered if she had the faith necessary to stay in Smitten. Maybe she wasn't that kind of believer. New York might be the best thing for her because the city asked so little of her.

# CHAPTER SIX

. . . . . . . . . . . . . . . . . . . . . . . . . . .

*T*uesday morning the sun hoisted itself high and bright in the sky. Nearly a week had passed, and Devlin Stovich had yet to return one of Julia's many phone calls. It was like a seventh-grade Sadie Hawkins dance all over again, only this time she instinctively understood male rejection. The truth that she may have misjudged Devlin's character wounded her to the core. She would have testified for him in a court of law. She had to find out exactly what Zak had learned about him. Regardless of his answer, New York would only be an option if she found another spa to work in. And without Devlin's recommendation, she wondered if that was even possible.

She hoped that whatever Zak told her would provide some kind of prophecy for her future and the spa, but she was quickly running out of hope. Usually time in prayer or time exercising with her friends restored her faith and motivation, but this time it felt as though God had her in a holding pattern and she had no idea why. She had run the numbers and costs for the business and wondered if maybe she should give the grill a second look.

With a twofold purpose, Julia resolved to schlep on over to the grill and talk to Zak. She parked her car in the gravel parking lot and sniffed in the deep, fresh air. At that moment she didn't miss a single thing about New York. The grill really did have the ideal location, just outside of town and on the pond. She felt her tense stomach relax just by being in the beautiful surroundings.

She'd dressed more practically this visit, in jeans and closed-toe wedges so that the sawdust wouldn't get into her shoes. She fastened her one-button blazer and started up the steps.

The sound of a hammer, the whirl of a drill all caught her attention when she approached the double red doors, propped slightly open by an antique metal iron. She tried to knock for attention before pushing the door open, but the sound of tools at work continued. She knocked louder.

"Hello! Zak?"

The pounding continued, and she coughed at the dust.

"Zak?" she called again and peered inside. She shielded her eyes as she stepped from the bright sunlight into the darkened room. The sound of the hammer and drill got louder, and the smell of freshly cut wood filled her nostrils. Sawdust littered the pine plank floors, but its fresh salmon-pink color told her it was new and the result of labor.

Natalie's boyfriend, Carson, was crouched over a hammer. He caught sight of her shoes and looked up. Carson was a broad-shouldered man whose body said he was well acquainted with physical labor. He owned the local fishing cabins on the lake as well as the local hardware store. By Smitten standards, that made him the town mogul.

"Julia," Carson said. "What are you doing here?"

"I might ask you the same thing. I thought the fishing cabins would be full about now."

"They are, except for the ones currently under renovation.

I'm helping Zak make some changes around this place. We can't let you girls have all the fun now, can we? Some days I don't even feel like it's necessary to be at the hardware store. I know all the customers and they pay their tabs at the end of the month. I should just leave the door unlocked, except now we've got all these strangers running about town."

Julia laughed. "Is Zak here?"

"He's around somewhere. He's got a new guy coming in after the Fourth of July holiday, but for now it's just the two of us. I'd tell you to grab a saw if you weren't dressed for a city luncheon." Carson chuckled.

"What kind of changes is he planning?"

"You'll have to ask him. He's on the deck, I think." Carson pointed his hammer toward the back of the room.

Julia maneuvered through the obstacle course of two-by-fours until she reached the back door. Zak wore protective eye goggles and was drilling something into the exterior wall. She opened the door and yelled, but he'd seen her and stopped the machine.

"Julia. You look beautiful. You always look beautiful. What brings you down to the Smitten slums?"

"I wanted to finish our conversation from the other day."

"Does that mean—"

"What are you doing to the grill?"

He wiped his forehead with the back of his hand. "Making some renovations. I want to be ready for ski season and, you know, Sawyer's wedding. I'm getting rid of the stumps. Bought real chairs. I imagine the wedding will bring a lot more women to town, and I just think it's time to give this place more of a woman's touch."

She nodded. "Shouldn't you have a woman here, then?"

"Is that an offer? You do have that gift of making things prettier. Spreading your pixie dust, I guess you'd say."

"I don't know anything about the restaurant business."

"I didn't know anything about the spa business until I looked up the setup of your spa in New York."

"You mean Devlin's spa."

He cleared his throat. "You want something to drink?"

"No, thanks."

"I would." He grinned.

She crossed her arms and shook her head. "You have no shame."

"I don't, but I do have a deep thirst. It's hot out here. I'm putting up an awning so I can serve out here in the summers."

"I'll be back," she said, trying to take Natalie's advice and show a little bit of humility. Maybe that's what her faith was missing. She walked through the large room and entered the kitchen. The commercial stainless steel refrigerator stood against the back wall, and to her surprise the fridge and the kitchen itself were spotless. She found a glass on a shelf, opened the ice machine, and dug the glass through until it was filled. She thought of Carson at that moment and did the same for him. Then she filled both glasses with water. Her eye caught a lemon on the countertop, and she sliced through it and put a citrus twist in both cups. "I am Betty Crocker," she said to herself. She carried the glasses through the restaurant and handed one to Carson.

"Thanks." He smiled, drank the water in one gulp, and handed the cup back to her. She set it on a table and went back outside to the deck.

Zak gazed briefly at her, then fired up his drill and finished with his screw.

"Your water." She held it out to him with a small curtsy. He set down the drill and took the glass from her.

"Sit down," he said as he took the chair to her left.

"What are you building?"

"A covering for the deck."

"I meant inside. I thought you were just getting new decor."

"I'm dividing the building so I can rent out part of it. I'd like to offer up a more inviting atmosphere, you know, for the women."

"You're avoiding my question. What are you building?"

"A new start. Until I can think of a reason to open the mill again. Get these men back to work."

"Ah, you're evading my question."

"Did you get hold of Devlin?" Zak fired the drill up when it was time for her to answer. Then he peered up at her from under his tousled brown hair with his deep-set, magnetic eyes.

"No, I didn't, but something tells me you knew that."

Zak smirked. "Maybe. I'll just say it doesn't surprise me." Zak chugged some of his water. "Devlin doesn't own that spa. That's what I found out on Google."

She laughed. "Of course he does. It's one of the best spas in New York. You can pay more and not get the glowing skin that Devlin's procedure gives you. Those women can't afford to have pocked skin for a day because of a facial."

Zak's mouth made an O shape and he put his fingers to his chin. "I know! But then, who *can* afford that?"

She tried not to giggle. Zak Grant was nothing if not

charming, but then, what guy wouldn't be when he always got his way? Zak answered to no one that she could see, and his charm came at a cost as far as she was concerned. A cost that she couldn't afford. Falling for Zak's charm would mean abandoning her dreams and morphing into the "little woman"—not that he'd ever give her the opportunity.

"What do you mean he doesn't own that spa?"

"Mrs. Shapiro owns it." He stuck a screw between his lips and marked a spot for his next drill hole. "Devlin's a front man because it's apparently beneath her to own a spa. It's not his."

"Zak, I worked for him. He signed my checks."

"He never had money to invest in Smitten. It would have been Mrs. Shapiro's money, and quite frankly, I don't think she would have considered the idea. Devlin came out here for you."

"Devlin's not interested in me," Julia said. "He's not interested in any one woman. Which seems to be the kind of men I attract." She stared pointedly at him.

He ignored her slight. "Maybe he thought you'd be more relaxed in your natural setting. Let your guard down."

"I live with my parents. Where exactly would I let my guard down?"

"You don't think like a guy, Julia. Give me that much at least."

She opened her mouth, but she had nothing to say. Zak was right.

He answered more of her questions about the renovation. "I'm putting a wall up inside, covering the deck here so you can move massage tables out here in the summers. There will also be a wall separating the deck. Take my help, Julia."

"This is . . . this is for me? Zak, I told you, this isn't—"

Carson came outside. "Two massage tables were just delivered," he said to Zak. "You getting intimate with your ribs for barbecue, or can I assume those are for Julia?"

"Why?" She narrowed her gaze. "Why would you do this?"

Zak saw Julia's walls come down, if only slightly. His act of faith had worked, if only for that instant.

"Natalie told Carson you were considering going back to New York. I promised your brother you'd stay in Smitten. Your parents don't need to worry about both of you."

That wasn't exactly the whole truth. The truth was, he wanted to do what he could to keep her near to him. To prove that he wasn't the commitment-phobe she feared, nor the caveman her father pretended to be. He was, in fact, in love with her. He probably always had been, but that truth proved far too inconvenient with his history and his promise to Greg.

"Greg can't expect you to keep me in Smitten. That's too much to ask of your friendship. You can't control another person."

"True. But I can do whatever I can to make it easy for you to stay. You say this is your dream. Carson, Natalie, and I—we want to do what we can to make it come true for you."

"I—I don't know what to say."

Zak slapped his knee and stood. "Greg wired me money to pay for this."

She shook her head. "No, Zak. I can't take my brother's money. He's fighting a war. He'll have to come back, and he'll have his own war to find work here in Smitten."

He pulled a check out of his shirt pocket. "I didn't take it, Julia. I knew you'd never accept his money. I would never accept his money."

"Independence Day may be tomorrow, but it seems like it will never come for me. Why does everyone think I need to be taken care of?"

"We take care of our own in Smitten. Why do you see it as control when we do it for love?"

"I—I just do. I thought you'd closed down the grill for good. Until the mill reopened at least."

"Plans change. Look, I realize this place isn't good enough for you or your spa, but you can make it work until you're rolling in the dough." He exhaled roughly. "I don't know what else I can do to prove to you that I want you here. I want your spa in my restaurant. Doesn't that mean anything to you?"

She didn't move. Her slender frame faced the pond, and she gazed out onto the glassy water and slowly sat in one of the chairs. "Carson, you knew about this?"

Carson shrugged. "Natalie told me to get over here and help. I just do as I'm told." He laughed.

"Hey!" Zak pointed the drill at her like a firearm. "I never said I was out of business." He pulled the drill back as if he were cocking a gun. "I said I was working on a plan to reopen the mill. I needed to focus. You make me sound like some kind of failure. Can't you just say thank you?"

"The town *has* failed, hasn't it? Isn't that why we're trying something new?"

"You girls are pinning all your hopes on Sawyer's wedding and the air of romance . . . You know what your problem is, Julia?"

"Yes, you scaring off my investor and my spa smelling like barbecue—that seems to be my trouble. What makes you think you know the first thing about what I want in a spa? That you would just feel free to start building without any commitment on my part? What if I leave and go back to New York?"

"Your trouble is that you got it in your head that the men of this town are your enemies, instead of asking for help when you might need it. You need my help and you're too proud to admit it. Who has enough space for this spa? Who has a pond? Who has the building skill and, I might add, the Internet skill to steal the plans from your New York City spa and build it here? I didn't see Devlin offering anything more than his snooty opinion, which, I might remind you, also led you right back here."

He instantly regretted his words. She had recoiled at his tough stance and his blowing his own horn, as if he alone could keep her in Smitten. Devlin could easily offer Julia more if given the opportunity. That's why Zak had started the plans. Though his heart was in the right place, Julia saw his actions as manipulative and controlling; the very thing she feared the most, he had made real.

*Say it*, he told himself. *Tell her how you feel before she bolts again!*

"Who's deciding when I need help—you? I would have figured it out, Zak!"

He put the drill down and came toward her chair. She stood up and straightened her shoulders. She still only came up to his chest.

"You've been in New York too long if you trust those wimpy, feminine men over the real men of Smitten. Carson and people like him built this town. Your father built this town. Carson and I, we get what you girls want to do, but you're forgetting something."

"Are we?" She pressed her fist to her hip.

"You're forgetting us men. You're taking away our sense of pride, and you're trying to win some invisible contest. We're not your competition. We want you to succeed, but forgive us for wanting to look after our women and help where we can. As the men of Smitten, we see it as our duty, even if we do think the idea is harebrained."

"Harebrained!" She latched onto the only words she could fight, apparently.

"Do you want us to let the women take care of us? It's not in our DNA." He set the drill back down and drained the rest of his water glass.

She unclenched her jaw. "What if I told you that it wasn't in mine to sit back and be told what to do?"

"I'd tell you that sometimes it's in everyone's best interest to sit back and be told what to do." He took her by the hand. "Come in and see the plans."

He tightened his grip around her tiny wrist and led her into the restaurant/spa. "What?" he asked. He drank in her hard stare until her expression softened and the skin around her eyes crinkled into a smile.

"Thank you."

"Was that so hard?"

She coughed. "I feel sick to my stomach, actually."

He leaned down and kissed her on the cheek chastely. As her brother might do. "I'm proud of you anyway. We're going to do this together, Julia. We'll have each other's backs."

"If this is really going to be a spa, then I need to get busy. I need to get plans and—"

"All taken care of."

"What would you know about building a spa, Zak?"

"Everything I need to." He picked up blueprints and rolled them out on a table.

Julia recognized the floor plan. "This is Devlin's spa. How did you get these?"

"Correction. It's not Devlin's spa. I told you, it's owned by someone named Shapiro. Devlin's nothing more than a well-dressed con man. Well, and a manager, I suppose. The fact is he lied about it. Why?"

"Mrs. Shapiro is one of his clients, not the owner. She lent him her plane to come here." She seemed to question herself, while she answered him firmly.

Zak rolled his eyes. "Do you ever listen, Julia?"

"Zak, he trained me on the business aspects of the spa. Not to mention he's one of the best estheticians in the world, but he doesn't do that any longer. Only for Mrs. Shapiro."

"That may well be, but he doesn't own that spa in Manhattan. All I'm saying."

"That's what you knew? Why would he care if I knew that?"

"It wasn't his money to invest, Julia. What was his reasoning? Did it ever occur to you that he might want something more out of you than—"

"He's old enough to be my father!"

"We all know that never happens, an older man and a younger woman. Unthinkable! Especially in Manhattan."

She stared at the floor. "Are you . . . are you jealous?" she asked.

*Yes! Yes, I'm jealous. Yes, I want to kill him for messing with my sweet Julia.*

Zak pulled her in toward him until he felt her warm breath on his cheek. He wiped his hands on the front of his jeans and placed them on each side of her cheeks. Her lips were so close that he could taste them, but he heard Greg's name whispered in his ear and pulled away. "I need to get back to work."

"Do you want me here, Zak? In your building, I mean?"

He rolled up the blueprints and strode away from her rather than stare into those wide, beautiful eyes. "I want what's best for Smitten."

# CHAPTER SEVEN

· · · · · · · · · · · · · · · · · · · · · · · · · · ·

*I*ndependence Day brought the entire town of Smitten together for Main Street's parade and, later that night, the fireworks over the lake. The flowers in the window boxes along Main Street were all in bloom, and red, white, and blue ribbons draped from each of them festively. The town square's green clock had been wrapped with patriotic ribbons, and underneath it, Smitten's own Garner Sisters played their stringed instruments to their hearts' delight. No amount of lipstick or rouge circles had been spared, and they absolutely glittered in the morning sunlight.

As the parade began, Julia found a place outside Natalie's coffee shop beside Reese. She had so much to tell them about the spa, about her brother's money . . . about Zak . . . but Carson and Zoe, Natalie's cousin, stood nearby and Julia didn't dare spill her feelings for fear that everything might come out. So she said nothing and sat beside them on the brick curb.

"Did you decide on the in-line skates?"

"Yes," Reese said as she sipped her cinnamon latte. "Just a few more decisions and I might be ready to do this. Smitten needs an outfitters shop, don't you think?"

"We all think so. Even those of us without a passion for outdoor activities still need to stay fit. We want to look as good as the Garner Sisters as we age, don't we?"

Reese giggled. "I suppose we do. Speaking of health, how's your mom?"

"She's doing a lot better. She's even making breakfast now, though I do wish she'd sit down and let me wait on her for a change."

"Considering all she usually does, I suppose that's progress."

"True."

Zoe carried a tray and handed out muffin pieces from Natalie's shop. No doubt Natalie couldn't bear to leave Zoe in charge inside on such an important day. Though Zoe was twenty-seven, she tended to blurt out whatever she thought at the time.

Julia took a piece and popped it into her mouth. "Is Nat coming out for the parade? Mia will be crushed if she doesn't see her along the route."

"She'll be here when the parade starts. Mia's Sunday school class is fourth in the lineup, so she'll be out by then," Zoe answered.

"Where's Shelby?" Julia asked.

"She's walking with her students, remember?" Reese replied. "She's going to have them all dressed up as little brides in white lace to sell our idea to the men of this town. Hopefully they'll find it cute, and we'll offer them some hope."

"Or they'll aim the fireworks at us tonight instead of upward."

Reese laughed with her.

"Oh. My. Gosh. Little Julia Bourne, is that you down there? You're still so tiny!"

Julia looked up at the long, jean-clad legs in front of her until she reached the mane of long blond hair highlighted by the sun, which glowed as if the woman wore a supernatural halo.

"Amy Hastings," Julia stuttered. "You're back in Smitten?"

Time had perfected the woman's appearance as if she'd ripened like a fresh summer peach instead of aging like the rest of them. Julia ventured a gaze at Reese, who rolled her eyes.

"Only for the Fourth. I'll come back for Sawyer's wedding, naturally, but things are going so well in California, I barely have time to think about Smitten. It's still as charming as ever. I heard you girls have big plans, right? That is so cute, I just have to tell you."

"Right," Reese said.

"It's hard for me to think of Smitten as romantic, though, having grown up here. The men in California are so sophisticated. I love how they're not above using all the antiaging products or doing their best to stay fit. It's not like here, where guys use a bar of soap and think they're suddenly Don Juan. You can see how it's hard for me to view this place as romantic and not backwoods."

Julia stood. "Not really. I prefer manly men. I don't care to share my hair product with a guy. I'm funny that way."

Amy gave a polite laugh.

"So what brings you back?" And in her mind Julia added, *And what will make you leave again?*

"Do you remember Zak Grant?" Amy smiled. "What am I asking—of course you do. Your brother was his best friend! How is Greg?"

"He's in Afghanistan, but he's doing well," she said. "He flies a Black Hawk."

"The military?"

Julia nodded. "So you're here all the way from California to see Zak?"

*I'm not jealous. I'm not jealous. I'm not jealous.* She'd say it to herself as many times as she needed to hear it. Zak thought of her as his little sister, and besides, who wanted a Christian woman who thought of marriage as a plague? *No one that I can think of!* Julia didn't need romance. She needed to make the world more beautiful. That was her place in life.

"He's remodeling his restaurant. He wants to make it more intimate. So I guess I'm here to see the Smitten Grill."

"Oh?" She hoped her open-ended answer would lead to more information. Julia thought *she* was supposed to offer advice on the restaurant. Leave it to Zak to ask any female he thought would fall for his line.

Amy placed her slender, manicured hands on her chest. "Oh, you don't know. I forget you're so many years younger than I am. That's what I do. I design restaurant interiors in Los Angeles. Granted, Smitten is a world apart, but great restaurant design is universal. It had been some time since I'd seen my parents anyway, so I thought, why not help Zak? It's the least I can do, considering our history."

"What does great restaurant design mean?" She'd keep asking questions until she got the answer she wanted. Was Amy here with designs for the restaurant or designs on Zak? Though she couldn't imagine Zak sharing hair product with anyone, much less the bleached blonde in front of her.

"It makes all the difference in the flow of customers, how much they spend in the bar, how they'll linger over dessert. It's an art form. But forget about me . . . What's Greg's little sister been up to?"

"I've been in New York. I'm . . . I . . . facials." *Word salad.* She cringed at her inability to speak when nervous.

"She's an esthetician," Reese interrupted with a distinct flip of her ponytail. "Julia's done some of the biggest names in Manhattan and learned at the premier spa in the Upper East Side. Now she's here to bring her expertise to Smitten and, of course, Sawyer's fans."

"Sawyer, right. Didn't you and Sawyer used to date?" Amy asked Reese, and the look on her friend's face made Julia want to slap Amy for her heartless ploy. "That must be awkward, to have him bring his bride back here."

"Not really," Reese answered. "That was ages ago. I mean, do you even remember who you dated in high school, Julia?"

"Yes," Julia said. "Only because it was nobody, so it's not all that difficult to remember." She slunk down to sit again on the curb.

Amy bent her long legs and balanced on her toes to crouch beside them. "You always were so cute." Amy touched the side of Julia's face. "Oh my gosh, to have those dimples! No wonder I was so jealous of you."

"Jealous of me?" Julia asked. "Weren't you homecoming queen?" Dare she mention that she had won the regional chemistry fair?

"Only prom queen," she said.

Julia and her friends were the queens of Saturday night television, so it hardly mattered which title Amy wore.

"Zak always spoke so highly of you. He wanted to make sure you kept out of trouble, and it used to make me so jealous! I used to call you Saint Julia when he made me angry. I wanted him to care about me like that, but he thought of me as just another girl. You were like his sister, and he looked out for you. I hated that."

"So why'd you come back here for his restaurant?" Reese asked.

"My boyfriend wanted to know the same thing, but Zak's my friend and Smitten's my hometown. With Sawyer's wedding, there's a good chance we can all make our names known. When Sawyer eats at the Smitten Grill, I want my name quoted in *People* magazine alongside Zak's, right? Maybe I have something to prove to my hometown, who knows?" Amy rose to her full height, which seemed to go forever from Julia's curb viewpoint. "So, it was great to see you. Maybe I'll see you again before I leave. But if you're ever in California, come and see me. I could do a lot with your hair, Julia."

"Yeah, that'd be great." Julia wondered if she should explain about the spa and the grill, but what was the point? She watched Amy's sultry saunter as the blonde sashayed away from them. "She's hardly dressed for a parade."

Reese stared at her. "You're hardly one to talk about who is dressed appropriately in Smitten, but I'll give you a free pass on Amy. What a nightmare. Can you believe she brought up Sawyer and me?"

"I imagine there's going to be more of that with him coming back to town. They'll probably want to interview you as his past girlfriend. Maybe Amy did you a favor by reminding you to have an answer ready."

"Probably, but I hardly have any dirt on the guy. He's been gone for years. He's not even my friend on Facebook."

"I'm no fan of a man who doesn't see what I see in you, Reese, but I'm glad Sawyer's coming back. We need him."

"Speaking of distant pasts, I never thought about you and Zak before all this remodeling happened," Reese said.

"That's something you and Zak have in common."

"I kind of like the idea. He'd be—"

"Don't say it. He's like a big brother and now a landlord, and that's all he'll ever be."

"Touchy, touchy. It's not like we have single men to spare in this town. I think Natalie grabbed up the only one available."

"Well, Zak is one you can cross off my list. Yours, too, if you're smart. I wonder if they'll get back together while she's here." Julia's gaze fixated on the perky Amy.

"You heard her say she was engaged."

"A boyfriend. Not engaged," Julia corrected.

"See, you were listening. Don't go borrowing trouble, and now that I know you've got feelings for Zak, I'd say you should make your move tonight at the fireworks."

"I don't have feelings for Zak!"

"Denial is so cute."

"The parade's starting. Here come the Garner Sisters playing their stringed instruments. Ah, I'm home!"

Truthfully, the older women's presence ruffled Julia's romantic view of her future alone. Maybe independence wasn't entirely sunshine and lollipops. She didn't have a sister, for one thing, plus she had no musical talent. Natalie was practically engaged. Shelby was too sweet to be single forever, and Reese would meet some handsome brick of a man on the running path someday. So that left . . . cats for Julia. Lots and lots of cats. The future didn't look bright for her as an aging esthetician in Smitten. What if she didn't age well? Would anyone come to her for a facial after a certain age? If she allowed herself to muse on that thought too long, Zak's face came to mind. Her mother always said it was a blessing to not want what you couldn't have.

"I'm going for a walk," Julia said. And though she never would have admitted it, her legs strode toward Zak's grill. Maybe it was to check if that's where Amy was headed, and maybe it wasn't, but she couldn't have fought the urge if she'd tried.

Zak stood on the outside porch of his restaurant and waited for the festivities to start. He was too far from town to see all the fun, but the sounds would travel toward him. The noise of a Smitten celebration always made him feel part of something bigger. He should have taken the entire day off instead of the afternoon to help barbecue at the town picnic.

He imagined what Julia was doing up the street and what she might have worn to the parade. Something entirely inappropriate and traffic-stopping, no doubt. If he were honest, her very presence was all he cared about that day. Standing on the porch took him closer to her without the temptation that seeing her provided.

Every year the parade was led by Smitten's own Garner Sisters, Natalie's great-aunts, who played stringed instruments together in the square. They rode on a giant flatbed truck with patriotic streamers glued to every exposed area. Zak smiled at the thought of the scene, which never changed year after year. He supposed that's what he loved about Smitten.

A cheerful roar erupted in the crowd from town, and he knew the parade had begun. Carson had left to help Natalie with the coffee shop, and Zak felt alone. He wasn't in the mood to work. A familiar figure walked toward the restaurant, and it wasn't long before he recognized it as Amy Hastings. A thousand thoughts rushed through his head, the loudest being, *What could I have been thinking?* Amy, the most popular girl in school, made Zak cool with her presence, but he'd grown weary of explaining simple things to her. It wasn't fair to say she was dumb, but she was shallow. If life was a highway, Amy was its on-ramp. Hard to get up to speed in the short amount of road available.

She wore high heels, a tank top, and jeans on her long legs. Where Julia made the stilettos look sweet and about her style, Amy made them look as if she were asking for trouble. He realized at that moment she'd noticed him.

"Zak Grant, you're not at the parade."

"Hey, Amy. Lot of work to do on the restaurant."

"Did you get my suggestions via e-mail?"

"I did. I don't think they'd really work here, but I appreciated the advice."

"That's why I came. I knew you wouldn't listen to anything I had to say. I'm a professional, Zak. I make good money doing this."

"Oh, I believe it. Smitten's just different, that's all."

"The restaurant business is universal. That's why my plans work so well. They increase revenue, Zak. I can show you proof."

"I'm sure you can, but I've got the spa coming in, so I don't imagine you've got a lot of plans for a spa and grill."

"It's been done. Of course, you'll see more spa fare on the menu. Not a lot of meat—except for perhaps raw tuna, maybe scallops."

"Why are you here, Amy?"

"I told you. I'm here to help with the restaurant design. You ignored my e-mails."

"I didn't ignore them. I didn't want the help."

"Always and forever, Zak."

Amy's presence made Zak uncomfortable. He knew she had a boyfriend back in Los Angeles, but he also knew she had an insatiable desire for attention, and he didn't have time for her drama. "Say hi to your parents for me. I'm going to get back to work."

"Zak, you could at least show me around. I came all the way here to help."

"Sawyer's not going to mention the restaurant in interviews, Amy."

"Why not? Why wouldn't Sawyer do what he could to get national attention for his buddy's restaurant? It's the least he could do. Marketing is everything now. Do you have a Twitter account for the restaurant? You can Tweet when Sawyer is here. That would be huge; it would go out to all his followers."

"I appreciate that, Amy, but Sawyer's my friend. If he wants to come here for a quiet meal, I'm not going to advertise that he's here."

"In this economy, no one is above marketing. Especially free marketing."

"Amy, I don't mean to be rude, but I've been working for a long time this morning so I can get to the barbecue. I need to get back to work." He clamped the lock down, and Amy grabbed his elbow. He turned to see Julia standing twenty feet away, her gaze turned on the two of them. He called out to her, "Julia!"

But it was too late. She turned and ran back toward town.

Amy giggled. "You're still leading that poor girl around like a lost puppy, and you think *I* have issues. Have a heart. Let her go already."

# CHAPTER EIGHT

. . . . . . . . . . . . . . . . . . . . . . . . . .

*J*ulia saw the way Amy touched Zak's elbow. The familiar feeling of rejection washed over her. How many dances had she watched the two of them together? The lavender wreath still hung on the door amid all the chaos of the remodel. She focused on it and the purple flowers and wished she had the faith of little Mia. To trust as a child trusted—somewhere along the line, she'd lost Mia's blind faith ability, and she mourned its loss as she stared at the wreath. A true, trusting faith seemed like it only belonged to others.

As Zak and Amy noticed her, she turned and ran back toward town. How many times did she have to batter her head against the same wall? Zak Grant didn't love her. He never would, and it was time she lived in reality, not her dream world.

Julia's phone rang in that instant, and she silenced it as quickly as possible. "Hello," she answered breathily.

"Julia, is that you? It's Devlin."

She walked around the building to the parking lot behind Sweet Surrender, but the chaos of Smitten's parade could still be heard. "It's me. It's the Fourth of July, so it's a bit loud here. A lot of celebrating going on, you understand."

"It's the Fourth here too, but Manhattan never sleeps, as you know. I'm here at the spa working. We've got a big wedding party coming in tonight."

"Does this call mean you accept my apology? I wouldn't have brought you out here if I'd known what I do now."

"I have a business proposition for you."

"For me?" Her legs felt weak. "Is it in New York?"

"Naturally. I think we both understand where I stand on Smitten at the moment."

She said nothing about Mrs. Shapiro or the truth according to Zak. She gazed at the warm celebration going on up the street. She felt torn between two worlds, not really belonging to either.

"It seems your sleuth boyfriend has outed me. I don't own the spa, I just manage it for Mrs. Shapiro. Not that there's anything wrong with decent work, but I did allow you to believe the place was mine. I allowed everyone to believe that. It was better for everyone involved."

"Yes, I heard that. Though your success can hardly be doubted, Devlin. You've made that spa all that it is. I never questioned that. Or your sincerity."

"Mrs. Shapiro used her husband's money to invest in the business, and because she's seen such a great return on it, she wants to open another one. On the West Side. As you know, there are a lot of younger patrons on the West Side, and she'd like to tap into that with a younger, hipper spa created for them."

"Wow, that's a great idea!" But something in her stomach didn't feel the elation her voice carried.

"She wants you to head it up. Just like I head up the spa here in the Upper East Side. As far as anyone knows, it's your business. You run it, you're the face behind all its success. How do you feel about that?"

"I feel . . . I feel completely dumbstruck and honored."

"That's what I told her you'd say. So when do you think you can get back here?"

"It's not that easy, Devlin. Zak has started building the spa, and—"

"Did you ask him to do that?"

"Well, I—he did it to get me started. My friends—"

"Your friends are trying to make something of a nothing town on little more than a wing and a prayer. What I'm offering you . . . what Mrs. Shapiro is offering you, is what you said you wanted. Your own high-end spa. You'll be equipped with everything I have here, and you'll cater to a younger audience. It couldn't be more perfect for you, Julia. It's everything that I trained you for."

"But why didn't you tell me before you came to Smitten?"

"I didn't know Mrs. Shapiro wanted to open another spa. I was going to back you with my own money in Smitten, regardless of what your boyfriend thought. I believe in you and your abilities, but I don't know anything about how small towns work. I understand the island of Manhattan. I know this is a surefire hit. Would you trade that for what is, at best, a long shot?"

She walked back to the brick sidewalk of Main Street and focused on the green clock and the oversize wreath of faith hanging from beneath the clock's face. Was faith leaving logic behind and trusting? Or was that nothing more than stupidity? Didn't God say to be as wise as serpents? That meant using what information you'd been given, not just blindly going forth on a feeling.

"Give me a day to think about it, Devlin. It's a huge change, and I have to make sure my mother is well enough to be left on her own now."

"Your mother's a big girl. She can find the help she needs. She wouldn't want to hold her daughter back. I'll give you a day, no more. Mrs. Shapiro is ready to go on this, and don't think I can't find a replacement for you. But you know I want you, Julia. It's not your responsibility to save that town. You have to think about yourself! What will you do with your future if that town dies again?"

"I'll call you tomorrow."

"Think about what I said."

"How could I think about anything else?" She snapped her phone shut.

Amy's heels clicked along the brick sidewalk toward her. Julia knew it was too late to retreat, so she steeled herself for another uncomfortable conversation. Amy stared at her, shook her head, and kept walking. Julia walked slowly toward the grill. As she walked up the ramp, she took the small wreath from the door and held it.

Zak came to the door and looked at her through the wooden screen door. "I didn't ask Amy here."

She nodded, careful to avoid his penetrating deep hazel gaze. "I know."

Zak opened the door out for her to come in. She glanced about the room, and her spa took form in her mind. She could hear the trickling water from the corner fountain, smell the calming lavender and sensuous sandalwood. For a brief moment she envisioned the spa completely done, and even pictured Zoe, Natalie's cousin, answering calls at the front desk.

"Julia, are you all right?"

"Everything here in Smitten is uncertain. Will Sawyer's wedding bring tourists in droves? Will you be able to reopen the mill and run the grill? Will everyone's renovations—Carson's at the lodge and yours at the grill—pay off? New York is a sure thing for me, Zak."

He nodded.

"I know the market. I'd have Mrs. Shapiro's financial backing and Devlin's expertise whenever I got into trouble. All I have here is blind faith with a dash of hope." She stared at him from across the room. *And you, Zak.*

Zak's barrel chest made the room feel smaller. Intimate.

"That's all you have here in Smitten? What about your best friends? What about your family?" He stood next to her in the late morning sunlight, and without thought she reached for his cheek, covered by three days' worth of stubble.

She snapped her hand away. "I'm sorry," she said. "It's one of the quirks of my business. I'm interested in the texture of a person's skin, and my curiosity gets the best of me sometimes. You understand." She swallowed hard at his proximity, willing him to say what she needed to hear. *Give me a reason to stay, Zak.*

"What about me?"

She twisted away from his prying eyes. "If there was anything in my life that was uncertain, it's always been you, Zak Grant. I'll pay you back for the work you've done, if that's what you mean." Her voice trembled. "I'd better get home. I'm going to bring my supplies to the lake before the fireworks and offer free skin consultations."

"Why? I mean, if you're not staying, why offer the people of Smitten anything?"

She searched for an answer. "Maybe you're right. I have to be able to support myself, Zak, and while I love Smitten, I can't pin my future on a long shot." She walked toward the door and turned back around. "Let me know what I owe you for all of this. They're still looking for a home for the new lingerie shop. Maybe you could rent this space to them."

As she reached the door, she squeezed Mia's wreath again. *Now faith is being sure of what we hope for and certain of what we do not see.* "I'm sorry, Zak."

Once outside, she felt sick to her stomach. She loved Zak Grant. There was no denying it, and she didn't love him like a big brother or a childhood friend. She loved him, and all it would have taken was one small word from him and she would have stayed. Her faith would have been restored in Smitten. She didn't want his building. She didn't want his construction expertise. She wanted him. But to stay there and work alongside him every day? To watch him flirt with patrons and waitresses? That was a future she couldn't handle. No matter how much faith she mustered up inside of herself.

"Good-bye, Zak."

# CHAPTER NINE

. . . . . . . . . . . . . . . . . . . . . . . . . . .

*T*imber Lake, with its blooming wildflowers and magnificent backdrop of the surrounding mountains, shone salmon-pink in the evening light. The entire town gathered around the lake, and on center stage, Violet and her sisters played their stringed instruments festively. As far as the sisters were concerned, every year was 1945 and there was no reason to stop celebrating the end of World War II.

Julia was surprised at how much energy those three women could muster when they had an audience. Applause was like a battery to their souls.

Natalie sat with Mia on a checkered blanket, and the little girl ate a hot dog and slurped a lemonade.

"Well, you two look like you've had a good day."

Mia nodded, her mouth full of food.

"That's her third hot dog," Natalie said. "But they're nitrate-free. Zak had the good sense to listen to me on that. Do you want a gluten-free cookie?" Natalie lifted her picnic basket.

"Uh, no thanks." Julia tried to find the best way to tell Natalie she'd be leaving town.

"I think I've really perfected it this time."

"I'm sure they're great. I have to watch my waistline, you know." She patted her tummy. "Can't bend over a big belly and give a proper facial."

"Julia Bourne, you don't have an ounce of fat on you either. You and Reese seem determined to make the rest of us believe you're not perfect."

"I'm definitely not perfect. I don't want a cookie, Nat." Julia looked over and noticed Zak behind a portable barbecue flipping hamburgers. He smiled at her, and her stomach fluttered. "Zak never said he'd be here. I thought he'd be working on the renovations."

"Everyone needs a break, and this is his way of giving back to the community. I think it's awesome he's here," Natalie said. "Did you go by and see the work he and Carson did?"

"Oh yeah. It's great. I mean, they've really outdone themselves. But, Nat, I need to tell you something. Well, you and Reese and Shelby too."

"I thought you were bringing your facial supplies to do skin consultations. Didn't you tell me that?"

"I was going to, but I have a confession to make, and you're not going to like it, so I didn't want to bring anything you might use as a weapon."

"Well, today would have been perfect to introduce the town to what you do. Carson said the spa is going to be ready by August. Aren't you amazed how these men have come through for the romance destination? I'm so proud of them, because they've come such a long way in their thinking. They're not too proud to admit when they're wrong. Says a lot about the men of Smitten. Personally, I think there're no better men on earth."

"Hmm. If I were dating a man like Carson, I might feel that way too." Julia became sidetracked by a gaggle of ducks around a small boy who fed them pieces of his hamburger bun. "I'll miss it here."

"Julia?"

"Huh?"

"Don't you think the men have come a long way?"

"Totally," she agreed.

"The whole town has come so far," Natalie continued. "I'm delighted when I look at how quaint Main Street looks with its twinkling lights at night and the flower boxes all perfectly kept. The way Carson and Zak are working together to renovate . . . It's like this town knows how to be there for each other."

"Uh-huh," Julia said absently.

"I heard next year on the Fourth we're going to have a hot-air balloon parade. It's going to be something."

Julia stared up into the clear blue sky. "Natalie, I'm not staying."

"For the fireworks? Do you know how hard Carson worked to pull together this show on a shoestring budget? Of course you're staying. Sit down. We've got room on the blanket. Mia, honey, move over and make room for Julia."

"No, I mean in Smitten. I'm not staying in Smitten. I had an offer today from Devlin. He wants me to open a new spa in New York and—I took it as a sign."

"A bigger sign than Zak and Carson building you a spa? A bigger sign than Zak going on the Internet and ordering you bamboo massage tables? A bigger sign than that?"

Mia put down her soda can and shook her head. "No, that's not where you're supposed to be, Miss Julia."

"Mia, you little sweetheart. I wish I had your faith, honey, but I just—well, there are reasons that you're too little to understand. Miss Julia has to earn a living and be independent in ways that I'm not sure Smitten can provide for me. I provide a service that I'm not sure the people of Smitten need."

"Then the tourists need it, isn't that right, Aunt Nat? I saw the wreath on the door at Zak's." Mia stood up. "Do you know what it means, Miss Julia? It stands for eternity. 'Cause God will always take care of us."

"Help me out here, Nat," Julia said.

Natalie's lips flattened. "You're on your own. We've all done our parts. Zak made space for you, and he and Carson are working their tails off to get that spa ready for you. How can you be so selfish as to walk out on us now? Carson!" she called out. "Carson, can you take Mia to find Reese and Shelby? Julia needs to talk to all of us."

"Sure," Carson said, and the hulking man lifted Mia as if she were no more than a packet of sugar, then went off into the crowd.

"I'm not running away, and I haven't told my parents yet, but I can send them money this way and they can enjoy their retirement years. Nat, you have Mia and Carson here for you. There's a reason for you to stay and make it work. What's here for me? Zak's ever-revolving door of girlfriends? And a spa with no clients that smells like barbecued ribs? This isn't right."

"That's what this is about—Zak? Your mind moves quicker than mercury, and when it does, you don't make wise decisions. You run, but part of relationships is sticking around when it gets tough."

"I can't go there every day, Nat. I love Zak," she admitted. "He's doing my brother a favor, and he thinks it's cute to flirt with me, when it breaks my heart. I wish I wasn't so weak, but I am. I don't want to watch him date and marry someone else. I'm not like you, Nat. I don't have your fortitude."

"Have you told him you love him? I'll let you go without another word if you've told him."

"I can't tell him that. I'd never hear the end of it. My brother always told me to leave him alone, that he wasn't interested. Maybe that's what draws me to him. I never was very good at doing what I was told."

Natalie laughed. "Are you serious? Oh my goodness, the drama. Girl!"

"What's so funny?" Reese came alongside them in her track pants and red, white, and blue T-shirt. Reese always appeared as if she might be forced at gunpoint to run a 10k at any given moment. "Hey, Julia, where's your stuff? I wanted my free skin consultation."

"She didn't bring it. Julia thinks Zak put together a spa for her because he feels guilty, and she's threatening to go back to New York where the Devil man offered her her own spa."

"What? First off, what would Zak have to feel guilty about?" Reese asked. "Besides, have you met Zak? He's not exactly the type to do anything he doesn't want to do. Can you say *problems with authority*?"

Shelby appeared then with Penelope in a red, white, and blue rhinestone collar. "What's going on?"

"Julia thinks Zak built the spa because Greg asked him to do it so she wouldn't go back to New York and leave her parents alone to worry about both of them. She gets out guilt-free, and Zak is stuck with half a spa."

Now Reese laughed, and Julia felt her face getting warm.

"Julia, your father worries about his cable going out and if his dinner is on time. Get real. He can live without you. Your mother is doing fine."

"Reese, I'd expect you of all people to understand. Do you like how everyone looks at you with those puppy dog eyes because they think you're not over Sawyer Smitten?"

"Well, no. But, Julia, what Nat is trying to tell you is that Zak's in love with you. That's why he built the spa. We think maybe Carson getting himself a girlfriend gave Zak some gumption," Reese said.

"And we think he can't go after you because he promised Greg something. But you can go after him. That's our theory, so go put it to the test." Shelby nodded toward the grill.

Now it was Julia who laughed. "Zak Grant? In love with me? Ha! He had a funny way of showing it with Amy Hastings all those years."

"He didn't know it! He sees himself as the Lone Ranger, the man who doesn't need a woman. That doesn't mean he's not going to move heaven and earth to keep you near him. The two of you are both so stubborn. Neither one of you thinks you need another living soul, and rather than admit that as a weakness, you run and he makes excuses like 'doing what Greg wants.' Greg's across the world—he's not the boss of you."

"Well, that kind of love doesn't do anybody any good."

"So tell him that!" Reese said.

Natalie, Shelby, and Reese dared her with their darkened brows and laser stares.

"You want me to tell him that? Fine, I'll tell him that. I've got nothing to lose, right? I'll be in New York by week's end."

"That's right, nothing to lose. Not if you're going back to New York," Natalie said.

"I'm going to." Julia pretended to stand up, but Reese stood and lifted her from the picnic blanket.

"We're waiting," Reese said.

"I'm gonna do it," she said, but inwardly she wondered what she could say to Zak to get the desired reaction for the girls. Maybe she could just ask him for a hug and tell the girls he said they were just friends.

"Oh, for crying out loud, I'll do it." Natalie stood up.

"No!" Julia cried. "I'll go." She walked across the grass that surrounded Timber Lake and willed her mind to think of something to say as she approached. She pulled her hair back into a makeshift ponytail and tied it in a knot. She stood across the large, iron barbecue from Zak, a plume of smoke between them.

Zak cranked the grill up and away from the fire, and the smoke lessened. "Julia, you hungry?"

"No . . . well, yeah. Maybe."

"Hot dog or hamburger?" He bent into the smoke. "I've got some ribs for special folks. You want some ribs?"

She smiled. "A hot dog is fine. I heard they have no nitrates."

He handed her a plate with a grin. "Sergeant Natalie has spoken. I guess you heard. The condiments are over there on that checkered table."

"I like mustard," she said for some unknown reason. He

nodded as though she were simple, and for that moment she supposed she was.

"I like mustard too."

"And pie. You like my mom's pie with vanilla ice cream and Cool Whip."

"That's right. I do. Did you happen to bring me some?" He moved around the grill and looked at her legs. "I also like it served in stilettos." He winked.

"Ballet flats this evening, for the fireworks," she said. "Hard to walk in the grass in stilettos."

"It's hard to walk anywhere in Smitten in stilettos. Not that this ever stopped you."

"Pie. I, uh . . . no, I didn't bring any pie, but my mom made some. Peach. If, you know. If you want to come by after the fireworks, I could serve you some."

"In stilettos?"

She turned to look back at her friends.

"Julia, is there something you want to say to me?"

She met the warmth in his eyes and became lost in the way they crinkled at the edges, and he conjured one dimple on his left cheek from years of his crooked smile.

"Nothing. Thanks for the hot dog."

"No, no. You're not getting away that easily. Spill it. I have half a spa in my restaurant that says you owe me the truth."

She stared at the pink of the hot dog. "You really know how to barbecue, don't you?"

"Julia."

"I don't really want to go to New York," she blubbered. "But I'm afraid to stay."

"Smitten is your home. Why would you be afraid to stay?"

"Because I love you, Zak. Not like a big brother, and not like a friend. I love you like someone I want to be around me for the rest of my life, and if you can't see me as more than Greg's little sister, I don't want to stay and be hurt day after day."

"I have been waiting an eternity for you to say those words to me." He put the utensil down and took the hot dog from her and placed it on a nearby table. "John, can you man the grill for a minute?"

"Yeah, no problem," his friend answered.

"What if I can't make the spa work, and your business fails because of me?"

Zak raked his fingers into Julia's hair and placed his palms on her cheeks. "Julia, I wouldn't care if we both failed, if you were by my side—but I don't think that would happen."

She sniffled. "No, don't flirt with me. You'll only make it worse. I know you promised my brother that you'd look after me, but—"

"I also promised your brother that I wouldn't court you until he got home and could see my intentions were right, but I don't intend to keep that promise, so I'm not as honorable as you give me credit for. I think I may have stretched the truth to a man in uniform. A man I respect greatly."

She dared not smile. "You're teasing me. Like you used to do when I was little and I'd watch you and Greg go out for the night. You'd muss my hair up and leave."

"No, not teasing. Julia, I have loved you for as long as I can remember. I found hundreds of excuses to tell myself it wasn't true, because it wasn't convenient. I tried the concept of honor. Sometimes I chose anger. I blamed you when you left for New York and decided that you were shallow, just like Amy. Once I even decided if you couldn't bake a pie like your mother, you weren't worthy of such devotion."

She felt the warmth of his words and snuggled into the crook of his neck, which smelled like barbecue smoke. She felt the vibrations of his voice in his chest.

"But the more reasons I thought of, the more I realized I couldn't picture anyone else by my side for the long haul, and it was either you or eternal bachelorhood."

"The long haul?"

"It totally caught me by surprise, when you brought that New York idiot into my town, how I didn't want any other man investing in your business. It made me crazy, and before I knew it, I'd jumped on the opportunity to cut my grill in half and build you a spa. I ran out of excuses at that point, don't you think?"

"You didn't say anything this morning when I told you I was leaving for New York."

"I know your parents. I know where your fear of being controlled comes from, Julia. I felt disgusted that I hadn't given you a choice on the spa—just started building it like you'd do what you were told. I was controlling things to get them the way I wanted them, and that isn't love. I decided I had to let you go if that's what you wanted."

"But somehow you knew I didn't."

"I had faith. I had faith enough for both of us." He pulled her closer and lifted her chin. He pressed his lips to hers. The outside world faded away as she lived in the moment she'd dreamt about since eighth grade. All right, maybe sixth grade.

"I thought the fireworks weren't supposed to start until it got dark," she said.

"These fireworks aren't going away if I have anything to say about it."

She heard her friends screaming encouragement in the background, and their shouts made her laugh.

"Sounds like my friends have something to say about it too."

She snuggled into Zak's embrace, and it was so much better than she'd imagined it all those years. She saw Mia smiling at her, and she realized the beautiful gift of Smitten's faith in God, led by a little child. Sometimes Julia ran low on faith, as if God's grace might dry up like Sugarcreek Mountain in the summer, but God's grace was unrelenting and overflowing. She smiled broadly toward her friends, thankful that when she'd run dry on faith, she could rely on God and the faith of others to fill her up again. She didn't have to walk alone. Sometimes, trusting in God meant trusting in the people he had placed in her life. Besides . . . independence was overrated.

# EPILOGUE

. . . . . . . . . . . . . . . . . . . . . . . . . .

*T*he Smitten Spa & Grill celebrated its grand opening on the last Saturday in August. Julia wore a
lime green Lilly Pulitzer summer shift that con-
trasted well against the pale greens and earthy browns of the
spa. She wore a light cashmere wrap over her shoulders. She'd
bought Zak a navy Hugo Boss suit, and he looked better than
any New York businessman she'd met. As she straightened his
tie, she kissed his cheek. "You look gorgeous."

"Enjoy it, because tomorrow it's jeans and a T-shirt."

She giggled. "Fine by me." She stared out the window of
the restaurant toward Smitten's Main Street, where flower
boxes brimmed with summer blooms. Tourists sprinkled the
town sidewalk, and she felt a fresh wave of satisfaction at the
committee's work.

"I have to admit it, Julia. You girls did it. We have more
tourists walking our streets than we've had in years."

"Sometimes all it takes is a little faith." She smiled broadly
at him. "And maybe a good verbal whack upside the head now
and again."

"Are we ready to open the doors?"

"Not just yet," she moaned. "Let me live in the moment
where it's just you and me and we're not surrounded by sawdust and dirt."

"We've been working toward this day for nearly two

months! All our friends and family are waiting out there to watch us succeed."

"I'll miss our cozy spa and grill where it's just us. Now we have to let people in, and it won't be the same."

"Even if both the restaurant and the spa are filled with patrons and we're making money hand over fist, it will always be just you and me here anyway," he said with a fist pump to his heart. "That's where we've been blessed."

"I'm so glad you had faith in me when I didn't."

"You had faith in me when I didn't. We'll just keep returning the favor to each other."

Zak pulled open both doors together. "Welcome, Smitten, to the grand reopening of Smitten's only spa and grill!"

Julia's knees went weak as she caught sight of her brother in full uniform. "Greg?"

Greg hugged her and lifted her off the ground. "I'm home, little sis. I needed to make sure this guy acted honorably."

She grasped her brother around his neck and held on tightly.

"I'm so glad you're home!"

"I had to come home for the wedding. All of them."

Zak bent on one knee in front of her. "Julia Bourne, will you do me the honor of becoming my wife?"

A roar went up from the crowd, and Julia's hand trembled as she held it out and said, "Yes, yes, a million times yes!"

"But it has to be after ours." Julia's mother held out her hand. A new sparkling diamond glimmered on her ring finger.

"Mom?"

"Your dad and I decided we'd get into the spirit of things and recommit our love."

Julia swayed on her heels and felt the world spinning around her as she tried to take it all in. Her parents' love story was something she'd never understand. But then, she didn't need to. She only needed to know that her path would be different. But she would learn to bake a pie—and if there was ever a man worth getting into an apron and stilettos for, it was Zak Grant.

# Shelby: You've Got a Friend

Diann Hunt

# CHAPTER ONE

· · · · · · · · · · · · · · · · · · · · · · · · · · · ·

*S*helby Evans spotted the fire truck at her house and knew instinctively this was not going to be a good Monday.

Maybe she'd been a little distracted on her walk in the park, but she didn't think she'd been gone that long. But it was such a beautiful September day and she had taken her journal, run into a couple of acquaintances, stopped for a bagel . . .

Clutching Penelope, her seven-pound Shih-poo, Shelby stepped over the neighbor kid's bicycle on her front walk. Penelope barked at the intrusion of the monstrous truck parked in her driveway and the men winding up the heavy hose.

Nick Majors touched Shelby's arm, catching her by surprise. She swiveled around to face him.

"What's going on?"

"Your neighbor reported smoke coming from your house."

Shelby gasped.

"It's contained in your dining room. Not too much damage—smoke damage mostly. The fire had just started when we got here."

She reached for the door and pushed it open. Thick smoke lingered inside the house, causing her to cough. "If this is 'not too much,' I'd hate to see what real damage looks like."

"What are you doing in here?" A firefighter dressed in a cumbersome uniform, a fire extinguisher on his back, gave her a forbidding look.

Nick stood behind her. "It's all right, Captain. She lives here."

Thankfully, Nick was a volunteer fireman and could plead her case. She'd be upset if she couldn't at least see the damage for herself.

Holding a dainty handkerchief loosely over Penelope's nose, Shelby held the dog close and looked around her dining room area. Water on her floor and dining room table. Wet walls. Though it could have been much worse, the scene overwhelmed her.

She spotted wet broken pieces of wood on the floor and cupped them in her hands. "This was the clock you made me."

"Don't worry about it. I'll make you another one for Christmas," Nick said.

The pieces spilled from her hands, and she choked back her emotions. Burying her face in Penelope's soft, clean fur, Shelby stepped back outside, away from the acrid smell, and took in long, deep breaths.

Classes for Social Graces were scheduled to start in two weeks. In this very place. With an apartment-like setup, Shelby lived in the upstairs of her Victorian home and used the downstairs for the school. It had been the perfect arrangement.

Until now.

Shelby had invested most of her money into the house to make it functional for her purposes, so she had little to use toward renting another place while this one was repaired. Her sewing business provided enough, but offered little extra. Social Graces, the place where she taught young girls how to become ladies, was more of a calling than a moneymaker.

She'd have to call her insurance company, then contact someone to clean up the mess.

"We'll figure it all out," Nick said.

Shelby nodded. Just having him near sent a rush of relief through her. He was right. They'd figure it out. And God would help her get through this, one step at a time. The tension eased from her shoulders.

The captain came out of the house, talked to Shelby again about what would happen next, and left.

"I have to wash my truck, and then we could stop at the coffee shop to talk things over. You need to get away from this place, the smoke and all, so you can think. Want to go?"

"Aren't you on duty?"

"I came when the pager went off, but they had enough responders when I got here. Since things are quieting down, Captain just told me I could go."

One of the other firemen called him over. Shelby watched them as they talked. She didn't like the growing frown on Nick's face or the way he stomped back toward her.

"They found out where the fire started."

"Oh?" She had the distinct feeling she didn't want to hear this.

"You left the glue gun on in the dining room, Shelby. How many times have I told you when you're finished to turn it off and unplug it?"

A flicker of irritation gained momentum—especially when she noticed several people looking their way. "I'm sorry,

Mr. Safety, but not all of us qualify for the Smokey the Bear Award."

"How can you defend yourself when we're talking life and death here?"

"I'm not defending myself. I'm just saying we don't all think of things the way you do. I messed up. So sue me."

His gaze pinned her in place. "I don't believe this." He rubbed a hand across the back of his neck.

Shelby knew it was her fault, but he didn't have to point it out so everyone could hear. "Look, Nick, I appreciate your concern, but you're not a superhero. Deal with it." She whirled around and attempted to walk away, but he grabbed her arm.

"Listen, we're both a little tense right now. Let's go to the coffee shop and talk about the repairs."

Shelby lifted her chin. "I need to change my exercise clothes and put Penelope upstairs away from the smoke." Her anger was really with herself, but when backed in a corner, she couldn't help taking it out on Nick.

"To be safe, you'd better take Penelope to a neighbor's house, at least for today. Then you can get some fans and dehumidifiers in there to help with the smell."

Shelby sighed. "Yeah, I guess you're right."

Once she had changed her clothes and taken Penelope to a neighbor's house, she rejoined Nick. They climbed into his old black Chevy truck and drove past the quaint storefronts that lined Main Street. Shoppers strolled from the fudge shop to the clothing boutique. Any other time she would have stopped at Sweet Surrender to soothe her pain with chocolate, but even that failed to tempt her. What was she going to do? This catastrophe would derail all her plans.

Nick swerved into the do-it-yourself car wash. "Be right back."

"Want some help?"

"No, thanks. I can handle it."

Shelby sighed. Why couldn't he get his truck washed at an automatic wash like normal people? She watched as he pulled some rags from the back of the truck and set to work sloshing soap around the vehicle. His arms looked strong, capable. She supposed Nick's determination to do things himself was what kept him so fit. He grabbed a brush and scrubbed the hubcaps. She decided "fit" looked nice on him.

After the rinse, polish, and dry, he rejoined her in the truck.

The remaining water sloshed off the wheel guards as Nick nosed the truck carefully onto the street and into traffic. The coffee shop was about a five-minute drive away.

As they stepped inside the shop, a wreath of grapevines and dried lavender shifted on the front door. Nick grunted at it, but Shelby ignored him. One problem at a time. That was all she could handle today.

Bold coffee smells greeted them. Adjusting the ruffled border of her periwinkle sweater, Shelby dipped into her small pocketbook and pulled out her debit card.

Nick motioned it away. "This one is on me."

Natalie Mansfield waved at them from behind the counter. "Be there in a sec."

"Thanks." Shelby fingered the small notepad in her hand while they waited.

"Hey, Shelby. Peppermint tea, or are you going to break

down and have coffee today?" Natalie gave a big smile, but it faded quickly as she looked at Shelby. "What's wrong?"

When Shelby hesitated, Nick jumped in and explained what had happened.

"Oh, Shelby, no. I'm so sorry, sweetie. Let me get your— tea, is it?"

Shelby nodded.

"I'll bring it out." Natalie took Nick's order while Shelby found a table for them.

Once seated, Shelby took a quick glance at her friend in the navy T-shirt, work boots, and long jeans. With dark hair that shagged a little long in back and drooped lazily over his ears, she couldn't deny Nick was handsome in a rugged sort of way. Strong jaw, deep-set dark eyes. But the stubble? What made a man want to leave little bits of hair on his face? It was like dark confetti strewn about that no one bothered to clean up. Once a mountain man, always a mountain man. How would he ever find a woman, looking like that?

"So have you played your Christmas music yet? It is September, you know." Nick pulled out a chair and sat down.

Shelby smiled. "Maybe once or twice."

"Good girl."

"How about you? Decorated any trees lately?" They both knew they were avoiding discussion of the inevitable.

"Not yet. But soon. Very soon." He winked.

"Would you stop talking Christmas already? It's not even Halloween yet, for crying out loud," Natalie said, easing a cup of tea to Shelby and a plain coffee toward Nick.

Nick laughed. "I can't exactly fault a woman for enjoying Christmas. After all, that is my line of work."

Natalie shook her head. "All right, you two, let's get down to business. What are you going to do about your classes, Shelby? Don't they start in a couple of weeks?"

"Yeah. I thought I would ask Rose if I could hold the classes at her house until the repairs are finished."

"Good," Natalie said. "Now, what about the repairs? Any idea who to hire?"

Shelby turned to Nick. "You mentioned you know someone?"

Just then several customers walked through the door and headed toward the counter.

"Uh-oh, gotta get back to work. Let me know if you need anything, Shelby."

"Okay. Thanks, Nat."

"Griffen Parker is back in town. He's a good contractor and a great guy. I think he knows a little about fire restoration too. We could see if he's available," Nick said.

"Didn't he do the work on Carson's cabins?"

"Yeah. Want me to call him for you?"

"That would be great. Thanks, Nick."

He shrugged and took another drink of his coffee. "I'd better get back over to your house and take another look, in case something else came up."

She had to admire the way he took charge of things for her at a time when she could hardly think straight. "Yeah, I need to talk to Rose. Call me the minute you hear from Griffen."

"Will do. You ready to go?"

"Yeah." She said good-bye to Natalie and followed Nick out the door.

"Thanks for your help, Nick. I'm sorry you always have to come to my rescue."

"Why are you sorry? I want you to count on me."

"But I can't expect you to always fix things for me. You have your own life."

"That's what friends do, Shelby. Period. I want you to come to me for anything you need."

Shelby saw the disappointment on Nick's face, so she said nothing further. Besides, as much as she hated to admit it, she did need him.

Those flowered wreaths had been springing up all over town for months. Nick grunted. Losing the mill was one thing, but now Smitten was on its way to being the laughingstock of the state.

Rolling down the roadway, Nick's truck chugged and groaned. Its big tires crunched and stirred up gravel dust behind the taillights. With a crank of the handle, he rolled up his window from the chill. He needed to finish his cup of hot coffee to get his mind off of what those women were trying to do to the town. He let out a sigh. He knew they meant well, but this was *his* town. He'd lived here all his life, and he couldn't stand by and just let them turn it into a "girly" town, could he?

His thoughts turned to Shelby and the way she had looked at her house. Her eyes, dark pools shadowed with fear beneath thick fringy lashes, the tinge of pink that stained her cheeks. In one protective moment, he wanted to scoop her dainty form into his arms and hold her close.

He shook his head. *You're thinking nonsense, dude.*

Passing the church, he spotted the lavender wreaths on the front doors. His sour mood zipped back into place. Seemed to him the church should stay neutral on such matters. Regardless of what the pastor said about the wreaths standing for faith in the town's survival, the fact that little Mia came up with the idea told him it was a nod toward the women and their ridiculous idea to make Smitten a romance capital. If he'd wanted to live in a love capital, he'd have moved to the Poconos.

Women. The big ones and the little ones were all the same. He should thank his lucky stars he didn't have any around his house. He took a careful swig from his paper cup, then let out the kind of sigh that came with thinking ahead.

Frank Sinatra's voice called from his cell phone, and Nick clicked his finger on his Bluetooth. "Hello?"

"Nick?"

"Yeah."

"This is Catherine Givens."

His body sprang to attention. He hadn't talked to his mother-in-law since the day of the divorce. She hadn't been exactly civil at the time.

"Hi, Mrs. Givens." The words felt strange as they slipped off his tongue. He had called her Catherine once upon a time.

A cold pause hovered between them, causing a thread of fear to wind through him. "Is Willow all right?"

His twelve-year-old daughter barely talked to him when he called her each week, and she acknowledged his gifts with forced thanks. Still, he loved her deeply. Unfortunately, there was more than miles between them.

"Willow is fine. It's Camilla."

He could only imagine what his ex-wife had gotten herself into now. She and her high-society friends always seemed to stir up something.

"What about her?" He braced himself. When things like this came up, it usually cost him money.

"She's dead." The way she said that, as though Camilla had the nerve to intrude upon her organized plans, sent a momentary wave of compassion through him for his ex-wife. He didn't know what to say. Though there had been no love lost between them in the last few years, she was at one time his wife and would always be the mother of his child.

Nick eased his truck to the side of the road so the vehicles behind him could pass.

"Did you hear me?"

"I heard," he said, his tongue thick, throat dry. Say what you would about Camilla, he'd never imagined her . . . dead. "What happened?" he whispered.

"A yachting accident."

He took a minute to digest the news. Then another thought crashed into his head like a tree downed in a storm. "Where's Willow?"

"She's with me."

He bristled. "I'll come get her."

"Yes, I supposed you would. Of course, Charles and I would be happy to have her stay here, but we travel so much and she would . . ."

*Get in the way. Like mother, like daughter.* "I'm her father. She should be here."

"Yes."

Just as he suspected, no argument. The sooner he got Willow, the better. Poor thing. She hardly knew him, and now she had lost her mother. He'd make it up to her somehow. He had to.

He took down the particulars on the funeral and made arrangements to take Willow home with him afterward. He clicked off his cell phone and realized his hands were shaking.

☙

"Are you all right, honey? I've been out of town and just heard the news." Shelby's next-door neighbor stood at the front door.

Shelby held the open door. "Come on in."

Rose Garner, Natalie's great-aunt, stepped inside. Her silver hair, threaded with black strands, was pulled back into a flawless knot at the nape of her long neck. Her complexion, fresh and glowing, made her look twenty years younger than her age of seventy-eight. A soft white blouse and trim dark pants gave her tall, lithe body an elegant appearance that matched her gentle nature.

Shelby took her into the dining room and showed her the damage.

"My, my." She turned to Shelby. "I'm just so thankful you're all right."

"I'm thankful that none of my sewing projects were ruined. Several of the outfits have deadlines, and that would have really put me behind."

Rose nodded.

"Would you like to go upstairs?"

"No, thank you, sweetie. I can't stay. I just wanted to make sure you were all right." They stepped back outside. "By the way, what are you going to do about your classes?"

"Well, I wanted to talk to you about that—"

"Yes, of course you may hold your classes at my house," Rose said with a smile.

"You're such a blessing. Just like your niece." Shelby smiled, thinking how Natalie and Rose shared the same spirit. "Thank you, Rose."

"The blessing is mine." Rose gave Shelby a hug. "While I'm thinking of it, do you still want my help when you get to the dining etiquette section?"

"Absolutely," Shelby said.

"Wonderful. Have you found someone to do the repairs?"

"Nick contacted Griffen Parker for me, and he's agreed to do the job."

"Nick is quite the gentleman."

Shelby thought that an interesting comment. Nick was a great friend, no doubt about it, but "gentleman"? Somehow an ax-wielding, whiskered mountain man did not conjure up a gentleman in her mind.

"Well, I'd better get going. We'll talk later about the classes. Bring over whatever you need anytime. I'll get my dining room ready."

Shelby waved good-bye and stepped back inside, wondering where to begin.

# CHAPTER TWO

. . . . . . . . . . . . . . . . . . . . . . . . . .

y Saturday afternoon Shelby had managed to bring some order to her dining room despite the damage brought on by the smoke and fire. The dehumidifiers and fans had helped with the smell, making it possible for her to stay in the upstairs of her home.

She could kick herself for being so irresponsible with the glue gun. She sighed. No use going there now. Fortunately, Griffen would be coming on Monday, and it wouldn't take too long to get the repairs finished. She hadn't been able to get in touch with Nick since he set everything up for her.

Sitting at her sewing machine, she put the finishing touches on Penelope's Christmas outfit. Penelope resembled a cream puff with button eyes, and would look beyond adorable in the red cotton T-shirt adorned with boa and tulle.

"Come here, Penelope," Shelby called. The dog pranced over to Shelby and lifted her head in eager expectation. Shelby pulled the outfit onto her dog and looked on with amusement as Penelope circled about like a doggy ballerina.

The doorbell rang then, and Shelby and Penelope went downstairs to answer it. Rose stood on the front step.

"I wanted to talk over some recipes with you. Do you have time?" she asked.

"Sure. Let's go upstairs."

They went to the living room and settled on the plump sofa cushions facing one another.

"How lovely. You have a fire going already."

"Yes. This big old house is drafty and I'm always cold—the damp air from fighting the fire doesn't help."

"Or the fans and open windows."

"Right. Though I confess the thought of starting a fire bothered me a bit."

Rose grinned. "I can understand why."

"Would you like something to drink?"

"No, thank you." The logs crackled in the flames. "I thought I'd make little finger sandwiches for the high tea."

"You don't need to do that, Rose. You'll be busy playing your violin for the occasion."

"But I want to do both. I enjoy helping the girls."

"You don't know how much I appreciate that."

Penelope jumped up on the sofa between the two women, tutu in place. Shelby watched the older woman interact with Penelope and whispered a prayer of thanks to God for bringing Rose into her life. They had met one night at the town square, right after Shelby had moved into town. The Garner Sisters had played, and Shelby thanked them for their performance and struck up a conversation. Shelby hit it off with all of them, but especially Rose. She supposed it was because Rose had a kind voice—like Shelby's mother.

"Well, I must say it's very exciting to see what you girls are up to with the town. I do believe you're sprucing things up." Rose smiled her approval.

"Yes, it is exciting. Have you been to Julia's spa yet?"

Rose shook her head. "Oh no. That's for you young things."

"You have to go. It's amazing." Shelby explained the ins and outs of a spa experience and pretty much convinced her friend to go. "I wish everyone was as excited about the changes in town as you, Rose."

"What? Oh, you mean the handful of men who are grumbling about it?" Rose waved her hand in dismissal. "They're nothing to worry about. They haven't done anything to make a go of it—why not give someone else a chance? Besides, that noise seems to be dying down."

"Well, Nick Majors sure hasn't lost his grumble."

"Is he back yet?" Rose asked.

"Back? Where did he go?"

Rose frowned. "You haven't heard? His ex-wife died, and he went to pick up his daughter."

"Oh my." Shelby took a moment to digest the news. "I'm so sorry to hear that." Nick didn't talk much about his daughter.

"Sweet little thing. Pretty too. About twelve years old, I would say. She lives in Boston with her mother—well, she did. The way I understand it, she'll be moving back here with Nick. It will be an adjustment for both of them, to say the least."

"How do you know all this?"

"I've been a friend of the family for years. Knew Nick when he was just a little tyke."

For some reason, the idea of Nick as a little boy warmed her. Shelby hoped he and his daughter would have a better relationship than she had with her father.

"Twelve years old is a tough time to switch families," Rose said.

"Twelve years old," Shelby whispered, with a clench in her

heart. She knew another child who would have been twelve this year . . . if the child had survived.

Once Willow's belongings were safely anchored down with bungee cables in the back of Nick's truck, he and Willow said their good-byes to her grandparents and climbed in. He turned the key in the ignition and glanced at Willow.

"You need to buckle up," he said.

She rolled her eyes and made a dramatic sweep of the belt across her chest.

Willow hardly spoke a word the entire trip home. Nick didn't know if she was grieving over her mother, worried about her new life with him, or just pouting about something. Her one-word answers to his attempts at conversation left little room for bonding, and he eventually gave up.

The moon hung low over Sugarcreek Mountain by the time he pulled the truck up to his cabin. The steel truck door protested when he climbed out and stretched his long legs on the hard ground. He let out a sigh. His heart squeezed for his only child. The future would offer challenges for both of them.

She was a beautiful girl, if he did say so himself. Long wavy brown hair, soft blue eyes, and a definite flair with fashion, just like her mother. Even he could see that. There was a certain gracefulness in the way she walked—not like a gawky kid.

With Willow's suitcases in hand, Nick led the way to the front door. The chilled air was sweet with the smell of balsam and Fraser firs. He drank it in. One of the many reasons he loved living here. He unlocked the door and flung it wide open and reached for the light switch.

His laptop was on the sofa. Shoes and socks littered the hardwood floor, along with a potato chip bag and chip crumbs. Beyond the living room, the kitchen sink was full of soiled dishes, and a couple of opened cans sat on the counter, their jagged-edged metal lids sticking straight up.

Willow looked around, wide-eyed—in fear or surprise, he couldn't say.

Nick cleared his throat. "I didn't have a lot of time to clean things up before I left."

She didn't answer.

"Well, I know it's late, so I'll just show you your room and we can talk some tomorrow."

Willow nodded.

No sooner had he closed the front door than someone rapped on it. Nick frowned. Who would be calling tonight? He walked over and opened the door.

"Shelby."

She held out a plate of cookies. "Hi, Nick. I'm sorry to call so late. I stopped by earlier, but you weren't home yet."

He opened his mouth to invite her in, but Willow's voice stopped him.

"That's because it took forever to get here. Dad wouldn't go over fifty on the interstate."

Clearly amused, Shelby looked at Nick. "No kidding?"

"I couldn't go much faster and still be safe, what with all her stuff tied down in the back of the truck." He glanced at Willow. "What is all that stuff anyway?"

"Just my life, that's all."

Willow rolled her eyes again—a gesture that Nick suspected was going to grow old quickly. But she'd just spoken more words in the last minute than she had the entire trip home.

"I'm so sorry about your mother, Willow." Shelby stepped inside and handed the plate of goodies to Willow. "I'm Shelby Evans. Your dad is a good friend of mine."

Willow nodded.

"Can I get you something to drink, Shelby?" Nick said.

"Oh, no thanks. I need to get home." She pulled her sweater tighter around her. "It's chilly tonight."

"Cold weather will be upon us before you know it," he said. "That reminds me, I noticed the seal around your door frame was pulling loose, and also you have some air coming through the bottom. You'll need that caulked before winter. I'll take care of it. It will save on your heating bill."

"Thanks, Nick. You take good care of me."

"That's what friends do," he said with a smile, pointing to the plate of cookies.

Just then Shelby's cell phone rang. With a glance at the caller ID, she said, "I'm sorry, I'd better get this." She clicked on the phone. "Hi, Rose. Everything okay? . . . Oh dear . . . No, of course, I understand. Don't worry about it. I'll figure out something. We'll talk tomorrow." She clicked off.

"Something wrong?" Nick asked.

"The pipe to Rose's water filter was corroded and burst while she was in Stowe today. Her kitchen floor and hallway are flooded. She has to clean it up and get new flooring. She was going to host my classes while the repairs were made to my house. Looks like I'll have to find another place."

Nick rubbed the back of his neck. "You could hold your classes in my outbuilding."

Shelby brightened. "Really?"

"Why not? It's pretty good-sized, and it's heated. It's the one I use to display candles, lights, ornaments—Christmas decorations for sale. Remember?"

"Of course."

"I'm not using it at the moment. Probably about the time I'll need it, your place will be up and running again."

"That's so sweet of you to offer, Nick." Shelby thought a moment. "I'll agree to it if you let me help you on the tree farm when things get busy. At that point, my classes will be over till January, and I'll be available."

"Deal," he said with a wide smile. "But just so you know, if you work on the farm, you might have to get dirty."

Shelby gave a mock shudder. "I think I can manage."

"You'll have to wear jeans."

"I don't wear jeans."

"You can't go around the farm with nice clothes on, Shelby. You'll ruin them," he said.

Shelby glanced at Willow, who just stood there staring at both of the adults. "I think we have time to talk about that one, don't we?" Shelby turned her attention to Willow. "Anyway, the school bus stop is right down from my house, if you ever want to get off and visit me. My house is the one that has a sign out front that says Social Graces."

"Thanks."

Nick thought he saw a flicker of interest in Willow's eyes.

"Well, that's all. Just wanted to introduce myself and bring a welcoming gift. Again, I'm so sorry for your loss. Both of you."

"Thanks, Shelby." Nick walked her to the door. "I appreciate it."

Shelby stepped outside. "See you later. And thanks again for the use of your building."

Nick waved and watched her go.

"I'm going to bed now," Willow said as he closed the front door.

He said good night and noted the firewood in the basket was low. "I'm going to cut some wood. I'll be outside if you need me."

"Have you talked with Nick since he brought his daughter home?" Natalie asked as she, Julia, Reese, and Shelby took a walk around Timber Lake.

"Poor kid. That's tough to lose your mom and your home all at the same time," Reese said.

The others struggled to catch up to her.

"Yeah. Maybe you can 'mother' her, Shelby. After all, you have no real risk of involvement with Nick. You've said so yourself," Julia said with a wink.

"Nick is a good friend. That's all he'll ever be," Shelby said. "No matter how much the three of you want it to be otherwise."

"But you're perfect for each other," Reese said.

Shelby stepped over a stick. "You can't base a marriage on a mutual fixation on Christmas."

"It's a start," Natalie said. "Besides, he's so cute."

"Come on, you guys. The man has chin stubble. You know I can't handle that. And he probably eats from a can."

The girls laughed.

"He's just a friend," Shelby said.

"Whatever," Julia said. "Still, friendship is a pretty good place to start. Who's to say what will happen once you start working on his property?"

"Now, cut that out. Our goal is to save the town, not get me married off," Shelby said.

"You do look cute together," Reese said.

They all laughed, the laughter of good friends sharing together.

Natalie shrugged. "Oh well, girls, we tried."

"I have news," Reese said, changing the subject. "I've taken steps toward the purchase of my outfitters shop. I've applied for financing to see how much I qualify for."

Natalie's eyes grew as wide as chocolate cupcakes, with the same sweet sparkle. "That's wonderful!"

The women talked excitedly about how they could help. Their conversation finally dwindled as they attempted to catch their breath while keeping up with Reese's walking pace.

"My skin is drying out already, and it's not even winter," Julia said, touching her cheeks.

"Mine too. The good news is I'm coming into the spa soon for my facial." Shelby grinned at Julia.

"Oh, good. When you come, plan on staying for lunch at the grill."

"Sorry, friend, but I don't eat goopy hamburgers, even for my best friends." Shelby laughed.

"You don't know what you're missing," Reese said.

"I'm willing to take my chances."

Natalie sighed. "Girls, if she won't risk a hamburger, there's no hope of her taking a chance on love."

Laughter rang through the air, and Shelby wondered if they knew just how true that was.

After the morning walk, Shelby showered and dressed. She passed the day finishing her current project, a dress and leggings that a young girl would pick up this evening, then worked on her class plans. Hopefully she'd get a few more students before registration was closed.

She walked into the kitchen to get a glass of iced tea when the phone rang.

"Hello?"

"Hi, Shelby. This is Dad."

Her stomach tightened. "Dad. How are you?"

"I just got the scarf and cap you knitted me for Father's Day. Thanks."

"But I sent that months ago."

"Yeah, it just got to me. You sent it to Minnesota. I'm in Florida now."

He'd moved . . . again. "Sorry. Guess you won't have much use for a cap and scarf there."

He laughed. "Oh, that's no problem. I'm just tired of this dead-end job," he said. "I'm thinking of looking for something else."

She could recite this conversation by heart. "There in Florida?"

"Oh, I don't know. I have an old army buddy in Tennessee. He told me they're hiring where he works."

*Same old, same old.*

"Dad, when are you going to settle down?"

Why couldn't she just let it go? He'd never change.

"Why do I need to, Shelby? I'm not hurting anybody."

*Not now. But what about all those schools you dragged me through?*

"You could move here with me, Dad. I have a huge house—" It was the right thing to say. But what would she do if he accepted?

"I won't mooch off my daughter."

They both knew it had nothing to do with that. He couldn't—*wouldn't* settle down. It was just as well. It would be like living with a stranger.

"Well, I just wanted to thank you for the gifts. They're nice."

"Um, you're welcome." Why was it always so awkward to talk to him? "Let me know if you move again," she said. "We should, you know, stay in touch." Sad that she had to say that to her own father.

"Will do. Talk to you later, kiddo."

"Okay. See you, Dad."

Shelby clicked off the phone and stared at it in her hand. The one thing she wanted more than anything was a relationship with her dad, but with her mother gone, she doubted it would ever happen.

Her thoughts flew to Nick and Willow. She prayed it would go better for them. Maybe she could help . . .

# CHAPTER THREE

. . . . . . . . . . . . . . . . . . . . . . . . . . . . .

*E*llie Draper wore her forty-two years with pure joy. Round, puffy cheeks stained with pink gave her a jolly image. And who wouldn't be in a constant state of bliss running a fudge shop? A hairnet pulled her cropped dark waves tight against her head. A full-length white apron, streaked with chocolate, covered her plump torso. She wiped her hands on a cotton cloth. "Shelby, so good to see you."

"Morning, Ellie. Is it all right if I post a flyer on your bulletin board?"

"You know you can. You don't even have to ask. I think it's a wonderful thing that you're doing, helping young girls the way you do. God bless you for that."

"Thank you." Shelby stepped up to the display case and looked at the candy. "Oh my."

Ellie chuckled. "Now you know why I have such a time with my weight." Her hand flew to her mouth, followed by another jovial chuckle. "Guess I shouldn't say that. It's bad for business."

"I haven't had your peanut butter fudge in a very long time." Shelby eyed the candy with longing.

"Then it's high time you did." Ellie reached for a bag, gave it a quick snap to open it, and scooped a couple pieces of fudge inside. She shut the display door and handed Shelby the bag.

"How much?"

Ellie waved her off. "Consider it an unexpected blessing."

That was Ellie, always thinking of others.

"I walked around the lake with the girls this morning, so a little indulgence can't hurt. Thanks."

"You're welcome. I'd give you a hug, but I don't suppose you'd want chocolate all over that beautiful sweater you're wearing." She waved good-bye and had gone back to stocking fudge before Shelby reached the door.

She stepped out of Sweet Surrender and came face-to-face with Nick and Willow. "Hey, what are you up to?"

"Oh, I'm looking into getting new windows for my house," he said. "Since we were in town, Willow wanted to look around."

"Windows, huh?"

"Yeah. The locks don't work on half of them, and I want to make sure Willow has a lock on hers. Too many weirdos out there."

Willow looked uncomfortable with her dad's overprotective attitude.

"New windows would help with winter too," Shelby said.

"True enough. Listen, Shelby, I thought Saturday might be a good day to start moving tables and whatever you need for your classes. Does that work for you?"

"Works fine. Are you sure you're still up for it? I mean, you've got a lot on your plate right now."

"Nothing I can't handle. I'll be by around nine o'clock Saturday, and we'll get started."

"Thanks so much, Nick."

Shelby took another look at Willow. The girl's thick, wavy

brown hair stopped at her waist. Her expression reminded Shelby of Nick, but the bright blue eyes beneath dark, thick lashes must have come from Willow's mother. Nick's eyes were brown. Chocolate brown. Almost liquidy smooth, like melted chocolate.

Willow wore a newsboy cap, a frilly blue and black dress with matching leggings, and tan boots.

"I love your outfit, Willow," Shelby said. "Did you know I'm a seamstress? Maybe you can come over sometime and give me your opinion on a couple of outfits I've been considering."

Willow nodded shyly. "You said you run that etiquette school too?"

"Yes, I do."

"I was signed up for one in Boston. It would have started at the end of this month."

"Well, I don't know why you couldn't come to mine instead."

Willow's gaze shot up. "Really?" She looked hopefully toward her dad, but Nick said nothing.

"Sign-up is right now for the next class," Shelby said, trying to nudge Nick into giving his approval.

Still nothing.

"And with your dad so graciously letting me use his building for my classes, we'll be right there on his property. So you'd just walk across the yard to go to class. Oh, and of course, your class sessions would be free."

"Could I go, Dad?" Willow practically whispered.

Nick frowned at Shelby. What was the deal?

"Willow, I was hoping for some chocolate-covered cherries."

He pulled out his wallet and gave her a ten-dollar bill. "Would you mind getting some for us while I talk to Shelby for a minute?"

Taking the money, Willow headed inside the store.

"Well, good to see you, Nick," Shelby said, hoping to make a quick getaway. She turned to go.

"Oh no, you don't," he said, grabbing her arm.

"What?"

"Shouldn't you have asked me first?"

"I'm sorry about that. We've never talked about it, Nick, but I don't have a great relationship with my dad. I was hoping maybe I could help you with Willow. Give you some pointers on what might have helped me when I was a kid."

"You could have done that without the school thing."

"The school thing? What do you mean?"

"I don't want to fill her mind with all that mumbo-jumbo high-society stuff."

"It has nothing to do with 'high society,' but everything to do with behaving like a lady. In another year she may not want to take those classes. Don't you want your daughter to learn some manners?"

"No offense, Shelby, but you don't have any kids of your own. I'd appreciate it if you'd let me handle this."

"Wow. Okay. So that's a no, then, on the free classes?"

"Yes, that's a no."

Just then Willow stepped out of the candy store and looked at them both.

"Shelby, we'll see you on Saturday," Nick said. He grabbed Willow's hand and practically pulled her away with him while Shelby looked on, utterly confused.

Saturday morning Shelby watched as Nick checked each cable around her things in his truck bed for the umpteenth time. She could have had everything in the building and completely settled by now, but he had to check and recheck. If there were an award for safety observance, Nick would win it hands down.

At least he didn't seem miffed with her anymore, and for that she was grateful. But he hadn't changed his mind either, and she was hoping she'd get a chance to talk him into letting Willow take her classes after all. She just hadn't figured out how.

When they arrived at Nick's place, Nick had another guy there to help him unload the truck. Willow joined Shelby, and they carried in the chairs while the guys hauled the tables. Once the tables were in their places, chairs crowded around them, blackboard hung, and dishware stacked on shelves, everything was ready to go—or should have been. But as Shelby looked everything over, she couldn't get over the institutional look of it all. It would never do. She couldn't wallpaper or paint, but she could add things that she could take with her once she moved out.

Nick's cell phone rang. He pulled it out of his pocket and flipped it open. "Hello?"

Shelby moved a couple of files into her desk drawer.

"Today?"

The urgency in his voice made Shelby look up. Nick was rubbing his neck as though it ached.

"Give us time to get packed and on our way. Okay, see you later." He snapped his phone closed.

"You okay?" Shelby asked.

He sighed. "Yeah. I have to go back to Boston to settle some affairs for Camilla—on behalf of Willow."

"You're leaving today?"

"Depends on how long it takes me to get ready. At the very latest, tomorrow morning."

"Do I have to go, Dad?" Willow asked.

"Don't you want to see your grandma and grandpa?"

She shook her head slightly, as though she didn't want to be disrespectful.

"Well, you can't stay here by yourself."

"She can stay with me." The words were out of Shelby's mouth before she could stop them.

Willow brightened. Nick frowned.

"I'd love to have her, Nick. She can help me get this room ready for the students—if she's game?" Shelby smiled at the young girl.

"Can I, Dad? Please?"

Nick waited, clearly weighing the situation on all sides. "I guess it's all right," he said finally. "If you're sure, Shelby. I'll be gone for several days."

"That's fine. It will be fun."

He scratched the stubble on his chin, and Shelby gave an involuntary shiver. Oh, how she'd love to get her hands on a razor right about now.

"All right, then. I guess it's settled," he said, though there was still hesitation in his voice.

"How did you like going to the church here?" Shelby asked Willow as they walked to the car in the church parking lot.

"I like it better than the one in Boston. We stayed in with the adults there. It was boring."

"Did you like the youth pastor?"

"Yeah. He's cool."

Shelby smiled. "I'm glad." They settled in the car. "So how does Parmesan chicken with asparagus sound?" Shelby placed her key in the ignition and turned to Willow, who said nothing.

They locked eyes.

"Pizza?"

Willow gave a vigorous nod.

Shelby laughed. "Okay, pizza it is."

After lunch Shelby and Willow went back to Shelby's house. Willow sat in the living room and flipped channels on the TV while Shelby worked at her sewing machine in a corner of the room—a temporary work space until her dining room repairs were finished.

"What do you think of this?" She held up a peasant-style dress in vibrant colors of gold, pink, and cream, complete with short puffy sleeves and a gathered skirt below an empire waist.

Willow's eyes widened. "Oh, I love it." She jumped up from the sofa and came over to inspect it. "You know what would look cool is if you made some ruffled leggings to go with it."

"I like the way you think," Shelby said.

"There's a boutique in Boston that sells clothes like this. Mom used to buy them for me and for her friend's daughter." A shadow crossed her face.

Shelby put her hand on Willow's arm. "I'm sorry, Willow. I know you must miss her very much."

Willow nodded.

"Do you sew?"

"A little," Willow said. "I took lessons from a lady in town."

"Really? A wonderful experience for someone your age," Shelby said. "Do you think you could make some headbands for me if I show you how? They'll basically be a band with a big flower."

"I'd love to."

"Well, it just so happens I have a spare sewing machine."

The two of them spent the afternoon sewing and talking together. By the time they were done, Willow had completed her first headband.

"What do you think?"

It was a black band with a thick black-and-white ruffled flower attached.

"Oh my goodness, I love it, Willow! You did an amazing job," Shelby said as she looked it over. "We may have to go into business together."

The look of pleasure on Willow's face touched Shelby's heart. "I'm cold. How about we get some hot chocolate and sit in front of the fireplace?"

Willow's face brightened. "Yeah."

Once the hot chocolate was ready, Shelby loaded Willow's cup with miniature marshmallows and sprinkled a couple in her own. Then they went into the living room to sit in front of the fire.

"I wonder how Dad's getting along," Willow said before taking a sip from her mug.

"I'm sure he's fine. Do you mind terribly staying here?"

"No, no," Willow said. "I'm having fun. It's just that . . ." Her voice trailed.

The girl had already lost one parent, Shelby realized; she was bound to worry when the other one wasn't around.

"I'm sure he's fine. He'll be home on Tuesday."

Willow nodded and took another drink.

"I know you haven't spent a lot of time with him, but you're lucky to have a dad like him, you know?"

Willow was silent for a moment. "Does your dad live in town?"

"It's funny you should ask. I'm not sure *where* my dad lives. He moves around a lot."

Willow looked down at the floor. "It seems like dads are never around when you need them."

Shelby's heart squeezed. "Sometimes they can't help it."

"Sometimes they can."

Shelby couldn't argue with that. One glance at Willow, and Shelby's heart determined all the more to make things work for that little girl and her father. They would not have the same type of relationship Shelby had with her dad.

She would see to it.

# CHAPTER FOUR

· · · · · · · · · · · · · · · · · · · · · · · · · · ·

$\mathcal{S}$helby had just poured her morning tea when the phone rang. She glanced at Willow, who sat on the sofa watching television.

"Hello?"

"Hey, Shelby. This is Nick. I hate to do this to you, but Camilla's attorney has a family emergency today and can't see me until tomorrow to go over Willow's trust fund. Could she stay with you until Wednesday?"

"Absolutely. We're having a great time together."

"Really?"

"Really." Shelby turned to Willow. "Honey, your dad is on the phone."

Willow got up and took the phone from Shelby. "Hi, Dad."

Shelby carried her cup of tea into the kitchen to give them some privacy. She couldn't hear what Willow was saying, but she treasured the sweet little voice that wafted into the kitchen. Her own daughter would have been Willow's age.

Oh, she didn't know for sure she had carried a daughter, but she'd always imagined she had a girl. The doctor didn't say one way or the other, and she had been afraid to ask.

How many times had she thought of her precious baby over the years? The precious baby that her father had ordered her to have removed from her body.

*It's like a wisdom tooth, Shelby. Might not bother you now, but it'll cause you trouble later on. Best to take care of things while you can.*

She could still see her mother's tears, hear her pleading with her dad. But he would have none of it. Said he would not pay for her mistake. She had to "remove" the baby or he would kick her out of the house . . . and she had nowhere else to go.

The truth was, she and her mother had feared her dad. He had never hurt them, but sometimes he acted as though he would, and his words did as much damage as any fist she could imagine. Her love and respect for him had died that day, along with her child. Had the Lord not made a difference in her life, she would have walked away from him and never looked back.

"You okay?" Willow stood in the doorway of the kitchen.

Shelby jumped. "I didn't hear you coming, Willow. Everything all right with your dad?"

"Yeah."

When Willow offered nothing further, Shelby said, "How about we go shopping today for curtain material for the two windows in your dad's building? He won't want to keep them up there, but I figure I could hang them until the school is out of there." She wiggled her eyebrows.

Willow grinned. "Sounds good to me."

They spent the morning looking for fabric in Smitten and nearby Stowe, then they came back home and set to work. Shelby worked on the curtains while Willow finger-knitted a cap for her friend back in Boston.

"I'm so impressed that you know how to do that."

"It's fun," Willow said. "I love to work with yarn and material."

"Do you ever crochet or knit with needles?"

"I crochet with a hook. My girlfriend's mom got me started and then fixed me up with YouTube to watch videos on how to do certain stitches. Way cool," she said. "I only finger-knit, though. I don't use needles."

"Oh my goodness, Willow, we can have such fun making things together. You could even crochet some flowers for my headbands—if you wanted to. Of course, I'd pay you for your efforts."

Willow beamed. "Really? That would be great. My very first real job."

Shelby laughed. "We'd better get to work."

By evening Shelby had finished sewing the chintz curtains with a cream background and bright red flowers. Frilly ruffles curled the edges. Spreading out the curtains on her bed, she looked them over.

"Oh, those are pretty," Willow said, entering her room.

"Yeah? Are you tired, or do you want to go with me tonight to hang them in the building?"

"I'll go."

"Great. We'll stop by for some fancy drinks at the coffee shop afterward. How about that?"

Willow nodded and grinned.

"Grab your jacket and let's go."

When Nick pulled up to his house Wednesday afternoon, he spotted Willow stepping onto the porch and waved.

"Hey, how's it going, kiddo?" He wanted to hug her but

wasn't sure how she would respond. He'd heard Shelby call Willow "honey" when he'd called them the other night, and it still baffled him. How did women bond so easily? Pulling up all the courage he could muster, he went over and put his arms slightly around her. She barely leaned in to him. He dropped his arms and gave her a quick pat on the shoulder. "Good to see you."

"Welcome home," Shelby called, walking out of the building. Her hair was swept up in a ponytail, she wore a ruffled blouse and glitzy belt, and her trim, long legs were eased into tailored navy pants. Sometimes she reminded him of a Barbie doll with brown hair. He wondered who the lucky Ken would be. One thing for certain, the man had better treat Shelby right. Nick would stand by her through thick and thin, no matter what.

"Thanks."

"When you get a minute, you'll have to see how we've spruced up your building," Shelby said.

He wasn't sure he liked the sound of that.

"I'll come now. No hurry to drag my luggage from the truck." He stepped over the solid ground, hardened by autumn's chill, and followed her into his building. It *was* his building, wasn't it? He looked around at the flowered curtains and the fancy tablecloth on a long table that held a candelabra as the centerpiece. Fancy dishes, lined with sparkling silverware and crystal-looking glasses, had no place in his building.

"What do you think?"

"I think this room will never be the same."

"Thanks," she said, obviously misinterpreting his comment for a compliment.

He held his tongue. He'd get his building back soon

enough and turn it back into the Christmas display room for
which it was intended.

"I'd better get my luggage." He headed toward the door,
and that was when he spotted it—the lavender wreath he'd seen
hanging on doors all around town. The same lavender wreath
he'd said he would never allow on his property.

Couldn't these women understand—he appreciated they
were trying to save the town, but why did it have to become a
girly town to be saved? He did not want flowery wreaths on
his doors. Was that too much to ask?

"Daddy, you have to come see the house." Willow pulled
on his jacket sleeve.

They'd messed with his house? If Shelby had put so much
as a votive candle on one of his stands . . .

*Stay calm, Nick. Stay calm.*

Step, step, step, closer to the house. He'd given the woman
use of his outbuilding for her classes. He had not given her
permission to take over his house. Step, step, step.

Willow pushed the front door open and led him through
the house.

Decorations in harvest colors, pumpkins and leaves, clut-
tered his stands, kitchen table, and one wall. A big pumpkin,
carved and smiling, sat perched beside his fireplace. Small
vases of flowers sat at the kitchen and bathroom sinks.

"Well, what do you think?" Shelby asked.

He turned to her. "Doggone it, Shelby, I gave you permission to use my Christmas shop, not take over my house!"

"But—"

"If I wanted this place to look like a girls' dorm, I would
have made it that way myself."

"But—"

"I'm sorry, but I just can't have this girly stuff all over my house." His arm gave a long wave, indicating the living room. "This is my house. *My* house. It was just fine the way it was."

"But, Daddy—"

"And another thing—that wreath is coming down. You're taking advantage of my friendship, Shelby, and that's just not right. You know how I feel about this whole town-changing thing."

"Daddy—"

"Not now, Willow."

Disappointment shadowed Shelby's expression. "Willow fixed up the house for you," she said. Without another word, she walked out.

Nick turned to his daughter, whose eyes were filled with tears. "Willow, I'm sorry. I didn't—"

Crying, Willow turned, ran to her bedroom, and slammed her door closed.

Nick headed after Shelby, who was getting into her car. "Oh, just like that you leave?" he said before she could get her door closed.

"What?"

"You stir up this whole mess and then just walk away?"

"*I* stirred up this whole mess? What are you talking about?"

"You could have told me Willow did the decorating."

"Are you kidding me? You didn't let us get a word in edgewise."

"Whatever."

"Look, Nick, I don't know what your deal is, but you'd

better work things out with your daughter." Shelby closed her car door, started the engine, and pulled out of the drive.

Nick went back inside and sank into the leather sofa. He leaned his head into his palm. How could he possibly fix this? He'd blabbed on and on about how bad the house looked . . . and his daughter had helped with it. She had taken the time to decorate it and looked at him with hopeful eyes, and all he had done was tear it down.

He released a long sigh. No Father of the Year Award for him. What did he know about women and girls? Obviously, he didn't know a thing, or his wife wouldn't have left him.

One thing he knew. He couldn't sit around the house and do nothing when he felt this way.

He walked to Willow's room and rapped on her door. "Willow?"

No answer.

"I need to go into town. You want to go with me?"

No answer.

"Listen, I know you need some time. If you don't want to go, I understand. I'll be gone about an hour. Will you be all right?"

He waited a minute and finally heard footsteps approach the door. Willow opened it and looked at him through red, puffy eyes.

"I'm so sorry, honey. I blew off my trap without thinking things through. I thought Shelby had done it all, and I didn't like her taking control of my home, you know?"

Willow reluctantly nodded.

"You forgive me?"

Another slight nod.

With hesitation, Nick reached for her, not sure if she would respond, but when Willow stepped into his arms, he pulled her close. "I'm so sorry, baby. I'm so sorry."

Once Nick was certain Willow was okay, he went to the auto parts store to pick up new windshield wipers for his truck. After that, he stopped by the hardware store to pick up some caulk to fix Shelby's door, whether she deserved it or not. Griffen and Carson were there.

"Hey, great to see you, buddy," Griffen said when Nick stepped into the store.

Carson looked up from helping a customer and waved.

"You too. Glad to see you got smart and came back to Smitten." Nick gave him a playful shove.

Griffen shook his head. "Don't get any ideas. I'm not sure I'm staying."

"Then why did you come back?"

"To help with the town revamp."

Nick could hardly believe his ears. "You're going along with all this love mumbo jumbo?"

"Well, sure. I'm for anything that will save the town. Aren't you?"

"If you're all for saving the town, why aren't you staying?"

"It's complicated."

Nick had known Griffen long enough to know that when he didn't want to talk about something, he really didn't.

"Hey, thanks for recommending me for Shelby's repair job. I appreciate the work."

"Listen, about that . . ."

"Uh-oh, don't tell me I'm laid off already."

"No, no, nothing like that."

"What is it, then?"

"Oh, nothing. Everything." Nick explained about his ex-wife, his daughter, and the latest fiasco with Shelby turning his outbuilding into Cinderella's castle and then encouraging Willow to feminize his house.

"First off, I'm sorry to hear about your ex-wife, Nick. That's rough."

"Yeah. We've been over for years, but she was still the mother of my kid, you know?"

"Yeah." Griffen looked through the boxes of nails on display and finally picked up a box. He walked over to the hammers, and Nick followed him.

"As for the Cinderella castle thing, you might be over-reacting. All she did was set up the room for her classes, right?"

"Yeah, I thought of that."

"And the house thing, well, I don't see what the big deal is."

Nick frowned, not liking where this was going.

Griffen held up his hands. "Well, the way I see it, you're getting onto Shelby and Willow for trying to make your home into something it's not—but, man, you're trying to make them into something they're not. Do you want your friends and your daughter to pretend for you? To walk on eggshells around you?"

Nick's jaw cramped. "It would just be better for all of us if she got back into her own work space." He thought a moment. "As a matter of fact, do you need any help with the work at her house? I don't want any money. It would ease the tension between Shelby and me if we could get things back to normal—meaning, get her back to work at home."

"Are you sure you're not just trying to be around her more?"

"Now cut that out."

Griffen laughed. "All right, all right. You can help me out if you don't ride me about the safety goggles."

Nick frowned. "I need to get home and check on the trees. See you at Shelby's."

# CHAPTER FIVE

$\mathcal{S}$helby dried her hands on the dish towel and opened the front door. "Nick, what are you doing here?" She glanced at his tool belt.

"I told Griffen I'd come over and help him today. I've got my pager if they need me at the station, and the farm is under control." He shrugged. "I know you'd like to have things back to normal as soon as possible. So here I am."

"Oh, okay. I'll take you to Griffen."

"Wait." Nick grabbed her arm so that she turned to him. "I'm sorry about what happened last night. I was tired from the drive, and seeing those flowers everywhere, then the wreath—well, it doesn't matter. None of it matters. I shouldn't have responded like that, and I'm sorry."

His comments not only surprised her, they touched her heart. "Thank you, Nick. I'm sorry too. I'll take the curtains down, and I'll—"

Nick shook his head. "No. I told you to do what you needed to do to prepare the building for your classes. You leave everything up. When your classes are over, then you can take it all down."

She was going to ask him about the wreath, but decided that since he didn't mention it, neither would she. That way she could keep it up a few more days until he absolutely forced her to take it down.

"So we're good?" he said.

Shelby smiled. "We're good." It warmed her to think that her friendship mattered to him. "I hope you don't mind my asking, but have you squared things with Willow too?"

"Yeah." He ran his hand through his hair. "Boy, I sure messed that up."

"From what I hear, all parents make mistakes." Without a thought, her hand went to her belly.

"Yeah, I guess." He paused. "How did it go with you and Willow while I was gone?"

"We had a wonderful time. She's such a great kid, Nick." Shelby had meant to encourage him, but when his expression sagged, she was sorry she'd said it.

"Yeah, I don't deserve her."

"Like I said, all parents make mistakes."

"I'm just so green at this. I have no idea how to be a full-time father. I mean, I can hold a five-minute conversation on the phone, but I've never had to do much beyond that. Even when I went there to spend time with her, she always brought a friend along. We were both uncomfortable, I guess."

"It just takes time." Shelby put her hand on his arm and looked him in the eye. "You'll get there."

"Maybe I'll buy a couple of books on parenting. That might help."

"Great idea."

He fingered his tool belt. "So when do your classes start?"

She breathed easier at the change of subject. "Tuesday, October second. I normally start a little earlier, but with the fire and all, it couldn't be helped. I'll be out of your hair before Thanksgiving. Will that give you enough time for what you need to do?"

"Yeah, that will be fine."

"Okay, good. And remember we only meet on Tuesday evenings, so we won't be there every day."

They stood in silence for a moment.

"Well, I guess I'd better get to work." He hesitated, then leaned over and hugged her. "Thanks again, Shelby. You're a good sport."

Shelby stood and watched as he walked toward her dining room. Maybe she'd open some windows. She suddenly felt very warm.

Shelby finished cutting out the pattern for the shirt she was making for her dad for Christmas. She hoped last year's sizes still worked. Carefully lifting each piece, she placed them in the order in which she would sew them and threaded her machine. She couldn't get away from the thought that she should call and check on him. It took great effort to reach out to her dad, but she knew the Lord wanted that of her. Still, her obedience might have more of an impact if she did it with a cheerful heart.

Resentment filled every word she spoke to him, but it seemed the Lord would not let her get away from it. Each time she made excuses and shoved her dad to the back of her mind, God seemed to bring him front and center. She reached for the phone.

"Hi, Dad. I was beginning to think you'd already moved."

"Nope, not yet. But I plan to in three weeks."

"Tennessee?"

"Uh, no. Actually, I'm headed up your way."

Her stomach cramped. "My way?"

"Yeah, about fifty miles north of you."

"Really?"

"You okay with that?"

"Why wouldn't I be?"

Silence.

"Do you need help moving?"

"No, I don't have much to bring. I'll get different furniture. The stuff here is getting old. I'm just gonna sell it lock, stock, and barrel."

Shelby tried to find the words, but her mind was a blank screen. "So will you let me know when you get moved in?"

"Yeah. Hey, listen, I've gotta go. The UPS guy is here." He hung up.

Shelby plopped down in her living room chair, and Penelope jumped up in her lap. While her thoughts ran the gamut, she stroked Penelope's fur. It was one thing to have to call her dad now and then. It was quite another to have him fifty miles away.

But why was she worried? It wasn't as though he would come to see her. He might be fifty miles away, but she wouldn't know it any more than if he still lived in Florida. Her dad kept to himself.

Always.

"So did you learn anything, squirt?" Nick asked, ruffling Willow's hair after Shelby's first class. Once he had apparently realized he'd have to pick and choose his battles, he'd given in to her pleading to attend.

"Don't, Daddy." Willow smoothed her hair down.

Nick shared a glance with Shelby that seemed to say, *What did I do?* She'd have to tell him later that girls didn't like getting their hair messed up.

"Tell him what you learned, Willow," Shelby said.

"A lady has good posture, sits and stands properly, and walks gracefully." Willow demonstrated as she talked, and she and Shelby giggled.

Nick's jaw dropped. "You mean there's a right and wrong way to do all that?"

Shelby laughed. "Yes, Nick, there is."

He scratched his jaw. "I suppose I've been doing it wrong all these years. How's this?" He grabbed Shelby's purse and walked across the room, hand on his hip, with a feminine swing to his strut.

Shelby and Willow laughed, and he swiveled around. "What? Didn't I do it right?"

"Oh, you. You're making fun of us," Shelby said, gathering her things.

"Just teasing." He grinned. "How about we go into the house for some hot apple cider?"

"That would be nice," Shelby said, intensely aware that Nick's hand was on the small of her back as he escorted her to his house, with Willow walking beside them.

Warmth from the crackling fire greeted her the moment she entered the front door.

"Now before you get any ideas, I started the fire in the fireplace just before I came out to get you guys. I know better than to leave a fire going when we're out of the house," Nick said.

"I never doubted it," Shelby said.

Nick's house was positively lovely with its rustic charm. The more she saw it, the more it appealed to her. Normally she preferred the frilly things of life, it was true, yet there was a simple beauty to his log cabin that she hadn't appreciated before.

The fact that he'd left Willow's decorations in place touched Shelby.

Spiced cider scented the room, splashing the air with the true aroma of autumn. Michael Bublé's voice sang softly from the CD player.

"This is nice, Nick. Really nice."

"Thanks," he said, pulling down mugs from his cupboard.

"And you didn't think you were a good dad," Shelby said, easing onto one of the stools at the counter.

"Good dad?" He looked confused.

"You know, going to all this trouble for Willow. Spiced cider and all that. That's really sweet and thoughtful."

"Oh, uh, yeah."

Shelby wondered at the confusion on his face, but quickly forgot it as she took in the surroundings.

"Here you are," he said, passing her a mug of steaming hot cider.

"Wait. Are you wearing a new sweater?" Shelby couldn't believe her eyes. Nick normally wore sweatshirts and T-shirts; she rarely saw him in a nice sweater other than at church.

"You mean my wardrobe is so sparse you notice when I buy a new sweater?"

Shelby took a tiny sip from her mug. "I'm afraid so," she said with a teasing grin. "It looks nice with your eyes."

"Really?" He stood taller and batted his lashes. "Guess I'll have to wear it more often."

She chuckled. Did she imagine it, or did his eyes linger on her a little longer than necessary?

He coughed, then turned his attention to one of the mugs. "Willow, your cider is ready," he called out.

Willow settled in the living room and watched something on television while Nick and Shelby stayed at the kitchen table. Nick stared into his mug.

"Something wrong?"

"Oh, just wondering how I can generate some more money. I know the Lord will provide, but with Willow coming up on her teen years, I know life's about to get expensive." He took a drink from his mug.

"That's true." Shelby thought a moment. "Have you considered adding events to your farm?"

"What do you mean?"

"You know, hayrides, hot chocolate with Santa, pumpkin hunts, educational tours to stir up interest, that sort of thing?"

Nick stared at her.

"What?"

"How'd you get so smart?"

Shelby laughed. "Haven't you heard of such things through the Christmas Tree Farm Association?"

"Yeah, I guess I have. Just didn't need the hassle of it all.

But with the mill closing, I won't be selling as much lumber, so I guess I need to consider it. It would bring in more outsiders if I offered those things. You know, people outside of Smitten."

"And you would be helping to save the town, all at the same time." She smiled, hoping she hadn't offended him.

"Yeah. My manly contribution." He winked.

They talked awhile longer of different ways he could spruce up his farm. Though Shelby always enjoyed spending time with Nick, tonight seemed special somehow. She didn't want to look at why yet. Maybe later. Taking in the sweet spicy aroma of the cider and soaking in the pleasure of Nick's company made her wish she didn't have to go home to an empty house.

Willow stepped into the kitchen, dressed in her pajamas.

"Whoa," Nick said. "Don't you think it's a little rude to put on your pajamas while we have company? That company being the lady of etiquette, no less?"

Shelby laughed. "Oh, come on, I'm not that snooty."

Willow looked at her dad. "It's Shelby, Dad. She's not company. She's family."

Shelby nearly dropped her mug. It seemed the whole world paused with Willow's statement. Nick's gaze locked with hers.

"I guess she is, at that."

Were her hands shaking? And she couldn't swallow. It was as though she had a ball of cotton in her mouth. Was she getting sick?

"If you'll excuse me, may I use your bathroom?"

"Sure, it's right in there." Nick pointed the way.

Shelby eased her way into the room, closing the door

behind her. She leaned against the wall a moment to catch her breath. Finally she pulled a handkerchief from her pocketbook, dampened it with water, and wiped the back of her neck. What was the matter with her? She mentally went over what she had eaten during the day. It couldn't be lack of food.

Then she remembered the feel of Nick's hand on her back. The look in his eyes when Willow paid her such a high compliment—well, it unsettled her, that was all. She was reading something into it that wasn't there.

Turning on the faucet, she dampened her cloth some more and dotted her face. She looked at herself in the mirror. "What is the matter with you?" she whispered to her reflection. "He's your friend. That's it." She paused, still staring at her reflection. "And besides that, he has whiskers!"

She took a deep breath and prepared to leave the room with her mind made up. She would do absolutely nothing to jeopardize her friendship with Nick.

No matter what her changing heart told her.

# CHAPTER SIX

. . . . . . . . . . . . . . . . . . . . . . . . . .

*Y*ou all right this morning?" Natalie asked, breathless, as they jogged around the river walk, Reese's exercise of choice.

Birds chirped and plumped their feathers in the cool morning air.

"Yeah, why?" Shelby jumped over a bump on the path. They were barely into their jog and already she had to shed her jacket. She hated to sweat.

"I was about to ask the same thing," Reese said. "You're awful quiet today."

"Just got a lot on my mind." If they only knew . . . but Shelby wasn't about to tell them. How could she when she didn't know herself? Besides, she didn't have enough breath to talk and jog at the same time.

"Like what?" Julia asked. "We spill our guts to you—it's only fair that you should do the same."

Shelby laughed. "That's Julia. Cuts right to the heart of the matter." She took a deep breath—for survival. "Well, I talked to my dad, and I guess he's moving up here now. Not to Smitten, but close by." Another breath. "In fact, now that I think about it, he didn't say exactly where. About fifty miles north."

"Is that a problem?" Natalie asked.

"We've just never been . . . close." She hadn't talked much

with her friends about the relationship—or lack thereof—that she had with her dad.

"Well, at least he won't be in town. It's not like you'll be around him all the time," Reese said.

"Yeah, I guess."

"There's more. I can hear it in your voice," Natalie said.

"It's called lack of oxygen," Shelby said.

They laughed.

"Dad and I have a history. Not a very good one."

"Have you prayed about it?" Natalie asked.

"Yes."

"Don't stop. God is working."

Shelby just nodded. She wondered how much God could work when she was holding back. But what was she holding back? She'd already forgiven her father for making her have the abortion, hadn't she? And for the way he ignored her after that, as though he couldn't stand the sight of her because of her "sin." God had forgiven her, but her dad couldn't seem to do it.

"Did you hear me?" Reese said.

"What? I'm sorry. Still thinking about Dad," Shelby said.

"I wanted to know how it was going, working at Nick's place."

She wished they'd quit making her talk. At this rate, she'd need an oxygen tank before the jog was over. "It's going all right. He said I could bring my sewing machine to the building and work there while Griffen works on my house. All that noise and dust is driving me crazy."

"Is he still helping Griffen?" Julia asked.

"Every now and then." Her pulse kicked up a notch—most

likely from the jogging, but she wasn't completely convinced. She couldn't imagine what was going on in her that was changing her feelings toward Nick. No matter what, she had to let it go. He thought of her as a mere friend, and if she made him uncomfortable, she'd lose his friendship. She couldn't bear the thought. Forcing her mind to stop rambling, she looked up to see the girls looking at her.

"What?"

"Oh, nothing," Reese said. "Nothing at all." A smirk played at the corner of Reese's mouth. Shelby ignored it.

"How's the spa business, Julia?" Shelby asked.

"Going okay. I've had a few women come in who said they were in town for their honeymoon. They wanted to see the place where the famous Sawyer Smitten was getting married."

"Woo-hoo, that's what we want to hear," Natalie said. "Word's getting out! I've had some couples coming into the coffee shop from out of town too. So fun to watch people in love."

"Have you given them any of your gluten-free cookies?" Julia asked.

"No."

"Don't." Julia, Shelby, and Reese all spoke at once.

"Hey!"

"Just kidding," Shelby said. "But maybe wait till you get them perfected."

"I'm getting closer every day," Natalie said. "Hey, Reese, have you thought about the Palmer building for your outfitters shop?"

"I was thinking about scheduling an appointment to look at it," Reese said.

"Better not wait too long. The new Smitten will be up and

running once that wedding takes place, and you'll want to be in on the action."

"Natalie, our eternal optimist," Julia said, shaking her head.

"Everything hinges on that wedding," Reese said. "It will make or break this town."

"Things will work out, you'll see," Natalie said with full confidence.

These were exciting times for the town of Smitten. Shelby could feel it. She couldn't help sensing good days were ahead for all of them—if she didn't blow it with Nick.

Nick grabbed his jacket and went to Willow's room to tell her he was walking in the woods, but just as he lifted his fist to rap on the door, he heard crying. He stood there a minute, not knowing what to do. He hadn't lived with a woman for so long, he'd forgotten how to deal with them. And even then, Camilla left before their first anniversary. Willow was the only good thing to come from that marriage.

He whispered a prayer to the Lord for strength and wisdom, then knocked softly on the door. "Willow, may I come in?"

There was a pause, and then a soft "Yes."

When he opened the door, she was sitting on her bed, eyes red and swollen, scarlet streaks on her face. He walked over and sat down beside her. Placing her hand between his own, he looked at her.

"You want to talk about it?"

Big sloppy tears spilled over her lashes and down her cheeks. "I miss Mom."

His heart hurt with her words. He wanted to make her all better. Make the bad stuff go away. But he couldn't.

"I know," he said quietly.

"She never stayed home. I always missed her. But now . . . we'll never really get to know each other."

"I'm sorry." So Camilla had treated her own daughter the same way she had treated him. He'd make it up to Willow. He didn't know how, but he would.

"Listen, I'm fairly new to this whole dad thing, but I want to do it right. It's great to have you here with me. I want to be what you need, but I'll make mistakes. That's just how I am."

Her smile in his direction melted his heart.

"Just know that no matter what, I will always love you," he said. "Deal?"

"Deal."

He pulled her into a strong hug, and she hugged him back. Not just any hug, but a real dad-daughter kind of hug. The type of hug that said *We're family*.

"I was just getting ready to take a walk through the trees, check on how things are doing. Want to go with me? We won't stay real long."

"Okay." She grabbed a tissue from her nightstand.

"What are your plans for today?" he asked, rising to his feet.

"I thought I'd work on some more headbands for Shelby. I've started crocheting a rose for one. I think she'll like it." Willow walked over and pulled a half-crocheted flower out of her dresser drawer. "What do you think?"

Though he couldn't make heads or tails of it, one look at

her sweet face and he couldn't stop gushing. "It's beautiful. You did this yourself?"

"Yeah."

"Shelby will be so pleased." He gave her a sideways hug. "I'm proud of you, kid."

"Thanks, Dad."

"Grab your jacket and let's go."

❦

The firs gave off their sweet aroma, filling the air with Christmas as Nick and Willow walked through the maze of trees. "We have trees growing at varying intervals. Some were just planted this year. Others are a couple of years old, and so on."

"How long does it take for a tree to grow big enough to become a Christmas tree?" she asked.

"About eight years." He stopped and flipped a tag out on a tree.

"Do you put tags on all these yourself?"

"I have part-time people who come and help me," Nick said. "We usually do that in September."

"Maybe I can help next year." She looked up at him, excitement flushing her cheeks.

"That would be great." He reached over to rough up her hair and stopped himself.

Willow laughed. "Now you're getting the hang of it."

Nick laughed out loud with her. He looked around the area. "Looks like I need to mow again. Won't be long, and I won't have to do it again until next spring."

"What kind of trees are these, Dad?"

"Balsam and Fraser firs."

"I love the smell," Willow said, taking in a deep breath.

"Yeah, me too." Nick smiled.

"Makes me excited for Christmas."

"I like people like you. They keep my farm going."

"What do you do for Christmas? I mean, before I came along, did you stay by yourself or go visit Grandpa and Grandma in South Carolina?"

"Sometimes they come here. They know I can't leave the place. Too many people want trees at the last minute. I'm busy through Christmas Eve."

"Oh, that sounds like fun!"

"Really? That wouldn't bother you?"

"No. I love helping other people have fun at Christmas. I used to go to fancy parties that Grandma and Grandpa Givens or Mom set up. I hated them. There were hardly ever any kids around, and when there were, they were stuck-up and didn't want to do anything fun."

"Well, we'll have to work on that. Speaking of which, have you made any friends at school?"

"Yeah, a couple."

"Anytime you want to have someone over, it's fine with me," he said.

"Thanks, Dad."

As they talked along the way, Nick stopped here and there to shear up unruly branches and carefully maintain the familiar Christmas tree shape.

"I like Shelby," Willow said.

"Yeah, she's a good friend." A twig snapped beneath his boot.

"Is that all?"

"Yeah, why?"

Willow shrugged. "Just seems like you two like each other more than that."

"What is this . . . women's intuition?" he asked.

Her face lit up. "Something like that."

"We've been friends since Shelby moved into town. Never been anything more than that."

"So you say."

Willow's comment tickled his funny bone. What kind of insight did this kid have? "She's nice to have around, I will say that," he said more in a manner of thinking out loud than in response to Willow's comment. He found her gaze on him. "I'll let you know if anything changes, squirt. How's that?" He grinned.

"I think you already have."

"I think it's time we went back to get some lunch, Little Miss Matchmaker."

"Okay," Willow said, easing her dainty fingers into his big, rough hand as they headed back to the house.

# CHAPTER SEVEN

· · · · · · · · · · · · · · · · · · · · · · · · · ·

*T*hanks again for letting me bring my sewing machine out here, Nick. I can work so much better without all the racket of saws and hammers rumbling through the house," Shelby said as she got out of her car and headed toward Nick's outbuilding.

"What about your dog?"

"Penelope?" Shelby grinned. "A neighbor girl is checking in on her."

He nodded. "Before you get started, how about joining me for some coffee?" He lifted his cup.

She'd take any excuse to spend some more time with him. "It's enough that you've let me come here. You don't have to serve me coffee too."

"Just two friends having coffee before work." He wiggled his eyebrows.

A twinge of disappointment crossed her heart, though she couldn't say why. That's what they were, just two friends. "Well, if you make it tea, you're on."

He wrinkled his nose. "I don't have any tea."

Shelby pulled a packet out of her purse. "It just so happens I carry my own stash."

Nick grinned. "Great. Let's go."

Ignoring the butterflies in her stomach, she followed him to the house, taking in his long-legged stride, his swinging muscular arms. She forced herself to look away. Sunshine spilled over the treetops, shrouding them in a whitewashed glow. Birds called from thick branches. Pine mixed with the fresh scent of autumn tickled her senses. Though the air was cold, the warmth of Nick's home embraced her the moment she stepped inside.

Willow greeted them. "Can I come over to the building and work with you while Dad's out in the forest?"

Shelby glanced at Nick, who smiled assent, then turned to Willow. "You certainly may," she said. "I would love the company."

"Great. I'll go get dressed." Willow took off so fast in her stocking feet that she almost slipped on the hardwood floor.

"I've never seen a kid so excited to work. Nice of you to let her use your spare sewing machine, by the way." Nick walked over to his teakettle, poured tap water from the faucet, and placed it on the stove to boil. He filled his coffeemaker with coffee and water and went back to join her. "I didn't even know she could sew or do that thing with yarn—"

"You mean crochet?"

"Whatever it's called."

Shelby laughed. "She's very good at it. Talented kid you've got there."

Nick stretched to his full six foot three, tucked his thumbs under his arms, and said, "What can I say? She takes after her old man."

"I don't doubt it for a minute."

Nick slid into a chair across the table from Shelby.

She took a deep breath. "I wanted to talk to you this morning about something."

"Uh-oh, that doesn't sound good."

"Well, it's like this. I thought I had a place to hold my high tea for the girls, but it's fallen through. We hadn't talked about anything other than holding my classes here, and I wasn't sure how you would feel if we held the tea here too."

"What's a high tea?" he asked, glancing toward the tea-kettle and coffeemaker.

"It's the final event of our class. The girls learn how to host a tea. This time we're inviting some extra people besides parents—teachers, pastors, grandparents, aunts and uncles. Each girl will host a table of up to eight guests—people, including their parents, who have impacted their lives."

"That sounds nice."

"Since Willow is new to Smitten, she can fill up her table with some of my friends. The event will raise money for the town."

He looked at her. "You raise money?" He drummed his fingers on the table.

"Yes. People have to buy a ticket to attend, and they'll be given an opportunity to donate money toward revamping Smitten as well. It's our way of giving back."

"Sure, you can use the building. Should be large enough for your needs, and there's plenty of room for parking too."

"That's what I thought. Thanks, Nick." Her tense shoulders relaxed slightly. "The other thing is, it's a formal affair. The dads will escort their daughters into the room while each one is announced."

Nick whistled. "Poor guys." His fingers stopped abruptly. "Wait." He looked up at her as though he'd swallowed a chicken bone.

Shelby giggled.

"Me?" He pointed to his chest. "I have to do this with Willow? I have to dress in a suit and tie?"

Just then Willow walked into the kitchen. She came up behind him and hugged his neck. "Won't it be fun, Dad? The first time we've really done something special together. Don't worry, though. I have plenty of nice dresses to choose from. You won't need to buy me anything."

Shelby's heart grew tender toward this thoughtful child who was clearly becoming a lovely young lady.

Nick sighed. "Well, if I'm going to dress up for anyone, I'd only do it for you," he said. He looked at Willow and winked.

Seemingly satisfied, Willow took her toast and went into the living room.

"You don't mind if we have the tea here, then?"

"No, that's fine. As long as you're out of there by Thanksgiving, we're good. I have to get my building set up with Christmas decorations for sale, garland ropes, a few wreaths, all that, because the day after Thanksgiving we're open for business."

"I understand. Thanks so much, Nick. You're the greatest friend ever."

He grinned and rubbed his whiskers. "Yeah, whatever."

Gaining courage, Shelby ventured on. "You might want to shave before the big event. Just an idea."

His eyes grew wide. "What? Wait. A. Minute." He frowned. "Now you're crossing the line. I'll wear a tie, but these whiskers stay."

Shelby held up her hands. "Okay, okay. But I have to know, are you like Tom Selleck—don't want to be seen without your mustache kind of thing?" She was teasing now, and by the look on his face, she could tell he knew it.

"Maybe."

"Might be nice to see what you look like underneath all that stubble."

The teakettle whistled. Nick got up and poured Shelby's hot water into the mug and handed it to her. She dipped her peppermint tea bag into the steaming water and let it steep.

They continued to discuss the big event and the Christmas tree farm. When Shelby had finished her tea, she pulled on her jacket and got up.

"Thanks for the tea, Nick. That was nice."

"You're welcome. It serves a purpose, you know."

"The tea?"

"The hair." He rubbed his stubble.

She crossed her arms in front of her. "Oh? What purpose is that?"

"It keeps me warm in the winter months."

"What about the summer months?"

"Uh, then too. All that air-conditioning, you know."

She laughed. "I've got to get to work." She headed for the door, fighting the urge, with every step, to stay right there with Nick.

Nick kissed Willow before he walked out the door to head into the woods. He'd joked with Shelby, but he wasn't the least bit happy that he had to dress up for the girly tea. But what could he do? It was important to Willow, so he'd have to follow through. If only he hadn't opened his big mouth and offered his building, he wouldn't be in this mess. Willow wouldn't even be in Shelby's class.

A tinge of shame pricked him. It was clear Willow was enjoying herself. He should be supporting his daughter rather than complaining about dressing up. It was no big deal. His boots scuffed the path as he checked trees for insects and any sign of disease or distress. With a deep inhale, he breathed in nature the way God intended it. Other guys could have their fancy clothes and cars. He wasn't wired that way. He had tried to explain that to Camilla, but she never accepted it. She had wanted a man who would wine and dine her, wear fancy clothes, smell like a perfume factory. For a while he'd tried to do things her way, but once he realized he'd never measure up to her image for him, he gave up. She used to grumble, "You can change the clothes, but you can't change the man."

So why bother?

And another thing. He wasn't about to start shaving every day. He wouldn't ever shave if he didn't have to, but he wasn't going for the Santa Claus look. Hey, maybe he should give that some thought, given the Christmas tree farm and all.

Nick headed back to the house. He glanced into Willow's room as he walked by and spotted the pictures she wanted hung on the wall. He needed to get a new level since he loaned out his old one to someone and hadn't gotten it back. He'd run into town, get a new level, then dash back while Shelby was still there. It would give him an excuse to stay nearby.

He let Shelby and Willow know where he was going, then pulled his truck up to Carson's hardware store. He glanced at the wreath on the door as he went inside, muttering under his breath.

"Hey, Nick," Carson said. Griffen was there too.

"Don't you ever work?" Nick teased Griffen. "This is the second time I've caught you in here."

"I could say the same for you," Griffen threw back.

Nick laughed. "Good point."

"What brings you in?" Carson asked.

"Need a level."

Carson pointed to where they were shelved.

"Hey, Carson, I'm curious about something. I already know Griffen's position on this, but I have to know what you really think deep down—aside from Natalie's view—about the women making this a girly town."

Carson laughed. "They're not making it a girly town. They're making it a romantic town. There's a difference. Besides, I'm good with it. Natalie helped me to see that anything that helps the town is worth pursuing. So I put aside my manly pride, and here we are." He nudged Nick with his elbow. "Romance isn't only a girl thing, you know."

Nick groaned while Griffen and Carson laughed.

"Come on, dude. It's not so hard to give in." Carson slapped him on the back. "Remember, it's for the good of the town."

"Yeah, I guess." By the time Nick finished talking with the guys, he felt like a class-A jerk for being so stubborn about it all. He'd just have to let this one go. Digging in his boots wasn't going to change anything.

*⊗*

"Hey, fancy meeting you here," Nick said, catching up with Shelby.

Shelby turned, and her stomach did a flip. She hadn't talked much to Nick in the past week or so. She'd been busy planning for the upcoming tea, and he'd been busy getting his trees ready for their busy Christmas season.

"Hello." She flashed a smile.

"So what brings you to the town square on a Friday night?" he said.

"I love to hear the Garner Sisters play. It's so relaxing."

Nick shoved a hand in his pocket. "Yeah, it is nice."

"Wait. I thought you were a jazz man."

Nick lifted his chin. "I have a bit of culture, ma'am." He bowed, took her hand, and pressed his lips against it, nearly taking Shelby's breath away.

"Oh my," she said, pretending to fan herself with all the charm of Scarlett O'Hara. Little did he know she was only partially pretending. "Where's Willow?"

"She's at a friend's house tonight. I just dropped her off and spotted you, so I stopped."

"Aha! So you aren't here just for the culture."

He winced. "Busted."

"Well, are you going to stay?"

"Sure. Why not."

"Want to sit over there?" She pointed to a spot not far from the string trio.

"Looks good."

They walked over, and she spread a blanket on the ground. "I'm sorry, I only brought enough tea for myself. I would have brought more had I known you were going to join me."

"No problem. I don't need anything." He patted his stomach.

She laughed, taking in the fact that his shirt had a nice crisp look to it and his casual khaki pants, not jeans, had a pressed crease down the middle.

Who was this man?

"I've got to say I'm surprised by the hair," Nick said, pointing to her ponytail. "That's only the second time I think I've ever seen you wear it that way."

"I let down my guard every now and then," she teased. "Especially on a beautiful fall night like this one." She tugged on her sweater.

"Listen, I want to apologize for being a jerk about the whole town makeover. You can leave that wreath on the door. I've just had to work through my manly pride."

Shelby let out a good laugh. "Really? Somehow I never saw you as the proud type."

"Ouch."

"Oh no." She leaned over and touched his arm. "I meant that in a good way."

"How are the plans coming for the high tea?"

"With Rose's help, I'm getting the menu pulled together."

"Good. Do you have enough tables?"

"The rental place in town will be delivering tables and linens the day of the tea. Should be fun."

"Any entertainment?"

She pointed to the string trio. "Best in town."

"Sounds like you have it all worked out."

"I hope so. I tend to get a little stressed as the day draws near."

"Thanks for the warning," he said.

"Hey, there's the dad of one of my students. He's a widower too. You should meet him. Ryan, would you like to join us?"

Ryan Stevenson greeted Shelby and Nick and settled into a place on their blanket. They made small talk until the music started.

She hadn't wanted to invite Ryan, but she needed a distraction from Nick. She couldn't say why, but she was out of sorts. Uncomfortable. She looked forward to this event every Friday night, but tonight she struggled to get lost in the music. No matter how hard she tried to rein them in, her thoughts kept going to Nick and the fact he was sitting so close to her, his woodsy scent tantalizing her.

The music filled the air, but Nick hardly noticed. He couldn't figure out what was going on inside his head. Why had he taken care to put on khaki pants and a nice shirt? Yes, he knew he would be driving by the concert and most likely would spot Shelby—or he had hoped he would. And that was what he couldn't figure out—why he wanted to see her.

He moved it around in his mind. They were friends, and they hadn't talked much lately. Maybe that was it. Yet Nick couldn't get past feeling that something was stirring between them—at least on his part. He glanced at the dude sitting with them and tried not to show his irritation. Why did she invite that guy to sit with them? She obviously didn't care if they were alone—which irritated him to no end.

He'd better be careful. They'd been friends too long to mess things up now.

Still, the churning inside his belly didn't feel like friendship.

# CHAPTER EIGHT

· · · · · · · · · · · · · · · · · · · · · · · · ·

*A* gentle October breeze fluttered through the limbs of balsam firs, sending a sweet Christmas perfume into the air. Shelby's boots crunched pebbles into the hardened patch of earth designated as Nick's driveway as she went to the building where she held her classes.

No sooner had she placed the materials on the table than the girls started to file into the building and seat themselves at the chairs around the tables. Though it was a Saturday, they had come together specifically to work on invitations for their high tea.

One by one the girls settled into work. Shelby walked around the tables and checked on their progress as they cut out the printed form of the woman in the dress that they would then stitch into place on the invitation. Shelby's occasional hobby of scrapbooking was paying off.

"Since we only have two sewing machines, you'll have to take turns. While others are at the machines, if you've finished cutting out the woman in the dress, you can cut out the paper for the ruffle, which we will sew into place at the bottom of the dress."

"Does this look right, Miss Shelby?" one student asked.

"Yes, Madison, it looks wonderful."

Papers scattered about, scissors in hands, the girls chatted excitedly, each one raising her voice to be heard over the others.

"Let's keep our talking soft, girls." Shelby inched toward a student and leaned in. "Cally, you'll need to straighten the background paper before you sew it on."

Shelby continued walking, her small heels clacking against the cement as she made her way around the tables. She drew in a breath of the cinnamon candle on her desk that scented the room and thought about her time with Nick last night.

He had been so relaxed. He was the same great friend he had always been, but now she noticed the curve of his jaw, the strength in his arms, the chocolate brown of his eyes. Why hadn't she noticed those things before? Something in his grin made her stomach flip just to think of it.

"Okay, girls, make sure you watch those scalloped edges. Keep them nice and trimmed."

Shelby was pleased with the progress the girls were making on the invitations—until one of them let out an earsplitting scream.

"What in the world?" Shelby turned in the direction of the sewing machines. "Willow, honey, what is it?"

Willow cried and held up her index finger—with the broken needle pierced clear through it.

Shelby's breath caught. "Madison, quickly, go get Mr. Majors."

The little girl ran out the door.

In another moment Nick dashed inside, spotted Willow crying, and rushed to her side.

"I'm not sure what happened, exactly. She was sewing and—"

Nick frowned at Shelby, scooped Willow into his arms, and ran out to his truck without a word.

After the last student left, Shelby waited awhile and

straightened the room, hoping she'd catch Willow and Nick when they returned. She had tried to contact him on his cell phone, but her call went straight into voice mail. Cell service was always spotty in this part of the state. Once everyone was gone, she decided to go to the hospital and see if she could find them. But just as she stepped out of the building and headed toward her car, Nick pulled up in his truck.

"How is she?" Shelby asked when she reached the car.

"She's going to be all right. Though she'll most likely lose feeling in the tip of her finger."

"I'm so sorry, Willow," Shelby said as she and Nick walked with her into the house.

Once Willow was placed comfortably in her bed so she could sleep off her pain medicine, Shelby followed Nick out of the room.

"Well, I guess I'd better go," Shelby said.

Nick rubbed the back of his neck. His face was flushed. "What happened out there?"

"She was sewing, Nick, and her finger got in the way of the needle. It can happen if you aren't careful."

"Oh, so it was her fault? Don't you watch what your students are doing? Kids can get hurt."

"I'm aware of that, but—"

"You can't leave them alone for a minute. You should know that. If you're going to work with children—"

"Nick, I—"

"I can't talk about it right now." He walked over and opened the door for her.

Words gathered in her throat, then dissolved with one swallow. "I'm sorry," she whispered as she walked past him.

Nick ran his fingers through his hair and slumped down on his couch. He didn't know why he reacted that way to Shelby. He knew it wasn't her fault. It was just seeing Willow in pain and feeling so helpless himself, he had to get mad at somebody, and she was the only one around.

That was a lame excuse, and he knew it. But it was also the truth. He was mad. Mad that his daughter was hurt, and he wanted to blame someone. Though he knew accidents happened and he knew Willow's negligence had brought it on, he could hardly blame her when she was in a world of pain already.

The more he thought about it, the more he realized there was more going on inside him than this. The situation brought to mind the thing that he wrestled with the most.

He couldn't always protect those whom he loved from pain.

Shelby stopped by the grocery store on the way home and spotted Reese.

"Hey, girl."

Reese turned around. "Hi, Shelby." They pushed their carts down the aisle together.

"You all right? You look a little upset."

Shelby forced a smile. "I'm fine. It's been a long day."

"How's the remodel coming along?"

"Going faster than I'd hoped."

"Griffen doing a nice job?" Reese asked.

Griffen and Reese had been good friends since high school. Where you saw one playing basketball, you saw the other. The two of them were well matched athletically.

"He's doing a great job. He'll be done in no time."

"Then you'll have to leave Nick's and move your school back to your place." Reese gave Shelby a sideways glance and lifted a teasing grin.

"Don't get me started."

They finished their shopping and walked out to the parking lot together.

"Wow, who's that?" Reese said.

Shelby looked up from digging for her car keys in her purse and followed Reese's gaze across the parking lot toward a man carrying two bags of groceries. He wore a baseball cap and a snug black T-shirt that revealed bulging biceps.

"Isn't that Griffen?" Shelby said.

"What? No." Reese leaned forward, squinting.

The man in question unloaded his bags into a truck, then walked around to the driver's side, clearly visible. Reese's mouth went slack, then she snapped it shut, looking away from her best buddy. Her face turned a pretty shade of pink.

Shelby felt a bubble of laughter building, but she pressed her lips together, smothering its release.

Reese pointed a finger at Shelby. "Not one word."

"Now you know how I feel," Shelby said. "I won't tease you if you won't tease me."

"Deal," Reese said.

They said good-bye, and by the time Shelby reached home, fatigue had swept over her. She could barely manage to drag herself into the house. Even Penelope's little happy dance at seeing her failed to lift her spirits. A heaviness weighed on Shelby's chest.

Willow would be fine, she knew that. But the anger on Nick's face . . . she had never seen that before. Not that way. And it was all directed at her. Dropping her keys and groceries on the counter, she went into the bedroom to change. She was too tired to eat dinner.

Putting on pink running pants and a matching pullover with ruffled cuffs on the sleeves, she headed to the kitchen to put away the groceries, make some tea, and then call it a night. Despite all the work they'd done on the invitations, she'd still need to address them and get them in the mail. But she could address them tomorrow and mail them on Monday. She had time.

Penelope barely had time to settle into her pajama bottoms and curl up on the sofa, and Shelby had just sat down next to her, cup of tea in hand, when the doorbell rang. Hope surged through her. Maybe Nick was coming to apologize—though Shelby wasn't at all sure he would leave Willow. Maybe Willow was up and feeling better. She walked downstairs to the door with Penelope following, doggy toenails clacking daintily against the hardwood floor.

With a renewed spirit, Shelby smiled and opened the door. One look at the visitor, and all life seemed to drain to her toes.

"Hi, Shelby. Aren't you going to invite me inside?"

Reluctantly she stepped aside. "Dad, what are you doing here?"

"Can't a man come see his daughter?"

"Well, of course. It's just so unexpected."

They never hugged, so she wasn't sure what to do. That's when she noticed he had something with him.

Luggage.

He followed her gaze. "I don't want to presume. If you can direct me to a hotel, I'll be happy to stay there."

"Don't be silly," she said. "I'd love to have you stay here—how long did you say?"

"I didn't. But it would just be a little while."

Little while. As in days, weeks, months? Years?

"What about that job you had lined up?"

"Oh, that. It didn't work out. They'd hired someone else before I got there. Guess they needed me a week earlier, and I didn't realize it."

"I'm sorry, Dad."

"Oh well. It's not as though I had to have it to survive."

Shelby led him upstairs and flipped on the lights in the guest room. "I just cleaned this room yesterday. It should work well for you."

"It looks nice, Shelby. Real nice." He rolled his luggage to the foot of the bed. "Don't want to be a bother, but do you have anything to eat? I'm starved."

This day just kept getting better.

*You see this, right, Lord?*

"No, Willow, you are not going." Nick stormed across the floor toward the kitchen. The door hinge squeaked, and he turned around.

Shelby stood in the doorway, embarrassed that she'd

caught them in a family moment. "I'm so sorry. I knocked and heard you say something. I assumed it was to tell me to come in."

"What do you need?" He didn't say that in an I-want-to-help-you kind of way. He said it in a hurry-up-I'm-busy sort of way.

"I just wanted to drop these off for Willow. She left them in class." Shelby walked over and handed Willow the tickets she had ordered.

"See what I mean? You can't even keep track of tickets. How can I expect you to be careful at a ski resort?" Nick turned on Shelby. "And that's another thing. Why in the world would you invite Willow on a ski trip? Can you guarantee to me that you will watch her 24/7?"

"I—" Shelby stuttered.

"Dad, I'm twelve years old!"

"She could fall and break a leg—"

"But I—"

"—hit a tree, get a concussion—"

"Nick, I—"

"—get kidnapped by some psycho weirdo person."

He *looked* like Nick Majors, but right at this moment, Shelby had her doubts. She stared at him.

"Well, can you guarantee none of those things will happen to my daughter?"

Shelby blew out a sigh. "No. But I—"

"Then she's not going. I won't have her well-being compromised."

"I'm not a baby. Stop treating me like one!" Willow stormed off to her bedroom and slammed the door behind her.

"I was trying to tell you, Nick. I merely suggested we should go sometime. We didn't set a definite date."

He paused as though to catch his breath. "I'm sorry, Shelby, but you need to talk to me about these things first. I'm trying to get a handle on things, but I need to think it through. I have to protect her at all costs."

She would not point out that his overprotective attitude could cost him a relationship with his daughter. She turned on her heels and left.

Nick was making her absolutely crazy. She wanted to help Willow, but she wasn't sure how to go about it. All this time she thought she'd known Nick, but obviously the good-friend role was far different from the father thing. Shelby was quickly losing faith in the family unit.

Once she got home, she shoved the front door closed behind her, allowing a gust of cold air to swish through the entryway and blow a grocery list off the hallway stand. The grocery list she had forgotten to take with her so they could eat tonight.

"Welcome home." Her dad stood in the hallway, holding a glass of iced tea in his hand. "What did you have in mind for dinner?"

"I need to get changed," she said. "It's been a long day."

He shrugged and walked back into the living room. Shelby watched him and felt a tinge of regret for her biting tone, but she was entitled to a bad day, wasn't she? Besides, since when was she responsible for his dinner? She hadn't expected him to come to her home. And aside from that, he still hadn't told her what he was doing there. How long was he planning to stay anyway? If history had told her anything, she didn't need to worry that he would stay there forever. He never stayed anywhere longer than a couple of months. But the very idea of a couple of months made her skin prickly.

Shelby walked into her room, closed the door, leaned against it, and shut her eyes. Maybe if she stayed there, this whole mess would go away.

# CHAPTER NINE

· · · · · · · · · · · · · · · · · · · · · · · · · ·

$\mathcal{N}$ick sat on the edge of his bed. What on earth had gotten into him lately? Yes, he was worried about protecting Willow at all costs, and that needle incident brought all his fears to light. But it was more than that. Much more.

Shelby.

Something about her lately had changed. Or maybe he had changed the way he looked at her. They'd always teased one another, but he'd never thought of her as anything more than a friend. Yes, he'd noticed her beauty, but he always considered her far beyond his reach. And no doubt she was. Still, Friday night when they'd listened to the Garner Sisters, he and Shelby had connected in a fresh way. Something in her smile, her sweet voice, the way she interacted with others. He didn't want to be her "friend" anymore.

And that irritated the daylights out of him.

Not only was he not good enough for the likes of Shelby, who no doubt had never done a wrong thing in her entire life, but she would never give a second glance at him had they not developed a friendship. If she knew his thoughts were running amok this way, she would most likely cut all ties with him. He had to stop.

Maybe it was because Willow had moved into his house. It made him look beyond his bachelor existence. He was a family man now. And didn't a family need a woman in the house? Not that that was the only reason he was noticing Shelby. No, no. It was much more than that. The silky feel of her hair between his fingers when he pulled a pine needle from it . . . the curve of her soft neck . . . the way the stars sparkled in her eyes.

Why would she ever give him a second glance? He rubbed the stubble on his chin. Why indeed?

"You, my man, need to talk to her," he said aloud. "With any luck, an apology—again—will keep you in her good graces. Though if you keep blowing it, she may count you out altogether." He stood up and started to leave the room, then looked back at his reflection in the dresser mirror. He shook his index finger at it. "And another thing—stop acting like a lovesick teenager."

"Who are you talking to, Dad?" Willow asked when he walked into the living room.

"Myself. It's what old people do."

"You're scaring me."

"Sometimes I scare myself." He put his hands on Willow's shoulders. "Listen, about the whole skiing thing—I'm sorry I came down so hard on you."

"You're going to have to get used to me growing up."

He sighed. "I know. I'll work on it, okay?"

"Okay."

He smiled and gave her a hug. Being a dad had its rewards. "Would you be all right if I drove into town for a little bit?"

"Going to see Shelby?" She grinned.

"Well, I just wanted to see how the repairs were coming, since I haven't helped Griffen for a few days."

He could tell by the look on Willow's face she wasn't buying it, but he ignored her.

"I'll take my cell phone. You can call if you need me."

"I'll be fine."

"Yes, I believe you will." He put on a jacket, kissed her good-bye, and closed the door behind him. When he pulled up to Shelby's driveway, he saw the strange car and remembered that her dad was there. He smacked his palm to his forehead. All this way for nothing. He started to pull out when he saw Shelby looking through the lacy sheers at the window.

No turning back now. He cut the engine and got out of the truck. The front door opened as he climbed the steps onto the porch.

"Hey, Nick."

At least she was still talking to him. That gave him a bit of hope. "I, uh, was passing through and thought I'd stop and see how the repairs were coming along."

"They're coming along fine," she said, full suspicion in her voice. "Dad's asleep in the downstairs living room right now, and I hate to wake him. Can I show you later?"

"Oh yeah, sure, no problem."

"I was just headed out the door to go for a walk in town. Want to go?"

"Sure. I'll drive."

They slipped into the truck and Nick drove to town, maneuvered the truck up to the curb, and turned off the engine. He looked at her. "Listen, Shelby, I don't know what's gotten into me lately. And it seems like I'm taking everything out on you. I'm sorry."

Shelby smiled. "We've both been under pressure."

They got out of the truck and strolled along the lamplit sidewalk. A few townsfolk were out and about.

He wanted to say more, but one look at Shelby and all words scattered from his brain.

"The moon is beautiful tonight," she said, gazing up at the sky.

"It sure is." They took a few steps in silence. "So are you ready for your big night?"

"I think we're fairly set to go. Of course, next week will be the busiest."

"Yeah. Will your dad be here for that?"

Shelby turned a surprised glance his way. "I don't think he'll still be here. My goodness, I hope not. I have enough on my plate without worrying about him."

"Oh, sorry. I just thought since the other dads would be escorting their daughters, and your dad is in town, and you're the teacher—"

"I don't think so."

"Uh-oh. Things not going well?"

"Let's just say we have a history, as I think I've told you. Not the greatest daughter-dad relationship around. That's why, I suppose, I was a little too anxious to help you."

"Are you trying to patch things up with him?"

"We just have to kind of go from here, you know?"

"You mean, forget the past and forge ahead?"

"Something like that. Can we talk about something else?"

"Sorry. Didn't mean to pry."

They settled on a wooden bench at the edge of the walk. A tub of mums rested beneath the lamplight just ahead of them.

"I know I overreacted on that ski deal. It's just that this parent thing is so scary." He looked at his big calloused hands. "What if something happens to her? What if I do it all wrong?"

Shelby touched his arm. "Nick, no one is perfect. Remember, all parents make mistakes. You have to give yourself some grace."

He shrugged. After a long pause he said, "Anyway, I'm sorry I've been so hard on you."

"All is forgiven." She smiled.

They talked awhile longer and then headed back to the truck. Nick reached over to open her door, and their gazes locked. Moonbeams danced in her eyes. "You look beautiful tonight." His breath caught in his throat, but the way she looked up at him gave him courage.

Without so much as a wisp of another breath, Nick gently pulled her to him, then leaned down and pressed his lips against hers. Her mouth was as sweet and intoxicating as he had imagined it would be. Reluctantly he let her go. Neither said much on the ride home, but Nick's heart told him plenty. His heart had moved to a place it had never been before—at least not in a very long time.

Tonight, something different definitely stirred deep within him toward Shelby . . . and it wasn't friendship.

The following week Shelby was so busy finalizing the details for the tea, she didn't have time to sort out her feelings about the kiss with Nick and all it entailed. He'd been busy at the tree farm, so they'd merely passed one another from time to time, which was a good thing for right now. Good for both of them to think things through.

People scurried around the room, setting tables, hanging

tulle, placing centerpieces and candlesticks. Shelby could hardly believe the class was over and this was the grand finale. The time had passed so quickly.

Once the final touches were in place, she rushed home to dress for the occasion in a long, elegant black dress. She pulled her hair up into a fashionable twist, fastened pearl earrings and necklace in place, stepped into her fragile heels, and hurried back to Nick's place.

The room was fragrant with the scent of tasty desserts. Candlelight flickered about, casting shadows in the room.

"We just lit those," Rose said proudly as Shelby greeted her.

Natalie appeared in a beautiful wine-colored floor-length dress and sparkling jewelry. She carried a tray of desserts. "Gluten-free brownies that are guaranteed to be the hit of the tea," she announced with pride.

"I wouldn't doubt it for a moment," Shelby said, relieving her friend from the load and taking them to the food table.

There was a hum of car engines and the crunch of tires on gravel, and people spilled out of their automobiles and entered the building. It seemed most of Smitten was present, dressed in elegant evening wear and fine-tailored suits. The students looked the loveliest of all, fine young ladies scrubbed to perfection and glowing with their first dashes of makeup.

When it was time to start, Shelby took her place at the microphone. Everyone found a seat, and at Rose's nod the Garner Sisters began to play chamber music. Shelby introduced each student, with her father as her escort, and two by two they filed across the front of the room, glittering, smiling, and delivering postures and entrances above reproach.

Finally, just as Shelby wondered if Willow and Nick were coming, they walked through the doorway. Her lungs seemed to hold her air captive, and she hesitated long enough for the audience to notice. Nick stood there in a black suit, hair cut in the latest style, and . . . clean-shaven. Not a hair on his face anywhere. Shelby thought she would melt into a puddle at his feet.

When she paused, he held her gaze, obviously wondering why she was taking so long to introduce them. Somehow she managed to get the girls and their escorts introduced and gave words of praise for the girls' hard work. Just as she was about to tell everyone the fine music would continue during the meal, Rose walked over and whispered to her to go stand by the door.

"Ladies and gentlemen," Rose said, "Miss Evans didn't know she too would have an escort this evening, but he has arrived. I would like to introduce you to Miss Shelby Evans and her handsome escort, her father, Mark Evans."

Shelby's breath caught as the door opened and her dad stepped into view, dressed in a suit and tie and looking the handsomest she had ever seen him in her entire life. The audience clapped as he held out his arm and she slipped her gloved hand into it. All her life she had dreamed of her dad showing up for a school play, a ball game, a choir program, but he never came. Finally she had quit dreaming.

Hot tears stung her eyes. She swallowed hard to keep her emotions in check. This was the girls' night, and she would not take anything away from them.

But there was no denying that tonight she felt like a true princess. Her dad stepped up beside Willow, leaving Shelby standing between him and Nick. And at that very moment she realized it; they were the two men she loved most in all the world.

"Are you sure you're warm enough?" Nick asked as they sat on a bench in his yard following the tea.

"I'm sure."

"We can go back into the warm building, or my house, if you want."

"I'm fine, really."

He put his arm around her and held her close. "Do you mind?"

She shook her head and smiled. "Nick, I love the look." She tickled his chin.

"I did it for you, you know."

Her pulse quickened as his lips met hers once, then again, and again.

"All this time, how did I not see it?" He grinned. "You, me, us."

She laughed. "I didn't see it either. But you were and are a great friend."

"I'll never be happy with just that anymore." Like soft whispers, he placed light kisses on the side of her face. He reached up and pulled a pin from her hair. "You looked beautiful tonight, but you never look more beautiful"—he slipped out another pin—"than when"—then another—"your hair is down." And another.

Her skin tingled at his touch as her hair fell softly around her shoulders. Her hand reached up to straighten it, and he caught it in his own.

"Let me," he said.

He lifted her hair between his fingers and worked his way through it, tucking here, lingering there.

Her heart drummed hard against her chest. Nick bent over and kissed her with an intensity that seemed to grow stronger with every second that ticked by. His lips tasted salty, his muscles strong and taut beneath her hands. She reveled in the tingle of his breath against her face, until she finally forced herself to pull away.

"I'm sorry, I don't know what came over me," he said.

She stood. "Let's walk."

He joined her. "Were you surprised when your dad showed up?"

"That is an understatement." She worked to relax her breathing, to shove aside the moments they had just shared—moments she knew she would relive a hundred times before sleep would overtake her tonight.

He laughed. "I could see it on your face."

"You don't know our story. Maybe it's time I told you."

As they walked beneath the starry sky, wandering through the maze of fir trees, she shared her story of the forbidden passion as a teenager, the pregnancy, and the abortion.

Nick stopped in his tracks. "You had an abortion?"

"Well, not by choice." She started to walk again, but Nick didn't move an inch.

"Doesn't everyone have a choice?"

She turned back around. "I didn't. Not if I wanted a place to live and eat. Dad would have thrown me out."

"I just don't understand how you could do that."

"It wasn't what I wanted to do, don't you get that? A piece of me died that day too. Thoughts of my baby haunt me every day. But when I met Jesus—"

"Shelby, I know that had to be hard for you. I'm sorry for what you endured. But . . . I need time to think this through. I thought things were different—you were different. After all this time—"

"But, Nick, you don't understand."

"No, no, I get it. I do." He ran his hand through his hair. "I just need time to digest it, okay?"

Tears scalded her eyes. The burning in her heart radiated through her chest, making her feel weak, vulnerable, lonely, unworthy . . . and unfairly judged.

"*You* need time to digest it? Who do you think you are, Nick? *For all have sinned and fall short of the glory of God.* Did you know that? *All.* You can judge me all you want, but I've been forgiven by the One who matters." Tears ran down her cheeks, and she flipped them away. "How could I have been so wrong about you?"

The judgment seemed to leave his eyes, but it was too late. He'd made his feelings clear.

With a heavy heart, Shelby turned and walked back to her car.

# CHAPTER TEN

. . . . . . . . . . . . . . . . . . . . . . . . . . . .

$\mathcal{S}$helby eased out of bed the next morning, careful not to jar her aching head. Inching her way into the bathroom, she pulled out some pain relievers, grabbed a nearby cup, and washed the pills down with water. She had hardly slept all night.

This was Nick's fault.

Pots and pans rattled in the kitchen, alerting her that her dad was already up. She glanced at her alarm clock. Ten o'clock. She couldn't remember when she had slept in that late before.

She hurried—as much as her headache would allow—through a shower and got dressed. She shoved thoughts of Nick aside and reveled instead in her dad's appearance at the tea and how wonderful it had been to have him by her side. His gesture last night gave her hope that maybe one day they could have a real father-daughter relationship.

Once she was dressed, she paused for prayer. Her heart ached beyond belief, knowing that Nick judged her so harshly without understanding her pain in those days. She wasn't proud of her past, but there wasn't anything she could do to change it now. Maybe she should have run away those years ago, defied her father, kept the baby. But where would she have gone? How could she have supported a child with no job, no money, no home? She hadn't seen a way out. She had been at her father's mercy.

Thankfully, she served a merciful heavenly Father who loved her still. If only she had known him back in those days. She wouldn't have gotten herself into such an awful mess.

Once she talked it over with the Lord, she got up from her knees, took a deep breath, and walked out to meet her dad.

There were two plates set on the table, along with platters laden with eggs, bacon, toast, and biscuits and gravy.

Shelby blinked in disbelief. "Dad, what's all this?"

"Where I come from, they call it breakfast," he said with a smile. "Care to join me?"

They sat down together. Her dad folded his hands, bowed his head, and prayed over the meal while Shelby sat absolutely dumbfounded. Never in her life had she heard her dad pray. When the prayer was over, he looked up at her and winked, flipped his napkin on his lap, and filled his plate.

They had small talk over their meal, and then her dad reached over and touched her hand. "Shelby, can we go into the living room? I'd like to talk to you."

She had no idea what was coming, but one thing was certain: he was full of surprises this morning. When did her dad start praying? Was he a believer now, or was it more of a nice gesture that people did at mealtime?

They settled onto the sofa, and her father turned to her. Cupping her hand into his, he looked straight into her eyes without a blink.

"I was wrong. Those many years ago. So wrong. I made you get rid of my only grandchild." Tears filled his eyes, and he shook his head, breaking eye contact as he squeezed them shut and let the tears spill down his face. "How could I have put you through that?"

A hairline crack seemed to break through the wall of Shelby's hardened heart, gaining momentum as the sincerity of her dad's confession enveloped and healed her brokenness.

"I'm so, so sorry, Shelby. Please forgive me." He pulled his hand away and grabbed a handkerchief from his pocket to wipe his nose. "I've been the worst father ever, but I want to change that, if you'll let me."

Shelby hadn't said a word the entire time. None came to mind. Not a single one.

"I was so intent on doing what I wanted when you were young, I missed out on everything. And your mother . . ." More tears. "What I put that woman through, moving all the time, my selfishness . . ."

This time Shelby reached out to him and grabbed his hand. "That's in the past, Dad. Mom loved you, and she didn't mind moving. She told me so more than once."

"She did?"

Shelby nodded.

"I found the Lord, Shelby. He has changed my heart, and if you'll let me, I want to try again."

They hugged one another. "Oh, Dad, I've missed you. I've always wanted you around."

"You know why I stayed away?" he asked.

She nodded, blotting her own face with a nearby tissue. "I shamed you. I know you couldn't bear the sight of me."

"What? Oh my, no, Shelby. No!" He pulled her into his arms. "I was ashamed of myself. Of what I had made you do with that precious baby. Each time I looked at you, I felt the pain of what I'd done."

Shelby lingered in the warmth of her father's arms,

allowing the healing balm of his touch and his words to flow through her.

Her dad pulled back and looked into her eyes. "When I saw you with those young ladies, how they looked up to you, how you nurtured them, I realized you would have been a wonderful mother. And I believe you will be, someday. God willing." He hesitated and then said with a raised brow, "Maybe sooner than you think."

"Shelby, Willow's run away." Nick's voice cracked over the phone.

The panic in his voice frightened her. "Where are you?"

"I'm at home."

"I'll be right there." They'd had their falling out only last night, but it seemed a lifetime ago. Shelby hung up the phone and ran to the closet to grab her jacket.

"What's wrong?" her dad asked.

"Willow's gone. Nick doesn't know where she is."

"Uh-oh. What can I do to help?"

"Maybe ask around if anyone has seen her. I don't know. I'm going to Nick's right now."

She exceeded every speed limit on her way to the tree farm. No sooner had Shelby pulled her car into the driveway than Nick rushed out to meet her. He pulled her into his arms. "I've made such a mess of this."

"It'll be all right, Nick. She couldn't have gone far. Why don't you tell me what happened?"

He pulled away, and they walked toward the house as he

filled her in. "Before we went to bed last night, she said she knew there was something wrong between us. She told me I was stupid if I let you go."

Shelby looked down at her hands.

"I told her she was a little girl and didn't understand things, and it sort of escalated from there. Angry words about losing her mother, her home, how nothing ever turned out right. All that."

"Do you think she could be in the woods?"

"I don't think so. She knows how dangerous it can be to get lost in the woods. The police are sending out officers to look for her. Usually they wait for a person to be gone twenty-four hours, but since I know the chief, they agreed to do this for me." He looked at her. "I really blew it."

"No time for regrets," Shelby said, suddenly finding a strength she didn't know she possessed. "Let's make a plan."

Before they could decide what to do, two police cars pulled up, followed by other cars belonging to Nick's friends.

"Shelby's dad spread the word around town. We want to help," Griffen said.

The woods quickly filled with friends and officers searching for Willow. Shelby stayed at Nick's house in case she showed up or they received any calls, but the morning melted away without any word.

The front door opened, and she looked up to see the anguish on Nick's face when he and some of the others returned without Willow. He sagged onto the sofa and covered his face with his hands.

The phone rang then, and Shelby answered it.

"Yes? . . . Uh-huh . . . Okay, we'll be right there." She

hung up the phone and smiled at Nick. "They found her. She's at the church."

Cheers went up around the room, and everyone quickly dispersed. When Nick and Shelby reached the church, Willow ran into her dad's embrace.

Nick stooped down to look her in the eyes. "Where have you been, honey? I've been so worried."

"I got up this morning and walked to the church."

"You walked all the way here?"

She nodded. "You said some things only God could fix. So I came here to talk to him."

Nick's jaw dropped.

"Pastor told me I could talk to God anywhere. I knew that, but I figured I'd really get his attention if I was at his house," Willow said.

Shelby's heart squeezed at the faith of Nick's precious daughter.

When the pastor took Willow into his office to give her a Bible, her very first one, Nick turned to Shelby. "Can you ever forgive my judgmental, hardheaded, self-righteous, stubborn attitude?"

His penitent tone touched her more than she wanted to admit. She looked up at him. "I won't lie to you. Your reaction cut deeply." The pain in his eyes seemed genuine, but could she trust him?

"I had no right. I reacted, like you said. I've always wanted a boatload of kids, and the thought of—well, as I said, I had no right. You were right, we all sin. That's where God's grace comes in. There is nothing he won't forgive, and I ought to know. I have my own shameful past. Thank God when we ask for forgiveness, he gives us a clean slate. Can you ever forgive me?" His eyes were pleading, his expression sincere and longing, his face—still clean of stubble.

Forgiveness. She'd extended it to her father. How could she not give it to the man she loved? "Of course I forgive you," she whispered.

"I have a clean slate?"

"A clean slate," she said.

Nick's relief was visible on his face, and he pulled her to him. "I love you so much."

Shelby closed her eyes and let the words wash over her as naturally as if they'd said them to one another every day. She opened her eyes and stared into his handsome, clean-shaven face. "I love you too."

His heart seemed to smile through his eyes. "I've been wanting to hear that for weeks."

Shelby nestled against his broad chest and inhaled the clean aroma of a man. Her man.

The pastor cleared his throat as he and Willow walked into the room.

Nick and Shelby smiled and pulled apart. Willow's eyes widened at the sight of them together, and she rushed over between them. They huddled into a group hug. Shelby held Willow tight, and she wondered if this was how it felt to be a real mother. Maybe one day she would know.

Nick looked from Willow to Shelby. "Let's go home."

Shelby wasn't yet sure what "home" would mean for all of them. But for now, being with the man she loved and the daughter for whom she'd always longed was enough.

# Reese: All Along

## Denise Hunter

# CHAPTER ONE

· · · · · · · · · · · · · · · · · · · · · · · · · ·

*R*eese Mackenzie swept her hand over the old wall as if she could perceive the secrets beneath it. Regardless of what the ugly wallpaper hid, in two months she'd be living her dream.

"You should definitely take the walls down," Griffen Parker said. He closed the space between them and knocked on the drywall. "Bet there's brick under there."

Reese met his clear blue eyes. A dark lock of hair fell over his forehead and battled with his eyelashes.

"I'd planned on painting. You never know what's behind these old walls. The only way to find out is to knock them down, and once you do that, there's no turning back."

"Can't be worse than this," he said, running his hand over the Pepto-Bismol wallpaper. "Besides, it'll take forever to remove this stuff."

He was right about that, but she hated changing boats midstream. "I'll think about it."

She couldn't believe the Palmer Building was all hers now. Well, hers and the bank's. There was so much work to do, and so many unknowns. She'd been planning this forever, but that didn't stop the worry from jangling on her nerves.

Reese crossed the open space, her Merrell boots barely making a sound on the wooden planks. "You don't see a problem structurally with opening up the second floor?"

He pocketed his hands in his vest coat. "Nope. The bones are solid."

Reese glanced around the space, her imagination kicking in. "I want lots of cubbies and shelving."

"Of course you do."

"A place for everything."

"I expected no less."

It was going to take a lot of time. She hoped it wouldn't put Griffen in a bind with his other clients. She knew he'd do anything for her, but she'd never take advantage of their friendship.

She studied his face. He'd changed since he left Smitten three years earlier. His hair was longer, dangling over his forehead and curling up on the ends. And he always seemed to be sporting a five o'clock shadow. Probably didn't have time to shave, with all his projects.

"You sure you have time for all this—you'd tell me if you didn't, right?"

He cocked a grin. "Always have time for my favorite girl. I'll finish the town's gazebo tomorrow, and I figured this project would be my last. I'm all yours for the next two months."

"Only if you're absolutely, positively sure . . ."

"You want it in blood?"

She shot him a look, then returned to her perusal of her very own building. "That would leave me a week to arrange the merchandise before the wedding. I'll be ready in plenty of time to assist the wedding guests with all their recreational needs."

She'd already ordered everything from ski poles to canoes. Opened boxes filled her spare rooms, and a variety of boats

and bikes had usurped her car's spot in the garage. Each ship-
ment filled her with excitement . . . and worry. What if this
whole plan was one massive failure? *Please, God. You know we're
trying to step out on faith here, right?*

"Obviously, you'll need new plumbing. And the heating
system is archaic."

"Just write it up and give me a ballpark figure." She nailed
him with a look. "And be fair. I'm not a charity case."

He tipped a grin her way. "Speaking of ballpark, I've been
home for almost eight months, and you haven't even been over
to shoot hoops yet. What's up with that? What d'ya say—have
time for some one-on-one?" He put up an invisible shot. "My
place came with a court, you know."

He was renting the old Halverson place, which had been
on the market since the mill closed.

"In case you haven't noticed, it's winter. Besides, I'm having coffee with the girls in an hour, and I was going to browse
a new sporting goods catalog."

"New plan." He nudged her. "Come on, it's almost forty,
and the ground's clear. We have almost an hour of daylight,
and you've been stuck behind a desk all day."

"Not anymore," she fairly sang. Today had been her last
day as the receptionist for Smitten Accounting. Her col-
leagues had ordered some chocolate heaven from Piece of
Cake to celebrate her new start.

He pulled her toward the door. "You can catch me up on
the scuttlebutt on the way."

She flipped off the lights on her way out and pulled the
old door with its wavy paneled glass. The wreath bounced
against the door as it hit the jamb.

"Here's the scuttlebutt," she said, donning her Thinsulate gloves. "Natalie's practically engaged, Julia's planning her wedding, Shelby and Nick are glued at the hip, and I've become the resident town spinster."

Griffen chuckled and ruffled her hair. "Aw, poor little Reese Cup. Feeling left out of the lovers' loop?"

She took her knit cap from her pocket and pulled it on, sighing. "Nah, I'm happy for them."

Reese would've been the first married if things had been different. Her whole life would be different if she and Sawyer had worked out. *Reese Smitten*. So it didn't exactly roll off the tongue. Didn't matter now anyway. He was set to marry a Hollywood beauty and save the town of Smitten in one fell swoop.

They crossed the brick street, dodging the diagonally parked cars in front of Smitten Hardware. The town was decked out for Christmas. Garlands spiraled up streetlamps and swagged across storefronts. Window boxes of poinsettias decked the buildings, and sparkling new ornaments dangled from the newly planted pine trees in the town square.

This would all be gone by Sawyer's wedding. The multicolored lights would be replaced with twinkling white ones, and the poinsettias would be traded in for artificial sprays of white peonies or something. What would it be like, seeing Sawyer again, with someone else? Marrying someone else?

"Whatever happened with you and Sawyer after I left? You never said."

"How do you do that?"

"What?"

"Read my mind."

He shrugged and turned a crooked grin on her, exhaling a puff of fog between them. His nose was already pink.

Ahead of them, a couple turned into Natalie's shop. Reese and Griffen continued to the corner and turned up Maple, heading toward his place. She hadn't forgotten his question, and he knew her well enough to know she'd get back to it eventually.

She and Sawyer . . . it seemed like a lifetime ago.

She shrugged, picking up their conversation. "Once he won *Country's Best*, everything changed, you know? He was offered a recording contract. He could hardly turn it down." Realizing she was still making excuses for him, she sighed. It didn't help that his new fiancée, with her blond hair and greenish eyes, looked a lot like his old one. Well. The shorter, less glamorous version.

"And you couldn't leave your mom."

"I was all she had." The Parkinson's had already taken her mom's mobility by then. It had been the hardest thing she'd ever experienced, watching her mom waste away.

"I'm sorry I wasn't here when she passed. You don't know how much I regret that."

"It's okay. I had the girls. I was just worried when I couldn't reach you."

Griffen had been on a Habitat for Humanity project somewhere in Mexico, and she hadn't located him until after the funeral.

"I'm sorry." He looked miserable.

"Bygones," she said, their favorite word from their high school days.

That earned her a smile.

They turned up his gravel lane and walked toward the two-story structure he'd rented.

"That thing's big enough for a family of ten."

"It was available—and cheap. Besides, I always liked the old place. Who knows, maybe I'll buy it someday."

"You planning on ten kids?"

"Maybe."

"Might want to start with a wife."

"I plan on it." He tossed her a grin, and Reese felt a jolt at the thought of Griffen with a wife. She'd been his for so long—okay, not *his*, but still. A wife wouldn't appreciate another woman in his life, even if they were just best buddies.

She recalled the day last fall when she'd noticed him across the grocery store parking lot. The attraction she'd felt before she'd recognized him, the comment she'd made to Shelby. Even now, her face went ten degrees hotter. She glanced at Griffen, hoping he'd attribute the flush of her cheeks to the cold.

He slipped inside the detached garage and flipped a switch. The light by the door flickered on with a buzz. She set down her purse and checked out the court, a concrete slab with a wooden pole and a backboard that had seen better days. At least the net was still there.

Griffen exited the building, dribbling the basketball toward the court. "Gotta warn you. I've been practicing."

Reese pulled off her gloves and rubbed her hands together. She bent her knees in a defensive position as he approached. "I'm so scared."

"You should be." He darted around her, but she blocked his path, waving her arms.

"You're still fast."

"May be a spinster, but I'm an active—"

He sidestepped and made an easy layup. *Swish.*

He jumped around her and grabbed the ball, swaggering back. "Like I said. Should I take it down a notch for you?"

He threw the ball, and she caught it at her chest, leveling him with a look as she dribbled the ball out. "You're gonna be the one begging for mercy, pal."

"Bring it on, sister."

Thirty minutes later their coats were discarded in a heap, they were fogging up the court, and they were tied at sixteen. What Reese lacked in size, she made up for in accuracy and speed.

She put a guard on Griffen all the way to the basket. He put up a shot that banked off the board and bounced on the rim before going in.

"'Bout time," she said. He'd missed his last three.

He gave her ponytail a tug. "Still up by one, Reese Cup."

She dribbled the ball out, then back toward him. "Not for long."

He crouched as she approached, his eyes on hers. She was going to dart around him and go in for an easy layup.

He swatted at the ball, and she dribbled it through her legs, catching it with her other hand.

"Nice move."

He swatted again, this time getting the prize.

She growled as he checked the ball out, then got between him and the basket before he could move in for an easy layup. She had to force the jump shot, his weakness. She pressed in, squeezing. He couldn't get around her—she was too fast. Smallness had its advantages.

He faked left, but she was there. He faked right. She

chuckled. He spun and darted forward. She was fast, right there in front of him, but he didn't anticipate that.

His body plunged into hers as he went in for the layup. She was falling backward. He caught her around the waist, pulling her toward him. His feet tangled with hers. She grabbed onto his shirt.

But it was too late. They were both going down.

Reese hit the ground hard. Griffen landed on her, and her breath left in one sudden expulsion. "Umph."

She felt the fall a full second later.

"Reese!" Griffen slid off to the side.

The sky overhead was darkening. The skeletal branch of an oak tree jutted across the blue canvas.

"Are you okay?" Griffen asked. "Reese?"

"Give me a minute." At least she hadn't hit her head. Had she? Her backside killed. Her shoulder blade hurt. Nothing too bad, she didn't think.

Assessing her injuries, she became aware of Griffen's body, still pressed against her side. A strange sensation moved through her limbs, winging its way to her stomach, where a ribbon of warmth unfurled. Her heart thudded heavily in her chest.

What the—

"Reese, talk to me. Did you hit your head?" He propped his weight on his elbow and brushed a loose strand of hair from her face.

The sensation sent a shiver down her spine, and she realized with dismay that she wanted him to touch her again.

"I'm fine," she croaked.

So. Not. Fine. She met his eyes, dazed, confused, but not by the fall.

His brows furrowed. "What hurts?"

She closed her eyes before he could read what was there. Better he think her hurt than crazy. And it was crazy. This was Griffen, for pity's sake.

He turned her face toward him. "Reese."

She brushed his hand away. "Quit. I'm fine." She needed to leave, needed to ice her head whether she'd hit it or not.

"Maybe you should lie—"

"I said I'm fine!" She pushed at him, and he rolled away, standing.

He held out his hand, but she ignored it. No more touching. Not until she checked into the psych ward. Man, she was such a freak. This was *Griffen*. She rose gingerly to her feet, brushed the gravel bits from her palms.

"I'm sorry, Reese. Did you hit your head? Come inside, we'll ice it."

She checked her watch. "I have to go."

He took her elbow. "You're hurt."

She pulled away, glaring.

He backed off, his eyes widening. "I'm sorry. I shouldn't have been so aggressive."

She sighed and waved him off, then went to gather her coat and purse. Twilight had closed in and a cacophony of night sounds had begun. Or maybe that was in her head.

"Reese . . ." She heard the worry in his voice, and some part of her reacted to that.

She turned, walking backward. "It's okay. I'm fine." Now that she was putting space between them. She held out her arms, exhibit A. "See?"

The furrowed brow remained.

Reese offered what she hoped was a normal smile. "See you Monday."

Griffen watched Reese walk away until she faded into the darkness of Maple Street. He picked up the basketball and slammed it into the cement, stopping the ball when it rebounded.

Idiot! Why'd he have to take the stupid game so seriously? He never should've charged into her like that. Now she was mad and probably hurt too.

He walked to the garage, tossed the ball inside, and flipped off the light. Darkness followed him as he retrieved his coat and entered his house through the side entrance. He closed the door and leaned against it. His heart was still racing, whether from the game, the fall, or what came after, who knew?

His mind zipped through the conversations they'd had earlier. The renovation project, her spinster comment . . . He wondered again if she still had feelings for Sawyer. His attempt to draw her out had been pointless. She'd changed the subject pretty quick.

He hoped Reese wasn't hurt. She was a tough girl, always had been. He'd seen her play through a sprained wrist and even the flu once when the regional championship was at stake.

What if she'd hit her head? She'd had a dazed look in her eyes as she'd stared back at him. Great. She might have a concussion, and he'd just let her walk back to town alone.

He banged his head on the door behind him. Once, twice, three times. He'd give her a few minutes to get to the coffee shop, then he'd text her and make sure she'd arrived safely.

He'd thought he was so good, playing ball with her like the old days, teasing her, taunting her. Then he'd trampled all over her like a big clumsy oaf. If he kept that up, she'd never figure it out.

Yeah, that's what he should do. Knock her down and bruise her up every time he saw her. Then she'd never guess the truth: that he'd fallen madly, crazily, and irrevocably in love with his best friend.

# CHAPTER TWO

. . . . . . . . . . . . . . . . . . . . . . . . . . . . .

*R*eese pulled her cinnamon latte closer and wrapped her hand around the mug's warmth. The heat stung her scraped palm. She couldn't get her mind off Griffen and those strange feelings that had coursed through her. It made her feel . . . guilty. He was her buddy, for pity's sake. It was so wrong.

"So the reason I asked you all here . . ." Natalie was saying. Her dark eyes twinkled with excitement. She pulled her hand from under her leg and waggled her fingers in the air.

A bright diamond glittered under the coffee shop lights.

"You're engaged!" Shelby slipped her long, elegant arms around Natalie.

"Congratulations!" Reese squeezed her hand.

Julia's dimples deepened. "About time." She pulled Natalie's hand closer and peered at the substantial diamond. "But worth the wait."

"He asked me last night. He took me to Michael's on the Hill, near Stowe, for dinner. He'd asked the chef to make a gluten-free dessert, and when it came the ring was on top, tucked in a little whipped cream cloud. He said—get this—that he couldn't imagine his forever without me in it."

Shelby sighed. "That's so romantic."

Natalie patted Shelby's hand. "You're next. I can just feel it."

The girls ramped up a conversation on wedding dates and venues.

Ten minutes later, they were listing the pros and cons of a summer wedding when Reese heard a text come in. She pulled her phone from its pocket and glanced at the screen.

Griffen. Her heart kicked her rib cage as she opened the phone.

*Are you sure you're okay? I really am sorry.*

She pondered her response. She'd just text a quick *I'm fine* and get back to the girls. Somehow, though, she couldn't make her fingers move. The words blurred on the screen as she relived the fall in slow motion.

She could hardly remember how it happened. Their feet had tangled up or something, and he'd reached for her. He'd pulled her smack against his body before gravity pulled them both down. And then he was on top of her, pressed against the length of her, all warm and . . . solid.

She did not just shiver.

She glanced around the table, suddenly worried the girls would see her every thought scrawled across her face.

They were staring at her. She realized someone had just said her name.

"What?" she asked, her eyes bouncing from Julia to Shelby and back to Natalie, who cocked a brow. *"What?"*

"Sheesh," Julia said. "What's got you so uptight?"

"Are you okay, honey?" Shelby asked.

"I'm fine." Good grief, how many times would she say that tonight? She sent off the text, then closed her phone and tossed it into the cavity of her bag.

"Did you see that?" Natalie asked.

"Yep," Julia said.

"Something's wrong," Natalie said. "You just tossed your phone in your purse."

"Without regard for its proper place," Shelby added.

"Nothing's wrong." Reese frowned at the girls. "This is Natalie's night. And besides . . ." One more time. "I'm *fine*."

"She's got that look in her eyes." Julia took a sip of tea.

"I see it too." Natalie put her bling away. "What happened?"

Couldn't she even have one little moment of stupid without the girls finding out?

Shelby smiled knowingly. "It's a man."

"Definitely a man," Julia said.

"It's not a man." She lowered her voice. "It's Griffen."

"Uh, Griffen is a man," Julia said. "In case you haven't noticed."

She had noticed. Boy, had she noticed. Reese shook her head as if she could shake away the unbuddy-like thought.

"What happened, honey?" Shelby asked. "Was his quote too high?"

"This isn't about a quote." Natalie leaned in. "Look, she's blushing. Tell all, and quick before Zoe needs my help."

"There's nothing to tell. It was silly."

"*What* was silly?" Julia asked.

They were like a dog with a bone. Might as well get it over with. They'd never leave it alone.

"It was nothing—just something strange that happened before I got here. Griffen and I were playing ball, and our feet got tangled up. We fell. He kinda landed on top of me, and we were lying there and—I don't know. It was just . . . weird."

"Weird . . ." Julia hiked a brow. "Or good?"

Reese frowned. "Weird. And good. It was weird *because* it was good."

Natalie's dark eyes twinkled. "I knew it! I knew this would happen."

Reese folded her arms. "Knew what would happen?"

"Men and women can't be just friends." Natalie punctuated the thought with a nod of certainty.

"I beg your pardon. Griff and I have been friends most of our lives."

"Until now." Shelby gave an unladylike snort, then straightened when Reese nailed her with a look. "Besides, look at Nick and me. We were just friends too."

"It's not like that. It was just an aberration. I probably hit my head and knocked a few marbles loose."

"How did it feel?" Shelby asked. "The Griffen thing, not the marbles."

Reese shrugged, remembering. She remembered his touch on her skin, remembered wanting him to touch her again. "It was like he wasn't Griff—like he was a man."

Julia raised a finger. "Uh, once again—"

"I know he's a man!" Reese said too loudly, then looked around and slouched deep into the leather cushions.

"What about Griffen?" Shelby asked. "How did he react?"

"He was afraid he'd hurt me. He kept asking if I was okay."

"Do you think he had the same thoughts?" Natalie asked.

"No!" Good grief, she was never going to live this down. "And not one word to him about this. It would make things awkward and totally ruin a great friendship."

"We won't say a word," Natalie said. "But don't rule out

the possibility of something more, Reese. Some of the best marriages start with friendship."

Marriage? Had her friend lost her mind?

Shelby smiled dreamily. "I think you'd make the cutest couple."

She couldn't believe they were talking this way—about her and Griffen. The love bug had bitten them all hard.

"You're all too love-struck to be objective. He's my buddy. I've never even thought of us together that way. *Never.*"

Reese scanned the group, stopping at Shelby, remembering again the day she'd spotted Griffen across the grocery store parking lot. Shelby was remembering too—she could see it in her friend's eyes. That was different. She hadn't known it was Griffen she was ogling.

Reese looked at Julia. "What about you? Aren't you going to chime in too?"

Julia set her teacup down, smiled saucily, and shrugged her slight shoulders. "Never say never."

# CHAPTER THREE

·························

*L*unchtime," Reese said.

She draped the old dusty counter with a clean sheet of plastic and started unpacking the cooler. From the radio in the corner, Bing Crosby crooned about a white Christmas.

Griffen grabbed the jug of water and splashed it over his hands in the sink.

She scanned her store. Chunks of drywall littered the drop cloths, two-by-fours were stacked haphazardly against one wall, and a fine layer of dust coated everything. Griffen had warned her it would look worse before it looked better. He wasn't kidding.

He'd talked her into removing the walls. He had a way of doing that—talking her into things. And she had to admit, when she saw the brick behind them, she was glad he'd changed her mind.

He pulled up a stool and took a seat across from her. "Looks good." They'd taken turns packing a lunch, and today's fare was her treat. Club sandwiches on whole wheat bread, fresh fruit, and Doritos—his favorite.

Griffen said grace, then popped the tab on his Coke. "Okay, what gives? You've been nothing but quiet for two weeks."

His blue eyes plowed into hers, and she made a deal of arranging the lettuce and tomato on her sandwich. She hated this. What she'd hoped was a temporary aberration, a moment of insanity, had followed her around for two weeks like an orphaned puppy. And being with him every waking hour of the day wasn't helping.

"It'll be okay," he said. "I'll have you up and running on time."

"I know you will."

"If it's not that, what is it?"

She should've taken the lifeline he'd offered. He had drywall dust in his hair, and a streak of something dark across his cheek. In short, he looked adorable.

She pressed her lips together.

He put his hand over hers. It was still cool from the water and rough against the back of her hand. "You worried about opening the store?"

She pulled her hand away and picked up her sandwich. "What if I made the wrong decision? It's a lot of money, and what do I know about running a business?"

"You've planned this down to the smallest detail. And what you don't know, Natalie can teach you."

Her friend had already helped her with incorporating and all the business stuff Reese had been afraid of.

"What if the town doesn't take off like we hoped? Natalie is sure it will, but you know Natalie. She's so optimistic she's practically delusional—and I mean that in the nicest way."

Griffen smiled, a half grin that kicked her in the gut. Why hadn't she ever noticed the way his eyes crinkled when he smiled, the way his long lashes tangled at the corners?

Holy moly. If he knew what she was thinking right now, she'd die a thousand deaths.

"We've already got tourists. The wedding and media will seal the deal. You'll see."

"Hope you're right." She took a bite of her sandwich.

"I'm proud of you for stepping out on faith. You won't regret it."

"If this is what stepping out on faith feels like, I see why I've never been a big fan."

"You know what they say, 'If you could do it on your own, you wouldn't need God.'"

Easy for Griffen to say. He'd moved to Pennsylvania and traveled the world on mission projects. She couldn't imagine having that kind of courage, being that spontaneous.

They ate in silence. Griffen took down his sandwich and half of hers when she shoved it to the side.

When he finished, he began clearing his trash. "What's that big box out back? I almost tripped over it this morning."

"Ice skates and lots of them. They arrived last night. I'm gonna have to get the back lot fenced in soon so I can start moving stuff over. My garage looks like a bicycle factory exploded."

Griffen drained the last of his Coke. "Let's go skating Saturday night."

"What?" She'd heard him, just needed a few seconds to fabricate a decent excuse.

"We can try out your new skates on the town square."

Wasn't it enough she had to fight these feelings five days a week? She took a bite of pineapple, chewed and swallowed without tasting. It was just the kind of thing they'd always done. But it was different now. Way different.

He stood and slipped into his parka. "Have to run to the hardware store. What d'ya say? We on for Saturday?"

Reese cleared her trash, searching high and low for an excuse. Why couldn't she have plans? A date? She was a reasonably attractive young woman, wasn't she? She wondered if one of the girls was free. Probably all had dates with their new loves.

Griffen raised his brows, waiting. The song on the radio ended, ushering in a beat of silence.

"Sure." She bit the inside of her mouth. Hard. What was she doing? How long did she think she could hide her feelings when they were together 24/7?

"Great. Won't be long." He exited the shop. She watched him cross the plate-glass window, then dropped her head in her folded arms and moaned.

Why did things have to get so complicated? Everything had been just hunky-dory before. She had a great friend, the best contractor for her new shop, and a buddy to challenge her on the court and slopes, all wrapped in one convenient package.

Now all she had were confusion, awkward moments, and constant tension from trying to hide her feelings. The chorus of "You're All I Want for Christmas" built as Bing Crosby belted it out.

Swell. She knew just how he felt.

"Reese?"

Her head popped up. Shelby had stepped inside and pulled the door shut behind her. Her dark hair was flecked with flurries. She wore a cute peacoat with dark trendy slacks.

Reese suddenly felt like a slob in her jeans and stained sweatshirt. "Hey, Shelby."

"What's wrong?" Shelby approached, dusted off the stool Griffen had occupied, and sat down.

She hadn't mentioned her problem to the girls since that first night. She was hoping it would blow over. Instead it seemed to be blowing up. Right in her face. How long could she hide her attraction from Griffen? And what would he do when he found out?

"I stopped by to check out your progress."

*Progress?* She blinked.

"On the store," Shelby clarified, glancing around. "It's coming along. I like the open loft concept. You found brick behind the walls like you were hoping."

"Yep."

Bing crooned on as they looked around, then Shelby's eyes settled on hers. "Want to talk about it?"

Reese looked into her friend's warm brown eyes and felt her defenses fall for the first time in weeks. She palmed her face. "What is wrong with me?"

Shelby rubbed her arm. "Nothing's wrong with you, honey. Your feelings are just changing. There's no crime in that."

"But I don't want them to. I feel tense all the time and awkward and afraid he's going to realize what's going on in my head. Everything was better before."

"Maybe God has something different in mind."

"Well, he failed to inform Griffen."

Shelby chuckled softly. "It might take some time. You've always been able to talk to him about anything. What if you just told him how you feel—got it out there on the table?"

Reese dropped her hands. "No. That is not the plan."

"You can't plan everything, honey. God is the real planner."

Just the thought of Griffen knowing, of how that would change things between them, made heat crawl up her neck and anxiety snake through her veins. He would distance himself from her, maybe even feel sorry for her.

Ick.

She shook her head. "I'm not losing his friendship over my temporary insanity."

Shelby gave a sympathetic smile. "There's nothing insane about having feelings for an incredible man."

Shelby hadn't known Griffen long, but she'd heard plenty of stories. And she was right. "He is pretty incredible, isn't he."

"I'm just saying, be open to whatever God has in store. You never know. I mean, I never expected my friendship with Nick to change the way it did."

It sounded great in theory, but that didn't change the facts. "Griffen doesn't see me that way. To him, I'm just his best buddy."

"Well, that's how you saw him until a couple weeks ago."

True. Reese picked up the pencil on the counter and tapped it on her lip. "If only the same thing would happen to him." It had struck out of the blue, like a lightning bolt. Maybe Griffen would get a lightning bolt too. Too bad something like that couldn't be manufactured.

Could it?

Shelby propped her elbows on the plastic. "Isn't Sawyer coming home soon for Christmas?"

"That's what I heard. He's taking a break from touring from Christmas through the wedding."

"Maybe seeing your ex-fiancé will do something inside Griffen."

"I don't think so. It didn't seem to matter when we were engaged. And clearly Sawyer's no threat now."

"You're probably right. Well, we'll just have to pray God opens Griffen's eyes."

An idea formed in Reese's mind. "Or . . ."

Shelby raised her delicately arched brows. "Or . . ."

"Or I could help Griffen along just a little." Now that she thought about it, the idea was growing on her. She absently bit the metal pencil tip.

Shelby narrowed her eyes. "What's going on in that blond head of yours?"

"He sees me as a buddy, right? And I want him to see me as a woman."

"Right . . ."

"Well, there's nothing like a date to make a man see a woman as a lady."

"You're going to ask him out?"

"Heck no. I'm going to ask someone else out. He'll see me with another man and realize he wants me for himself." Okay, maybe that was simplifying things a tad. Reese shrugged. "Well. It might work."

"I don't know. Sometimes these things can get out of hand. Feelings can get hurt."

Reese gnawed on the pencil. Shelby was right. "But if I were honest with the other guy, then there'd be nothing to lose."

"I suppose . . ."

Reese was already searching her mental database for the right man. He had to be available and able to keep a secret. Good looks wouldn't hurt either.

She smiled. "Joshua Campbell. He's perfect. Nice look-ing, friendly, and available. Plus he owes me big-time. I taught him how to ski so he didn't fall on his face in front of Betsy Harmeyer."

"Isn't Betsy married?"

Reese waved her off. "It was a few years ago. Josh is per-fect, and I'm sure he'll help me out. I'll ask him today."

After Shelby left, Reese went back to work, a new bounce in her step. *Okay, God, new plan. Please make Griffen notice me. Please?*

# Chapter Four

. . . . . . . . . . . . . . . . . . . . . . . . . .

*G*riffen slid to a stop, sending a spray of ice toward Reese. "Nice skates. You spared no expense."

"They're made to last."

They shared the rink with a handful of tourists and a couple he remembered vaguely from high school. A tall man in a bulky coat lumbered across the ice in the shadowed corner. He lost his balance, and his arms windmilled before he regained his footing.

An old-fashioned waltzy song leaked from the speakers.

Griffen watched Reese execute a graceful turn. She looked beyond cute under the twinkling lights that danced in the trees around the rink. She finished the twirl and took a bow. Her cheeks were flushed with cold, and a relaxed smile curved her full lips.

"You become a ballerina while I was away?"

"As if I'd be caught dead in a tutu."

"I'd pay money to see it."

"Don't hold your breath."

Tonight she wore her usual jeans and a baby blue North Face parka. A fuzzy black hat covered her low ponytail and kept her ears warm.

"The gazebo looks awesome over there," she said. "I love the scrolling on the eaves. Look, it's already in use."

Someone had lit the structure with white Christmas lights.

During the warm months, the Garner Sisters would play from there on weekend evenings, replacing the canned music. Right now, a couple cuddled on the bench. When he'd been building it, he'd dreamed of Reese and him cuddling there under the stars. But then, he was always dreaming about Reese and him.

He was thinking of telling her soon. It was the reason he'd returned to Smitten. Well, that and to help the town rebuild. He watched her do another spin. Maybe he'd tell her tonight if he found the right moment. His heart bucked at the thought.

The timing never seemed right. When he'd realized his feelings three years earlier, she'd been dating Sawyer. Then, to his dismay, they'd become engaged. That was when he'd known he had to leave town. He couldn't stand by and watch the woman he'd fallen in love with begin her life with someone else.

The man in the gazebo had lowered his head toward the woman.

"Look, they're smooching," Reese said.

He looked at Reese instead. Her lips curved in a dreamy smile that gave him courage. If not now, when? She already loved him. How big a gap could there be between "love" and "in love"? He'd never know what could be if he didn't take a leap of faith.

He pushed off, closing the distance between them, pocketing his hands when he realized they were shaking.

"Reese . . ."

She turned those dreamy eyes on him, and for a moment his world stopped. His breath seized in his lungs. Even her frozen exhale seemed to hang in the air between them.

*Say it, Parker. Tell her that she's captured you, heart and soul. That you love every little thing about her. That you can't bear to face another day without her knowing.*

He opened his mouth to deliver the words that had been three years in coming.

*Thwack.*

A body barreled into Reese. Griffen reached out but she was gone, swept up in a tangle of arms and legs. They fought for balance, spinning and chopping at the air.

Finally they came to a standstill, facing one another. And that's when Griffen got a look at the man who'd nearly swept Reese off her feet—in more ways than one.

Sawyer Smitten. Griffen recognized him the same time Reese did. He watched her lips part, her eyes widen.

"Sawyer." His name left her lips on a sigh.

"Reese. Good heavens, I'm so sorry. I'm a klutz on these things." He'd picked up a southern accent somewhere. Probably all those country songs he crooned.

Reese gave a high-pitched laugh—her nervous laugh. She and Sawyer still gripped each other's forearms, and Griffen wanted to tear them apart, but he couldn't seem to move.

"I hadn't heard you were back."

Was he imagining the breathiness in her voice?

"Just arrived today. I'm on break until we kick off the tour here in Smitten." He managed to pull his eyes from Reese and scan the square. "Can't believe what y'all have done with the town. Heard it was your idea, your planning."

Reese did her nervous laugh again and shrugged. "No, no. Everyone worked together."

"Some of the men gave you a hard time, I hear," Sawyer said, a flirtatious twinkle in his eyes.

"Not so much anymore. They're coming around."

Did they not realize they were practically folded into each other's arms? He wondered if Reese liked the changes in Sawyer. The neat sideburns, the shadow of a goatee. Some women went for that country singer look, he supposed.

Sawyer finally noticed him. His eyes widened in recognition. "Griffen Parker." He extended his hand, which at least meant letting loose of Reese.

"Didn't recognize you without your cowboy hat. Good to see you, Sawyer." Griffen shook his hand. "Congratulations on your career successes—and your upcoming nuptials." In case either of them needed the reminder.

"Thanks. Yeah, a lot going on these days. So you're back in Smitten for a while?"

Griffen stood close to Reese in case she swooned. "For as long as I'm needed." He telegraphed a message with his eyes, but Sawyer was already back to Reese.

"You're opening that sporting goods store you always dreamed of."

"An outfitters shop."

He nodded. "Well. Good for you."

"I bought the old Palmer building. You'll have to swing by and see it when it's finished. It's going to be great."

*My best buddy Griffen is renovating it,* Griffen added to himself. *You know, the one who didn't leave me for fame and fortune.*

"I'll do that." Sawyer caught her hand. "It was good seeing you again. We'll have to catch up sometime."

"I'd like that."

"Well, listen, I'll let you two get back to it. I think I can make it back to my boots without fracturing my skull."

Nervous laugh. "See you around, Sawyer."

He could hardly wait.

"Bye now."

Griffen watched Smitten's claim to fame scuttle over the ice, watched Reese watching him go, and wondered if the woman he loved wasn't still in love with a man who now belonged to someone else.

# CHAPTER FIVE

. . . . . . . . . . . . . . . . . . . . . . . .

*I*t's too cold for this," Natalie said, her feet pounding the river walk pavement behind Reese.

"Four months ago you were complaining it was too hot," Reese called, her fogged breath dropping over her shoulder like a cape.

"Well, we were running up a mountain," Natalie said between breaths. "And it's Christmas Eve—shouldn't we get holidays off?"

"Christmas Eve morning. It's not a holiday until tonight."

"Speaking of Christmas," Shelby said. "I can't wait till you girls see Penelope's Christmas outfit."

"Why am I suddenly picturing her in red velvet and a white beard?" Reese asked.

Shelby laughed. "No, no. More like a red boa and white tulle."

Julia shook her head. "You have no shame."

"She made it in September," Natalie said. "Slow down, woman—it's too hard to talk while we're running."

Shelby had fallen in step beside her, and Natalie stage-whispered to her, "How can a woman with such short legs move so fast?"

"I heard that." Reese traded a smile with Natalie.

Reese slowed her pace and they jogged in silence for a few minutes, none of them fully awake yet. Shelby seemed different these days. Not just in love—she was at peace. Reese thought about all her friend had been through with the teenage pregnancy and her fateful decision. She was so glad Shelby had shared her burden with them. She could only respect a woman who pushed past a painful mistake and let God do a new work.

A sluggish fog hung over the river, mingling with flurries that fell from a gray abyss. Snow nested on the evergreen branches lining the river walk, and in the distance Sugarcreek Mountain rose majestically into the clouds. She'd have to take her new skis up there soon. There was a fluffy layer of snow just waiting for her on Switchback Pass. If she could only find the time.

"So what time are we meeting?" Julia asked. They were exchanging gifts at Natalie's shop later.

"Three?" Natalie suggested.

"Can't," Reese said. "I have to put in a full day."

"I have a couple clients this afternoon too." Julia pocketed her gloves.

They agreed on five, which would give the other girls time to spend the rest of Christmas Eve with their men and families.

After a while they slowed to a walk. Natalie and Shelby caught up, and the four spanned the deserted path. The rhythmic pounding of their sneakers and their huffs of air broke the otherwise silent morning.

"I heard Sawyer was back in town," Julia said as they cooled down.

"He came into the coffee shop last night."

Reese could feel her friends' eyes on her. "I already know. We ran into each other Saturday night at the ice rink. Literally."

"Are you okay?" Shelby asked.

Reese knew she wasn't referring to the collision. It was the first time she'd seen Sawyer since they'd broken their engagement, having deftly avoided him when he'd passed through town in the spring.

She shrugged. "It was awkward, but we got through it. Griffen was there too, which only made it more awkward."

"Do you think you're over him?" Natalie asked.

Julia's dimple appeared with an ornery smile. "Sawyer or Griffen?"

Reese shot her a look, then addressed Natalie. "Oh yeah. That boat has sailed." She'd known she was over Sawyer, but seeing him had confirmed it. "Griffen, though—that's another story."

"What'd you get him for Christmas?" Shelby asked.

Reese had thought long and hard about that one. In the past they'd exchanged trinkets. While he was away it had dwindled down to Christmas cards.

"A Catamount sweatshirt."

"What's that?" Shelby asked.

"The University of Vermont mascot," Natalie said. "Griffen played on their hockey team."

Shelby nodded. "That's a safe gift."

"Personal, but not too personal," Julia said.

"Good, that's what I was going for."

"You should've gotten him a photo frame," Natalie said. "And put a picture of you two in it with a note that says"—she swiped her hand across the sky—"*Friends make the best lovers.*"

Shelby and Julia laughed.

Reese felt a flush climbing her neck. "That's real subtle."

They paused for Natalie to tie her shoe, then picked up the pace again.

"You should know," Reese said, "that I'll be going to the New Year's Eve bash with Joshua Campbell. And we'll probably be going out a lot in the near future."

"Joshua Campbell . . . ?" Natalie said.

"Did I miss something?" Julia asked.

Reese waved off their curiosity. "Nothing like that. It's all part of my plan to help Griffen see me as more than his little buddy."

"Yeah, now he'll see you as Josh's girlfriend," Julia said.

"I had to do something. Besides, Josh knows the score. He's just helping me out."

"I think you should tell Griffen the truth, Reese," Natalie said. "Why play games when you can just be honest?"

"Because honesty could cause an irreparable fracture in a very important relationship."

"Well, your plan might not work, and then you'll be back to square one."

"Even so, at least our friendship will be intact."

Natalie shook her head. "It's like those walls you busted down. You were afraid what you'd find behind them, but you found just what you'd hoped for."

"This isn't a wall, it's a relationship."

"But sometimes you have to take a chance."

Reese knew she was wasting her breath. If something like this had happened to Natalie, her friend would bust right through the wall. But Reese wasn't Natalie, and she had to do things her own way. Better safe than sorry.

# CHAPTER SIX

. . . . . . . . . . . . . . . . . . . . . . . . .

*R*eese picked up the store's sign, Griffen's Christmas gift to her, and moved it out of harm's way. She didn't know when he'd found the time to make it, but it was gorgeous. "Outdoor Adventures" it read in yellow-trimmed burgundy letters. The multilayered wooden shingle, a mix of natural wood and hunter green paint, would look great hanging under the green canopy she was adding over the entryway.

He'd seemed pleased with his Catamount sweatshirt, but if Reese had hoped for some kind of moment during the gift exchange, those hopes had been dashed. He'd given her a quick hug, then tousled her hair for good measure.

Across the store, he was now prying the last of the drywall from the studs. The shop was a disaster, even though she'd been cleaning up behind him. The mess was driving her crazy.

She had to admit, the newly exposed brick walls looked great, or would once they sucked the dust away. The brick added the old-timey look she'd been hoping for. That, combined with the thick wooden trusses exposed on the second floor, made for a nice rustic look. The lofted second floor was open now and well supported with a beam.

He set down the pry bar and pulled off his gloves and filter mask. The air was thick with drywall dust that clogged Reese's throat even through her mask.

"That's the last of it," Griffen said, retrieving a bottle of water from the cooler behind the old counter. He handed her one.

"Thank goodness." There wasn't a clean surface in the room. Reese pulled off her mask and took a long drink.

"We'll need to roll up the plastic carefully. The Shop-Vac will handle the rest, but there's no sense doing that until the dust settles. At least the messy part is over." He cocked a grin at her. "It's driving you nuts, isn't it?"

She thought of denying it, but why bother? He knew her too well. "A bit."

"A bit." He chuckled, then tugged her ponytail, releasing a cloud of dust. "Am I making a big old mess for Little Reese Cup?" he said, baby talking.

She gave him a shove that was only half playful. "What else is new?"

He sank down on the dirty floor behind the counter, finished his water in one long drink, then pulled out his cell phone.

"Good grief, what happened in here?" Joshua Campbell entered the shop with a blast of cold air. He shut the door behind him and waved his hand in front of his face.

"Drywall dust," she said.

What was he doing here? Maybe he'd come to get an early start on their Griffen plan. She peeked over the counter where Griffen was texting from his spot on the floor and scowled. Good luck with that.

She cleared the dust from her throat and beamed at Josh. "I've got my outfit all picked out for New Year's on the Square. I bought a new hat just for—" She stopped as Josh's face fell. "What?"

"Listen, Reese, about that . . ."

He was canceling, she just knew it. Like she wanted Griffen to hear another man dumping her. Sure, that would make him interested.

"Let's go outside and get some fresh air," she said.

"Stop!" Josh stepped back, colliding with the door. "I have mono. I just left the doctor's office. That's what I came to tell you."

Reese saw her plan going up in smoke, watched the mental fire burning and all hope drifting skyward in a great black cloud.

Then she looked at Josh and realized that the poor man faced at least several weeks of illness. "I'm sorry. That's a bummer."

Still, she had to get him out of there. He hadn't noticed Griffen tucked away behind the counter, and what if he said something stupid? "Okay, we'll talk about this later. You go home and rest up, and don't worry about New Year's."

"You know it's not just New Year's, right? I'm afraid—"

Reese shook her head frantically.

"—Operation Jealousy will have to be put on hold indefinitely."

Josh had never been good with subtleties. Reese winced. Still, at least he hadn't said Griffen's name. And he was busy texting, right? He probably hadn't heard.

She shook her head at Josh again, made a throat-cutting motion.

But Josh was looking out the plate-glass window now at the flecks of snow drifting to the ground. "The doctor said I was contagious, and honestly, I feel like crap, so—"

"Of course you do. You go on home. Don't give it another thought." She was about to push him out the door, germs be darned.

"We'll pick it up when I'm over this if you can't find someone else to help. I know how you feel about—"

Reese hacked loudly. A prolonged choking kind of hack, accompanied by eyes wide enough to alert the most clueless of people.

Josh jumped, then frowned at her.

"Drywall dust." She added one more hack for good measure.

Josh's eyes left hers, moved just to her right, then widened. "Oh . . . Hi, Griffen." Josh felt for the door handle. "Uh, well, I really have to go. And rest. At home. Catch you later, Reese. You too, Griffen."

He moved incredibly fast for a guy with mono. The door thwacked shut behind him. He ducked against the cold, crossing in front of the plate-glass window.

*Thanks a lot, pal.*

Reese's stomach had fallen somewhere between her knees and ankles. She heard Griffen moving behind the counter, heard the crunch of drywall pieces under his work boots.

"What was that about?"

She turned, ready with a fake smile, then remembered her mask and snapped it over her mouth instead. "What?"

Two creases etched the space between Griffen's brows. He gestured toward the door. "That."

"He has mono."

"I gathered that."

"We were going to spend New Year's Eve together."

"I'm not deaf, Reese. Operation Jealousy?"

*Oh, you heard that?*

*Think, Reese. Fast.* Something. Anything. Her brain readily dumped all logical thought. Griffen was looking through her with those blue lasers of his, and she couldn't string together two coherent thoughts.

Something flickered in the pool of blue just before his eyes narrowed. "You *are* still in love with him."

"What? Who?"

He reached over the counter and pulled her mask, letting it dangle from the elastic string. "Sawyer."

She shook her head. "No."

"Don't deny it. I was there last Saturday, remember? What, you've come up with some cockamamie plot to make him jealous? To make him see what he's missing before it's too late?"

"Uh . . ." It was the best she could do. Her mind spun with options. Let Griffen believe it, tell him the truth, or tell him it wasn't Sawyer but someone else. Then he'd want to know who. It all led back to him, and she couldn't go there. Not yet.

"He's engaged, Reese."

"I know that."

Griffen propped his hands on his hips, looked away. A shadow flickered on his jaw over a streak of white dust.

She had to do something. She couldn't let him think she still loved Sawyer. But she couldn't let him know how she felt about him either. It would ruin everything. No more casual games of B-ball, no more friendly chats, no more easy laughter and banter. All of that would be gone . . . and they'd still be stuck working together all day, every day.

He looked at her again, and she swore she could see right to the core. She tried for an innocent expression but feared she wasn't fooling anyone.

"You and your plans. Have you considered the repercussions?"

"Repercussions?"

"What if you succeed? What if you break up Sawyer and his fiancée—what then?"

"What do you mean?"

"The wedding, Reese. The whole town is counting on it. What'll become of Smitten—of your store—if there's no wedding?"

"Hmm. That's something to consider."

"You think?" He ran his hand through his hair. Dust showered his shoulders. Griffen paced to the brick wall, kicking a chunk of drywall out of his way. He returned, stopping in front of her. "I can't believe you're doing this."

She couldn't either. She thought of what Natalie had said. That she should just tell him the truth. That she had feelings that went way beyond the friendship they'd always shared. That right now she wanted to run her fingers through his hair, melt into his arms, taste of his lips.

She should just pretend she was Natalie and say it. But what if it ruined everything? What if she tore down the wall and there was nothing but a hollow space? What then?

At the thought of failure, adrenaline shot through her, speeding her heart rate, drying her mouth. The temperature of her face had shot up several degrees, and her cheeks burned like fire. She had to say something, do something—and not any of the things she yearned to do.

"Josh is sick." Okay, so she wasn't making sense. No wonder he was looking at her like that.

"And now you're going to find someone else, is that it?"

Was it? "Well . . ."

"You think he just needs to see you with another man, and all the feelings you have for him will magically appear in him?"

"Uh, well . . . that was the plan." *Sort of. Only for you, not Sawyer.*

He paced again, shaking his head this time. He breathed a laugh.

Now he thought she was in love with Sawyer and wanted him badly enough to ruin Smitten. Not only was she in love with someone else's man, but she was selfish to boot. Perfect. She wanted to curl up in a ball and cry.

Griffen turned and shoved his hands in his pockets. "All right. I'll do it."

"Do what?"

"You need someone—a date." He lifted his shoulders. "I'll do it. I'll take Josh's place."

Her eyes widened. "What?"

Her and Griffen dating? Hugging, holding hands . . . kissing? All for someone else's benefit?

Then again . . .

"Why not me? We're always together anyway. Besides, lots of people say we'd make a cute couple."

She did a double take. "They do?"

He scowled. "Don't look so surprised. I'm a good catch."

"And so humble too." Reese turned toward the counter and reached for her water. She needed a minute to think without him reading her every thought. She took a slow sip.

Maybe this would work. Maybe this plan was better than *her* plan. Maybe after a few dates, pretending he had feelings for her, he'd develop real feelings for her. It could happen, couldn't it? Meanwhile, it would be just this side of torture for her, but what other option did she have?

"What do you think?" he asked.

Reese set her water down and turned, leaning back on the counter. "I think it might be just the ticket."

# CHAPTER SEVEN

· · · · · · · · · · · · · · · · · · · · · · · · ·

*T*his was not the way his first date with Reese was supposed to go.

One, they were supposed to be alone, preferably in a quiet restaurant at a table for two, with candlelight flickering nearby and quiet music in the background.

Two, they were supposed to be holding hands and gazing into each other's eyes and talking about how amazing it was that they'd found love after all these years of friendship.

Three, she was supposed to know it was a real date.

Instead they were sipping hot chocolate with three hundred of their closest neighbors and a handful of tourists on the town square, bundled in parkas, knit caps, and thick gloves. A lively tune flowed from hidden speakers, he hadn't so much as touched Reese, and all they'd talked about was Sawyer Smitten, who seemed to be within sight every second of this long night.

But, Griffen reminded himself, this was not a real date at all, and no one was more aware of that fact than he.

He sipped his hot chocolate, now tepid at best, and leaned back on the bench, watching the ice skaters. Reese waved at Shelby and Nick, who glided hand in hand across the ice. Beside them Willow took a spin, her spindly arms stretched out.

Every town had its New Year's rituals. Smitten's was pretty simple. Have dinner with friends, go see the annual play at the chapel, then wander out to the town square for sleigh rides and free hot chocolate.

The town square clock was the center of attention tonight. Spotlights lit the old green timepiece, and a fat garland spiraled up the post past the lavender wreath and culminated in a big red bow.

Sleigh bells jingled in the distance, and he located the sled over his shoulder. "Go for a ride? The line's dwindled down."

Reese glanced toward the hot chocolate stand where Sawyer was holding court for twenty of his closest fans. He wore a cowboy hat tonight and matching cowboy boots. Griffen wondered when his fiancée was going to arrive. Couldn't be soon enough for him. Maybe when Kate Owens came, Reese would end this silly charade.

"We'd never make it back by midnight."

"Probably right." But he knew what she was really thinking. What's the point of going someplace Sawyer couldn't see them?

He smothered a sigh. *Patience, Parker.* This wasn't going to happen quickly, if it happened at all. She fancied herself in love with Sawyer. He wasn't sure how—they'd been apart for three years, after all.

Then again, he'd been away just as long, and his feelings for Reese hadn't diminished.

"People are used to seeing us together," she said.

"True."

Reese looked soft and feminine tonight. She wore a fuzzy pink cap that set off her hazel eyes. Her blond ponytail looked soft as a silk sheet falling down her back. She had a tiny cleft in her chin that he'd always thought would fit his thumb perfectly—but had never had the nerve to check.

She looked toward the hot chocolate booth. "Maybe you should, I don't know, put your arm around me or something."

His heart tripped over his ribs like a clumsy schoolboy over his shoestrings. "That wouldn't make you feel weird?"

"Kidding me? It would keep me warm. It's freezing out here."

Griffen slid his arm around her. Should he let his hand hang loose or cup her shoulder and pull her closer? No question which he longed to do. Still, he had to control himself. Keep it casual. Remember this was for show.

She took the decision from his hands when she scooched into his side, close enough to share body heat, close enough to make his mouth go dry.

"There, that's better, don't you think?" she asked.

Not for his peace of mind. Not for his sanity. Not for his—

"Sure."

For show. This was for show. He could do this. How else would he ever awaken in Reese the same feelings she'd awakened in him years ago?

One minute Reese was snuggled in Griffen's arms, and the next she spied Natalie barreling across the square toward them, a beaming smile on her face.

Reese hadn't had a chance to inform her friends of the latest development in her plan. It took all of two seconds to piece together what Natalie assumed upon seeing her and

Griffen snuggled on the bench. She had to intercept her and fast.

Reese sprang to her feet. "Uh, I'll get us some warm hot chocolate."

"I can get it."

She waved him off. "No, I got it."

She ignored Griffen's befuddled expression and headed toward the chocolate stand, where she met up with Natalie.

Her friend gave her a hearty hug. "You told him! I'm proud of you. You look so cute together."

Reese pulled away. "Uh, it's not quite how it looks."

She filled Natalie in on the details of Josh's mono and Griffen's subsequent offer. By the end of the explanation, her voice had dwindled to nothing. She ended with a *What else could I do?* shrug.

Lines had sprouted across Natalie's forehead. She fisted her hands on the curve of her hips. "What have you done?"

"What was I supposed to do? Never mind. Don't answer that."

"Reese!" Sawyer approached and gave her a sideways hug. "Natalie, good to see you. Where'd Carson get off to? That brother of mine is harder to catch up with than an alley cat."

"He and Mia are saving us a spot near the clock. When does your fiancée arrive? I thought she might join you for the holidays."

"Not till after, I'm afraid. She had work obligations and couldn't get away yet. We're both counting the days, though. And you'll be happy to know I got that 'Smitten' song written before I left Nashville. Think y'all will like it."

Natalie clapped. "Oh, I can't wait to hear it!"

"You'll have to wait till the wedding like everyone else, Miss Natalie. Even Kate hasn't heard it yet."

Sawyer really did have a devastating smile. It was a wonder it didn't do anything for Reese anymore. Instead, she pictured Griffen's grin, half-cocked and dangerous.

They made small talk for a few minutes before Natalie's aunt joined them. "I took Joshua Campbell a casserole earlier this evening," Violet said. "That was so nice of you to put together a meal schedule for him, Reese."

"How's he feeling?" Natalie asked.

"Didn't even get off the couch, poor dear. He sure appreciates those meals, though."

A moment later, Violet stole Sawyer away. It was closing in on midnight, and Reese owed Griffen a hot chocolate. Natalie gave her one last disapproving look before turning to find Carson and Mia in the gathering crowd.

By the time Reese made it to the stand, they were closing down, so she headed back to Griffen empty-handed.

"Sorry, I was too late."

He stood and tossed his empty cup in the bin. "Just as well. It's almost time."

Reese checked her watch. "Just a few minutes."

Griffen took her hand and pulled her toward the crowd. He'd taken off his gloves, and Reese wished she'd removed her own, wished she could feel his warm, strong hand against hers.

They settled into the back of the group. It was times like these Reese hated being short. She couldn't even see the face of the clock over the broad shoulders in front of her.

"Should I put you on my shoulders?" Griffen asked.

She shot him a look, then tugged him toward the center of the crowd behind a family with children.

"There, that's better." Reese could see the clock face at least, though she had to admit she was more focused on the hand wrapped around hers than the ones on the clock.

The crowd tightened as more people joined the throng, a mass of people huddled on the square for warmth. The clamor of chatter quieted as the minute hand inched its way toward midnight.

Her arm against Griffen's side tingled with warmth, or something else. Most likely something else.

"I hope the New Year brings you everything you want," Griffen said.

She looked at him, at the glow of light on his face, the sparkle of sincerity in those familiar eyes, and thought in that instant that he was the only thing she really wanted. That if he could just see her in the same way she saw him, she could deal with anything that came her way.

"You too, Griff."

His eyes strayed, caught by some movement or something behind her. The corner of his lips fell into a straight line before he looked ahead to the clock as the crowd began the countdown.

"Ten."

What had changed his countenance?

"Nine . . . eight . . . seven."

She counted down mechanically, her mind awhirl, anticipating the hug Griffen always gave her at midnight, at least used to, when neither of them had a New Year's date.

"Three . . . two . . . one . . . Happy New Year!" the crowd rang out. The chapel bells chimed.

Reese turned with a ready smile, but Griffen wasn't reaching out for a hug. And he wasn't smiling. He pulled his hand from hers, and her heart bottomed out.

There was a look in his eyes she hadn't seen before. Her own smile slipped.

Then he took her chin and tilted it up. She met his half-lidded gaze as he lowered his lips to hers. They brushed across hers, warm and tender.

Time stopped. The world hushed. The earth froze on its axis. She forgot to breathe, forgot to think, forgot to—

And then it was over. Griffen pulled away, taking something of hers with him. Her heart, she realized with sudden clarity.

His eyes bore some indefinable emotion. They slid to the right before coming back to her. The muscle in his jaw flinched.

"Might as well give him an eyeful, right?"

She followed his eyes to where Sawyer stood, mere feet away, hugging his younger cousin, lifting her off her feet, making her laugh.

For just a moment she'd let herself believe the kiss was real. Silly her. Griffen was only playing a part. It was what she'd wanted, wasn't it? But somehow that realization didn't stop the sting of tears or the hard lump that swelled in her throat.

# CHAPTER EIGHT

· · · · · · · · · · · · · · · · · · · · · · · · · · ·

*R*eese bucketed the stiff brush and stretched her aching fingers. The brick was clean and ready for shelving. Now that she'd cleared away the drywall dust, she could better envision the finished results. She liked what she saw. Removing the walls and opening the second floor made the space feel roomier. The brick walls and beams lent a rugged feel that was perfect for an outfitters shop.

Across the room, Griffen nailed a wooden slab into place over the support beam. The hammer rang loudly in the empty room. Once they polished the wood floor and finished the plumbing, they'd be ready to install shelving.

In the four days since their kiss, Reese had been unable to shake the memory. It didn't help that they were together constantly or that they'd become Smitten's newest hot couple— a complication she hadn't foreseen. It seemed everyone in Smitten had seen them snuggling or heard of their midnight kiss. They couldn't stop talking about it.

And Reese couldn't stop thinking about it. At the worst times, she found her eyes drifting to his lips and remembering the feel of them on hers. Found herself wondering when another opportunity would arise.

Then she'd remind herself that the kiss wasn't real and chide herself for going down Fantasy Lane. She'd wondered a hundred times how Griffen felt about the kiss. If he'd been repulsed at the thought of kissing his best friend. If he'd gone home and washed his mouth out with soap.

Not a pleasant thought.

Reese wiped her forehead and tightened her ponytail. In between hammer swings, Griffen tossed her a grin. She must look a wreck. She was caked in dust and sweat. For once she wanted to look like a girl, not the tomboy he'd known all his life. She couldn't even wash up, since the plumbing was disassembled while they waited for parts.

The walls were closing in, and she felt her sanity slipping inch by inch. She had to get out of there. She headed toward the counter, where she'd stowed her purse. "I'm going for a coffee break. Want something?"

"Nah, I'm good."

After slipping into her coat, she exited the shop and headed down the deserted sidewalk. The Christmas decorations had disappeared, and a light layer of snow coated the ground. A lone car meandered past, the only noise on the otherwise still Friday afternoon.

The cold wind bit hard, and Reese tucked her nose into her scarf as she crossed the street. When she reached Natalie's shop, she ducked inside and breathed in the warm, java-scented air. A soft melody filtered from the speakers, the only noise in the empty shop.

Natalie peeked through the kitchen doorway. "Hey, Reese."

"Can I wash up in your bathroom?"

"Help yourself."

After Reese had washed her hands and splashed the dust from her face, she tidied her ponytail. Feeling presentable again, she entered the shop, detecting a new aroma.

"You're just in time to taste my newest batch."

Natalie approached the back side of the counter bearing something wrapped in a napkin. Reese smothered a groan at the sight of yet another gluten-free cookie attempt.

"Stop scowling. You'll like this one."

Reese took the cookie and studied it. It looked normal enough.

"It's not going to bite you," Natalie said. "Want your usual?"

"Please." Reese slapped three dollars on the counter and carried the cookie to their corner. She sank into the chair and took a cautious bite.

Hmm. Not bad. Pretty good, actually.

"You like it!" Natalie hollered over the whir of the espresso machine.

Reese chewed, swallowed, and braced herself for the aftertaste as the machine went quiet. The only lingering taste was of sweet cookie goodness.

"I have to hand it to you, Nat—I can't tell it's gluten-free from the taste."

Natalie punched the air. "Yes!"

Reese looked at the cookie. "The texture, though . . ."

"What's wrong with the texture?"

"It's . . . I don't know . . . kinda weird."

"Well, rats." Natalie poured the shots into a mug, her engagement diamond flashing under the spotlights. "I'm getting close, though. Have you heard from Shelby? I've been trying to reach her." Natalie set down her latte, removed her flour-splattered apron, and sank into her favorite chair.

"Nope." Reese took a sip of her latte. "Mmmm, good.

Maybe she and Nick went skiing or something. I'm sure Nick needs a break from the tree farm about now, and with all the help Shelby gave him over Christmas, I'm sure she's exhausted."

"She still has her school to run."

"You know Shelby, though. She's probably in a funk because Christmas is over."

The door opened, and Sawyer entered with a blast of frigid air. He tipped his cowboy hat at them. "Ladies."

The girls greeted him.

Natalie sprang up. "Have a seat. What can I get you?"

Sawyer ordered a black coffee and sank into the chair across from Reese. It seemed crazy that the man she'd nearly married was now a national star and would soon be Natalie's brother-in-law.

"So . . ." Sawyer said with a knowing twinkle in his eyes. "You and Griffen, huh?"

Sawyer had been a little suspicious of her friendship with Griffen once upon a time, despite her denials. This was getting complicated.

"I assure you, Griffen and I were strictly platonic when you and I were dating."

He nodded, his lips twitching. "Sure you were."

Reese scowled. "Our feelings are a very recent development." So recent Griffen wasn't even aware of them yet.

Sawyer's smile broke loose. "I'm just giving you a hard time. I'm nothing but happy for you, Reese. I happen to believe everything worked out just as God intended."

He seemed sincere. "You're right. And I'm happy for you too." She toasted him with her latte cup. "The town eagerly awaits your wedding day."

She was anticipating it as much as anyone. Her whole savings was at stake. And her heart. If she didn't make Griffen notice her by then, the jig was up. He was leaving town and her chance would be gone. Poof!

Natalie set Sawyer's coffee down and took a load off.

"Thanks, Natalie. Put it on my tab?"

"It's on the house. Least I can do for the man who's single-handedly saving the village."

He waved her off. "It's a team effort. Everyone's doing their part, right down to little Mia."

"It's so quiet, though," Reese said.

"Should I turn up the music?"

"I mean the town. Since New Year's this place is dead. I gotta say, I'm getting a little worried."

"It'll be fine." Natalie brushed her hair behind her ears. "All tourist destinations have low seasons. Hard to believe the wedding is only six weeks away. The media will be here to show Smitten to the world . . ." She patted Sawyer's arm. "And all your fancy-schmancy friends will go home and rave about our little jewel in the mountains."

"Hope you're right."

A timer went off, and Natalie dashed off toward the kitchen.

"I love her optimism." Reese played with the napkin. "But I have to be realistic. Every dime I have is wrapped up in my new store. I don't know what I'll do if the plan doesn't work. What any of us will do."

"If it makes you feel better, my concert is already sold out. And all the major media are coming. We've got interviews lined up right up to the wedding, and we'll plug the town. It'll be fine." He set his hand on hers and gave a friendly squeeze. "It's a wonder what a little media coverage can accomplish. You'll see."

The door opened and Griffen entered, his eyes settling over her and Sawyer like a cold blast of air.

As Griffen entered the coffee shop, the sweet smell of baking brownies wafted toward his nose, lifting his spirits and the corners of his mouth. He spotted Reese in her usual seat.

And then he spotted Sawyer. The man's hand rested on Reese's. A protective reflex kicked in so hard, Griffen knotted his hands into fists to keep himself from diving across the table and landing Sawyer flat on his back.

"Griffen." Reese's lips lifted as Griffen's smile slipped.

Lover boy pulled his hand away. *Smart move, buddy*.

"How ya doing, Griffen?" Sawyer asked.

"Not bad." Griffen sat close to Reese and draped his arm casually around her shoulders.

"I said I'd bring you back something." Reese's smile looked unnatural.

"Well, I missed you." He leaned toward her and pressed a kiss to her cheek. It was what she wanted, right? To make Sawyer see what he was missing? Well, Griffen could manage that just fine.

Reese took a sip of her drink as a pretty blush colored her cheeks.

"So, Sawyer . . . when does the lucky lady arrive in town?" Griffen asked.

"A couple weeks. She's tying up things at work, but she's looking forward to finishing the wedding preparations."

"You must be counting the minutes."

Sawyer nodded. "I am. I am. Congrats on . . ." He waved a finger between Reese and Griffen. "You know—you two."

"Yeah." Griffen tightened his hold on Reese, pulling her into his side. "It's amazing the way it all came together. Isn't it, honey?"

Reese gave her high-pitched laugh. "Amazing."

They sipped their drinks, ushering in an awkward pause. Griffen became aware of Reese's body snuggled tightly against his side. Her firm curves, the smell of her hair, sweet apples with musky undertones. Ragged little breaths, puffing warm air against his hand, which dangled from her shoulder.

He was unprepared for the rush of adrenaline, the feel-good chemicals, and his body's reactions to the chemistry. Well, it was his own fault, wasn't it? He was the one who'd wanted to show Sawyer whose girl she was.

"Hi, Griffen." Natalie set a black coffee and a brownie in front of him.

"Thanks, Natalie. How'd you know I was after one of these?"

"Would you like one, Sawyer?" Natalie asked.

"No, thanks." He patted his solid middle. "Have to watch the girlish figure."

"How come they get the good stuff?" Reese said.

"You're my taster—that's a privilege—but I'll get you one." Natalie started to get up.

"Don't bother," Griffen said. "I'll share."

He picked up the brownie and held it to Reese's mouth as Natalie sank back down.

Something flickered in Reese's eyes as her lips parted for the bite. He watched her teeth sink into the warm treat. Her full lips pursed as she chewed the dainty bite. A dab of melted chocolate perched on her lower lip.

He reached out and brushed it away with the flick of his thumb, then casually sucked the chocolate from his own. *How do you like that, Sawyer Smitten?*

Reese's eyes widened.

Natalie cleared her throat. "So . . . we were just talking about how the town was coming along."

"I was telling Reese the concert is already sold out," Sawyer said.

Griffen took a bite of brownie as Sawyer went on about the media circus they had planned. His mind was elsewhere. Namely on the cute little thing tucked into his side.

He took another bite and offered Reese the rest. When she shook her head, he shrugged and finished it off.

Reese slanted him a look. *What's gotten into you?*

He raised his brows and lifted his shoulders ever so slightly. *Isn't this what you wanted, Miss Operation Jealousy?*

He wasn't sure what was up with the hand-holding thing he'd walked in on, but he'd rallied big-time if he said so himself. And he had to admit, it wasn't all bad, being with Reese and Sawyer. Gave him an excuse to do everything he'd wanted to do for three years. And if he were honest, it felt kinda good, rubbing it into old Sawyer over there. He already had a fiancée and a gaggle of worshipping fans—would it be too much to ask to leave this one for him?

". . . the one thing I'm worried about," Sawyer was saying.

"It'll be fine," Natalie said.

"You know I don't ski, Reese. And the media will be there watching me making a fool of myself."

"It'll be great for the town, though," Natalie said. "The guests wouldn't get the full effect of Smitten without sampling our slopes."

"Maybe I can just sit out," Sawyer said.

"You can't do that," Natalie said. "You should be leading the pack. Smitten's our home and skiing's our game—so to speak."

An idea popped into Griffen's head and out his mouth. "We can teach you."

He felt Reese's head jerk toward him.

"I was a part-time instructor in high school, remember?" Griffen said.

Sawyer shook his head. "You saw me on skates. Put me on skis, multiply that by ten, and you'll get an idea what we're working with."

"I could teach a monkey to ski. And Reese here, well, she's a natural. You know that—and she has all the gear too."

Griffen looked at Reese and was treated to her *What the heck?* look.

"I think that's a great idea," Natalie said.

Reese frowned. "You do?"

"Well, we can't have our resident star looking like a hippo on wheels."

Sawyer gave a self-deprecating smile. "Gee, thanks."

"Oh, you know what I mean," Natalie said. "And Griffen's right. If Reese taught me to ski, she can teach anyone. Between the two of them, they'll have you looking like a pro in no time."

"I don't know . . ."

"What d'ya have to lose?" Griffen asked. "You can't get any worse."

Sawyer laughed. "That's true." Thoughtful lines appeared on his brow. "Though the idea of embarrassing myself in front of our fellow Smittenites doesn't appeal either."

"Know what? The Bellinghams are old friends of the family. I'm sure they'd give us access to the mountain before they open one morning. We'd have total privacy."

Sawyer rubbed his jaw. "Really? Well, that's tempting. You know, Kate's been worried the ski day was a mistake. It might be nice to surprise her."

Natalie leaned forward. "Oh, you should totally do that! She'll be so impressed."

Sawyer nodded thoughtfully. "All right. I'm game if you two are."

Griffen tightened his grip on Reese. "We're happy to help. Aren't we, honey?"

Reese gave her high-pitched laugh. "Uh—sure. Happy to help."

# CHAPTER NINE

. . . . . . . . . . . . . . . . . . . . . . . . . . . .

*G*riffen released the rope and skied toward the peak of the bunny hill. The morning was quiet except for the grinding sound of the rope tow and the *shhhh* of three pairs of skis slicing through fresh snow. His breath released a puff of fog. It couldn't be more than fifteen degrees, and even wearing one of Reese's quality ski suits, he was feeling it.

After an hour, Sawyer had managed the plow and straight run. They'd given him instructions on pointing his way down the slope, and this was his first go.

"Okay," Reese said. "I'll head down first. Watch me and follow."

Griffen watched her descend the gentle slope, her athletic body gliding back and forth effortlessly.

"She makes it look so easy," Sawyer said, pulling his ski mask into place.

"You'll be fine."

"Here goes nothing." Sawyer pushed off, going straight at first, then trying a turn.

The morning hadn't gone quite the way Griffen had hoped. There was little time for displays of affection when they were busy keeping a six-foot-two guy on his feet.

It was gratifying to be the competent one, though, and he was enjoying the fact that today Sawyer hardly resembled the country music star all the women went gaga over. Without his

cowboy hat he looked like a regular guy; and on skis, well, he looked like a giraffe with broken kneecaps. How could a guy, so at ease onstage, be so awkward on the slopes?

Griffen watched Sawyer totter when his skis crossed. He was losing control. "Plow!" he called, but he didn't think Sawyer heard because he was skiing a straight run now and quickly gaining speed.

Griffen pushed off. "Plow!" he called again.

But Sawyer was picking up speed and heading toward Reese, his ski poles waving wildly.

Oblivious to Sawyer's proximity, Reese cut back to the left, right into Sawyer's path.

"Reese!" Sawyer yelled, and she must've heard because she looked back just in time for the collision.

Sawyer snatched her around the middle as he hit her and leaned backward. Their skis clacked together, then there was a thud as they hit the ground. Their skis and poles went flying. Reese landed on top of Sawyer, and he grunted.

"Reese!" Griffen surged forward, not liking their stillness. But then Reese flopped off to the side. When he slid to a stop, they were laughing like maniacs.

"I take it you're fine," he said, aware his voice was frostier than the air.

They were laughing too hard to notice. Griffen collected their things, remembering his own recent collision with Reese. She hadn't found it so amusing then. In fact, if memory served, she'd been a smidge testy. But then, that collision had been with him, not her beloved Sawyer.

Griffen dropped their skis and poles beside them. Sawyer was flicking the snow from Reese's hat. Her cheeks were rosy pink, her eyes twinkling.

"Right. Going inside to warm up." Because clearly they were having enough fun without him. Clearly Griffen was only in the way.

Reese worked with Sawyer until he could successfully point his way down the bunny hill. She'd expected Griffen to return by now, but after a while she realized he was giving them alone time—which was what he thought she wanted. She *had* enjoyed Sawyer's company this morning, just not the way Griffen supposed. And fact was, she'd felt guilty being so alone with Sawyer on the slopes when he was engaged to someone else.

She skied back to the lodge, leaving Sawyer to practice his new skill. Inside, the lodge was quiet and lit only by the bank of windows facing the slopes. Griffen sat in front of the stone fireplace, staring into the cold grate. On the table behind him sat a cup of coffee he must've made himself.

He didn't seem to notice her approach. Smiling, Reese snuck up behind him and covered his eyes. "Guess who?"

He pulled away, hardly looking at her, and she recalled his departing words on the slope—or rather, the tone in which he'd said them.

Reese plunked down beside him on the bench and rubbed her cold hands together. The mock plan to win Sawyer probably seemed to be working from his perspective, which was exactly what they'd set out to do.

"You seem to be making headway." He didn't sound entirely pleased.

"I guess."

"What do you mean? You were rolling in the snow like a couple of lovebirds." His mouth smiled, but his eyes didn't follow.

"Well. It's a start."

He nodded. "And then what?"

"What do you mean?"

He looked at her then, those piercing blue eyes, and she knew exactly what he meant. The wedding. The town's only hope. Her plan, if it succeeded, would ruin it all, and they both knew it.

She felt like a dog for even pretending to attempt it. He must think she was selfish to the extreme. It was right there in his eyes, and she hated it. *God, I wanted Griffen to notice me, but I'm making a mess of it. Now he thinks I'm a jerk.*

A lock of hair had flipped over his forehead and tangled in his long lashes. She fought the urge to brush it away, fisting her hands. She looked back into his eyes, and that's when it hit her.

She loved him. Not just loved him—she was *in* love with him. Two totally different things. How had it happened so quickly? The line between "love" and "in love" was much thinner than she'd thought.

"What?" he asked.

And she was suddenly sure her every emotion must be sketched on her face.

"Nothing." She cupped her cold hands over her mouth and warmed them with her breath. How ironic, the way her feelings had flip-flopped. She now felt only friendship toward the man she used to love, and was in love with the man who used to be her friend.

Maybe she should just tell him. Right now. End the charade. Get it off her chest once and for all. *Griffen, I don't love Sawyer . . . I love you.*

See, she even had the words. They were right there. She opened her mouth to say them, willing the words to make the short journey from her brain to her tongue.

But fear reached up and snatched them from her throat. Only air escaped her parted lips.

He looked away, his jaw twitching.

*What a tangled web we weave when first we practice to deceive.* The old quote scrolled across her brain like a TV crawler.

Griffen was probably hating her, hating himself for his own part in this scheme. Maybe it was time to end this charade. If she couldn't tell him her feelings, she could at least let him off the hook.

"You know," she said, "why don't we just call it quits."

"What do you mean?"

She tucked her hands in her pockets, warming them. "You don't want to do this anymore. I get it. I can take it from here."

"Get someone else to help, you mean."

She shrugged. Hadn't thought that far ahead, but the mere thought of another charade left her exhausted. Weren't things complicated enough?

"No," Griffen said. "Said I'd help, and I will."

He still didn't look too happy about it, but Reese was at a loss as to how to fix the mess. She bumped his shoulder, trying to lighten the mood. "You sure?"

Griffen stood and pulled his gloves from his pockets. "I'm sure."

# CHAPTER TEN

. . . . . . . . . . . . . . . . . . . . . . . . . . . .

*T*he new bells jangled as the door to Reese's shop opened. Shelby entered, brushing bits of snow from her shoulders.

Reese shut off the drill and handed it to Griffen. "Hey, Shelby."

Shelby stopped in her tracks. "Oh my goodness, it's finished!"

Reese perused the space, trying to see it with fresh eyes. It looked just as she'd imagined. The wide wooden floorboards were spotless, and the plumbing and heat were functional. Tomorrow she'd do a good cleaning, and soon the shop would be packed with merchandise and, hopefully, customers.

"Just about," Griffen said, heading toward the cooler for a water break. "We're still waiting on the new countertop, and we need to get it wired for Internet."

Reese's eyes followed him longingly. It was already the last week in January. *Eighteen more days.* She could hear the ticking clock and was helpless to stop it.

"I love the new canopy and the sign you made, Griffen. I don't know how you found the time."

"Anything for my best girl."

How many times had he called her that? Now the old pet name was nothing but a punch in the gut.

Shelby gave her a sympathetic smile, then ran her gloved hand along the smooth wooden shelving. "It's all coming together. Your shop is ready, the media are booked, and the bride has arrived."

Kate Owens was quickly winning over the town. She was as sweet as she was beautiful. The *Smitten Gazette* had run a nice feature on her three days earlier.

"I can't believe it's two and a half weeks away."

"Me neither. Hey, the reason I'm here—I just spoke with Nat, and we thought we might call an impromptu meeting of the girls since we missed last week."

"We're about finished for the day, I guess. Besides, I need to get out of these fumes." She looked at Griffen, half tempted to invite him along.

"Go on. I want to get that last shelf up. I'll lock up when I'm done."

So much for that idea.

"Great. Thanks, Griff."

Shelby texted Natalie while Reese slipped into her coat and grabbed her purse. As they headed outside, sadness bloomed deep inside Reese. All this time together, all the subterfuge and public displays of affection, and where was she? Square one.

Shelby pocketed her phone. "Isn't it beautiful?"

Reese emerged from her self-pity long enough to look around. Flurries fell, coating the village with a fresh white blanket. Lights twinkled from shop windows, glowing softly on the snow.

"It is beautiful." The village was silent, except for the snow crunching under their feet. Smitten was so empty. Hardly a body in sight, and it was nearing the weekend. Where were the lovers? Shouldn't things be picking up at least a little? A thread of worry inched through her.

Her eyes fell on the wreath gracing Sweet Surrender's entrance, and guilt pricked at the door of her heart. She should have more faith. Why was it so hard to just believe?

If only real faith were as easy as hanging a wreath. Hadn't she hung hers? And yet the doubt remained. She woke in the middle of the night sometimes, fear clawing at her throat. What if it didn't work? What if she lost everything she'd saved? What if, despite all their efforts, the town died, and a year from now Smitten was nothing but a ghost town?

What if she lost not only her shop but Griffen too? The ticking clock grew louder each day. At such times, what could she do but pray? It was out of her hands now. She couldn't make tourists come, and she couldn't make Griffen love her.

*Give me faith, Jesus. Help my unbelief.*

When they reached the coffee shop, Reese held the door for Shelby. They entered the warm, cozy shop and shucked their winter gear in the corner. Julia and Natalie greeted them as they sank into the cushy leather.

She hated to be a wet blanket, but that's how she felt tonight. Not even the sweet smell of freshly baked cookies lifted her spirits. She reached for the cup of comfort Natalie set at her fingertips. "Thanks, Nat."

Natalie took one look at her face, and her brown eyes softened. "You look tired. Are you okay?" She looked at Shelby for a clue, but Shelby just lifted her delicate shoulders.

Reese hated to admit her lack of faith, even to her best friends. Why pull them down? Instead she focused on her other worry. On the love of her life who would slip out of town, out of her grip, in a matter of days.

"It's Griffen."

"Things not going well?" Natalie asked.

Reese shook her head.

"I thought for sure after that day when we sat in here with Sawyer, he was coming around. I mean, for crying out loud, he ate chocolate off your lips."

Julia's brows jumped. "What?"

"Do tell," Shelby said.

"It was . . ." Natalie fanned her face. "Wow."

A gurgle escaped Reese's throat. "And yet, when we're alone, nothing. It was all for show. Turns out Griffen is quite the actor. The love of my life is helping me get another man's attention, and he seems to be more than happy to do so."

Reese dropped her head into her hands. What had she been thinking? This was torture. What was more hurtful than the man you loved handing you on a platter to another man?

She felt someone smoothing her hair. Shelby probably. She should warn her about the thick coat of dust.

"Poor baby," Natalie murmured. "What can we do?"

"She needs a makeover," Julia said.

"Thanks a lot," Reese said into her hands.

"Well, that ponytail," Julia said. "Really, it practically screams *one of the guys*."

Reese lifted her head. "I'm remodeling a building."

"Please," Julia said. "You've had your hair in a ponytail for fifteen years."

Reese pursed her lips. She wished she could deny it but, well . . .

"A makeover for the wedding," Shelby said. "I love it."

Natalie leaned forward, eyes twinkling, clearly ready to jump on board the Makeover Express. "She'll need a mani and pedi and a facial, of course. I'll do her makeup after Julia fixes her skin."

Reese felt her cheeks. Her skin was one of her best features, or so she'd thought. "What's wrong with my skin?"

"You have great skin. But I can make it glow."

"What are you planning to wear for the wedding?" Natalie asked.

"Wear? I don't know. The wedding's over two weeks away. I'll probably hit the thrift store next week."

Julia closed her eyes in a long blink. "I'll pretend I didn't hear that."

"I'm only going to wear it once."

Natalie set her hand over Reese's, her diamond flashing under the lights. *Show-off.*

"It's your best shot to make Griffen see you as a woman," she said. "Do you really want to be wearing, well, that horrid shade you're wearing now, for instance?"

Reese glanced down at her sweatshirt. "What's wrong with orange?"

"That's it," Natalie said. "I'm taking you dress shopping—and not at the thrift store."

"And I'm scheduling spa time the morning of the wedding."

"You're closed that day."

"Not anymore. Emergency makeover time."

"I'll be busy at my shop—or I'm hoping to be."

"It'll only take a few hours, and everyone else will be getting ready for the wedding too."

"I can fill in at the shop," Shelby said.

"We're going to make you so beautiful you'll knock his socks off," Natalie said.

Shelby clapped. "This is going to be so fun!"

Reese wasn't sure she liked being an emergency, but her friends' hopeful smiles were contagious.

"This calls for a celebration." Natalie hopped up. "Desserts on the house."

Reese was still down about Griffen. This was no time for Natalie's gluten-free cookies. "I think I speak for all of us when I say, 'Brownies, please.'"

Natalie's laugh carried back to them. "Don't worry. I made a batch of cookies for my aunts, so I made some extras for us."

Julia and Shelby began planning out Reese's spa day and were still at it when Natalie returned with a plate of gooey cookies.

"I'm so spoiling my dinner," Julia said.

"Me too." Of course, when dinner was a can of bean-with-bacon soup and a banana, that wasn't saying much.

"Guess what?" Natalie sank into the sofa and bit into a cookie. "A reporter from the Associated Press called Carson today. He's coming to Smitten to interview him about the town next week."

"That's wonderful!" Shelby said. "A little prewedding advertising won't hurt."

"That's what I thought."

They talked about last-minute plans for their own businesses as they geared up for the wedding guests. Smitten's business owners had met the week before to discuss the importance of exceptional service during the wedding weekend. When Reese checked her watch, she was surprised almost an hour had passed.

She wiped the crumbs from her lips. "Thanks for the cookies, Nat."

"Yeah, they hit the spot," Julia said.

"Totally worth breaking my diet for," Shelby added.

Reese pushed back. "Think I'll check in at the shop and see if Griffen's still there."

"Wait," Natalie said. "I have an announcement." She looked like she was about to go into liftoff sequence. "The cookies . . ." She made eye contact with each of them, stretching the moment. "They were gluten-free." She fairly sang the last part.

Silence spanned the space. Reese swiped the inside of her mouth for an aftertaste. Nope. She hadn't noticed a texture issue either.

"No way," Julia said.

"Yay!" Shelby clapped. "You did it."

Reese smiled. "Have to hand it to you, I couldn't tell the difference. Way to go, Nat. Just in time for tourists."

"They'll be on the shelves first thing tomorrow morning. Just wanted to make sure they passed the taste test."

Reese looked at the empty chocolate-smudged plate. "I'd say they passed with flying colors."

# Chapter Eleven

. . . . . . . . . . . . . . . . . . . . . . . . .

*R*eese helped Griffen square the new countertop that had finally arrived the day before: an extravagant slab of speckled granite. It had taken three men plus Reese to set the piece, but it was a beauty. She ran her fingers over the smooth edges.

Behind her, Griffen cleared his throat. "Excuse me."

One of his hands was on the slab beside her. She could feel the heat of his body nearly touching her back.

"Oh. Sorry." She jumped out of his way, her heart rate betraying her. She watched him finish squaring the piece. He set the level and checked. Her eyes roamed from his broad shoulders down to the sturdy span of his waist and she sighed.

The counter was the last thing. The last missing piece of the puzzle. The shop was sparkling clean and ready for merchandise. With one week to go before the wedding, she was on track for her grand opening.

But after the counter was installed, Griffen's work here was done.

Her phone vibrated in her pocket, and Reese checked it before answering.

"Hey, Nat."

Her friend screamed something, but Reese couldn't tell what. "Wait, Nat, slow down—what happened?"

"The guy, the newspaper guy, his article, it's in all the papers!"

"What?"

"The Associated Press reporter! The one who interviewed Carson—his article on Smitten has been picked up by tons of newspapers nationwide. It's all about—well, I'll send you the link. You have to read it!"

"That's awesome!"

Griffen was looking at her with raised brows. She covered the phone. "The AP article went nationwide."

He nodded, gave a thumbs-up, and went back to work.

"It's everywhere, and I mean everywhere," Natalie was saying. "The *Chicago Tribune*, a paper in Charlotte, and Boston, and Nashville, and just everywhere!"

"Wow, that's amazing. And it's positive?"

"Reservations are coming into Carson's office by the dozens. I have to go help answer phones, but I'm sending it now. Go read it. You won't believe it."

Reese pocketed her phone and entered her office. "She sent the link."

Griffen followed her into the small space. Her computer, set up a few days prior, sat in the middle of her ancient desk from home. She sank into the chair and opened her e-mail while Griffen positioned himself behind her.

"She said the article's all over the whole country. Can you believe it?"

He pointed. "There's the link."

A moment later, the *Washington Post* page opened. A photo of the snow-speckled village topped the article.

Griffen leaned low to read it, his breath tickling the back of her ear. His elbows jutted out on each side of her.

*Focus, girl.* Maybe if she read aloud, he'd move his tempting self. She shifted forward and began reading.

"The Little Town That Could." She smiled. "I like that." She cleared her throat and began.

"Once upon a time there was a tiny village named Smitten, snug at the base of Sugarcreek Mountain in northern Vermont. The town, home to country-singing sensation Sawyer Smitten, thrived due to its booming milling industry.

"One day the economy turned bad, and the little town lost its major employer. The town's engine had faltered, and the residents feared Smitten was months away from dying. But an idea swept through the village: *What if we turn Smitten into a romantic getaway destination?* Nearby ski slopes, cozy cabins, and a secluded lake made it the ideal location for a romantic rendezvous . . . not to mention the very name of the town. The engine roared to life.

"An idea was born, but could the town pull off the major transition? Some feared not. Enter a little girl with a big faith. Five-year-old Mia Mansfield was in Sunday school when she heard a story of faith. She took it upon herself to pray for her village. Then little Mia hung a lavender wreath on her door, a symbol of her faith that Smitten would not only survive but thrive once again. Word spread, and wreaths began appearing on doorways throughout the tiny village.

"And then Sawyer Smitten and his Hollywood fiancée Kate Owens decided on a Valentine's Day wedding in Smitten. The villagers' hopes soared. Wealthy guests and media were just what the town needed to put Smitten on the map. The little engine began a long uphill climb.

"Renovations began: a new ice rink was installed on the town square, the river walk was revamped, the Carriage House bed-and-breakfast hung its shingle, the chapel was restored to its former glory, and new stores opened—a sweet shop, a spa, an artisan gallery, and an outfitters store, all catering to traveling lovebirds. The town emptied its coffers, then raised more money and emptied them once again. As the money drained, so did their faith. But the villagers looked to the wreaths, hanging on nearly every door in town, to remind them of their faith.

"Now, with renovations complete and the wedding around the corner, all the residents of Smitten, Vermont, can do is wait. The destiny of their village is only a week away, a short but steep climb to the top of the hill.

"When asked if she thought the town could pull off its monumental task, little Mia smiled confidently and said, 'I think we can.'"

Hope flowed through Reese. It was a wonderful, heart-warming story. She leaned back and smiled over her shoulder. "What a great article—"

Griffen was still there, a mere breath away, his head propped on his arm. She inhaled, and the faint scent of his musky soap teased her senses. Their eyes locked, and she felt her smile slipping away. The moment drew out, lingering in the air, a moment that would either land nimbly on Something Meaningful or sprawl awkwardly on the floor between them.

"Reese . . ." His eyes were pools of liquid, pulling her into their warm depths. "You're buzzing."

It took three full seconds for his meaning to kick in. Her phone vibrated in her pocket. She popped from the chair and pulled out her phone, her heart scampering away to hide beneath her ribs.

"Yeah," she said, answering it, her voice breathless.

"Did you hear?"

"Sawyer. Yeah. Yeah, I just read the article. Great, huh?"

Noises sounded behind her, but she didn't dare turn around. Didn't want Griffen to see the flush that heated her cheeks.

"I'll say."

"Nat said the phones are lighting up at Carson's office."

"He told me. I'd say things are going better than anyone expected."

"I'd say so."

At least some things were. She could hear Griffen working in the store, and turned to face her empty office.

"Well, all eyes are on Smitten now," Sawyer said.

"I think you're right."

"Hey, I also wanted to thank you again for the ski lesson. I've been practicing on my own, and I think I can pull it off without embarrassing myself too badly."

"That's great, Sawyer."

"Thank Griffen for me too. You guys make a great couple."

Her heart gave a little squeeze. "Will do."

"Listen, I gotta run, but I know you were worried, so thought I'd call."

"Thanks. See you around."

Reese sank onto the window ledge, her legs shaky from

the adrenaline rush. Was Griffen weirded out by the moment they'd just shared? Had he guessed her feelings? Had she seen something in his eyes, or had she only imagined what she longed to see?

She should just go tell him. Walk into the room, turn him around, and tell him she was in love with him, not Sawyer. Maybe she'd pull it off this time.

But even as the thought formed, even as the ticking clock grew louder and seemed to pick up speed, her fingers gripped tight on the windowsill and refused to let go.

# CHAPTER TWELVE

. . . . . . . . . . . . . . . . . . . . . . . . . . .

*L*ook down." Natalie came at Reese with a fat mascara wand.

Reese obeyed, then felt the tug of the wand on her upper lashes. After Julia's ministrations at her beautiful new spa, her skin did indeed glow. From there, they'd moved to Reese's house, where Natalie began her work on Reese. She was nearly finished with the makeup but hadn't let her subject so much as peek in the mirror.

Natalie fanned her lashes dry. "Okay, look up."

Reese looked at the ceiling. "You're not caking it on, are you? I want to be recognizable, you know."

"Relax. I'm just bringing out your natural beauty."

Reese snorted, then shifted in the chair.

"Sit still."

"You almost done?"

Natalie pulled her hand away, capped the mascara, then came at her with a tube of rose-colored lipstick. "Do this." She parted her lips.

Reese did the same, sighing. She was nervous and tired. Her shop's grand opening three days earlier had been a huge success, thanks in part to the Associated Press article.

Wedding guests had begun trickling into town, checking in at the newly completed Timber Lake Lodge on Carson's old property and at the Maple Valley Inn where the mill had been and into Carson's refurbished cabins out by the lake.

The ski event had gone off without a hitch, and this morning's edition of several New England newspapers featured a photo of Sawyer and Kate on the slopes.

No skiing for Reese, though. Outdoor Adventures had been hopping right through the concert on the square the night before. She'd hoped to catch some of Sawyer's show but had ended up working late. She'd had to settle for hearing his band through the shop windows and peeking out the door during brief lulls. They'd set up an enormous tent, complete with commercial-size heaters. The tourists seemed to have had a blast.

This morning had been a blur too, as many of the wedding guests rented ski equipment, snowmobiles, and skates. The shop was closed now, but she hoped Shelby hadn't regretted filling in for her this afternoon.

Natalie's shop had been bustling as well, and there were similar reports from other business owners, all of whom were working hard to please the tourists.

The media had arrived in full force that afternoon, and Carson, Sawyer, and Mia had been busy granting interviews. Cameramen stood on street corners, media vans clogged Main Street, and there'd been nothing but rave reviews so far from the guests. Smitten seemed to be on its way to a successful future.

*Thank you, Jesus. You've been so good to us.*

Natalie dragged the lipstick across her lower lip, tugging. "Wait till you see Mia in her flower girl dress. Oh my goodness. So adorable."

"I'll bet she looks like a little princess."

"She does. And Carson . . . well, let's just say he's not looking so bad in his tux."

"I'll take your word for it."

Natalie leaned back, assessing her work, and gave a final nod.

"Now the dress." Natalie capped the lipstick, then took the garment from Reese's bedroom door.

They'd spent four painful hours at the boutique the previous Saturday. Reese had tried on every dress in the store, frowning at the lace and ruffles that made her feel like a little girl playing dress-up.

Natalie handed her the dress and went to put away the makeup while Reese slipped into it.

"Careful of your hair," Natalie called over her shoulder.

They'd finally settled on a satin icy pink number that hit just above the knee. The structured A-line dress, elegant in simplicity, was devoid of ruffles and lace, thank goodness. Its only adornment was a white ribbon sash that encircled the empire waistline. Reese slid her arms through the straps and clutched the bodice to her chest.

"Zip me up?"

Natalie bustled into the room, and moments later the dress clung to Reese's middle, flaring gently over the curve of her hips.

"Beautiful! I forgot what a great figure you have—buried the way it always is under yards of sweatshirt material. Put these on." Natalie handed her the flesh-colored heels that she'd insisted would make Reese's legs appear longer.

She slipped them on. "Can I look now?" Reese wanted to get this over with.

"Not yet." Natalie handed her the matching wrap. "Here."

Part of her wanted to get the whole evening over with. Griffen wasn't leaving until next week, but tonight felt very much like her last chance. It was a lot of pressure to put on a layer of makeup and some satiny material. What if it wasn't enough? What if, no matter what she wore, no matter how she looked, Griffen only saw her as one of the guys? His best buddy?

"Stop frowning. You look gorgeous." Natalie grabbed Reese's hand and tugged.

Reese followed her to the freestanding mirror that waited in the corner of the room.

Griffen grabbed the bouquet of flowers from the passenger seat and exited his SUV. Reese lived in a red Craftsman-style house just outside of town, in her childhood home. He couldn't have counted the hours they'd spent shooting hoops on the court by her detached garage, or the hours shoveling snow in her neighborhood to raise some pocket cash.

The cement walkway to her porch was cleared of snow, revealing cracks and crevices caused by burgeoning roots from nearby maple trees. He neared the porch and took the steps slowly, tugging at the tight collar of his dress shirt. He couldn't recall being so nervous, having such mixed feelings about a date.

On one hand, he was getting to spend time with his favorite girl. On the other, she was trying to win another man's heart. Or had she given up, being that it was the evening of the wedding, and so far her plan seemed to have gained her nothing—hand-holding at the coffee shop notwithstanding.

He wondered how she felt tonight at the prospect of watching the man she loved pledge his love to another.

*How do you think she feels, Parker?* Hadn't he left town three years ago, just so he didn't have to endure the same? Hadn't the thought of Sawyer and Reese's wedding been enough to drive him from his hometown? It was reason for the tulips in his hand. He'd wanted to get her something for Valentine's, and hoped the bouquet might make her feel special on an otherwise painful day.

He drew a deep breath and knocked on the old door, gearing himself up for a difficult evening. She'd probably be a mess by the end of the night, but he'd be there for her. Of course he would.

It was time for him to face facts, though. Time for him to give up the fantasy that Reese would ever return his feelings. He'd go back to Pennsylvania, back to his sparse little apartment, back to his job. Smitten was on its way to a successful future. They didn't need him anymore.

And neither did Reese.

He heard movement inside. He'd better think of something to say or he'd get tongue-tied at the sight of her and say something stupid.

*Reese. You look like an angel.* Stupid *and* corny.

*Hey, you clean up well.* He gave a sharp shake of his head. Why not just give her a high five?

*Happy Valentine's Day, pretty lady.* Hmm. He tilted his head, thinking. Not bad. Casual, but complimentary. He wiped his damp palms down his pant legs.

The door opened, and Natalie beamed at him.

"Griffen, look at you, all dolled up!"

She wore a blue dress, and her dark hair was caught up on her head.

"You look great, Natalie."

"Thanks." She pulled him inside and turned toward the stairway.

Griffen followed her eyes toward the vision in pink that was descending. His jaw went slack.

Reese. Not athletic, little buddy Reese, but stunning, womanly Reese.

Silky curls trickled over her bare shoulders like a golden waterfall. The shimmery dress clung to her slim torso, then skimmed past her hips, stopping at the top of her knees.

His eyes strayed back to her face. She looked softer, more delicate. Her eyes took center stage. He'd never seen them so bright and sparkly.

His heart marched up into his throat and rendered him speechless.

She reached the bottom of the steps and stood, her small hand gripping the boxed newel post.

*Say something, Parker.*

"Reese . . ." *Brilliant, you know her name.*

What was that line again? He swallowed, a joke since his throat was as dry as a plate of sawdust, then remembered the flowers in his hand. *Valentine's Day.*

Smiling, he held them out. "Happy Valentine's Day, pretty lady."

Her eyes smiled first, then spread to her lips. "You rehearsed that."

"I did."

"I'll forgive you since you brought me tulips." She took the flowers from him. "My favorite. Thanks."

He couldn't seem to take his eyes off her. "But I have to admit my line seems woefully short of reality. You look . . . wow, Reese."

She looked down at the tulips, a pretty blush blooming on her cheeks. "Thank you. You're looking pretty dapper yourself."

Natalie appeared, buttoning her coat. "I'm going to run now. Oooh, pretty flowers." She gave Reese a wink. "See you two at the chapel."

After Natalie left, Reese found a vase in a kitchen cupboard.

Griffen took the opportunity to look her over one more time. He could probably span her tiny waist with his hands if she ever let him that close. Reese was so strong and capable, he forgot how small she was sometimes.

She set the flowers on the table, then turned, tugging her lower lip with her teeth. He reminded himself that she had a difficult night ahead.

He squeezed her hand and found it cold. "You okay?"

When she nodded, Griffen helped her on with her coat and escorted her to his SUV. His heart thumped so loudly on the drive to the chapel, he wondered if she could feel the vibrations.

The church was bustling with activity. Lit from within, the stained-glass windows burst with color. They used the valet parking and entered the chapel behind a couple Griffen recognized from TV. The media were there, he knew, tucked away in the balcony as requested by the bride and groom.

They presented their invitations to security and moved forward into the sanctuary. The pews were already packed, but there was still room near the back.

"Wow," Reese whispered.

He followed her eyes to the front of the sanctuary. A white liner led down the center aisle to a candlelit altar covered with sprays of white and purple flowers. Swaths of silver fabric draped from the ceiling beams creating a soft, romantic look.

They took their seats on the aisle near the back and waited for the ceremony to begin. The Garner Sisters played at the corner of the stage, something slow and heartfelt. Someone must've dressed them, because the women were clothed in neutral shades of champagne, even Violet, though her red hair and lipstick stood out like a shining beacon.

Beside him, Reese fidgeted with her bracelet. She had to be hurting. He wished he had the words to comfort her. Instead, he gathered his courage and put his arm around her. Comfort. He was only trying to comfort her.

She looked up at him with wide eyes that looked vulnerable and afraid. Without thinking, he pulled her into his side. She settled there, his little Reese, with a soft sigh.

A moment later, the parents were seated. When the song ended, there was a brief pause while Sawyer and Carson, in their tuxes, shuffled out at the front.

The procession began with the melodic strains of the strings. The bridesmaids, clothed in silver dresses, glided down the aisle on the groomsmen's arms. After them, Mia appeared in the doorway, clutching a miniature bouquet. Her skirt was a white cloud, dotted with tiny purple flowers. The crowd's sigh was audible and quickly followed by a rapid fire of camera clicks from the side balcony. Mia reached into the basket and scattered what looked like a handful of sparkly snowflakes.

"Look," Reese whispered. "She's wearing a lavender wreath."

Sure enough, a delicate wreath topped the girl's curly hair. The little girl with a big faith had captured the hearts of America.

When Mia reached the front, there was a pause as the song ended. A shuffling sounded in the doorway behind them, then the familiar strains of the "Wedding March" began. The crowd rose to its feet. Griffen and Reese followed.

Kate Owens appeared in the doorway, draped in an elaborate white gown. Her shining eyes and wide smile were trained straight ahead. She began walking, and the guests turned as she passed them. Regardless of the press, of the crowded sanctuary, it was clear Kate only had eyes for Sawyer. The groom, likewise, only had eyes for his bride.

When she reached the front, the pastor instructed them to be seated. He began talking, and Griffen realized he was building to the question. How had he forgotten about the question?

"We are gathered here today to celebrate one of life's most memorable moments, to recognize the gift of love, and to ask God's blessing on the unity of Sawyer and Kate in holy matrimony."

Reese wouldn't speak out. Would she? But hadn't that been one of the reasons he'd left before? Hadn't he been afraid that, in some weak and foolish moment, he'd blurt out his feelings and ruin Reese's special day?

Had she been devising a secret plan to announce her feelings for Sawyer today with all the world watching?

"Should there be anyone who has cause why this couple should not be united in holy matrimony, they must speak now or forever hold their peace."

The silence was sudden and sharp, like the crack of a whip. It was her last chance, and he prayed she wouldn't take it. He felt for her hand and gathered it in his own as if he could will her to let the moment pass. Her palm was cool and clammy. Her fingers twitched, and he tightened his grip. *Don't do it, Reese. Don't do it.*

"Who brings this woman to this man?"

Griffen expelled a breath he didn't realize he'd held. He glanced down at Reese. Her eyes were straight ahead, her jaw set. He imagined how he'd feel if he were witnessing Reese and Sawyer becoming one flesh, and his heart twisted. His poor little Reese. He would take the pain and make it his own if he could. He squeezed her hand, willing his strength to pass into her.

# CHAPTER THIRTEEN

. . . . . . . . . . . . . . . . . . . . . . . . . . . . .

*T*he reception was held in the beautiful Sugarcreek Ski Lodge, located ten minutes outside Smitten. Reese surveyed the lofted space from her seat at the table.

It didn't look remotely like the room she'd sat in with Griffen a month earlier after they'd given Sawyer his ski lesson. The lodge had been transformed into a winter wonderland. White lights dangled from the wooden trusses like twinkling icicles. Sprays of flowers anchored round tables that were covered in shimmering silver, and great clusters of white-painted branches flanked the stone walls.

Dinner had been served, the towering cake had been cut, the bridal bouquet thrown, and now guests danced on the parquet floor to the celebratory strains of the band. The media people had left, rushing to meet their deadlines. Tomorrow's papers and news programs would be littered with news of the celebrity wedding.

Reese scanned the crowd for her friends. On the dance floor, Carson held Mia in his arms and danced with Natalie at the same time. No doubt they were dreaming of the day they would become a family. With the adoption being finalized in a few short weeks and their summer wedding approaching, it wouldn't be long. The couple had come so far from the antagonistic relationship they'd shared a year ago. Natalie looked so happy, her cheeks flushed, her eyes sparkling. Reese was glad for her.

.A short distance away she spotted Shelby and Nick, gliding across the floor gracefully. The couple had eyes only for each other. Shelby had managed to talk Nick into a suit and a clean shave, and the way he was holding her, she didn't think he was going to let go anytime soon. If Reese's hunch was right, a proposal wouldn't be long in coming. Grace surely did cover a multitude of sins. Those two were proof of what happened when unconditional love stepped in.

She searched the crowd again and finally found Julia and Zak sitting by the enormous fireplace, their heads close together in conversation. Julia tossed her head back, laughing, and Zak ran his finger inside his collar, tugging. So different, those two, and yet so perfect together. Reese shook her head, amazed by the power of love and the unexpected blessings that God sent into her friends' lives.

The crowd on the dance floor applauded, drawing Reese's attention. Sawyer twirled his bride, then drew her into his arms with a great flourish. Reese thought back to the new song he'd sung during the ceremony. The whole chapel had seemed to melt. The lyrics to "Smitten" were lovely, the melody haunting, and somehow he'd written the words so you couldn't tell if he was singing about his woman or his hometown. But there was no doubt as he sang it tonight that the words were for his bride alone.

The words rang in Reese's ears even now.

*I'm just gonna say it*
*Gonna lay my heart,*

*There on the line*
*Every time I wrap my arms around you*
*Whisper in your ear,*
*I realize*

*That I'm smitten*
*Oh, I'm smitten*
*Yes I'm smitten*

*By your love.*

Kate had dabbed her eyes after he sang the last romantic words, and she wasn't the only one. Reese had no doubt the song was going to hit the charts upon its release.

Reese propped her chin on her palm and watched the newlyweds longingly. It wasn't that she wasn't happy for Sawyer. It was that she longed for that kind of love—the kind that was returned. Why had God let these feelings develop if Griffen wasn't going to return them?

He loved her, she didn't doubt that. But there was a vast difference between loving a friend and being thoroughly, well, smitten. It hurt to be the one who loved more. She wondered if God felt this way. *After all, our love for you really can't measure up to your extravagant love for us. I'm sorry, God. Let me love you like you love me. Make me smitten.*

Griffen appeared at her side with her drink and dropped into his chair. They were the only two left at the circular table.

"Thanks," she said.

When he followed her eyes to the dance floor, she peeked

at him through her lashes. A shadow flickered over his jaw as he watched the bride and groom dancing.

A moment later, he turned back to her. "I'm sorry things didn't work out the way you wanted."

His eyes were all melty, and she pulled hers away before she got sucked in. "I'll be fine." She threw in a brave smile for good measure.

She didn't want to talk about Sawyer Smitten and her supposed pathetic crush. "Hey, at least the town's going to make it, huh? The influx from the weekend will fill the coffers back up for that advertising campaign Carson wants to launch."

From the corner of her eye she saw him nod.

"Sure, sure. And your shop's going to do great. I'm proud of you, throwing it all on the line that way. I know it wasn't easy for you."

He did know her, better than anyone else, in fact. And yet, she had this secret thing she didn't dare tell him.

A lump grew in her throat. "Yeah, well, couldn't have done it without you, buddy." She winced. Why did she say that? That was the last thing she wanted him to think.

There was a pause as the song ended, then the band struck up a new tune. The lead singer lifted the microphone and crooned the words, "Someday . . . when I'm awfully low . . ."

She listened a moment, the poignancy of the words not lost on her.

Griffen leaned back in his chair and his thigh brushed hers, sending a flash of heat through her.

"I've decided to leave tomorrow," he said.

Her eyes flew to his, her stomach dropping somewhere in

the vicinity of her ankles. "What? I thought you were leaving next week."

"I was, but . . . I think I'll get an earlier start."

The hands of the ticking clock whirled forward, erasing hours, days. This couldn't be happening. "What's the rush?"

He looked toward the dance floor, shrugging. "My work here is done, you know?"

It was done, all right. He'd come to town, bowled her over, and made her love him.

"Like you said, Smitten will be fine. The revamping is complete." He tossed her a smile. "I'm taking my tools and going home."

*Don't forget my heart. You're taking that too.* The lump swelled, choking off an appropriate response.

So it was over. She'd lost her chance. And seeing her all dolled up hadn't changed a thing. Had she really thought it would?

There were no stars in his eyes tonight, only pity. No lingering caresses of a lover, only the comforting touches of a friend. He didn't love her. He only felt sorry for her.

Her eyes began to burn. She had to get out of here before she made a real fool of herself. She popped to her feet, turning. "I'm going to the ladies' room."

He angled a look her direction. "You okay?"

She waved his concern away. "Fine. Be right back."

She wove through the tables to the back of the lodge on wobbly legs. The hall by the restroom was crowded with loud, giddy women. Sweat beaded on the back of her neck. She couldn't go in there. She needed a moment alone. She needed air. She was suffocating in this tight dress.

Turning left, she pushed the door that led to a brick patio. Air washed over her, cooling her skin. She breathed, letting the chilly air fill her lungs.

Evergreens sheltered the patio from the wind and sparkled with white dancing lights. Their glow made the snow into a carpet of gold. Not to be outdone, the stars shimmered in the night sky. The temperature had warmed through the day, and she could hear the *drip, drip, drip* of icicles melting nearby.

Reese drew a deeper breath, and the expansion of her lungs almost choked her. He was leaving tomorrow. All these weeks she'd wasted trying to make him jealous, and for what? She'd lost her chance.

She spied a bench along the stone wall and lowered her weight onto it. The faint strains of "The Way You Look Tonight" bled through the walls. It didn't matter how she looked tonight. Not one iota.

The song ended, and all was quiet for a moment. The kind of hush that only a snow-shrouded landscape brought. Then the band struck up another tune.

The music grew louder when the door behind her opened. Natalie shivered as she approached the bench. "Brrr. What are you doing out here, and without a coat?"

"It's not so cold."

Natalie sank down beside her. They listened to the music for a moment. The dripping snowmelt, a woman's laughter from the hallway.

"He's leaving tomorrow," Reese said. What would it feel like to lose him? To have him living two states away? To wait a month just to hear his voice?

"Why don't you just tell him, Reese?"

As it always did, her heart raced at the thought of revealing her secret. Her mouth dried, and adrenaline raced through her veins like she was about to parachute from a plane instead of just admit her feelings.

Natalie brushed Reese's hair over her shoulder. "If he's leaving anyway, what does it matter? Even if it makes things awkward, you won't have to face him every day."

That was true. Still, there were the phone calls. Could she stand to hear the pity in his voice? To hear how bad he felt that he couldn't return her feelings? Not to mention the loss of his friendship. Things would never be the same.

"Remember when Julia was sure Zak didn't return her feelings, and we encouraged her to tell him? It worked out, didn't it? I know you don't like stepping off into the great unknown, but, honey, sometimes you have to step out in faith and trust God to work it out. Like we did with the town. It wasn't easy for any of us. But we laid it all on the line and left the results up to God. He's come through pretty well, hasn't he?"

Reese nodded. "You're right. I just can't seem to make myself do it. I've tried—I have. The words just get all crammed in my throat."

"Well, if he's leaving tomorrow, it's now or never." Natalie smiled sympathetically. "Speak now or forever hold your peace."

The wedding words took on a whole new meaning, and Reese gave a wry grin. Natalie was right, but how would she find the courage?

Natalie gathered Reese's hand in hers and bowed her head.

"Jesus, you've done amazing things. Right before our eyes, you've transformed our little town, saved it. We thank you for that. You're faithful and good, and you bless us with far more than we deserve. I pray for my friend right now. Give her the courage to follow your leading, whatever direction that may take her. Wrap your arms around her and comfort her." Natalie gave her a squeeze.

"Amen. Thanks, Nat."

Her friend rubbed her bare shoulders, warming them. "You do look beautiful tonight, honey. I saw the way Griffen looked at you when you were coming down those stairs."

Reese breathed a laugh. "He was shocked to see me without a ponytail and sneakers." Still, at the memory of that look, her flesh tingled.

"Maybe . . ."

The music grew louder, and they both turned to see Griffen exiting the building.

"There you are," he said.

Natalie gave Reese a sympathetic smile. "I'm heading back inside."

Reese turned a pleading look on her friend, who nevertheless sprang off the bench and passed Griffen.

"Carson's looking for you," he said.

"Thanks, Griffen." And then she was gone.

Reese stood, all nerves, her legs wobbling on these stupid heels Natalie had talked her into.

Griffen pulled off his jacket and held it open for her.

She slipped her arms into the sleeves and pulled the jacket tight. "Thanks." It smelled of Griffen, and before she could stop herself, she drew a deep whiff.

"You okay?"

She shrugged. "Sure."

He looked at her, those blue eyes plumbing the depths. "I can take you home if you want."

She looked away before he saw too much. "I told Natalie I'd stay and help with the coffee equipment."

He tucked his hands into his trouser pockets. "Go back inside?"

She needed time to process what Natalie had said. A little time to weigh the pros and cons one last time before she broke down a wall she could never rebuild.

"You go on. I'm fine—just need a few minutes."

He tilted his head, looking at her intently. Blue eyes had never looked so warm. She couldn't look away. They were pulling her like a magnet. She didn't *want* to look away. Who knew when they would look at her that way again?

He opened his arms. "Dance?"

That was unexpected. She had an immediate image of herself curled in his arms, her head against his chest, his arms circling her waist. Sheer torture.

"Out here?" She cleared the squeak from her voice.

He shrugged. "Why not?"

Torture, yes. But perhaps her last chance. *Oh, why not?*

She stepped into his arms. He set his hands at her waist. She placed hers on his shoulders. So it wasn't like she'd pictured it. She could still feel his body heat beneath her palms. Still feel his breath on her temples.

"You did real good tonight," he whispered. "I know it was hard."

He had no idea. The hardest part of her night had just

begun. Pros and cons. Pros and cons. She couldn't think with him so close. Could only think of him leaving tomorrow. Of days and weeks and months without seeing him again.

Sure, she'd done it before. But that was before she'd fallen totally and completely in love with him. Everything was different now.

Different for her. Him, not so much.

Her eyes began to burn, and tears followed too quickly to stop them.

Griffen leaned back, frowning. "Hey, now."

His thumb caught the tear that spilled over, but another followed, and another. She couldn't seem to stop the flow once it began.

"Don't cry, Reese Cup. It'll be okay. You'll see." He pulled her into his arms, cradling her. His heart beat strong and steady against her temple, and she felt his deep sigh.

Her tears dampened his shirt. He'd said it would be okay, but it wouldn't. He didn't even understand her tears—thought they were for someone else.

Natalie's words rang in her ears. *"Sometimes you have to step out in faith and trust God to work it out."*

Her heart pummeled her ribs, and her mouth went dry. It was now or never. *Speak now or forever hold your peace.* She sucked in a breath. Breathed a prayer.

Reese pulled away. They were barely swaying now. She clenched her fists against his shoulders and looked into his eyes.

Words. She needed words. A few of them, strung together coherently, preferably.

Creases appeared between his brows. "You need me to stay longer? I can stick around until next week."

"Yes." She needed him. A few extra days. More time, another chance to get his attention without having to put it all on the line.

What was she doing? Chickening out again? She shook her head. "No. No, you don't have to stay."

He frowned, those blue eyes questioning.

No wonder. She was as changeable as the wind. She closed her eyes, unable to think with him looking at her that way. She opened them again, focused on the tight knot of the black tie at his throat.

She unclenched her fists and laid her hands flat against his shoulders. She took a deep breath and forced herself to say the words.

"Thing is, Griffen . . . I'm, uh, not in love with Sawyer." Heat crept up her neck and into her cheeks. Her legs trembled with the surge of adrenaline.

The pause stretched out, practically begged for a peek at his face. But she couldn't. Not if she was going to get through this.

"I don't understand," he said.

Well, he would in a minute. For better or worse. She swallowed hard. "I know. It's—it's all my fault. I led you to believe it, or I let you believe it, really, that day when Josh walked in and canceled our date. But the truth is, the *real* truth, is that—"

*Be brave, Reese. You can do this. Deep breaths.*

She forced her eyes to his. "See, somewhere along the way, Griff, I—I fell in love with you. I'm sorry, I know this must be a big shock, and I didn't even want to tell you because I was so afraid of losing you as a friend. But then you assumed I wanted to win Sawyer back, and I thought if we just spent time together, your feelings might change too, and then tonight, I thought seeing me this way might make you see me as not just your little buddy but as a woman, but then you said you were leaving, and—"

His lips parted, stretched, and then he was laughing.

*Laughing.*

The response was a kick, hard and low. She shivered, but it wasn't from the cold. She didn't know what she'd expected, but it wasn't this. Angry tears burned her eyes.

She glared, shoved her palms into his shoulders, and stepped from his embrace. "You're laughing at me?"

As quickly as the laugh surfaced, it was gone. Griffen held his hands up. "No, honey, I'm not laughing at you."

"Well, it sure sounds like it."

He looked away, forked his fingers through his hair, leaving it all tousled and boyishly charming, drat him. Then he looked back at her, disbelief in every line on his forehead, looking at her as if he'd never seen her before.

This was humiliating enough without the sheer shock. Without the cruel laughter. She hugged her body against the cold. Yeah, that was it. The cold.

He put his hands on his hips. "You don't love Sawyer."

"No."

"You weren't trying to break up the wedding, get him back, all that."

*"No."*

"You—you love *me*."

She felt her lip wobble. "You need it in blood? And if you start laughing again, Griffen Parker, I'm going to slug you so hard—"

He pulled her close until she was a breath away. When

he took her chin and tilted her face, she saw a new look in his eyes.

"I've waited three years for this, lady," he whispered.

He brushed her lips with his own. His kiss was gentle and strong all at once. The anger and hurt drained away, and she melted into his arms. She palmed his freshly shaven face, gave back everything he was giving. Soaked in the familiar smell of him, the familiar feel of him that was both old and new.

He deepened the kiss, and her legs nearly buckled. How had she missed this all these years? He was right there all along. Something he said before rushed to her mind. Three years.

She pulled back, already missing his kiss. But just looking at him was pretty good too. "You said three years."

"I did, didn't I?"

"Before you left?"

He gave a little smile. "You were engaged, Reese. I couldn't watch the love of my life find her happily-ever-after with someone else."

His words struck her speechless. How could she not have known? If she had . . . Well, she didn't know what would've happened. Maybe her eyes would've been opened. But maybe not.

*You knew, though, didn't you, God? You had this planned all along.*

"I'm so sorry," she said. "I didn't feel this way until you came back—that day on the basketball court."

His eyes narrowed. "When I knocked you down?"

"Bowled me over, more like."

He looked at her with wonder in his eyes, joy in the curve of his lips, then he framed her face in his palms. "This is the best Valentine's Day present I ever got, by far."

She smiled. "Better than the I-Heart-You chocolate Miranda Willoughby gave you in ninth grade?"

"Way better."

"Better than the teddy bear from Laurel Perkins?"

"You couldn't dig up a better Valentine's Day present if you searched the world over." His eyes flickered over her. "And look, it's even wrapped in pink."

Her smile widened. "You noticed."

"Oh, I noticed all right." And then he kissed her again, making her knees go weak in two seconds flat.

Her fingers found the curls at the nape of his neck and threaded their way through. Joy bubbled deep inside her heart.

Some things were destined to happen, she supposed. Unlikely matches, unexpected beginnings, unforeseeable love. She might not have believed it a year ago, maybe not even a week ago, but now . . . well, anything was possible when you were smitten.

# ACKNOWLEDGMENTS

*N*ever has a book been more of a labor of love than *Smitten*! The four of us have had the best time writing this book together.

But we couldn't have done it without lots of help. We are so blessed to have been able to do this project with Thomas Nelson. They caught the vision right from the start and entered into a partnership with us with great enthusiasm. A big hug and thanks to publisher Allen Arnold who was quick to tell us he wanted this project. And a big thank-you to our editor, Ami McConnell, who knows each one of us intimately and was able to make suggestions to bring our characters to life. Our team has worked hard on the project all along so we will be showing our gratitude with hugs and DeBrand truffles to Marketing Director Eric Mullett, Publicity Manager Katie Bond, cover designer Kristen Vasgaard, Marketing Specialist Ashley Schneider, Publicist Ruthie Harper, and editors Becky Monds, Jodi Hughes, Natalie Hanemann, and Amanda Bostic. Our terrific sales team is already hard at work too and we couldn't do much without them! Love you all! And our agents, Karen Solem and Lee Hough, have been a huge help as we put together this very different story. Thanks, friends!

A special thanks to Rick Acker for spending precious conference time sitting and brainstorming with us last year.

He helped us flesh out our plot with some great suggestions. And our editor, L.B. Norton, was phenomenal on
this project. She caught the inconsistencies that no one else
could. And our families are always our backbones as we jug-
gle life and career.

Our biggest thank-you goes to God who brought the four
of us together in a bond of unbreakable friendship. We are all
so different, and yet one, in our love for Christ and for one
another.

# Reading Group Guide

. . . . . . . . . . . . . . . . . . . . . . . . . .

1. Which protagonist (Natalie, Julia, Shelby, or Reese) did you most relate to and why?

2. After a lack of stability early in life, Natalie craved being in one place. What made Smitten special to her? Have you ever felt like that about a place?

3. Natalie believed her sister's report about Carson. Have you ever believed gossip and wished you hadn't?

4. When Julia returns to Smitten, long-lost feelings for her brother's best friend Zak resurface. Has coming back to a familiar place ever brought back unresolved feelings? Did you have to deal with them the second time? How did you resolve them?

5. Julia loves her friends and her hometown, but going back to New York City feels easier. Have you ever had to make the harder choice to do the right thing? How did you know it was the right decision for you?

6. Julia has a strong independent streak, but ultimately discovers that counting on others can make life easier and more fulfilling. Have you ever tried to do something alone only to discover the lesson was in submitting to others? What was the outcome?

7. When the girls support Reese in her outfitter's store dreams, they do things they wouldn't otherwise be interested in—such as roller blading. Do you have friends who expand your world that way? How has it made you a better person?

8. Shelby had some major issues with her dad. Before they could have healing in their relationship, she had to truly forgive him. In fact, he had to forgive himself. Have you ever had a relationship like that? Did you choose to forgive (with God's help) and receive

healing, or are you still holding on to the bitterness? What can you do to let it go?

9. Sometimes life isn't fair. Circumstances can change in an instant. Nick's circumstances changed when his ex-wife died and his daughter, Willow, came to live with him. Despite the challenges, they settled into their new life together and shared a relationship they wouldn't have had otherwise. When life hands you challenges, do you fight them or do you try to learn from them and make your life better?

10. Shelby gained strength and support from her friends. She also offered that same support back to them. Do you have someone like that in your life? Are you that someone to someone else? Reach out today.

11. The more Shelby and Nick got to know each other, the more they had to work through in their relationship, but difficulties can bring growth in a relationship and make it stronger. Think of the relationships in your life. What has truly made them grow?

12. It's clear from the beginning of "All Along" that Reese Mackenzie is a planner, but it doesn't take long for her plan to make Griffen love her go awry. Have you ever been so committed to your own plans that God's will got lost somewhere along the way? How did you come to that realization? What happened as a result?

13. In what ways did Griffen balance Reese? Who provides balance for you, and in what ways?

14. Reese's faith falters as they approach Sawyer's wedding and the finalization of their plans for Smitten. Why do you think having faith can be so difficult? When was the last time your faith faltered? What got you through that time?

15. How did the friendship between Natalie, Julia, Shelby, and Reese serve as a support system spiritually, emotionally, and physically? Who is your support system and how do you hold each other up?

# SMITTEN WITH FRIENDSHIP

. . . . . . . . . . . . . . . . . . . . . . . . . . . . .

*H*ow do four best-selling authors collaborate on a highly-interconnected novella collection? Very carefully. And it helps when you're best friends.

**COLLEEN COBLE**: The four of us are more than writing partners—we're soul mates. We are so close we can finish sentences for each other. Kristin and Di are the funny ones who have crazy things happen to them. Denise is the deep thinker who keeps us all organized. I'm the mom of the group and mother everyone within an inch of their lives. That first picture of us all together at the coffee shop is on my website: colleencoble.com. If you think we've aged, don't tell us, okay?

**DIANN HUNT**: I confess to pouting over the fact that the three of them had written a novella collection or two together before I came along. I mentioned it once—okay, maybe twice—I've never been good at math—that I wanted to do a collection with them. I never dreamed it would happen.

**DENISE HUNTER**: When we were approached about doing a collection, we were so excited. I mean, the chance to do what we love, with the people we love? What could be better?

**COLLEEN**: An editor we all knew asked us if we'd consider doing a historical collection. We had never worked together on a project before and Diann really wanted to try that. For Di's sake, I asked Ami McConnell, my editor at Thomas Nelson, if we could do it (Denise and I had an exclusive contract and needed permission), but Ami wondered if we'd want to do something very different for Thomas Nelson instead. She went to Allen Arnold, our publisher, and he was enthusiastic. I talked to the girls and we brainstormed several ideas that might make a novel in four parts, which is what this story really is.

**AMI MCCONNELL (EDITOR)**: I've worked with each of these authors on their individual, full-length novels, so I knew the wealth of talent they had for creating captivating, inspiring romances. That excited me. But I also knew firsthand about their dynamic as a friendship circle. I met Colleen, Kristin, Diann, and Denise at a writer's conference years ago in California. I wanted readers to experience the energy, the laughter, the intense feeling of knowing and being known that they share. If we could capture that feeling and let the reader feel it vicariously along with some terrific romances, I knew we'd have a hit.

**KRISTIN BILLERBECK**: Writing can be such a lonely sport, and I missed the connection we'd had when working on earlier projects. We already work so well together brainstorming each other's books, so to work together on one book, where the ideas are coming so fast and furious? It was simply pure joy.

You can see us brainstorming and giggling at the SmittenVermont.com site.

**DIANN**: Since we found one another, loneliness is no more! The first person I called when I found out I had lymphoma was Colleen, who then called the other girls. Did I mention that Colleen called me on my cell phone at the hospital—as I was being rolled down the hall on a gurney after a biopsy—to tell me one of my books had finaled in the ACFW Book of the Year Contest? Through the years we had laughed a lot together and when it was time to cry, we did that together too, especially when I was diagnosed with ovarian cancer. But laughter always follows us.

**DENISE**: Especially when we visited you in the hospital, Di! And Colleen punched your morphine button when she thought she was calling the nurse. I tried to stop her. Really I did. But it was like one of those slow motion things where you're shouting n-o-o and nothing is coming out.

**COLLEEN**: It was an honest mistake! You girls will never let me live it down.

**DENISE**: Well, what do you expect when you drug our friend?

**DIANN**: I went to sleep happy.☺

**KRISTIN**: What would we do without one another? There are days when I don't know how I will make it through everything I have to do with four kids. The girls help me keep my sanity.

**COLLEEN**: And when Dave was diagnosed with prostate cancer this year, I cried on your shoulders. But you know what? I wouldn't trade walking the valleys with my friends for anything. Anyone can have a friend who laughs over coffee. But how many of us are blessed with friends who stick "closer than a brother," as scripture says, when the going gets tough?

**DENISE**: I have to take Justin to college in a few weeks. My first little chick out of the nest. The girls know how I like to know exactly what's going to happen. And this is outside my comfort zone. So get the DeBrand truffles ready, okay? I like the raspberry.

**DIANN**: DeBrands? Did someone say DeBrands? You can do it, D. We'll pray you through it. And get you DeBrands.☺

**AMI**: And I'm the fifth wheel, always, but you've taken me in—and it's been a bonding year for sure. I've prayed for each of you and felt your prayers this year as I've navigated a hard road, a tough divorce. Trials for all of us—and so much grace! You all have such different personalities and they complement one another. How does that work in real life?

**KRISTIN**: You mean how we're each like a character from *Winnie the Pooh*? Colleen blogged about it here: girlswriteout.blogspot.com/2010/11/plotting-of-smitten.html. We all laughed but she might be a little right. Though I will say Colleen is totally Tigger. Her cheerfulness can be positively annoying.

**DENISE**: You said it; I didn't.

**AMI**: So you sent in your ideas for a novella collection. Several, if I recall correctly. I'm a sucker for a good romance, so that was a given. Key for me was the setting. What setting would entice readers to settle in for four great romance stories? The notion of a small town—of knowing the names of the folks you pass on the street—that just makes me smile. When you all said "Vermont," I was swooning!

**DIANN**: I remember when we heard from you that *Smitten* was your pick from the ideas list we'd sent in. There was a lot of *whoohooo!-ing* over email, and I'm certain a trip to DeBrand's was mentioned.☺

**DENISE**: That might've been me because I was pulling for *Smitten*. You can just see the joy in all our faces in that photo we took when we signed the contract (DeniseHunterBooks.com). The whole concept of Smitten excited us all. It's about a town whose survival is threatened when their logging company closes. Then four friends devise a plan to turn Smitten, Vermont, into the country's premier honeymoon destination—and each finds a love of her own in the process.

**KRISTIN**: Why Vermont? We were looking for a setting that was highly romantic, but also remote enough where the idea of it being a "new" romantic destination spot worked. We also wanted to do a story for each season, so we needed a locale that had winter sports and summer recreation. Vermont just felt cozy and a fellow writer, Rick Acker, helped us brainstorm. His family owns a stand of trees in another state. So we liked the idea of a logging mill being abandoned and the townspeople rallying together to find new hope in their town. Community is so important to our book and to our friendship. Our image of an idyllic community naturally includes us together, something we can't be with life going on around us. But when we are together, it's like the image of community.

**DENISE**: We knew these stories would be highly inter-connected, with story threads running through the whole collection and with each of our heroines appearing in all four stories. I think it was Colleen who suggested we give our heroines our own basic personalities. We know each other well, so putting words in each others' mouths would be a piece of cake.

**COLLEEN**: I knew I wanted to get to write about Kristin's character, Julia, giving Natalie, my character, a pair of shoes. And how Diann's character, Shelby, loves her small dog and dresses it up. And how Denise's character, Reese, organizes her spices by alphabet. And okay, I admit I might have sprinkled a few other friends in there. Like Natalie was named for a certain editor friend at Thomas Nelson. And there is a certain Mrs. Deshler mentioned . . .

**DENISE**: We're not exactly like our characters though. My heroine Reese, for example, is an exercise nut. Now don't get me wrong, I'm a walker and all, but I don't jog, and I sure don't jog up mountains or play one-on-one basketball in the middle of winter.

**DIANN**: Well, since we're being honest here, I'm not exactly as elegant as my heroine, Shelby. I know that comes as a shock to you all. But I DO have a creampuff dog. Take a peek at Latte on my website at diannhunt.com. Isn't she adorable?

**COLLEEN**: In real life I hate conflict, so if I were really my character, I'd have asked Kristin's character to confront my hero, Carson. But for the sake of the story, my "Natalie" had to do that hard work! It worked well for her in the end . . .

**KRISTIN**: This book was so easy to write because we know each other so well. In fact, we even had Colleen's character saying the same thing in two of the stories. We simply know how the others will react. Colleen is comfortable being bossy (or the mother, depending on if you agree with her at that moment). She's also incredible with setting, so her taking the first story allowed the rest of us to follow that lead. Denise is the organizer, so she cleaned up all the loose ends by taking the last story in winter. Diann seems to find it appropriate to listen to Christmas carols in July and I do believe she starts decorating her tree around October, so she got to do that in the story. I got spring—because I've lived in California all my life and have no idea what a real winter looks like.

One way I'm significantly different from my character, Julia, though, is that I can only take nature in small doses, and the idea of small-town living gives me hives. So I'm glad to live in Smitten with my girls, but ultimately, I love being able to walk to Korean, Indian, or Japanese restaurants any time I feel like it.

**AMI**: We should've had you take winter so you would have to do some research!

**DENISE**: Like a trip to Indiana in February!

**DIANN**: I loved how the community came together to save the town, and the faith of a little girl led the way. Our Heavenly Father is so creative that way. He surprises us with answers to our prayers in ways we hadn't considered.

**DENISE**: That is so true. I was praying hard when we finished our stories, and it was time to send them to the other girls. Yikes. Was I the only one who was nervous? I mean, they knew what they were getting when they signed me up, but we were in this together, and I didn't want to let my pals down, you know?

**COLLEEN**: I think we were all a little nervous! Would this idea even work? But when I read through the entire story, I was struck by how our unique voices brought a distinct flavor to the whole. *Smitten* is just plain fun to read!

**DENISE**: Colleen, our fearless leader, compiled the stories into one document and hit Send. Then we waited patiently to hear from Ami. We did not email each other seeking reassurance. We did not bite our nails to the quick. And we never, not even once, turned to chocolate for comfort.

**AMI**: The manuscript was everything I'd hoped for: four individually compelling novellas that read together as if it were a cohesive experience. And the vicarious experience of friendship in a small town was just so lovely and so real! I never wanted to leave Smitten.

**KRISTIN**: The editorial process, which I thought would

be a nightmare, was incredibly easy. Ami and LB each gave us feedback and we simply made sure all our facts were straight and the characters/setting consistent.

**DENISE**: In many ways, *Smitten* is a celebration of our friendship, a celebration of enduring love, and a celebration of God's unexpected blessings, all wrapped up in one book. We hope our readers will feel part of that as they join us on a journey to a very special place called Smitten.

# RECIPES FROM NATALIE

. . . . . . . . . . . . . . . . . . . . . . . . . . .

## Mug Cake

2 tablespoons almond flour
1 1/2 teaspoons xylitol
1 tablespoon cocoa powder, heaping
1 egg
1 1/2 tablespoons half and half or cream
1 tablespoon butter or coconut oil
Splash of vanilla extract
1 large coffee mug

Mix all dry ingredients in mug, add egg and blend thoroughly. Add milk, oil, and vanilla and mix. Place in 1000-watt microwave for 90 seconds. Do not cover mug. Cake will rise. Let cool and place on a plate. Add a little whipped cream to the top.

# Cranberry Bars

1 1/2 cups raw pecans
10 dates, pitted
2 tablespoons coconut oil
1/4 teaspoon Celtic sea salt
6 cups fresh cranberries
1 cup agave nectar
1 tablespoon orange zest

Grind dates and pecans in food processor.
Add in oil and salt until mixture begins to form a ball.
Press crust into an 8x8-inch, greased baking dish.
Bake at 350° for 10–12 minutes until lightly browned.

**Cranberry Topping**

Stir together 4 cups cranberries, agave, and orange zest then bring mixture to a boil. Reduce heat and simmer until cranberries start to dissolve, about 10–15 minutes.

Add remaining 2 cups cranberries and cook for 5 more minutes with lid still on.

Remove mixture from heat and cool for 10 minutes before pouring over pecan crust.

Let set at least an hour.

# Cauliflower Pizza Crust

2 cups cooked, mashed cauliflower (I also use RAW
   cabbage run through the food processor)
3 eggs
1 cup mozzarella cheese

Spray a cookie sheet with non-stick spray. In a medium bowl, combine cauliflower, egg, and mozzarella. Press evenly on the pan. Sprinkle Italian seasonings across the top.

Bake at 450° for 15–20 minutes. Remove the pan from the oven. Spread tomato paste on the crust, more Italian seasonings, then toppings like cooked meats, mushrooms, and cheese. Place under a broiler at high heat just until the cheese is melted.

# Reese's Tips to Motivate Yourself to Exercise

· · · · · · · · · · · · · · · · · · · · · · · · · · · · · · · ·

Notice: It is always important to consult your physician before starting a daily exercise program.

1. Make a deal with yourself: You'll exercise for ten minutes and then you can quit. Getting started is the hardest part. Often you'll find yourself going longer once you get started.

2. Choose an exercise you enjoy. If you deplore jogging, you'll never do it. If aerobics gives you hives, you'll find excuses to skip. Dance, join a volleyball league, or go skating. Make it fun!

3. Buy a cute workout outfit that makes you look and feel great.

4. Put exercise on the schedule like all of your important appointments.

5. Exercise early in the day before other things (excuses) crowd it out.

6. Make exercising a multitasking event. Walk and socialize with your friends, jog and listen to your favorite tunes, hit the treadmill with a novel, go hiking and dream up ideas for your next project (bring a voice recorder!).

7. Partner with someone for built-in accountability.

8. Award yourself for meeting your goals—not with junk food!

9. Start small. Maybe ten minutes, three times a week. Build slowly to longer and more frequent activity until it becomes routine.

10. Change it up! Any activity done repetitively can get boring. Alternating activities will challenge the mind and body.

# Julia's Cranberry

# Exfoliating Mask

. . . . . . . . . . . . . . . . . . . . . . . . . . . . .

1 cup fresh cranberries
1/4 cup ground oatmeal
3 tablespoons fresh lemon
1 tablespoon fresh ginger
1/4 cup plain yogurt

Boil the cranberries and then let them cool.

Whirl the oatmeal in the blender so that it becomes a powder. Add the cranberries, lemon juice, ginger, and plain yogurt to the blender. Blend well. Use a clean makeup brush to "paint" the mask on and leave on for twenty to thirty minutes for a refreshing peel with fruit acids.

Store leftover mixture in an airtight container for next time you want your skin to feel fresh and rejuvenated.

# ABOUT THE AUTHORS

RITA finalist Colleen Coble is the author of several best-selling romantic suspense series, including the Mercy Falls series, the Lonestar series, and the Rock Harbor series. She lives with her husband, Dave, in Indiana.

visit ColleenCoble.com

Photo by
Joe Saxton

Photo by
Michael Hawk Photography

Christy Award finalist and two-time winner of the ACFW Book of the Year award, Kristin Billerbeck has appeared on the *Today Show* and has been featured in the *New York Times*. She lives with her family in Northern California.

visit KristinBillerbeck.com

Diann Hunt has lived in Indiana forever, been happily married forever, loves her family, chocolate, her friends, her dog, and, well, chocolate.

visit DiannHunt.com

Photo by
Clik Chick Photography

Photo by
Amber Zimmerman

Denise Hunter is the award-winning and best-selling author of several novels, including *A Cowboy's Touch*. She and her husband are raising three boys in Indiana.

visit DeniseHunterBooks.com